"I CAN TELL YOU WHO I AM, SIR," THE MAN SAID ANGRILY . . .

Arrhae broke out all over in cold sweat at the sound of him. She was not wearing a translator, and he spoke Federation Standard, and she understood him. Not that this should have been strange, of course. Arrhae's composure began to shatter, and she kept walking, steadily, to be well out of sight before it should do so completely.

"I'm Doctor Leonard E. McCoy," he said, and O Elements, it was a native Terran accent, from somewhere in the south of EnnAy, probably Florida or Georgia. Arrhae made herself keep walking, without reaction, without any slightest reaction to the language she had not heard from another being for eight years, and had stopped hearing even in her dreams.

"I'm a Commander in the United Federation of Planets' Starfleet—and what your people have done is a damned act of war!"

Look for *Star Trek* fiction from Pocket Books

A STAR TREK® NOVEL

THE ROMULAN WAY

DIANE DUANE AND PETER MORWOOD

PUBLISHED BY POCKET BOOKS NEW YORK

Another *Original* publication of POCKET BOOKS

POCKET BOOKS, a division of Simon & Schuster, Inc.
1230 Avenue of the Americas, New York, N.Y. 10020

ISBN: 0-671-63498-4

First Pocket Books printing August 1987

10 9 8 7 6 5 4 3 2 1

For the collaborator . . .

. . . isn't it *great*?

NOTE

The document following is a print-medium transcription of the "subjective-conceptual history" work *The Romulan Way*, copyright © Terise Haleakala-LoBrutto. The material originally appeared in substantially different form in *The Journal of the Federation Institute for the Study of Xenosociology*, Vol. LXII, Numbers 88–109.

Foreword

Among many issues we are still unsure of, one fact makes itself superevident: they were *never* "Romulans."

But one hundred years after our first tragic encounters with them, that is what we still call them. The Rihannsu find this a choice irony. Among the people of the Two Worlds, words, and particularly names, have an importance we have trouble taking seriously. A Rihanha asked about this would say that we have been interacting, not with them and their own name as it really is, but with a twisted word/name, an *aehallh* or monster-ghost, far from any true image. And how can one hope to prosper in one's relationships if they are spent talking to false images in the belief that they are real?

Eight years of life among the Rihannsu has dispelled some of the ghosts for me, but not all. Even thinking in their language is not enough to completely subsume the observer into that fierce, swift, incredibly alien mindset, born of a species bred to war, seemingly destined to peace, and then self-exiled to develop a bizarre synthesis of the two. It may be that only our children, exchanged with theirs in their old custom of *rrh-thanai,* hostage-fostering, will come home to us knowing not only their foster families' minds, but their hearts. And we will of course be shocked, after the fashion of parents everywhere, to find that our children are not wholly our own anymore. But if we can overcome that terror and truly listen to what those children say and do in our councils afterward, the wars between our peoples may be over at last.

Meanwhile, they continue, and this work is one of their by-products. It was begun as a mere piece of intelligence—newsgathering for a Federation frightened of a strange enemy and wanting weapons to turn against it from the inside. What became of the work, and the one who did it, makes a curious tale that will smack of expediency, opportunism, and treason to some that read it . . . mostly those unfamiliar with the exigencies of deep-cover work in hostile territory. Others may think they see that greatest and most irrationally feared of occupational hazards for sociologists—the scientist "going native." By way of dismissal, let me say that the presumption that one mindset is superior to another—an old one to a new one, a familiar one to a strange—is a value judgment of the rankest sort, one in which any sociologist would normally be ashamed to be caught . . . if his wits were about him. But for some reason this single loophole has been exempted from the rule, and the sociologist-observer's mindset is somehow supposed to remain unaltered by what goes on around him. Of this dangerous logical fallacy, let the reasoner beware.

The raw data that the observer was sent to gather is detailed in separate sections from those which tell how she gathered it. This way, those minded to skip the incidental history of the gathering may do so. But for those interested not only in the why of research among the Rihannsu but in the how as well, there is as much information about the culmination of those eight years as the Federation will allow to be released at this time. I hope that this writing may do something to hasten the day when our children will come home from summer on ch'Rihan and ch'Havran and tell us much more, including the important things, the heartmatters that cause Federations and Empires to blush and turn away, muttering that it's not their business.

About that, they will be right. It is not their business, but ours; for there are no governments, only people. May the day when they will fully be true come swiftly.

Terise Haleakala-LoBrutto

Chapter One

ARRHAE IR-MNAEHA T'KHELLIAN yawned, losing her sleep's last dream in the tawny light that lay warm across her face, bright on her eyelids. She was reluctant to open her eyes, both because of the golden-orange brightness outside them, and because Eisn's rising past her windowsill meant she had overslept and was late starting her duties. But there was no avoiding the light, and no avoiding the work. She rubbed her eyes to the point where she could open them, and sat up on her couch.

It was courtesy and euphemism to call anything so hard and plain a couch: but then, it could hardly be expected to be better. Being set in authority over the other servants and slaves did not entitle her to such luxuries as stuffed cushions and woven couch fittings. It was the stone pillow for Arrhae, and a couch of triple-thickness leather and whitewood, and a balding fur or two in far-sun weather: nothing more. And to be truthful, anything more would have sorted ill with the austerity of her room. It was no more than a place to wash and to sleep, preferably without dreams.

Arrhae sighed. She was much better off than most other servants in the household: but even for the sake of the chief servant, the House could not in honor afford to make toward the *hfehan* any gesture that might be construed as indulgence. *Or comfort,* Arrhae thought, rubbing at the kinks in her spine and looking with loathing toward the 'fresher—which as often as not ran only with cold water. Still, she did at least *have* one. And there was even a mirror, though that had been purchased with her own meager store of money. It wasn't so much a luxury as a necessity, for House

Khellian had rigid standards of dress for its servants. Those who supervised them were expected to set a good example.

And the one who supervised everything was *not* supposed to be last to appear in the morning. Arrhae went looking hurriedly for the scraping-stone. Granted that this morning's lateness was her first significant fall from grace; but having achieved a position of trust, Arrhae was reluctant to lose it by provoking the always-uncertain temper of her employer.

H'daen tr'Khellian was one of those middle-aged, embittered Praetors whose inherited rank and wealth had placed him where he was, but whose inability to make powerful friends—or more correctly, from what she had seen, to make friends at all—had prevented him from rising any further. In the Empire there were various means by which elevation could be attained through merit, or through . . . well, "pressure" was the polite term for it. But H'daen had no military honors in his past that he could use as influence, and no political or personal secrets to employ as leverage when influence failed. Even his wealth, though sufficient to keep this fine house in an appropriate style, fell far short of that necessary to buy Senatorial support and patronage. His home was a popular place to visit, much frequented by "acquaintances" who were always on the brink of tendering support for one Khellian project or another. But somehow the promised support never materialized, and Arrhae had too often overheard chance comments that told her it never would.

She stood there outside the 'fresher door with the scraping-stone and the oil bottle clutched in one hand, while she waved the other hopelessly around in the spray zone, waiting for a change in temperature. There was no use waiting: the 'fresher was running cold again, and Arrhae clambered in and made some of the fastest ablutions of her life. When she got out, her teeth were clattering together, and her skin had been blanched by the cold to several shades paler than its usual dusky olive. She scrubbed at herself with the rough bathfelt, and finally managed to stop her teeth chattering, then was almost sorry she had. The sounds of a frightful argument, violent already and escalating, were floating in from the kitchen, two halls and an anteroom away. She started struggling hurriedly into her clothes: she was still damp, and they clung to her and fought her and wrinkled. The uproar increased. She thought of how horrible it would be if the Head of House should stumble into the *fhaihuhhru* going on out there, and not find her there stopping it, or, more properly, keeping it from happening. *O Elements, avert it!*

"Stupid *hlai*-brained drunken wastrel!" someone shrieked from two halls and an anteroom away, and the sound made the paper panes in the window buzz. Arrhae winced, then gave up and clenched her fists and squeezed her eyes shut and swore.

This naturally made no difference to the shouting voices, but the momentary blasphemy left Arrhae with a sort of crooked satisfaction. As servants' manager, *hru'hfe*, she monitored not only performance but propriety, the small and large matters of honor that for slave or master were the lifeblood of a House. It was a small, wicked pleasure to commit the occasional impropriety herself: it always discharged more tension than it had a right to. Arrhae was calmer as she peeled herself out of her kilt and singlet and then, much more neatly, slipped back into them. Pleats fell as they should, her chiton's draping draped properly. She checked her braid, found it intact—at least *something* was behaving from the very start this morning. Then she stepped outside to face whatever briefly interesting enterprise the world held in store.

The argument escalated as she got closer to it. Bemused, then tickled by the noise, Arrhae discarded fear. If tr'Khellian himself were there, she would sweep into the scene and command it. If not—she considered choice wordings, possible shadings of voice and manner calculated to raise blisters. She smiled. She killed the

11

smile, lest she meet someone in the hall while in such unseemly mirth. Then, *"Eneh hwai'kllhwnia na imirrhlhhse!"* shouted a voice, Thue's voice, and the obscenity stung the blood into Arrhae's cheeks and all the humor out of her. The door was in front of her. She seized the latch and pulled it sideways, hard.

The force of the pull overrode the door's friction-slides dramatically: it shot back in its runners as if about to fly out of them, and fetched up against its stops with a very satisfying crash. Heads snapped around to stare, and a dropped utensil rang loudly in the sudden silence. Arrhae stood in the doorway, returning the stares with interest.

"His father never did *that*," she said, gentle-voiced. "Certainly not with a *kllhe*: it would never have stood for it." She moved smoothly past Thue and watched with satisfaction as her narrow face colored to dark emerald, as well it should have. "Pick up the spoon, Thue," she said without looking back, "and be glad I don't have one of the ostlers use it on your back. See that you come talk to me later about language fit for a great House, where a guest might hear you, or the Lord." She felt the angry, frightened eyes fixed on her back, and ignored them as she walked into the big room.

Arrhae left them standing there with their mouths open, and started prowling around the great ochre-tiled kitchen. It was in a mess, as she had well suspected. House breakfast was not for an hour yet, and it was just as well, because the coals weren't even in the grill, nor the earthenware pot fired or even scoured for the Lord's fowl porridge. *I must get up earlier. Another morning like this will be the ruin of the whole domestic staff. Still, something can be saved—* "I have had about enough," she said, running an idle hand over the broad clay tiles where meat was cut, "of this business with your daughter, Thue, and your son, HHirl. Settle it. Or I will have it settled for you. Surely they would be happier staying here than sold halfway around the planet. And they're not so bad for each other, truly. Think about it."

The silence in the kitchen got deeper. Arrhae peered up the chimney at the puddings and meatrolls hung there for smoking, counted them, noticed two missing, thought a minute about who in the kitchen was pregnant, decided that she could cover the loss, and said nothing. She wiped the firing-tiles with three fingers and picked up a smear of soot that should never have been allowed to collect, then cleaned her fingers absently on the whitest of the hanging polishing cloths, one that should have been much cleaner. The smear faced rather obviously toward the kitchen staff, all gathered together now by the big spit roaster and looking like they thought they were about to be threaded on it. "The baked goods only half started," said Arrhae gently, "and the roast ones not yet started, and the strong and the sweet still in the coldroom, and fastbreak only an hour from now. But there must have been other work in hand. Very busy at it, you must have been. So busy that you could spend the most important part of the working morning in discussion. I'm sure the Lord will understand, though, when his meal is half an hour late. *You* may explain it to him, Thue."

The terrified rustle gratified Arrhae—not for its own sake, but because she could hear silent mental resolutions being made to get work done in the future. Arrhae suppressed her smile again. She had seen many Rihannsu officers among the people who came to H'daen's house, and had profitably taken note of their methods. Some of them shouted, some of them purred: she had learned to use either method, and occasionally both. She dropped the lid back onto a pot of overboiled porridge with an ostentatious shudder that was only half feigned, and turned to narrow her eyes at Thue, the second cook, and tr'Aimne, the first one. "Or if you would prefer to bypass the explanations," she said, "I would start another firepot for the gruel, and use that fowl from yesterday, the batch we didn't cook, it's still good enough; the Lord won't notice, if you don't overcook it. If you do—" She fell silent, and peered into the dish processor: it, for a miracle, was empty—there were at least enough clean plates.

"I've heard you this morning," she said, shutting the processor's door. "Now you hear me. Put your minds to your work. Your Lord's honor rests as much with you as with his family. His honor rests as much in little things, scouring and cooking, as in great matters. Mind it—lest you find yourself caring for the honor of some hedge-lord in Iuruth with a hall that leaks rain and a byre for your bedroom."

The silence held. Arrhae looked at them all, not singling any one person out for eye contact, and went out through the great arched main doors that led to the halls and living quarters of the House. She didn't bother listening for the cursing and backbiting that would follow her exit: she had other things to worry about. For one, she should have reported to H'daen long before now. Arrhae made her way across the center court and into the wing reserved for tr'Khellian's private apartments, noting absently as she did so that two of the firepots in the lower corridor were failing and needed replacement, and that one of the tame *fvai* had evidently been indoors too long. . . . At least the busyness kept her from fretting too much.

The Lord's anteroom was empty, his bodyservants elsewhere on errands. Arrhae knocked on the couching-room door, heard the usual curt *"Ie,"* and stepped in.

"Fair morning, Lord," she said.

H'daen acknowledged her with no more than an abstracted grunt and a nod of the head that could have signified anything. He was absorbed in whatever was displayed on his reader; so absorbed that Arrhae felt immediately surplus to all requirements and would have faded decorously from the room had he not pointed at her and then rapped his finger on the table.

H'daen tr'Khellian was a man given to twitches, tics, and little gestures. This one meant simply "stay where you are," and Arrhae did just that, settling her stance so that she would not have to shift her weight to stay comfortable. She was mildly curious about what was on the reader screen, but she wasn't quite close enough to see its content. At least there were no recriminations for lateness. Not yet, anyway.

"Wine," said H'daen, not looking up from the screen. Its glow was carving gullies of shadow into the wrinkled skin of his face, and though she had known it for long enough, as if for the first time Arrhae realized that he was old. Very old. It was affectation that he still wore his iron-gray hair in the fringed military crop, and dressed in the boots and breeches more reminiscent of Fleet uniform than of any civilian wear. The affectation, and maybe the lost dream, of one who had never been anything worthy of note in the Imperial military and now, his hopes defeated by advancing years as they had been defeated by every other circumstance, never would. Arrhae looked at him as if through different eyes, and felt a stab of pity.

"Must I die of thirst?" H'daen snapped testily. "Give me the wine I asked for."

"At once, Lord." She went through the dim, worn tidiness of the couching room to the wine cabinet, and brought out a small urn good enough for morning but not so good as to provoke comment about waste. She brought down the Lord's white clay cup, noted with relief that it was scoured, brought it and the urn back to the table, and poured carefully, observing the proprieties of wine-drinking regardless of how parched H'daen might be. There were certain stylized ritual movements in the serving of the ancient drink, and if they were ignored, notice would be taken and ill luck surely follow. That was the story, anyway; whether there was any truth in something whose origins were lost in the confusion of legend and history that followed the Sundering was another matter entirely. Perhaps better to be safe; perhaps, equally, as well to honor the old ways in a time when the new ways had little of honor in them. She drew back the flask with that small, careful jerk and twist which prevented unsightly droplets of wine from staining her hands or the furnishings, set it down and stoppered it, and only then brought the cup to H'daen's desk.

He had been watching her, and as she approached he touched a control so that the reader's screen went dark and folded down out of sight. Arrhae didn't follow its movement with her eyes; it would have been most impolite, and besides, all her concentration was needed for the brimming winecup.

"You're a good girl, Arrhae," said H'daen suddenly. "I like you."

Arrhae set down the wine most carefully, not spilling any, and made the little half bow of courteous acceptance customary when presenting food or drink, to acknowledge the thanks of the recipient. It might also have acknowledged H'daen's compliment—or then again, it might not have. It was always safer to be equivocal.

"You run my household well, Arrhae," H'daen continued eventually, "and I trust you."

He touched the shuttered reader with one fingertip, unaware of the worried look that had crept into her eyes. A plainly confidential communication, and unexpected talk of trust and liking, made up an uneasy conjunction of which she would as soon have no part. It had the poisonous taint of intrigue about it, of meddling in the affairs of the great and powerful; of hazard, and danger, and death. Arrhae began to feel afraid.

H'daen tr'Khellian tapped out a code on the reader's touchpad, and its screen rose once more from the desk's recess. He read again what glowed there in amber on black, shifted so that he could give Arrhae his full attention, and smiled at her. She kept the roil of emotion off her face with a great effort, and succeeded in looking only intent and eager as a good head-of-servants should. H'daen's smile seemed to promise so many things that she wanted no part of that when he finally spoke, the truth was anticlimactic.

"It appears that this house will have important guests before nightfall. There is much requiring my attention before I"—the smile crossed his face again—"have to play the host, so I leave all the arrangements for their reception in your hands. It is most important to me, to this House, and to everyone in it. Don't fail me, Arrhae. Don't fail us."

H'daen turned away to scan the reader-screen one last time, and so didn't notice the undisguised relief on Arrhae's face.

Ch'Rihan was a perilous place; it had always been so—plotting and subtlety was almost an integral part of both private and political life—but now with the new, youthful aggressiveness in the Senate and the High Command, suicide, execution, and simple, plain natural causes were far more frequent than they had ever been before, and neither lowly rank nor lofty were any defense. With what she already knew about H'daen's ambition, it would have horrified but not really surprised her had she been asked to slip poison into someone's food or drink. . . .

Some vestige of concern must have manifested itself in her face, because H'daen was staring at her strangely when her attention returned to him. "Uh, yes, my Lord," she ventured as noncommittally as she dared, trying not to sound as if she had missed anything else he had said to her.

"Then 'yes' let it be!" The acerbic edge was back in his voice, a tone far more familiar to her—to any in House Khellian—than the almost-friendly fashion in which he had spoken before. "I told you to do it, not think about it, and certainly not on my time or in my private rooms. Go!"

Arrhae went.

There had been guests at the house many times before, and both intimate dinners for a few and banquets for many; but this was the first time that Arrhae had been given so little notice of the event. At least she had complete control of organization and—more important—purchase of produce. Armed with an estimate of numbers attending, quantities required, and a list of possible dishes that she had taken care to have approved, she set out with the chastened chief cook to do a little shopping.

The expedition involved more and harder work in a shorter time than Arrhae had experienced in a very long while—but it did have certain advantages. Foremost among those was the flitter. H'daen's authorization to use his personal vehicle was waiting for Arrhae when she emerged from the stores and pantries with a sheaf of notes in her hand and tr'Aimne in tow, and that authorization did as much to instill respect for her in the chief cook as any amount of severity and harsh language. None of the household staff were overly fond of H'daen tr'Khellian—but his temper had earned him wide respect.

Arrhae checked the usage-clearance documents several times before going closer than arm's length to the vehicle. Oh, she knew how to drive one—who didn't? —but given the present mood of the inner-city constables, she would sooner find an error or an oversight in the authorizations herself than let it be found by one of the traffic-control troopers. She listened to gossip, of course—again, who didn't?—but she gave small credence to the stories she had overheard from other high-house servants of strange goings-on in Command. Though there was always the possibility that Lhaesl tr'Khev had just been trying to impress her.

Arrhae smiled at *that* particular memory as she went through the vehicle-status sections of the documentation. Lhaesl was a good-looking young man, very good-looking indeed if one's tastes ran to floppy, clumsily endearing baby animals. He tried so very hard to be grown-up, and always failed—by not having lived long enough. On the last occasion that they met, he had managed to talk like a more or less sensible person in the intervals of fetching her a cup of ale and that plate of sticky little sweetmeats that had taken her so long to scrub from her fingers. She hadn't even liked the ale much, its harshness always left her throat feeling abraded, but to refuse the youngster's attentions with the brutality needed to make him notice would have been on the same level as kicking a puppy. So Arrhae had sat, sipping and coughing slightly, nibbling and adhering to things, and being a good listener as working for H'daen had taught her how. It was all nonsense, of course, a garble of starships and secrets, with important names scattered grandly through the narrative that would have meant much more to Arrhae had she known who these doubtless-worthy people were.

But gossip apart, there was an unspecified something wrong in i'Ramnau. Arrhae had visited the city twice in recent months, not then to buy and carry, but merely to supervise purchases that would later be delivered. Because of that she had traveled by *yhfi-ss'ue*, the less-than-loved public transport tubes. They always smelled—not bad, exactly, but odd; musty, as if they were overdue for a thorough washing inside and out. There had been times, especially when Eisn burned hot and close in the summer sky, when Arrhae would have dearly loved the supervising of the sanitary staff. That, however, was by the way. What had remained with her about those last journeys to the inner city was the difference between them. The first had been like all the others, boring, occasionally bumpy, and completely unremarkable. But the second . . .

That had been when the three tubecars had stopped, and settled, and been invaded by both city constables and military personnel, all with drawn sidearms. Arrhae had been very frightened. Her previous encounters with the Rihannsu military had been decorous meetings with officers of moderately high rank in House Khellian, where they were guests and she was responsible for their comfort. Then, looking down the bore of an issue blaster, the realization had been hammered home that not all soldiers were officers, and indeed that not all officers were gentlemen. What such uniformed brutes would do if they found her in a private flitter without complete and correct documentation didn't bear considering. . . .

She carded the papers at last and slipped them securely into her travel-tunic's pocket, then glanced at tr'Aimne, the cook. "Well, what are you waiting for?" she said in a fair imitation of H'daen tr'Khellian at his most irritable. "Get in!"

Without waiting for him, she popped the canopy and slipped sideways into the flitter's prime-chair, mentally reviewing the warmup protocols as she made herself comfortable. Once learned, never forgotten; while tr'Aimne was securing himself in the next seat—and being, she thought, as ostentatious as he dared about fastening his restraint harness—her fingers were already entering the clearance codes that would release the flitter's controls. Instrumentation lit up; all of it touch-pad operated systems rather than the modern voice-activators. H'daen's flitter might have been beautifully appointed inside, and fitted with a great many luxuries, but it was still, unmistakably, several years out-of-date. No matter, for today, old or not, it was hers.

Arrhae shifted the driver into first and felt a tiny lurch as A/G linears came on line to lift the flitter from its cradle. Ahead and above, the doors at the top of the ramp slid open, accompanying their movement with a dignified chime of warning gongs rather than the raucous hooting of sirens. H'daen was a man of taste, or considered himself as such, anyway. Out of the corner of her eye, Arrhae caught sight of tr'Aimne tightening his straps, and his lips moving silently. Tr'Aimne was not fond of driving, and little good at being driven. "You could get in the back if you really wanted to," Arrhae said. "That way you wouldn't have to watch. . . ."

Tr'Aimne said nothing, and didn't even look at her, but his knuckles went very pale where they gripped the harness-straps while his face flushed dark bronze-green. Arrhae shrugged, willing to let him brazen it out, and took the flitter out of the garage.

She didn't even do it as fast as she might have, but nonetheless tr'Aimne changed complexion again, for the worse. "Sorry," she said. It was of course too late to change the speed parameters—the master system had them, and in accordance with local speed laws, wouldn't let them be changed without groundbased countermand. "It won't be long," she said, but tr'Aimne made no reply. He was too busy holding on to the restraint straps and the grab-handles inside the flitter. Arrhae for her own part shrugged and kept her hands on the controls, just in case manual override might be needed. The system was fairly reliable, but sometimes it overloaded: and this was, after all, a holiday. . . .

With this in mind she had let the i'Ramnau traffic-control net have them from the very start of the trip rather than free-driving it: people did forget to file driveplans, and there had been some ugly accidents in the recent past on the city's high-level accessways. One of them had in fact resulted in her appointment as *hru'hfe s'Khellian,* and she would as soon not provide someone else with advancement by the same means.

The flitter brought them to i'Ramnau far faster than *yhfiss'ue* would have, and too fast for Arrhae's liking; she was enjoying herself as she had rarely since she began working for House Khellian. Both lifter and driver of the Varrhan-series flitters were more powerful than warranted by their size, and they were less vehicles to drive than to fly. Arrhae flew it, with great enthusiasm and considerable skill. When they grounded in the flitpark, and the far door popped, followed by tr'Aimne leaning out and making most unfortunate noises, she busied herself with her own straps and lists, and carefully didn't "notice."

Finally he was straightening his clothes and had most of his color back. "Are you all right?" she said.

"I . . . yes, *hru'hfe*. I think so." He coughed again, and then spat—close enough to her feet for insult's sake, and yet not close enough to let her make an issue of it.

Well, there it was, he certainly *had* taken it personally; and she didn't need a quarrel with the chief cook, not today of all days. Arrhae glanced at the spittle briefly, just long enough to make it clear she had noticed that its placing was no accident, and then looked at him wryly. "If I had *wanted* to make you unwell," she said, "I wouldn't have done so poor a job of it—you wouldn't be able to stand. Come, chief cook, pardon my eagerness. I so love to drive."

He nodded rather curtly, and together they gathered up the netbags for the few things they would be needing and headed for the market. Arrhae pushed the pace. They were already later than she would have preferred to be.

It was annoying that she had to be in such a Powers-driven hurry on Eitreih'hveinn, one of the nine major religious festivals of the Rihannsu year. No matter that the Farmers' Festival was one of her favorites: she had no time to enjoy it today. There was only one good thing about it, and Arrhae took full advantage—the produce for sale was going to be superb.

Tr'Aimne, to her mild annoyance, refused to enjoy the shopping trip. One would have thought the sight of so much gorgeous food would have filled any decent cook full of joy, but he generally dragged along behind Arrhae rather like a wet cloak trailed on the ground. *Maybe he's still not well,* she thought, and slowed down a little for his sake. But it made no difference, tr'Aimne was incivility itself at the merchants' and farmers' booths, and his manners began to improve only as they got closer to the expensive, exclusive stores near the city center. By that time they had acquired most of the staples they needed, in one form or another, and had begun to shop for the luxuries that made H'daen tr'Khellian's formal dinners the well-attended functions they were.

Rare delicacies, fine vintages, fragrant blossoms for the tables and the dining chamber. Some were easy to find—Arrhae enjoyed the simple pleasure of being able to point at anything that took her fancy regardless of its price, and striking the Khellian house-sigil nonchalantly onto whatever bills were pushed toward her—but others proved much more difficult. And one or two were quite impossible.

"What do you mean, out of stock? You always had *hlai'vnau* before, so why not now?"

The shopkeeper went through all the appropriate expressions and movements of regret—none of which, of course, put any cuts of meat in the empty cool-trays or did anything to calm Arrhae down. She had all but promised that the traditional holiday foods would be served at H'daen's table, and now here was this bucolic idiot telling her that he had sold every last scrap of wild *hlai* in the city. She was sure enough of that sweeping statement, because it could be bought nowhere else, at least nowhere else on this particular day. Only merchants approved by priestly mandate and subjected each year to the most stringent examinations were permitted to sell wild game on the day set aside to honor domestic produce and the people who provided it, and this man held the single such approval in i'Ramnau.

"Very well." Arrhae unclenched her fists, annoyed that she had let so much irritation be so obvious; tr'Aimne would doubtless delight in reporting it to his cronies. "Plain *hlai'hwy*, then." She leaned closer, smiling a carefully neutral smile that wasn't meant to reassure and didn't. "But do make sure they're properly cleaned. If any of Lord tr'Khellian's guests break their teeth on a stray scale, your reputation would certainly suffer."

If only H'daen's mansion was closer to a large city

23

instead of this mudhole. If only it weren't so fashionable to have a home in open country. If only . . . Arrhae dismissed the thoughts as not worth wasting brainspace on; H'daen lived where he lived, and that was all. *But why here?* the stubborn voice in her head persisted. *Nothing ever happens here. . . .*

The sound began as a rumble so low it was beyond the edge of hearing; Arrhae felt it more as a vibration in her bones and teeth. It persisted there for long enough to be dismissed to the unconscious, like computer hum or the white-noise song from an active viewscreen—and then it raced up through the scale to peak at an earsplitting atonal screech that chased its source across the sky as a military suborbital shuttle dropped vertically through the scattered clouds.

Nothing . . . ? Well, almost nothing, Arrhae thought. The shuttle snapped out of its descent pattern and made a leisurely curve out of sight; probably on approach to the Fleet landing field that lay halfway between i'Ramnau and H'daen's mansion. The echoes of its passage slapped between the city's buildings for many minutes afterward, but long before they died away completely Arrhae had finished the last of her purchases and made enough amiably threatening noises to insure that they would be delivered in good time, and was making her way back to the holding-bay where her flitter waited. *Another night,* she thought, *another dinner, probably another of H'daen's deals, struck but never completed. And with whom?*

Oh, well. A full belly at least . . .

Turning away from the dining chamber for perhaps the tenth time since she had told him everything was in readiness, H'daen tr'Khellian made his tenth gesture of approval toward his *hru'hfe.* Arrhae acknowledged—again—and tried to keep the good-humored appreciation on her face when it seemed determined to slip off and reveal the boredom beneath. H'daen's guests were late, very late indeed, and without even the courtesy of

advising their host of the reason why. The lateness was
unusual, the lateness combined with the rudeness nearly unheard of. H'daen knew it; the original enthusiasm
when he saw how well his instructions had been followed had long since eroded to an automatic wave of
the hand, and these past few times Arrhae was prepared to hear herself ordered to clear the place and
dump all the food. She privately gave him five more
minutes before the command was given. . . .

And then the door chime sounded loudly through the
silent house. Arrhae could not have said who moved
first or faster, H'daen or herself, but after the first three
steps he remembered his dignity and let her attend to
the guests, if guests they were, while he returned to his
study for what was probably a well-deserved swift
drink.

The callers were indeed the long-awaited dinner
companions: a man and a woman, both Fleet officers in
full uniform of scarlet and black. Looking past them
out into the darkness, Arrhae could see their transport
sitting in one of the mansion's parking bays, and for
some reason felt sure that it wasn't empty. The officers'
aides, or their driver, or a guard, or—Arrhae stamped
down on her curiosity before it went any further; the
transport wasn't her business.

"Llhei u'Rekkhai," she said in her best voice and
most mannered phase of language. "Aefvadh; rheh-
Hwael l'oenn-uoira." She stepped to one side so that
they could walk inside and straight to the laving-bowl
and fair cloths set out for refreshment after their
"arduous journey"; no more arduous than a stroll from
the military flitter, and no more for refreshment than
the token dabbing of face and fingertips, but a traditional courtesy to guests nonetheless.

"Sthea'hwill au-khia oal'lhlih mnei i H'daen
hru'fihrh Khellian . . . ?" said the woman.

Announce whom? thought Arrhae. *I don't know any
names yet!* "Nahi 'lai, llhei?"

One of the officers hesitated, a soft towel still in his

hands, fingers clenching momentarily at the interrogative lift of Arrhae's voice, then glanced swiftly at his companion.

"U'rreki tae-hna," she said absently, not especially interested. "Hfivann h'rau."

"Hra'vae?" he said slowly. There was wariness and suspicion in that voice, and Arrhae wondered why. Then the officer turned full around, staring at her with cold, secretive eyes as if trying to read more than what he saw in her face. "Hsei vah-udt?" The demand came out like a whipstroke.

"Arrhae i-Mnaeha t'Khellian, daise hru'hfe, Rekk—"

"Rhe've . . . ?" The man didn't sound convinced. "Khru va—"

"Ah, Subcommander, it's enough . . ." Though his companion spoke in a less formal mode, there was no mistaking the tacit warning in her voice. "This one is only doing her job, as are we all. And well she does it." She dipped her fingers into the bowl of scented water once more, then dried them off and waved their newly-acquired perfume appreciatively under her nose. "Very well indeed. Tell H'daen that Commander t'Radaik and Subcommander tr'Annhwi are here."

"Madam, sir, at once. There is drink here in the anteroom, and small foods for you." Arrhae opened a door off the hallway. "And servants to attend you." *There had better be,* she thought. Neither of H'daen's houseguests were the languid desk-captains she was used to; there was a quick and haughty anger about the man tr'Annhwi, but the lazy, controlled power of Commander t'Radaik was more disturbing still. The woman's every word, every gesture, bespoke a confidence in her strength or her rank that suggested both were far beyond what first sight might suggest. Arrhae bowed them through the doorway, saw that at least three of the other house servants were waiting with trays and cups and flagons, and slipped the door shut on her own silent sigh of relief.

She had cause, once or twice in the next hour, to enter or pass through the dining chamber, a place of dimmed lights and muted voices, where H'daen and his guests discussed what seemed matters of importance. Like any good servant, Arrhae could be selectively deaf when necessary, and moreover had little enough time to eavesdrop even had she more inclination to do so. The unexpected work created by her shopping trip meant that everything else was running hours behind—an inspection of the guestrooms, completion of her half-finished audit of the domestic purchase ledgers, and even getting herself something to eat. . . .

A successful raid on the kitchen produced a glare from tr'Aimne—also meat, bread, and a jug of ale, watered down until it was almost palatable. After making a swift reverence, Arrhae fell to with a will. She hadn't realized just how hungry she had become until the savor of the baked *hlai* reached her nostrils. She made short work of everything on her platter.

Not that it took long, because even the dinner which the three upstairs had eaten was no many-coursed banquet, for all its elegant presentation, and Arrhae's stolen meal was only a degree or so above leftover scraps. Yet set against the standards of everyday fare it was a feast indeed, if not in quantity, then at least by virtue of its quality and flavor. The Rihannsu were not—with a few exceptions—a wealthy people, reckoning riches more by honors won and past House glories than in cash and precious things. She ate off one such precious/not-precious article tonight: a dish that was part of the set made by H'daen's ancestor nine generations back from the remnants of her Warbird, after the vessel had safely returned to ch'Rihan after a nacelle accident that should have killed everyone aboard. It had been decommissioned and scrapped after that, but its memory as something that continued useful when all reason and logic said otherwise was contained, with a sardonic humor that Arrhae liked, in the dining-service made of its breached hull.

She was debating whether or not to venture down to the kitchen again for any more of whatever was left, when the summoning-bell went off, loudly enough to make her jump. Its normally decorous sound had been turned up to an earpiercing clangor like that of a warship's tocsin, and that, Arrhae knew, was something H'daen would not normally tolerate. Even as she scrambled to her feet, wiping her mouth and straightening her tunic, she was wondering *who, and how, and why . . . ?*

She found out.

Commander t'Radaik met her at the head of the stairs. No longer benevolent and defensive, the woman looked every inch what Arrhae had come to suspect she was: someone whose actual rank or status was far, far higher than that claimed or indicated by insignia. One of the guests at a dinner-party two years past had given her the same feeling—and it had been vindicated when the man, ostensibly a Senior Centurion, had announced his true rank of *khre'Riov* and his position in Imperial Intelligence, and had arrested Vaebn tr'Lhoell, another of the guests, on charges of espionage and treason. Arrhae and all the other house servants had been interrogated to learn if they had seen anything suspicious during the party, and since tr'Lhoell had negotiated her present post in House Khellian, she had been terrified lest some ulterior motive should come to light and indicate that she was somehow implicated in whatever crime he had intended.

T'Radaik had that same look of a mask having been removed, and Arrhae thought abruptly and horribly of H'daen's enigmatic offer to take her into his confidence. Once again the small worm of fear twisted into life within her belly, and she fought with all her strength to keep any expression that might be construed as guilt from becoming visible on her face.

There was more introspection than anything else on the Commander's face; she had the air of a person deep in thought, and at first didn't see Arrhae five steps below. Then she focused on Arrhae as coldly as a surveillance camera, and her eyes burned right through Arrhae's to the brain behind, seeming to read whatever secrets were hidden there—and disapprove of them all. *"Hru'hfe,"* she said, all business now, "which guest-chamber in this house has a lock that can be overridden from outside?"

Arrhae paused, wondering why such a place was required, needing to think about her answer and feeling foolish because of it. Commander t'Radaik watched her impatiently. "Come along, hurry up! H'daen tr'Khellian seems to think that you're reasonably intelligent. . . ."

"The Commander's pardon," Arrhae said, embarrassed, "but this house is such that none of the guest-rooms ever needed to be locked from outside. The storerooms, however, all—"

"Show me."

"I. . . . Of course. As the Commander wishes."

The store was very definitely a store; there was no way in which it could possibly be redefined as anything approaching *guest* quarters, and even terming it *living* quarters was questionable. But t'Radaik liked it. She inspected the barred and shuttered windows, the thickness of the door and how well it fitted to its jamb, and the all-important lock, pronouncing herself well-pleased with everything. "Have this place cleared, aired, warmed, and furnished," she said, sliding the heavy door shut and seeming most satisfied with the ponderous sound of its closure.

Arrhae tried not to stare, but decided at last that to swallow all her curiosity would be worse than to let a little out. "If the Commander permits—what purpose is there in all of this? It looks like a"—realization struck her and she wished suddenly that she hadn't begun to speak—"like a prison cell. . . ."

"Hru'hfe Arrhae t'Khellian." Commander t'Radaik

spoke softly. She didn't look at Arrhae, but she had the chill air of one fixing a face and a name securely in the memory. "Ask no questions, girl, and hear no lies." And the Commander looked at her a little sidelong. "H'daen makes much of your intelligence; he also says you can be trusted. Don't make a liar of him. Matters afoot in this house are no concern of servants, even trustworthy ones; if you love life, keep your questions to yourself."

She unclipped a communicator from her belt and said several words into it; they made no coherent sentence and were plainly a coded command, but the mere use of the device brought home to Arrhae the jolting realization that concealed by the uniform's half-cloak, t'Radaik was wearing a full equipment-harness. Including a holstered sidearm whose red primer-diodes glowed up at her like the hot eyes of some small, vicious animal.

Arrhae walked very quietly behind the Commander after that; well behind, avoiding notice as best she could but quite sure that she had drawn too much notice already. She replied to t'Radaik's occasional questions with unobtrusive monosyllables, ventured no opinions of her own, and heartily wished that she had kept her mouth shut earlier on. T'Radaik said nothing more regarding excessive curiosity, and seemed content to let Arrhae sweat over the possible consequences of her own error, or was once more engrossed in her own private thoughts and had dismissed the matter from her mind. Arrhae sent out a small, fervent prayer to all the Powers and Elements that such was the case, but she didn't dare believe it. Not yet, anyway.

Subcommander tr'Annhwi was waiting for t'Radaik, and the house door was open at his back. It was very dark outside; they were far enough from i'Ramnau for the city glow to be only a pallid thread on the horizon, and sometimes, if she had leisure after her work for the day was done, Arrhae liked to go outside on a clear night and look up toward the myriad stars and think very private thoughts to herself. But not tonight. Ariennye alone knew what was out there, or what would happen to any who tried to see without the authority of the two officers who now stalked past her with blasters drawn. The weapons' charge-tones sang an evil two-chord melody in Arrhae's ears, making her skin crawl and pushing any inclination toward curiosity very far down inside her mind. Feeling superfluous and, standing in a well-lit hallway looking out into the ominous dark, very exposed, she began to back away.

"H'ta-fvau!" snapped tr'Annhwi. He didn't turn around, much less level his blaster at her, but Arrhae knew without being told that it would be his immediate next move. She ventured a weak smile, and came back as bidden.

H'daen appeared from the dining chamber with traces of wine on his lips and chin. Arrhae glanced at him, and could see his hands trembling slightly; she wondered what he had been told to bring on such a fit of the shakes, and then decided that she really didn't want to know. There was already movement outside, the sound of approaching military boots, and Arrhae remembered her first suspicion that the military flitter was carrying more than just H'daen's two dinner guests. It seemed that she was to be proven right—but the reason for the other personnel and their secrecy was not something that she wanted to dwell upon. There was too much similarity between tr'Lhoell's arrest and now. Arrhae's fears had never truly died away, and now they returned full force to haunt her.

The metalwork of weapons and helmets glittered as six troopers filed into the front hall of H'daen tr'Khellian's house, but it was not the incongruous presence of soldiers that made Arrhae catch her breath. It was the figure in the midst of them, staring from side to side at his surroundings; a man whose craggy features and angry eyes could not conceal the apprehension that he held so well in check. A man who wore civilian clothing, out of place in so martial a company, and more out of place than any form of dress might make him . . .

Because he was not Rihannsu hominid, but Terran human.

If Arrhae stared, her staring was no more apparent than that of the rest of the household, most of whom had never seen an Earther before. Heard of them, yes; lost kin to them in one Fleet skirmish or another, quite probably. But never yet seen any face-to-face until now, when one stood in their own front hall and looked with faint disdain at the Fleet troopers who surrounded him. He looked at them all in turn: at H'daen, wiping the blue winestains from his face, at the house servants who had abandoned their duties cleaning up the dining chamber and who now stood gaping like so many fools, and at Arrhae.

She flinched from his direct gaze, so startlingly blue after the dark eyes of Rihannsu, and something about the way she flinched made him stare still harder. In the background of her confusion Arrhae could hear Commander t'Radaik's voice: ". . . a most important guest of the Imperium. Treat him well until the time for treating harshly comes around. . . ."

While in plain sight of all present, the man's hands moved together in a gesture that might have been and certainly appeared to be simple nervousness. Except that it wasn't. It was one of the Command Conditioning gestures by which one Federation Starfleet officer might know another when more straightforward means of identification were impossible. Such as when one or both were acting under cover in a hostile environment.

Such as now.

Arrhae remained quite still for a long moment, not daring to move even an eyelid for fear it should compound her self-betrayal. It had been so long since she had looked on faces that were other than alien. So long that she had almost forgotten who she really was, or what her purpose had originally been. Almost—but not quite. Her hands began to move almost of their own accord in the standard gesture of reply; and then she stopped short while a wave of trembling passed through her entire body. What if this were some trap and the presence of Commander t'Radaik no more than a means to insure that she betray herself? Arrhae dropped her hands and was still, or as still as her shuddering would let her be. She looked to H'daen.

"The Commander has bidden me prepare one of the locked stores as a secure guest accommodation," she heard her own voice saying as calmly as if the house were invaded daily by military people with prisoners in tow. "With your permission, I shall attend to it at once."

H'daen waved her away, not really listening to what she said. He was hanging on every word spoken by t'Radaik, seeing the chance of importance at long last for his house—and more immediately, for himself. "Who is *this*?" Arrhae heard him ask. She continued her steady walk away, not turning around no matter what was said, or who said it.

"*I* can tell you who I am, sir," the man said angrily . . . and Arrhae broke out all over in cold sweat at the sound of him. She was not wearing a translator, and he spoke Federation Standard, and she *understood* him. Not that this should have been strange, of course. Arrhae's composure began to shatter, and she kept walking, steadily, to be well out of sight before it should do so completely.

"I'm Dr. Leonard E. McCoy," he said, and, O Elements, it was a native Terran accent, from somewhere in the South of EnnAy, probably Florida or Georgia. Arrhae made herself keep walking without reaction, without the slightest reaction to the language she had not heard from another being for eight years, and had stopped hearing even in her dreams. "I'm a Commander in the United Federation of Planets' Starfleet—and what your people have done is a damned act of war!"

Chapter Two

Pasts

"I AM A Vulcan, bred to peace," said S'task long ago to the alien captor who asked him for his name and rank; and many a Vulcan has quoted him over the years since, ignoring both the fierce irony inherent in what S'task did to his captors while escaping them, and the pun on the poet's name. Or perhaps they are not ignoring either. The Vulcans are not so much a taciturn race as they have been painted, but a reserved one; their rich mindlife demands a privacy that less esper-talented species find suspect, and their altruism is based on that firmest of foundations, necessity. The declaration is not just a statement of preference, but a description of what has become necessary for them to survive as a species and as individuals.

It was not always this way. So much scholarship, drama, and fiction has been written about pre-Reformation Vulcan society that it is unnecessary and perhaps useless to say much more about it. The images of a brutal and savage splendor spreading over a desert world, a fierce and lavish culture full of bizarre and secretive ceremony, wonders and horrors wrought by the unleashed and uncontrolled power of mind—of blood sacrifices, massive battles, single and multiple combats on which kingdoms were staked, and (most often) of wild passions and doomed loves destroyed by mindlock, clan jealousies or mere ambition—all these have sunk as deep into mass-culture consciousness as the semi-mythical Ten Lordships of the Andorian Thaha Dynasty, or the cowboys-and-Indians Old West of Earth. And this Vulcan has approximately the same relationship as those to historical reality: being careful, here, to mean history as "what truly came to pass" rather than history as "what historians believe probably occurred."

We do know that Vulcan was on the brink of economic, political, and perhaps moral disaster before the Reformation: and that within three generations after it the planet was almost completely recovered and stable and at peace with itself as few worlds have been before or since. Something plainly happened that mere history can barely account for. On other worlds, where aggression seems to have a much lighter grip or never quite took hold—Duiya, for example, or Lahain—one could easily accept the appearance and swift appeal of a Surak. In Vulcan's case, if we knew nothing of the truth, we might be tempted to take his story for a fiction as wild as any yet written. But there is Surak, and there is the Reformation, and ready to hand before us is the world that resulted. What happened?

Some writers have looked at the man's history—of inflexible peace, utter compassion, a man who laid down his life for what he believed in, and died horribly, slain by the enemies he had been offering peace—and have seen in it parallels to situations on other worlds, where powers from Outside have seemed to come and redeem the hopelessly fallen. On this subject and this outlook, the Vulcans are absolutely silent. They refuse to deal with anything but the facts: that Surak arose and taught peace, died for it, and was followed by hundreds and thousands who did the same, until the whole world renounced unmastered passion and gave itself over to that which English scholars of Vulcan (and the Vulcans themselves) translate as "logic" but which is more accurately defined as "reality-truth." But Hirad and other commentators point out that "reality-truth" in pre-Reformation times also meant the presence of God, immanent in the real things of the world and therefore also in the workings of the reasoning mind. The only response the Vulcans have made on this has been T'Leia's rather dry observation that "reality-truth" by either definition also includes error—a thing all too real—and all those who commit it.

What the Vulcans also often decline to comment on is that the cool proud man who declared himself "bred to peace" is the same man who turned his back on Surak, his teacher, and on the world that had become Surak's: the man who led more than eighty thousand Vulcans out into the interstellar night in search of a place where they could practice their beliefs in what passed for peace among them. In a most unusual inversion, it was the old beliefs that went out hunting the new world: not persecuted, but gladly, angrily self-exiled. The Eighty Thousand and S'task were the first Rihannsu.

Less than eighteen thousand of them finally made planetfall on ch'Rihan: and their pride was sorely tested in the two thousand years between the Worldfall and the days when they arose again in their reinvented spacecraft to trouble both the fledgling Federation and its enemies. But arise they did: and since that time the Vulcans have looked in their direction with a terrible calm that some find most interesting. It may be true, as the doomed T'thusaih said, that neither race will be whole until they are reunited, and heal one another's wounds. But on this, too, the Vulcans have no comment, and the Rihannsu smile in scornful silence and sharpen their swords.

There are some historians who say that the great rift that divided Vulcans into Vulcans and Romulans grew, not from any influence within the planetary societies, but from xenophobia following their first contact with other intelligent species. This is one of those theories that must be approached from both sides. On the one hand, why should Vulcans show xenic reaction to intelligent species? After all, Vulcan falls among the twenty percent of all known worlds that are inhabited by more than one intelligence. Contact from prehistoric times with the sehlats, and with the various intelligences of the deep sand, should have adequately prepared the Vulcans for the shock of sentience in nonhominid form.

And their technology, that most elegant and effective combination of the physical and nonphysical sciences, was already turning toward starflight. By the time of Surak, the first landing on Vulcan's closest planetary neighbor was several centuries in the past, and mining expeditions to the other inner worlds of 40 Eridani were becoming, if not commonplace, at least not unusual. The thoughts of the whole planet were beginning to turn outward as philosophers and engineers postulated the likelihood of intelligent life forms living on other worlds. Vulcan science fiction of that period—couched in those favorite Vulcan literary forms, the epic poem and the serial syllogism—is some of the best literature to be found on any world, and it fanned to a blaze a whole world's smoldering interest in the stars. By the time one small group of Terrans was building the pyramids, serious research was going on among Vulcans of all nations in the physics and the psi-technologies that would support generation ships on their journeys to the nearest stars, sixteen and thirty lightyears away. Taken as a whole, this does not look much like xenophobia.

But there is more than one kind of xenophobia. Vulcan historians naturally do not admit to shame or embarrassment about anything, but their relative reticence about the times before the unification of the planet makes their attitude toward those times quite plain. In the oldest Vulcan societies, where all life was a struggle for survival against a terrible desert ecology, one had no need to fear the stranger who came suddenly out of nowhere. It was your neighbor who continually competed with you for water, food, and shelter. It was your neighbor who was your enemy.

Vulcan hospitality was (and still is) legendary. Vulcan enmity toward neighboring tribes, states, and nations passed out of legend into epic; their wars escalated with time and technology to astonishing proportions. Between the dawn of Earth's Bronze Age at Catal Huyuk, around 10,000 B.C., and the fall of the Spartans at Thermopylae, there was only one period of ten standard years during which as much as ten percent of Vulcan was *not* at war. Without Surak the planet would probably not exist today except as a ragged band of radioactive asteroids in the second orbit out from 40 Eri. Even with him it did not survive whole.

To do justice to another side of the xenophobia argument, it might be safe to say that the universe awaiting the Vulcans was not one they had ever imagined. It was ironic that the sudden beacon in their sky, the da'Nikhirch, or Eye of Fire, which stirred many Vulcans to even more intense interest in neighboring interstellar space, and which (some said) heralded the birth of Surak, was also to be the cause of such terrible anguish for the planet. No one has ever proved that it was a sunkiller bomb that made sigma-1014 Orionis go nova, but the destruction of the hearthworld of the Inshai Compact planets certainly suited the expansionist aims of their old enemies in trade, the "nonaligned" planets of the southern Orion Congeries.

With the great power and restraining influence of Inshai suddenly gone, a reign of terror began in those spaces. Wars, and economic and societal collapse, decimated planetary populations in waves of starvation and plague while the decentralized interstellar corporations, their fleets armed with planetcracker weapons, fought over trade routes and sources of raw materials—blackmailing worlds into submission, destroying those that would not submit. In the power vacuum the surviving Compact worlds could not maintain their influence, or their technology, much of which derived from Inshai. They, too, turned to extortion and conquest to survive. Formerly peaceful worlds like Etosha and depopulated ones like Duthul became the home bases of the companies and guilds who degenerated over centuries into the Orion pirates. And Vulcan looked out into the darkness, where these dangerous next-door neighbors were stirring, not realizing that they had already turned on the houselights for them. It was around the time of Surak's birth, when the FireEye's light reached Vulcan, that the first electromagnetic signals from Vulcan reached Etosha in their turn, and notice was taken.

Their first contacts with the Orion pirates, forty-five years later, would have been enough to disillusion even a Terran steeped in all old Earth's legends of bug-eyed monsters intent on stealing their women and subjugating their planet. The Vulcans had no such legends: they expected to deal with strangers hospitably, and courteously, though always from strength. They had no idea that their strengths were in areas that would mean nothing to the Duthulhiv pirates who first reached them.

The subterfuge used by the raiders had worked on many another world. They surveyed Vulcan for months, monitoring communications, learning the languages, and assessing the world's resources for marketability. Then initial contacts began, properly stumbling ones made by conventional radio from pirate scout craft transmitting from several lightweeks outside the system. The pirates used a simple series of trinary signal-pulses expressing atomic ratios and so forth. Their own records, preserved on Last Etosha, make it plain that no one ever cracked this code as swiftly as the Vulcans did. "It was almost as if they had been expecting it," one pirate scientist was reported to have said. Messages began to flow back and forth immediately.

When communication was established, the pirates offered peaceful trade and cultural opportunities; the first messages were debated for several standard months in councils around the planet. Several wars or declarations of wars were in fact put on hold, or postponed, while the officials conducting them were recalled to their capitals to assist in the discussions. Finally the Vulcans decided to receive the strangers as a united front. On this at least they were agreed, that their own position of strength would be stronger yet if they acted all together. If a more pressing reason for this lay in the minds of various parties—the idea that this way, no one faction would be allowed to get a jump on the others—then no one voiced it out loud.

The date for the first physical meeting was set: nine Irrheen of the Vulcan old-date 139954, equivalent in Terran dating to January 18–19, 22 B.C. There at the agreed landing place at Shi'Kahr—then a tiny village of a ritually neutral tribe—five hundred twenty-three of the great ones of Vulcan gathered: clan and tribal chieftains, priestesses and clerics, merchants, scientists and philosophers, who went out in all their splendor to meet the strangers in courtesy and bring them home in honor. What met them in turn, when the strangers' landing craft settled, were phasers that stunned those who were to be held for ransom or sold into slavery, and particle-beam weapons that blew to bloody rags those who tried to fight or escape.

By the merest accident, Surak was not there: an aircar malfunction had detained him at the port facility at ta'Valsh. When the news reached him, he immediately offered to go to the aliens and to "deal peace" with them. No government would support him in this, most specifically since half the nations on the planet that day were mourning their leaders: the other half were staring in rage at ransom demands radioed to them from the slaver ships in orbit.

Thus war broke out—'Ahkh, "the" War, Vulcans called it, thereby demoting all other wars before it to the rank of mere tribal feuds. No ransoms were paid—

and indeed if they had been, they would have beggared the planet. But the Vulcans knew from their own bitter experience with one another that once one paid Dane-geld, one never got rid of the Dane. The space fleets of the planet were then no more than unarmed trading ships: in one of those lacunae that puzzle historians, the Vulcans had never even thought of carrying their warfare into space. But the ships did not stay unarmed long, and some of the armaments were of the kind that would not show on any enemy's sensors. The chief psi-talents of the planet, great builders and architects, and technicians who had long mastered the subtleties of the undermind, went out in the ships and taught the Duthulhiv pirates that weapons weren't everything. Metal came unraveled in ships' hulls; pilots calmly locked their ships into suicidal courses, unheeding of the screams of the crews: and the Vulcans beamed images of the destruction back to Etosha, lest there should be any confusion about the cause. The message was meant to be plain: kill us, and die.

That meeting was to prove the rock on which Vulcan pacifism first and most violently ran aground. S'task's handling of it differed terribly from his master's, as they differed at that part of their lives on everything else. S'task was at the meeting at Shi'Kahr, one of those who was taken hostage. He it was who organized the in-ship rebellion that cost so many of the slavers their lives: he was the one who broke the back of the torturer left alone with him, broke into and sabotaged the ship's databanks, and then—after releasing the other hostages safely on Vulcan—crashed the luckless vessel into the pirate mothership at the cost of thousands of pirates' lives, and almost his own. Only his astonishing talent for calculation saved him, so that weeks later, after much anguished searching, he was picked up drifting in a lifepod in an L5 orbit, half starved, half dead of dehydration, but clinging to life through sheer rage. They brought him home, and Surak hurried to his couchside—to rebuke him. The words "I have lost my best student to madness" are the beginning of the breaking of the Vulcan species.

No writer has recorded those anguished conversations between Surak and S'task. From contemporaries we know only that they went on for days as the master tried to reason with the pupil, and increasingly discovered that the pupil had found reasons of his own which he was not willing to let go. Peace, S'task said, was not the way to deal with the universe that now awaited Vulcan. The only way to meet other species, obviously barbaric, was in power to match their own—power blatantly exhibited, and violently, if necessary. Over the next few months, through the information networks and "mindtrees" of the time, S'task spread his views, and his views began to spread without him. Surak's coalition and support base far outnumbered that of those holding S'task's opinion, but mere majorities have never much influenced Vulcans: and no one was really surprised when the riots began in late 139955. Several small cities were burned or wrecked, and Surak himself was almost killed in the disturbances in Nekhie, trying to deal peace with those who did not want it.

It was at this point that S'task went into seclusion, hunting solutions. He loved his master, though he had come to hate his reasoning: and he well saw that their disagreement would destroy any chance Vulcan would ever have of facing as a unified entity the powers watching it from outside. (This surveillance had been confirmed toward the end of 139954, when another ship from Etosha arrived—cloaked, it thought, against Vulcan detection. The ship's wreckage, preserved by the desert dryness through thousands of years, is still visible outside Te'Rikh, carefully kept clear of sand by the Vulcan planetary park authorities.)

The problem was a thorny one. S'task was no fool: though he was sure he was right, he knew that Surak felt that way, too, and one side or the other was bound to be tragically right rather than triumphantly so. One side or the other would eventually win the argument, but the price of the victory would be centuries of bloodshed, and a planet never wholly at one with itself. Once again the ancient pattern would reassert itself, and S'task's vision of Vulcan as one proud, strong world among many would degenerate into just one more thing to have a war over: the goal itself would be forgotten in the grudges that its partisans would spawn in others and nurture in themselves for hundreds of years. For this reason alone S'task was unwilling to push the issue to its logical conclusion, civil war. But another question, that of ethic, concerned him: he was still Surak's pupil, and as such acknowledged that no cause or goal, however good, could bear good fruit of so evil a beginning. "The structure of spacetime," Surak had said to him at their first meeting, "is more concerned with means than ends: beginnings must be clean to be of profit." S'task had taken this deeply to heart.

So he proposed a clean beginning, and the proposition made its way through the mindtrees and the nets like lightning. If the world was not working, S'task said, then those Vulcans dissatisfied with it should make another. Let them take the technology that the aliens had inadvertently brought them, and add their own science to it, and go hunting another world, where what they loved would be preserved in the way they thought it should be. Let there be another Vulcan: or rather, the *true* Vulcan, Vulcan as it *ought* to be.

The arguments went on for fifty years, while the fartravel ships were being built, while more pirate attacks were beaten back and the first radio signals from other species farther out were decoded. Slowly the Eighty Thousand rallied around S'task, and on 12 Ahhahr 140005 the first ship, *Rea's Helm*, left orbit and drove outward into a great silence that was not to be broken for two millennia. The last message from *Helm*, sent as it cut in its subdrivers, provoked much confusion. It was a single stave in the *steheht* mode. Like all other Vulcan poetry, its translation is never certain, but more translations of it have been attempted than of any verse except T'sahen's Stricture, and so the sense is fairly certain:

> Enthrone your pasts:
>> this done, fire and old blood
>> will find you again:
> better hearts' breaking
> than worlds'.

It was the Last Song, S'task's farewell to Vulcan, and the last poem he ever made: after it he cut the strings of his *ryill* and spoke no other song till he died. Some on Vulcan consider that a greater loss than the departure of the Eighty Thousand, or all the death that befell as they returned to the counsels of the Worlds two thousand years later.

In their absence, under Surak's tutelage, Vulcan became one. The irony has been much commented on, that the aliens who presented the threat that almost destroyed Vulcan were eventually the instrument of its unification, and the world which had never *not* been at war became the exemplar of peace. It has been said that evil frequently triumphs over good unless good is very, very careful. This is true: but it should be added that good frequently has help that looks evil on the surface of it, and that "even God's enemies are some way his own." Surak spent his life, and eventually gave his life, for an idea whose time had come—an idea the accomplishment of which would fill other planets, in future times, with envy or longing. But the other side of the idea, the lost side, the incomplete, the failed side, was never out of his mind, or Vulcan's. Among his writings after he died was found this stave:

> Dethrone the past:
>> this done, day comes up new

though empty-hearted:
O the long silence,
my son!

Chapter Three

HIS PRESENT CABIN was one of the most comfortable
berths that Leonard McCoy had enjoyed for a long
while. The ship was a civilian liner, not subject to
Starfleet regulations, and as an honored guest—and
first class passenger—he was getting the full treatment.
At a guess he'd put on half a kilo in the past three
weeks. Life on the USS *Enterprise* might not be so
luxurious, but it certainly kept a man in trim; well,
there'd be reassignment when this was over and he'd
finished all he had to do. Back with Jim Kirk and the
rest, "hopping galaxies" as somebody had once put it.
McCoy smiled a little at that. With *Vega* running in
otherspace at warp 3, what else was he doing but
hopping galaxies right now? Or star systems,
anyway. . . .

He pushed back from his desk and from the datapad
still keyed for comparative xenobiology, knuckling a
yawn to extinction as he watched information flick
across the screens on their way to hardcopy dump. To
all intents and purposes this was no more than a
busman's holiday. The zeta Reticuli orbital research
facility didn't need *him* for its setup inspection; any
senior medic from Starfleet Academy would have been
quite sufficient. But they wanted the famous Dr.
McCoy from the famous *Enterprise*—and Command
had agreed he should go.

So here he was, Leonard E. McCoy, fifty-year-old
medical whiz kid, traveling first class on a luxury
starliner, working on the learned dissertation he was

expected to present, getting no exercise, getting bored, and wishing he were somewhere else. There was such a thing as getting too much R & R, and he was getting it right now. . . .

The electronics squeaked politely at him as they finished transcribing, and produced a bound copy of his dissertation notes with the slightly self-deprecatory air of a chicken laying an egg. McCoy picked it up and thumbed through the pages, looking halfheartedly for typos so that he would have something worthwhile to grumble about. There weren't any. That was the whole point of textsetting onscreen, but it was always worth a look anyway. He hadn't forgotten the time when a glitch in the *Enterprise* sickbay processors had over-printed every fifth word of Jim Kirk's monthly health report with a random selection of the most favored obscenities in seven Federation languages. Jim had laughed, and even Spock had been observed to raise one eyebrow. McCoy, however, had been audibly, indeed volubly, embarrassed, and had made a pri-vate promise that such errors wouldn't get past him again. Hence his almost obsessive care over this particular piece of work. After presentation to the Facility's medical board it was going straight into the *I.C.Xmed. Journal,* and that august publication would find mistakes neither ironic nor amusing. He set the checked script down and looked at it thoughtfully. *Always the same. Four submissions accepted, printed, and praised to the stars—and I'm still like a cat on eggs about whether I've got it right or not. Oh, well, maybe the fifth will feel diff—*

Then the desk kicked down at his thighs and the whole ship jerked as viciously as a bone shaken by a dog.

That's impossible, a rational voice said at the back of his mind. *No it's not,* said the same voice an instant later as his stomach supplied more data. Something had flickered the *Vega's* artificial gravity net, slapping him—

and presumably everyone else aboard—from null-G to maybe 4 G's, and then back to 1-G standard all in the space of half a second. And that something had to be either a collision, or—

Proximity alarms began yelping as the liner shuddered out of warp and back to realspace.

Somebody had just fired on them!

Here we go, he thought. It was almost a relief, in a peculiar way. Maybe the trip was going to be worthwhile after all. . . .

McCoy hit two tabs simultaneously: one lit up the courtesy you-are-here starfield map on the back wall of his cabin, and the second unshuttered clearsteel ports set in the outer hull. Those he kept shut while the *Vega* was running at warpspeed; nobody—apart, of course, from Spock, who was the exception to so many rules— actually *chose* to look out at unfiltered otherspace. But he opened it up anyway, no matter how pointless that might seem in the interstellar void, because he wanted if at all possible to see whatever the hell was happening.

And he did.

For just a second there was only velvety dark pin-pricked by the light of distant stars. The swirl of motion came from nowhere, a wavering haze that first set those stars to dancing and then swallowed them as it condensed into a ship hanging less than five hundred meters away. Criminally close—although that would concern this vessel's captain not at all, if McCoy's memory of ship-silhouettes was accurate.

The Federation's five-klick traffic limit was not observed by Klingons.

At least *(at least?)* it wasn't the familiar brutal hunchbacked-vulture shape of an *Akif-* or *K't'inga*-class battlecruiser. This was smaller and more rakish, one of the *K'hanakh* class frigates—still with firepower capable of blowing a target into a cloud of free electrons if the word was given. But what in the name of all things holy was a Klingon raider doing this deep into Federation space? But they were much closer to the Romulan

Neutral Zone . . . and the Romulans often used Klingon ships. He would *much* rather that the ship was Romulan.

As if responding to his thought, the warship pivoted gently on its maneuvering thrusters and slid toward the *Vega* and McCoy. Already its outline was fading again. He got no more than a glimpse of the insignia painted across its underbelly—an abstract spread-winged bird of prey—before ship and painted bird alike were gone from sight. McCoy stared out at the emptiness of space for several minutes even though there was no longer anything much to see, then turned and lifted the bound dissertation with a reluctant feeling of relief. *Cloaking device,* he thought. *Well, that's that. We're rolling . . . it's just as well. . . . I hate public speaking anyway!*

McCoy grabbed his jacket from where he had thrown it and left the cabin at a dead run, almost too fast for the automatic door. He didn't know his way around the *Vega,* but right now he wanted to get to the Command bridge, and he wanted it fast. The ship's corridors were chaotic, full of panicky people, most of whom didn't know what was going on; McCoy had a feeling that if they *did* know, the situation would get rapidly worse. He managed to stop one of the liner's stewards—a Sulamid—as it whirled past him, and was dismayed to see the alternating blue-green patterns of its tentacles. This particular Sulamid was so scared that reflex was overriding the good manners which usually kept its emotional-display pigmentation under control.

"Sir sir not restrain, urgency prime/paramount thistime," it said hurriedly, trying to squirm past him.

"Just hold on there, mister," said McCoy, blocking as best he could. "Get me to the bridge; I've gotta speak to the captain."

"Prohibited passenger bridge access alltime, doublemost prohibited thistime absolute."

I'd hoped I wouldn't need this, but . . . McCoy reached inside his jacket and pulled out the flat case

containing his Starfleet ID, flipping it up in front of the
Sulamid's five nearest eye-stalks. "Passenger yes—
civilian not." He tried to keep the impatient growl out
of his voice and used holophrastic speech for quicker
understanding. "Authority override: rank, position,
knowledge previous situations same ongoing. Please
immediate bridge/captain contact *now!*"

The Sulamid stared with all eight of its eyes first at
the ID card and then at him. "Knowledge previous
situations/situation thistime?" it said hopefully.

Too damn many for comfort, son. "Knowledge yes.
See presence alive/healthy; confirm situations survived
yes? To captain speaking important hurry please."

Again the rustle, and a nervous writhing of three big
handling tentacles. Then the Sulamid came to a decision and flipped two of the tentacle-tips at the floor.
McCoy knew enough of this particular nonhominid
species' kinesics to recognize a despairing shrug when
he saw one. Starfleet or no Starfleet, it plainly expected
trouble from the captain. "Sir to bridge guide follow,"
it said, and made off without waiting for an answer.

*"—mind the damned procedures! Just get an all-band
distress squawk out on subspace before that's jammed
too—"*

*"—taken out all the drive systems! Impulse? You gotta
be joking—I said all, didn't I . . . ?"*

*"—our ID was running, I tell you! They knew we
weren't military traffic!"*

*"—which is why they attacked in the first place—d'you
think if we'd been a Starfleet cruiser they'd have dared
to—"*

"—who are they anyway . . . ?"

The bridge was in a state of lively turmoil when
McCoy and the reluctant Sulamid reached it, and they
went unnoticed for several seconds while the chaos
boiled around them. Then someone with executive
officer's stripes and a ferocious mustache swiveled his

chair and began to hammer data into a terminal-pad, saw something he didn't expect, and did a double-take to confirm it. "What the—! You! Who the hell are you? No—just get off the blasted bridge, mister! And I mean *right now!*"

"I know who they are," said McCoy, unperturbed by the yelling. "I saw them, and they're—"

"Captain Reaves! They're Orion pirates, sir!" shouted somebody at the comm board. "I caught an ID-transmission leak before they shut it down and—"

"Any visual contact?" The *Vega*'s captain kicked his Command chair around, saw McCoy, and favored him with a blistering glare, then dismissed the presence of intruders on his bridge in favor of more immediately important matters.

McCoy was not so easily ignored. "You'll not get a fix on that ship, Captain," he said, cutting through whatever reply the liner's flight crew might have made. "It's cloaked." He took advantage of the sudden silence to continue in a more restrained fashion. "Captain Reaves, it was pure luck that I looked through my viewport at where I did, when I did. I saw the ship drop out of warp and raise its cloaking device; we're under its phasers right now. . . ." His voice trailed off at the expression on the captain's face. "You don't believe me."

"Mister, I—"

"—that's doctor, Captain. Of medicine."

"All right. Doctor. So you *saw* this raider come out of warp and then you *saw* it disappear again. If you're a medical man"—and from his tone Reaves was doubtful —"you'll know how that sounds. Agreed?"

"Here." For the second time in five minutes McCoy flipped out his Starfleet authority and held it up in front of the captain's eyes. "Doctor, also Commander. I know what I'm talking about. I don't care if they ID as Orions, Gorn, or my old Aunt Matilda! There's a Klingon-built, Romulan-owned Bird of Prey frigate right outside your damned front door, so you'd better start listening. If they're jamming on wide-band subspace frequencies, then try a narrow-focus tachyon squirt—"

"A man of parts, Doctor." Reaves glanced toward two screens, swore softly, and looked quickly away from them. "Do you *really* know what you're talking about?"

McCoy bristled just a bit. "Enough for your comm officer to understand. Let me finish before you interr—"

"Terran Starliner Vega, *phasers are locked on target. Do not attempt to raise your shields. Prepare to receive a boarding party."*

The new interruption had nothing to do with the captain, or with anyone else on the liner's bridge. Battered almost to incoherence by the energy-sleet of an activated cloaking device, it crackled from a speaker module on the comm station's translator board. In the shocked stillness after the speaker cut out, *Vega's* people looked at one another and then, helplessly, at McCoy and Reaves.

The young officer manning the liner's external scanners didn't look. He hit a bank of activator-toggles with a sweep of his hand and said, "Visual, sir." Then he audibly caught his breath as the image he had tracked sprang to high-magnification life on the main screen.

The outline was vague at first, but rapidly became hard-edged reality. The warship decloaked—and they stared straight down the glowing maws of activated phaser conduits. That hailing transmission had been no idle threat; but then, neither Romulans nor Klingons were known for bluffing if superior firepower could be used instead.

"Oh, God," said someone very softly. Four columns of glittering crimson fire swirled to life on the bridge, and nobody needed to hear the reports that abruptly began spilling from *Vega's* internal communicators to know that the same thing was happening all over the liner. Each firespout collapsed into itself in a storm of glowing motes and became human.

No. Romulan.

Each trooper wore a helmet with his uniform and carried an ugly businesslike disruptor rifle, but the officer who accompanied them was bare-headed and held a phaser pistol nonchalantly in one hand. He looked about the bridge with that cool, neutral expression worn most commonly by Vulcans, then smiled at the man in the Command chair. "I am Subcommander tr'Annhwi, set in authority over Imperial Vessel *Avenger*," he said in good if heavily accented Federation Standard Anglish. "All aboard this ship are my prisoners."

"Reaves, J. Michael, Captain of civilian starliner *Vega*, out of Sigma Pavonis IV." The words were spoken calmly enough, but his fingers were clenched too tightly on the arms of his Command chair. "Subcommander, has there been a formal declaration of war between our governments? If not, then explain what you're doing aboard my ship."

"Your restraint does you credit, Captain h'Reeviss. It is a most wise attitude to adopt. I wish to see this vessel's crew roster, cargo manifests, and passenger listing."

"I'll see you in hell first, you bloody pirate!" Reaves wasn't even halfway out of his seat when a phaser-bolt melted the deck-plating between his feet.

"Carefully, Captain. Sit down." Subcommander tr'Annhwi's voice still carried its tone of cold amusement, but his smile was gone and the anger in his narrow eyes had killed whatever similarity he might have had to a calm, logic-governed Vulcan. "If you insult me again, you will die. If you try to attack me again, you will die. If you do anything other than by my order again, you will die. Is all of this quite clear, h'Reeviss, J. Maik-'ell?" The captain didn't reply, but tr'Annhwi nodded anyway. "Good. Run the information to this screen here; my antecenturion will do the rest."

McCoy watched, saying nothing, as columns of data began to scroll past tr'Annhwi's interested gaze. He turned an empty station-seat around and settled into it with the serenity of a man coming to terms with his own fate. *It must have felt like this back in the twentieth century when the doctor told you it was cancer,* he thought. *We've beaten the disease, but not the feeling.*

"These names: crew, or passengers?" tr'Annhwi asked. There was no reply until he touched his fingertips ominously to the firing-grip of his phaser, and even then Captain Reaves left the answer to one of his junior officers.

"The data is presented as you asked for it, Subcommander. Crew, then cargo, and passengers last of all." The young man contrived to be subtly insolent in his brief explanation, but tr'Annhwi either missed it or chose to let it pass.

"Very well," he said. "Proceed on my order. *Erein t'Hwaehrai, h'tah-fveinn lh'hde hnhaudr tlhei.* Commence, please." Every few seconds tr'Annhwi stopped the flow of data and waited while the antecenturion flickered her fingers across the keypads and took note of one item or another of interest to her commander. "The accuracy of these manifests will be checked, of course," he said over his shoulder. "No comments, Captain?"

"They're accurate," said Reaves sullenly.

"So you say." Tr'Annhwi tapped at the screen, which had completed its scrolling and gone dark. "Finished? Then screen off, and print it all." The antecenturion glanced at him quizzically. *"Lloann'na ta'khoi; t'Hwaehrai, haudet' s'tivh qiunn aedn'voi."*

"Ie, erei'Riov."

A printer sat humming to itself in the silence of the liner's bridge, and then dropped a sheaf of hard copy into Antecenturion t'Hwaehrai's waiting hands. She

leafed quickly through the flimsy pages to make sure
that tr'Annhwi's remarks had been emphasized properly, then handed them over to him.

"An eclectic assortment, is it not?" he muttered. It
would have sounded more like a voiced private observation had he not spoken in Anglish. "Let me see.
Hold *A*. Alcohol, beverage, one hundred fifty-seven
hektoliters." He tapped his teeth thoughtfully with a
scriber, considering, then marked the page and read
on. "Textiles—silk, wool, synthetics. Foodstuffs—
basic, luxury, gourmet, stasis-secured. Salt and spices,
total weight sixty-three kilos.

"Hold *B*. Pharmaceutical supplies." Another mark,
different this time by the way the scriber moved.
McCoy stiffened. "A rock sample, weight one and
one-half tonnes. Grain and associated phosphates, two
thousand four hundred forty-one tonnes. Machine
parts." This time as he scribbled something down,
tr'Annhwi was smiling to himself, a grim look. "Of
course machine parts."

McCoy relaxed a little. He was actually beginning to
believe that this was going to work.

"And finally, Hold *C*. Art treasures—paintings,
twenty; sculptures, three: helmeted head of a goddess,
in marble, Terran Hellenic period; convolutions representing thought, in extruded crystal, Hamalket second
T'r'lkt era; unfinished portrait, in several substances,
Deirr modern. Mail, one thousand eighteen items.
Alcohol, industrial, seven hundred ninety-five hektoliters."

Tr'Annhwi's smile was still there as he flicked a
disdainful finger at the cargo manifest and stared at
Captain Reaves. "Intoxicants *and* drugs. These goods
are subject to confiscation, Captain, and you to a fine."

Reaves wasn't about to take that sitting down, but
with the barrel of a disruptor rifle resting none too
lightly on either shoulder he had little choice but to stay
right where he was. Tr'Annhwi watched the impotent

fury on the Earther's face and grinned with pleasure. "You keep forgetting what I told you, Captain. Remember please, or you will surely die. Also, these 'machine parts'; come now, not even the Klingons bother using that label for gunrunning anymore. And by the way, no matter what your Federation Starfleet may think of us, the Imperium regards the unauthorized transportation of weapons in just the same way as all other civilized persons. Illegal. There will be another fine."

"This ship," said Reaves, speaking slowly and carefully as if reasoning with a clever two-year-old, "isn't carrying any form of illegal cargo. No drugs other than those requested by the new zeta Reticuli medical facility; no alcohol other than that indented for by the Malory-Lynne-Stephens mineral processing plant on Sisyphos—and no weapons, concealed or otherwise, Subcommander tr'Annhwi. Run a physical check of the cargo holds if you like."

"Oh, I will, Captain. But my thanks for your permission anyway. Of the four ships I have searched this past standard day, this one interests me most of all."

"What?"

"Singular as the honor may appear, you aren't my paramount reason for entering Federation space. Although this ship might well be. After reading your passenger list, who knows . . . ?"

"We've upward of four thousand passengers aboard this vessel, Subcommander. I trust that you've plenty of time."

"Enough to find the names I want. Afterward we shall determine if more time is necessary, perhaps to blow your ship apart. Run sections *K, M,* and *S.*"

Finally, McCoy thought, and regardless of his relief, began to sweat again. *Took the boy long enough. Thought I'd come all this way for nothing.*

Sensing the increase of tension, even though they didn't understand its source, the bridge crew of the

Vega watched Subcommander tr'Annhwi as he read through the three subsections of their vessel's passenger listing without comment or even drawing so much as an unnecessary breath. And then speed-scanned the entire list of four thousand two hundred and seventy-three names from beginning to end.

"What is the meaning of this question-symbol?" he said at last.

"That refers to a 'no-show' passenger," explained the junior officer who had been so delicately insulting at first. Uncomprehending eyebrows were raised, and he elaborated. "It's a passenger whose place has been booked in advance, and who then doesn't arrive to claim it."

"Ah." Tr'Annhwi uttered the sound in great satisfaction, as though many things were suddenly clear. "There are only twenty-one out of all the names shown here." He reached out for the single sheet that Antecenturion t'Hwaehrai had prepared in anticipation, and ran his fingertip down the single column of print. "Brickner, G.; Bryant, E.; B'tey'nn; Farey, K.; Farey, N.; Ferguson, B.; Friedman, D.; Gamble, C.; Gamble, D.; H'rewiss. . . . All of these persons were expected, but did not appear?"

"Yes."

"So. H'rewiss, yes; Johnson, T.; Kh'Avn-Araht; King, T.; Meacham, B.; Meier, W. *and* Meier, W. . . . Most interesting. Sadek; Sepulveda, R.; Siegel, K.; Talv'Lin; T'Pehr." The Romulan shuffled both sets of hardcopy data together, and there was a look of faint loathing on his face. "I can comprehend why Vulcans and a Tellarite might travel on a Terran-registered vessel, Captain. But some of these others are not"—everyone saw how he looked at the Sulamid steward—"not even *shaped* like you!"

"That isn't an issue under question, Subcommander," said Reaves, staring at tr'Annhwi, "and I recommend you not to start."

There was a brief silence, and then tr'Annhwi shrugged, apparently not understanding Reaves's reaction, and not caring that he didn't. "No matter. As you say, Captain. It is not under question."

He turned back to t'Hwaehrai at the computer terminal. "So," he said. "To work. I would think—would you not, Captain?—that some most interesting conclusions might be discovered if one correlated each passenger with his, her, or its supposed ports of embarkation and added on the cargo-loading manifests."

Reaves blinked, not making sense of the Romulan's words for a moment. Then realization dawned and he glanced from t'Hwaehrai, whose fingers were already pattering briskly at the terminal's access console, to the satisfied little smile that tr'Annhwi was wearing. "Whatever you're thinking, Subcommander," he said, "you're wrong."

"Am I? Perhaps. Or perhaps not."

"*Ta-hrenn, erei'Riov!*" Antecenturion t'Hwaehrai looked decidedly pleased with herself. "*Eh't ierra-tai rh'oiin hviur ihhaeth.*"

"*Hnafirh 'rau.*" Tr'Annhwi leaned over to read what was on the screen and his smile became a wide grin. "*Ie. Au'e rha. Khnai'ra rhissiuy, Erein.* Much as I expected to find, Captain," he said, "despite your protestations. You still insist that nobody on this ship has seen the passengers Sadek, T'Pehr, Kh'Avn-Araht, or the coincidentally identical Meiers?"

"Of course not. You saw the list yourself—all of those passengers failed to board before departure."

"Yet items of cargo were loaded at each port of embarkation, yes?"

"Yes."

"And the cargo holds of this starliner are maintained to the same pressure-temperature-gravity parameters as the life shell, yes?"

"Yes. . . ."

"So conceivably, if aware of this, any 'no-show'

57

passenger might be snugly ensconced within a cargo space, yes?"

"*No!*"

"You sound very sure of your facts, Captain h'-Reeviss. Most decisive. And since you are so certain, you will scarcely mind opening the holds to space for fifteen standard minutes."

"I will not!" Reaves thumped his clenched fist against the arm of his Command chair as violently as he dared while surrounded by armed and wary Romulan soldiers. "Maybe you don't realize," he said, forcing himself to behave more calmly, "that my contracts specify safe delivery of cargo."

"And perhaps *you* do not realize, Captain, that if you do not vent the holds, I shall. My weapons officer on *Avenger* is very skilled. You have five standard minutes in which to make your choice." Tr'Annhwi glanced at the image of his warship which filled *Vega*'s main screen and unclipped a communicator from his belt. "*Ra'kholh, hwaveyiir 'rhae: aihr erei'Riov tr'-Annhwi.*"

"*Ra'kholh, erei'Riov. Enarrain tr'Hheinia hrrau Oira. Aeuthn qiu oaii mnek'nra?*"

McCoy listened, and began to sweat. Perhaps Captain Reaves might have suspected, but nobody else on the bridge could know about the translator nestling snugly against the brachial nerve in his forearm. Certainly even the captain wasn't aware of how well it was working. After the Levaeri V incident, Starfleet's intradermal translators had been reprogrammed with augmented details of the Romulan/Rihanha language, even down to the then-current military slang. There was no slang being used here, on either side of the conversation, and even the bridge centurion's "all-well?" inquiry had been formally phrased. He guessed that Subcommander tr'Annhwi wasn't an officer who encouraged familiarity—or who made idle threats.

"*Ie, ie. Oiuu'n mnekha. Vaed'rae, Enarrain: rhi*

siuren dha, iehyyak 'haerh s'Vega rhudhe dvaer. Ssuej-d'ifv?"

Only the cargo spaces? McCoy shivered, and rubbed a film of moisture from his palms. No matter how good the Romulan gunnery officer was, he was far too close for that sort of precision fire with shipboard batteries. At less than five hundred meters, the weapon systems on the *Avenger* were more likely to crack *Vega* open like an eggshell than just puncture her holds.

Even so, McCoy thought to himself, *don't jump the gun. You have to give this a chance to look right . . . and give the boy a chance to chicken out.*

"Ie, ssuaj-ha', erei'Riov. Hn'haerht dvahr. Ra'kholh 'khoi." The frigate shifted slightly, bringing its main phasers to bear, and then faded from the screen in a flicker of static as someone on its bridge transmitted an override. It wasn't a view to inspire confidence—*Vega* as seen by the Romulan targeting computers, a schematic outline whose lower hull was marked in three places by the glowing orange diamonds of image-enhanced phaser locks.

"Five minutes and counting, Captain," said tr'-Annhwi, looking with unnecessary emphasis at the elapsed-time display onscreen. No matter that all the visible symbology was Romulan; this was easy enough to follow. And time was running out.

"Subcommander . . . !" There was an edge of desperation in Reaves's voice now, and he turned hurriedly to his own crew. "Number one, activate the loading-monitors at full and free mobility—cut in full internal lighting. Exec, patch the signals through to the main screen. Insert mode—over *that.* And for God's sake, hurry!"

It was common practice for a vessel's cargo spaces to have track-mounted surveillance cameras, and there was one in each of *Vega*'s holds. The pictures they transmitted were high-definition, good enough to read the labels on the bulk flasks of Saurian brandy in hold *A* or the stenciled "This way up" instruction on crated medicinal drugs. Certainly good enough to show if anything was amiss—or if anyone was there.

"Look, Subcommander! Can't you see? There's nothing that shouldn't be there!"

Tr'Annhwi looked, not especially interested, and began to turn away. "Three minutes," he said. And then his head snapped back toward the screen. "There! Something moved!"

"You're imagining—" Reaves started to say, but shut his teeth on the words as tr'Annhwi leveled a phaser at his face.

"Close your mouth or I'll burn another one in your head to keep it company," the Romulan snapped. And to the still-active communicator in his left hand: *"Ie'yyak-Hnah!"*

The screen went blank for an instant, then flicked back to a tactical sketch of a Federation liner with computer-graphic splatters of blue fire raking all across its belly.

And at the same instant, *Vega*'s substructure howled in protest as she was gutted. The vessel wrenched out of line in three dimensions at once, flinging both crew and intruders into bulkheads or onto the shuddering deck. Alarms and people alike were screaming. The bridge consoles overloaded in a convulsion of sparks and choking smoke, the screen was flashing HULL INTEGRITY VIOLATED and nobody was paying any attention. . . .

Leonard McCoy clambered stiffly to his feet, coughing the stink of seared insulation from his lungs. He was bruised and shaken, his spine hurt from the three-way whiplash, and he was appalled that the Romulans had actually made good their threat. In that one instant, in the warship of one state firing on the unarmed civilian vessel of another, it had gone beyond piracy to war. And he was right in the middle of it.

Or was he . . . ? The bridge extractors cut in and began to clear the smoke, and the first thing he saw was tr'Annhwi on hands and knees on the deck. The second was the expression on the Subcommander's face. It was a mingling of rage and terror such as McCoy had seldom seen on any face; terror at the consequences of a panicked action, and at the consequences yet to come, and fury at being placed in such a situation by all the circumstances which had led him there. Worst of all, the quickest way tr'Annhwi could cover his blunder would be by blowing *Vega* to subatomic particles. Maybe he might not be as ruthless as that, but his last overreaction and the way that he looked now made him more dangerous than the coldest, most efficient starship captain would ever be. Because tr'Annhwi had already shown that he might act without thinking, and he was scared enough to do it again—except that this time people were going to die. . . .

Unless he was distracted.

McCoy stood up, the first man on the bridge to do so, straightened his rumpled, smoke-stained jacket, and met the stares and the leveled weapons with as much equanimity as he could summon. "Subcommander tr'Annhwi, I'm on your list. The name's McCoy—of the *Enterprise*."

He had gone beyond butterflies in the stomach; it felt like three heavy cruisers on maneuvers in there, but it was still worth it just to see the way tr'Annhwi's face changed. At first the Romulan plainly didn't believe him, then wanted to believe and didn't dare, and finally decided to make quite sure.

The making-sure was brief, and fortunately painless. No matter that *Vega* bridge was smashed, the Romulan frigate's computers were still in perfect working order —and their intelligence data on a trio of much-sought Federation officers, there by no coincidence at all, made short work of providing a tri-D likeness. It arrived in a flicker and hum of transporter effect: a fat dossier with squat blocks of Rihanha charactery on its cover.

Tr'Annhwi looked at it; then at McCoy, then back at the dossier. McCoy already knew that Romulans frowned when deep in thought. If he hadn't, one look at the Subcommander would have made him sure of it, because the crease between tr'Annhwi's brows was indented deep enough to put his brain at risk.

The pictures under study weren't at first familiar, and seeing them only by inverted glimpses didn't help. *Where did they get . . . ?* McCoy started to wonder, then recognized the background details and guessed right. They had been taken from the deck-monitor system of the only—so far—Romulan vessel he had ever boarded (and even that had been a Klingon-built *Akif*-class D7 battlecruiser). *Hers . . . .* Ael's sister's daughter's ship, *Talon.* "She's your *niece?*" He could remember his own voice quite clearly, and its near-squeak of astonishment. Somehow one never thought of enemies with families; brothers or sisters, fathers or daughters. It made keeping them distanced, keeping them enemies that much easier.

And then all of a sudden there was one enemy who was Commander of a Warbird and at the same time an aunt—and a mother. *A mother who killed her own son in the name of honor and justice. Mhnei'sahe, they call it. I call it murder. And yet I stood by, knowing what she was about and pretending not to know, and not wanting to know. And I took her thanks afterward and said nothing.*

"Close enough," said tr'Annhwi grudgingly. There was a cheated air about him, as if having started violence he would as soon have gained his answers after more of it. "Take him." Two disruptors nudged McCoy, in chest and spine.

He looked down at the weapons with disdain—there was no longer any point in being scared, or at least obviously so—and glanced in the Subcommander's direction. "Are you expecting me to pull a phaser out of somewhere, sir? Or run? I've had ample time for both—yet here I am." He pushed the nearer, more aggressive rifle to one side and smiled just a bit at the helmeted young trooper who carried it. "Put that away, son, before somebody gets hurt. Subcommander tr'Annhwi, now that you've got what you came for, let these people"—his wave took in the bridge crew and by inference everyone else aboard *Vega*—"be about their business."

"No." The Romulan shook his head in a very Terran gesture of denial. "Dr. Mak'khoi, even without you I find this ship fascinating. Worth a closer look, especially—" His communicator squawked a summons, and when he opened a channel, the voice on the other end sounded very urgent.

"Subcommander, we have a long-range contact. ID is NCC-2252, Federation light cruiser Valiant. *Closing speed is warp seven. May I recommend immediate—"*

Tr'Annhwi made an irritable noise and his officer went silent. "Yes, another look indeed," he muttered, "but not here." The orders he snapped back at Centurion tr'Hheinha were too fast for McCoy's translator to make sense of all the words, but "rig for high-speed towing" came through quite plainly. As did "Battle Stations."

"This is an active shipping lane, Captain." Tr'Annhwi turned to Reaves, using Anglish again and plainly proud of his ability to speak it. *"Avenger* has made her presence known to three other vessels, but yours has taken up more time than my schedule allowed." He smiled, that thin and far from pleasant smile of a man with all the aces in his pocket. "Mine, and that of the Starfleet local-patrol ship. Normally we would have had some hours in hand, but our earlier acquaintances seem to have cried wolf-in-the-fold. We are therefore returning to more friendly space. With you and your ship as our guests."

"I won't let you—"

"By doing *what?*" This time tr'Annhwi didn't bother

with anything so overt as pointing his phaser at the outraged Captain. He just let the situation speak for itself; and it did so, very clearly.

Reaves tugged in a halfhearted way at his uniform tunic, more for something to do with his hands than through any hope of making the ripped and filthy garment anything like presentable. It was obvious that those hands wanted to reach out and take the smile clean off tr'Annhwi's face, together with his more prominent features. The Romulan could see it as clearly as everyone else on the bridge. But he—all of them—knew that it stopped at wanting. With holes already blown in his ship, Reaves wasn't about to take any further chances.

"Not to worry, Captain h'Reeviss." Tr'Annhwi made the placatory gesture of holstering his phaser, although he didn't order the other Romulans to follow suit. "Your crew and passengers have nothing to fear. After our experts on ch'Rihan have checked your ship properly, it will be repaired and all of you released to go your way." He looked a little sideways, at the only person on the bridge still held at ostentatious gunpoint. "All but the war criminal Mak'khoi." The communicator, still activated and in his hand, squeaked several worried noises involving approach vectors. Tr'Annhwi raised one eyebrow. "And he comes with me now. *Aihr erei'Riov*. Ra'kholh, *hteij 'rhae*."

"*Hteij 'rhae. Lhhwoi-sdei.*"

"*Hna'h. . . .*"

As the *Avenger*'s transporter beam engulfed him in scarlet shimmer, the last thing that McCoy saw was tr'Annhwi's smile—

—an unpleasant smile, that survived quite unscathed and if anything had grown wider during the transition.

"Welcome aboard, Doctor." The courtesy was decidedly mocking now, delivered by someone in an even greater position of strength than before. "This is

Avenger. Neither so large nor so impressive as *Enterprise,* but bearer of a worthy name. And an apt name, Dr. Mak'khoi"—the smile was fading fast—"because it is best you know that I had close kin serving on both *Rea's Helm* and *Battlequeen,* which your *Enterprise* destroyed. It would be joy and *mhnei'sahe* for me to take their death-vengeance upon you. Take him out of my sight."

McCoy doubted that it would do him any good to tell the Romulan that *Battlequeen* had been destroyed by Captain Rihaul's *Inaieu* and not by the *Enterprise* at all. Whatever was said would be the wrong thing to say, and in tr'Annhwi's present mercurial mood, saying anything at all was downright dangerous. He let two helmeted security troopers hustle him off toward what he presumed would be the brig, and was silently grateful that tr'Annhwi's orders required him alive, unharmed, and in one piece. McCoy had a feeling that without such orders, his time aboard the *Avenger* would be notably unpleasant. . . .

As he lay back on the thin, hard bunk, he could feel jolts running through the Romulan frigate as it engaged tractor beams and locked them on *Vega,* but the lurch as its warpfield was extended around the damaged vessel knocked him off the bunk and onto the deck beneath it. McCoy swore viciously, rubbed at two fresh and three renewed bruises, considered lying down again, and did. But until the warship was well under way and the subharmonic drone of her main drive was making his teeth shake in their sockets, he lay on the floor.

They entered Rihannsu homespace in ship's night. McCoy hadn't been asleep, just leaning back with his crossed arms behind his head, looking up into the darkness and thinking the sort of convoluted thoughts men think when they can't sleep. And then the darkness became bright, and tr'Annhwi stepped through the afterimage glow that was all that remained of the force-shielded door, and he was smiling again. McCoy was growing very tired of that smile.

"Well, here you are," the Romulan said.

There was something nauseating about an enemy commander trying to be avuncular, and McCoy's glare and nonStandard suggestion both escaped before he thought of what effect they might have on his continued health.

Tr'Annhwi's smile only widened even further. "Oh, not me, Doctor," he said. "Not for some while yet. But you, quite possibly—and certainly quite soon. They are capital charges, after all. Now get up. You *do* want to see your ultimate destination, don't you?"

McCoy did; he wanted to see anything, anywhere, just so long as it was different from the four walls of the cell where he had been for almost three days. "Which is?" he said, swinging his feet to the deck.

"Ch'Rihan," said tr'Annhwi. He said it again as the planet rotated slowly on the *Avenger*'s main screen, while he lounged in his center seat and McCoy stood uncomfortably flanked by armed guards right behind it. "We are now in a geosynchronous parking orbit above the city of i'Ramnau. The place where you will spend your last few days before going to Areinnye—the hell you wished on me with such feeling, Dr. Mak'khoi—by whatever painful route your judges decide. After they have done with you and the news is known, perhaps the Federation will be more respectful of Rihannsu space, and lives, and secrets."

"Subcommander"—one of the crewmen on the cramped little bridge swung his seat around and took a translator from his ear—"Fleet Intelligence personnel and a scanning team are en route from the surface. Commander t'Radaik requests that the prisoner be made ready for immediate transfer to her shuttle. You are invited to accompany him. I have readied Hangar Bay Three for immediate turnaround and—*what in the Elements' name!*"

The whole ship vibrated and alarms warbled briefly, but died as damage control reported in. "External visual—there." The *Vega,* locked into the same orbit as her captor, was wreathed in a swirling mist of liquid and letters that billowed from the rip in her belly and danced a Brownian-motion polka around the liner's hull.

"Captain h'Reeviss, what happened?" Tr'Annhwi sounded more embarrassed that an Intelligence officer should have seen this mess than concerned for the safety of his prize.

"You blew a hole in my bloody ship and then dragged her half across the galaxy, that's what happened!" crackled Reaves's voice. *"I'm only surprised the alcohol-cargo tanks lasted this long before—"*

"What losses, Captain? Was anyone hurt?"

"No—but no thanks to you, you—"

"Then what else? I see papers and liquid vapor—was that all?"

"Some of the artwork blew out—explosive decompression sent it into atmosphere—lost items worth more than you'll earn in a—"

"Good. No harm done." Tr'Annhwi didn't bother hiding his relief. "Now, Dr. Mak'khoi, if you would follow me . . . ?"

McCoy felt that the politeness of the request was rather offset by the vigor with which someone prodded a phaser into his back, but he followed anyway. It was better than being pushed the whole way to ch'Rihan.

None of them had said anything after tr'Annhwi's brief introduction, neither the Subcommander nor the cool-eyed female Commander who was uncomfortably like two other Romulan woman officers in her quiet self-assurance, and certainly not the six soldiers who had accompanied her up to *Avenger* and back down, and who had sat stolidly gazing at McCoy the whole day long. Though to tell the truth, he hadn't felt inclined to open a conversation himself. Odds were that the soldiers didn't wear translators, and there wasn't much to talk about. He hadn't seen a great deal of ch'Rihan after landing, and before that—well, one M-class planet seen from orbit looked very much like another.

They had been sitting in the back of an armored military flitter for what felt like hours now, and McCoy had become very glad of the little 'freshbooth built into the vehicle's tail-section. Once in a while he wondered simple things: *Is it day or night outside? Will there be food soon? What does a Romulan city look like . . . ?* because his mind wouldn't go blank no matter how he tried to force it, and unless he thought of ordinary needs, the doubts and terrors kept creeping back to harry him. Of course, that was what they wanted, and why they had left him like this, but knowing it and being able to do something about it were two entirely different things.

The mouse-squeak of a Romulan communicator was so sudden and unusual that for a moment McCoy couldn't place it. But the guards stood up, and two opened the rear hatch of the flitter to admit a blessed breath of nonrecirculated air, while the remaining four escorted him out. If "escorting" actually described being seized by the upper arms and manhandled like a parcel.

It was night outside indeed, and alien constellations burned above him in a clear, clean sky. The dwelling toward which he was being "escorted," for the two larger guards had not yet released their grip on him, was a low, rambling place that was itself star-spotted with light, some harsh and artificial but the rest a warm amber glow of live-flame torchieres.

The soldiers let him go at the foot of a short flight of stairs, and shifted to a parade march-step as they advanced up the steps alongside him. McCoy looked up at the building's open doorway and smiled briefly despite the untidy mixture of emotions that were filling him. *Wonderful,* he thought wryly, *a familiar, friendly face to welcome me.*

Tr'Annhwi was standing in the doorway wearing an expression fit to curdle milk, and the tall shape of Commander t'Radaik was right beside him. They were both armed, and not with phasers but with brutal-looking issue blasters. McCoy was simultaneously angry and amused. *Are they expecting trouble at this stage?* he thought. *Not from me, no sir!*

The hall inside was full of people, all Rihannsu, all staring hard, and McCoy felt uncomfortably like an animal put on show. He felt quite within his rights to stare back, at the soldiers and the officers, at the old man with wine on his chin, and at what had to be servants—

And suddenly, intently, at one in particular. A woman in servant's clothing, but with an elaborate garment over it that made him think of a fleet officer's half-cloak. But it wasn't her clothing. She had moved . . . *strangely* was the only way to describe it, and McCoy wondered something that was far from simple. *Is this the one? Am I in the right House after all?* His hands moved together in a recognition gesture, one that any Federation agent would spot immediately; its response was simple enough that she could reply at once, in plain sight. . . .

Except that she didn't. Oh, there was a fluttering of sorts as her fingers moved, but it wasn't the right movement. It wasn't any sort of gesture, just a twitch of nervousness. McCoy felt his guts give a little acid heave as the realization came home to him. Worst scenario. Very worst. Either this agent had gone the way Star-fleet Command suspected, spent so long in deep cover that she'd gone native and literally forgotten who and what she really was, or—or maybe there'd been some horrible mistake and he'd been brought to the wrong House, wishful thinking had misread her body kinesics, and she wasn't an agent at all.

His mouth moved as he spoke bold words, bolder than he'd dared to utter yet, because there was a feeling that he had nothing to lose by them anymore. Maybe he was alone there after all.

Maybe he *was* going to die.

Chapter Four

Preflight

NATURALLY ONE DOES not just say good-bye to one's planet, build a fleet of starships, and take off in them . . . though this is often the image of what happened on Vulcan during the Reformation.

S'task showed some canniness about handling Vulcan psychology when he slipped the concept of a massive off-planet migration quietly into the Vulcan communications nets and mindtrees rather than making an open, hard declaration right off the bat. "When people think an idea is theirs," he said later in his writings aboard *Rea's Helm*, "they take it so much the more to heart than if they think they got it from someone else, or worse, followed a great public trend. There is nothing people want to do more than to follow great trends, and nothing they want less to *seem* to be doing."

The declaration itself, the document to be known much later as the Statement of Intention of Flight, appeared first in the journal of the Vulcan Academy of Sciences—then an infant body of the Universities—under a title that translates approximately into Terran academic-journalistic idiom as "A Study of Socioeconomic Influences on Vulcan Space Exploration." It was a sober and scholarly investigation into the economic trends that had moved the various Vulcan space programs over a thousand years, and it discussed in depth one recurring trend with disquieting correlations to the aggressiveness taking place on the planet at a specific place and time. When a given part of the planet grew too crowded to adequately support its population with water, food, and shelter, said this theory, then wars broke out there as the neighboring tribes or nations fought for resources. When wars broke out, technology, both physical and nonphysical, flourished during the "war efforts" of the various sides. And after the war in question was over, the technology was spun off into the private sector, with a subsequent substantial increase in the ability of a given part of the planet to support its population . . . until the next peak in the cycle.

S'task was therefore the first Vulcan to manage to introduce into Vulcan mass consciousness a statement of what on Earth has come to be known as Heinlein's Law. The idea had, of course, occurred to many people at many times over Vulcan's history, but S'task was the first to spread the concept so widely, into that "threshold number" of minds necessary for a culture to begin working change on itself. And, whether on purpose or accidentally, S'task framed the concept as the conclusion of an exercise in logic—asking, at the end of the article, whether it would not be more logical simply to have the increase in technology and subsequent spinoff and omit the war.

Many who read this saw in the article a potential reconciliation between S'task and Surak, but the old teacher knew better. He is said to have wept after he first saw the presentation of it, knowing that his student, whether in spite or cunning, was using logic, Surak's great love and tool, as a weapon against him.

It is sometimes hard for humans to understand that logic as a way of life did not instantly descend upon the whole Vulcan people immediately after Surak announced that it would be a good thing. Very quickly, by historical standards, yes: but not overnight. There were many false starts, renunciations, debunkings, persecutions, and periods of what seemed massive inertia; and

71

the idea of the logical life went through many of the stages that other, less sweeping popular phenomena do. Around the time of the Statement of Intent, "reality-truth" was still truly only a fad among Vulcans, an "up-and-coming trend." This is something else that people, particularly humans, find hard to grasp. The difficulty is understandable, susceptible as we are to our own blindnesses to fads like the scientific method, and the various ways in which each new generation tends to twist the sciences to fit its own *zeitgeist*. Surak could see the time when reason would be truly internalized in the behavior of a whole population, and would guide the whole planet. But despite its validity as a tool, at the moment logic was only an easy gateway into people's minds because of its novelty status—and S'task was not ashamed to use it as such.

S'task also used the article to suggest something slightly radical: the idea that a largish planetary migration might be the tool necessary to curtail the planet's violence. If the whole planet's population were lessened, then the whole place would better be able to support the people who remained, and wars might be fewer. He never even mentioned the question of any philosophical disagreement, which was the root of the matter, and in truth it would have been inappropriate, in the context of the journal in question, to do so. As it was, the argument he used smacked of *a priori* reasoning, but its end product was something that too many people wanted to hear. This, too, is difficult to explain to humans—that despite their violent history, the Vulcans did not *like* violence, war, terror, or death. They simply had it . . . rather like the populations of many other planets that did not seem able to stop fighting. They wanted it to stop, or at least to slow down . . . and anything that seemed likely to do that seemed very good to them.

In any case, the article served to found the context for the Flight: the idea that not only *could* many thousands of people leave Vulcan, but they *should*.

Rather than having people trying to stop them from going, the Travelers found pressure on them to go. There were, of course, some factions pressured into going against their will, and they made their belated displeasure known in the counsels of ch'Rihan and ch'Havran much later, to the intense annoyance of the majority of the Rihannsu. Several of these "forgotten" factions are the reason that there sometimes seem to be numerous different versions of the "Romulan Empire," all espousing different aims and behaving in different ways. More of this later.

So the context was established in the popular mind that a sort of "New Vulcan" should be established somewhere far from the decadent excesses and "liberalism" of the old. Support for this viewpoint grew across the board during the fifteen years or so that the Argument officially lasted. But the part of the "board" hardest to convince was, of course, industry, and S'task had to concentrate his efforts on them for some years before achieving the results he needed.

S'task knew quite well that finding venture capital to build fifteen ships of a kind that had never been seen before—generation ships—was not going to be possible. So, as usual, he went around the problem to an unexpected solution.

The mindtrees and networks had for some years been discussing the question of who should go. By 139970 the number of the *seheik*, the "declared," was approaching twelve thousand. Into this context S'task inserted the suggestion that perhaps only those should go who were willing to give nearly everything they had in support of it. The suggestion was a risky one, but also wise: it began functioning to "shake out" those who were not completely committed to the move because of the philosophy behind it. Subscriptions began to pile up in the escrow accounts established by S'task's followers, and as they did so, concern built in the Vulcan financial community.

It was at the point where about eight thousand

people had made contributions varying from ten percent to a hundred percent of their estates, and construction had begun on *Rea's Helm* and *Farseeker,* that the community first began to seriously discuss what should be done about the Flight. Their concern was understandable . . . since the Travelers' movement was growing with a speed unprecedented until then. It had seemed only a fad until the 139980s, but by the end of that decade something like five percent of the population had committed to the Journey. Within the close order of eighteen years, as much as twenty to thirty percent of the total capital wealth on Vulcan might be completely removed from the banking and credit systems. The Vulcan financial ecology could not withstand such a blow: any withdrawal of funds and labor potential greater than eighteen percent would cause a depression too deep for the planet to ever recover from. Yet such a withdrawal was certainly coming, unless something was done to halt or slow the spread of the Traveler movement. At that time the question of financing enough ships to carry everyone was constantly in the nets, and attracting a great deal of attention to the issues of the Traveler cause itself, which in turn was causing more and more Vulcans to contribute their time and money to the cause.

The major banking cartels conferred over this problem for nearly a year, and then took the only action possible to them: one that cost them the equivalent of billions of credits, but both saved Vulcan from a depression and made them a great deal of money later. They financed the building of the starships themselves, as well as much necessary research and development. Crookedly, in a way S'task himself had not expected, his twist on the Heinlein principle began to prove itself. The technologies born in the shipbuilding paid for themselves many times over, since all the major patents were owned by the banking cartels. It is true that the banks gained a measure of control over the Journey by limiting the number of ships, and therefore of Travelers, and with the problem of transport solved, some of the attractiveness of the Journey as a "desperate cause" was lost, and the number of new subscribers to the Journey dropped off. But S'task was willing to accept this, and to grant the banks their small measure of control. He had what he wanted from them. Also, he, too, had been worrying about the economic impact of the Journey on Vulcan: he was angry at his homeworld, but not so much so as to want to reduce it to poverty.

Some have pointed out an unforeseen and unfortunate side effect of starting an interstellar colonization effort by subscription. Many fortunes large and small, many "nest eggs" and hoards of family money, went into the building fund even after the banks began financing the Journey. Many a family was bitterly divided over the issue, and much Vulcan fiction of this period revolves around the Sundering. Among those making the Journey, a peculiar mindset began to form, born of the poverty and scarcity that many of the Travelers had to suffer while waiting to leave Vulcan. Many of the Travelers came to feel that possession of more than one's daily needs was an evil, that one should share as necessary with those others also making the Journey and otherwise eschew personal possessions and wealth. Some cultural sociologists have stated the opinion that this "foundation context" of privation and scarcity as a thing somehow good and noble came to affect the Rihannsu later in their development. These sociologists suggest that had the Journey not started this way, the Rihannsu would not have had the problems with poverty and scarcity that they had later. But then again, neither would they have been Rihannsu as we now know them.

With design and construction funding finally available for the ships, serious consideration of where they should go could begin, had to, since this would influence the ships' design at every level. Mass interferometry and spectrometry of neighboring stars had been fairly encouraging. The area around 40 Eri contains several large congeries of stars, one a group of Population II blue and blue-white giants, and the two others both large collections of Pop I stars ranging through types G through M, with the occasional N, R, and S "carbon stars." There were at least twenty stars within five lightyears of Vulcan, another eighty within fifteen lightyears, and of both these groups, the mass interferometer indicated that some twenty had planets. The astronomers involved in the Journey had a merry time arguing over the optimum course, but finally agreement was reached on an initial twelve-year tour of the most likely close stars, with an optional fifty-year tour of the less well-scanned outer ones. There were five very likely candidates in the first sequence, three of them type M stars like Vulcan, the others a type K and a G9, rather more orange than yellow. All five had planets, several of them large ones Vulcan's size or larger, and the Vulcan version of Bode's Law indicated that each system had at least one planet at what (for Vulcans) was the right distance from its sun.

To help (or some said hinder) them, they also had some information salvaged from the computers of the crashed or captured Etoshan pirate ships, concerning the locations of populated planets. This data the Vulcans were generally inclined to mistrust, since the Etoshans had already lied to them. However, they did use the information in a negative way: they kept far away from any star mentioned in it. The Travelers did not want to be found by aliens again. All the courses plotted were to take them far from space known to the Etoshans.

With all this in mind, the ships built were designed as fairly short-term interstellar shuttle ships, with an option for use as generation vessels should both the first and second tours prove barren. Each ship was meant to carry about five thousand people in an arrangement of six cylinders clustered and bound together by access-ways and major "thoroughfares." The design of these craft closely approximates those used for some of the L5 colonies around Terra, except that gravity was provided artificially rather than by spin. Drive for the vessels was conventional iondrive with the Vulcan version of a Bussard ramjet (a piece of design they did not mind stealing from the Etoshans). Later on, when they discovered it during the Journey, the psi-assisted "bootstrap" method was also occasionally used, by which an adept instantly accelerated the whole vessel to .99999c, and then allowed the ship to coast "downhill" to the next star. This method was used only when there was an extreme emergency threatening the vessel; it tended to kill the adept performing it, and only a jump-trained adept could train others in the technique. Whichever method was used, the ship could use a given star's gravity well to slow it down, and then move on subdrive to the primary's planets: or if the star's planets looked unpromising, it could pick up momentum again by using the gravity well for the acceleration phase of a "slingshot" maneuver.

Ships were not the only thing being built, however. Many of the Travelers had realized that if they were going to truly become their own world rather than a sort of retread of the failed Vulcan, they would have to discard a great deal of their culture, and invent new institutions as replacements. The matter of choices took the whole fifteen years between the Statement of Intent and the launching of *Rea's Helm*, and to this day the controversy about some choices has not died down.

The records of the arguments on the nets, and transcriptions or paraphrasings of the discussions on the mindtrees, fill some six hundred rooms in the Archive on ch'Havran, and some hundreds of terabytes in the Vulcan Science Academy's history storage. Vulcan foods, literature, clothing styles, weapons, poetry, religions, social customs, furniture designs, fairy tales, art, science, and philosophy all were endlessly examined in a fifteen-year game of "lifeboat." Only the best, or the ideologically correct, were to be taken along on the Journey. No one person or committee was ever set up as the arbiter of taste: the roughly eighty thousand minds participating in the nets and the Travelers' mindtrees would argue themselves to a rough consensus, or to silence, and in either case each Traveler would decide for himself what to do about a given issue. Mostly they agreed, and it may be astonishing to Terrans how often these people did so. They were possibly more like-minded than we, or they, would like to admit, or else they were terrified by how closely their previous disagreement had brought their planet to disaster.

One thing they agreed on quickly was that they could not stop being Vulcan while they still spoke the language. A team of semanticists and poets, S'task among them, began building the Travelers' new language just after the ships' keels were flown. They did not, of course, try to divorce it completely from Vulcan, but they went back to the original Old High Vulcan roots and "aged" the words in another direction, as it were—producing a language as different from its ancient parent and the other "fullgrown" tongue as Basque is different from Spanish and their parent, Latin. The new tongue was a softer one, with fewer fricatives than Vulcan, and many aspirants; long broad vowels and liquid consonant combinations, both fairly rare in Vulcan, were made commonplace in the new language. To Terran ears it frequently sounds like a combination of Latin and Welsh. The language came strangely to Vulcan tongues at first, but its grammar and syntax were grossly similar, and over the years of Flight, the Travelers spoke it with increasing pleasure and pride. From it they took what was to be their new name, which by attachment became the language's also. *Seheik*, "the declared," became *rihanh* in the new language. This, in the adjective form, became *rihannsu*. The building of the language is often overlooked in studies of Rihannsu culture. It deserves more attention than there is room to give it here—the only "made" language ever to be successfully adopted by an entire planetary population.

But though this and many other good things were added to the Rihannsu culture, many things were also lost. The matriarchal cast of the civilization remained, though power would come to distribute itself rather differently from the council-of-tribes structure under which Vulcan had been operating for thousands of years. Much literature was condemned as "decadent" or "liberal" and left behind. A considerable amount of science scavenged from the Etoshans was relabeled as Vulcan. The encounter with the Etoshans itself, the trigger of all this, was retold as the foundation of the persecutions that caused the Travelers to leave the planet, and the "straw that broke the camel's back." When one looks at this bit of revisionist history, the xenophobia of "Romulans" becomes entirely understandable. Fifty generations of Rihannsu were taught that anything alien was probably bad, and vice versa. Earthmen saying "we come in peace" were not likely to be believed. The Etoshans had said the same thing.

For good or ill (though meaning good), the Travelers decided to rewrite history for their children and teach them all the same thing. Mostly it came to the idea, as stated above, that aliens were dangerous, that even their own people had once made a dangerous choice, but that they (the fortunate children) had been saved from it; they must take care not to let the same thing happen to them, or *their* children. And indeed to this day there are two words in Rihannsu for fact: "truth" and "told-truth."

There were, of course, cultural and artistic "smugglings." Not even the Vulcan-trained can police the thoughts of eighty thousand fiercely committed revolutionaries (or counterrevolutionaries). Bits of non-approved culture, science, and law sneaked in here and there. Some of them were the source of endless anguish. Some were afterward cherished as treasures.

One of these was S'task's own, and not even his own people could much blame him for it. As poets often are, he was a swordsman as well, and besides his wife and daughter and the clothes on his back, the only things he brought with him on the Journey were three swords by the smith S'harien.

S'harien was the greatest of all the smiths working by the edge of the desert that other species call Vulcan's Forge, and he was also something of an embarrassment to everyone who knew him. He lived for metal: beside it, nothing mattered to him, not his wife, not his children, not eating or drinking. He was usually rude and almost always unkempt (in Vulcan culture, the most unforgivable of bad habits), one of those people who is always being taken places twice . . . the second time to apologize. He was almost always forgiven, for this cranky, perpetually angry creature could create such beauty in steel as had never been seen before. "He works it as a god works flesh," said another smith, one of his contemporaries. Petty kings and tribal chieftains had often come offering everything they had to purchase his swords. He insulted them like beggars, and they took it. They had to: he was S'harien.

He was also a diehard reactionary. In a time when so many other Vulcan men were taking the five-letter names beginning with S and ending in K in token of their acceptance (or at least honoring) of "reality-truth" and its chief proponent, S'harien purposely took a pre-Reformation name, and an ill-omened one, "pierceblood." S'harien loved the old wars and the honorable bloodshed, and hated Surak's name, and would spit on his shadow if he saw it—so he told everyone. On his hundred and ninetieth birthday, hearing that Surak was nearby, he went to do so. And everyone became very confused when, a tenday later, S'harien very suddenly started buying up all his swords and melting them down, in ongoing renunciation of violence. Even Surak tried to stop him from doing this: a S'harien sword was a treasure of gorgeous and dangerous workmanship that even the most nonviolent heart could rest in without guilt. But S'harien was not to be dissuaded.

There was consternation late one night when a flitter docked outside S'task's quarters in the orbital ship-yards, and the short, dark, fierce shape in the pressure suit stepped through the airlock with a long bundle in his arms. The security people stared in astonishment. It was in fact Surak. They took him to S'task and made to leave, though very much desiring to stay: master and pupil had at that point not seen each other for six standard years. But Surak bade them stay, and handed the bundle to S'task. "Keep these safe, I pray you," he said in the Old High Vulcan of ceremony. And S'task, stricken by the formality of the language—or perhaps by the worn look of his old master—took the bundle, bowed deeply, and made no other answer. When he straightened, Surak was already on his way out.

The bundle contained three of the most priceless S'hariens on the planet, two of which had been thought to belong to kings, and one to the High Councillor, himself a bitter enemy of Surak's. How Surak had come by the swords no one ever found out, though various Vulcan families have (conflicting) tales of a shadowy shape who came to them around that time and begged them for "their sword's life." There was argument about keeping the swords, at first—they had after all come from Surak, and there were sore hearts who wanted no gifts from him: gifts, they said, bind. But S'task said a few quiet words in the swords' behalf in Meeting, some nights before the ships left, and put the issue to rest. In time the Travelers came to treasure the S'hariens greatly, as a gift from their most worthy adversary, and as beautiful things in their own right, but most of all as a symbol for the ancient glory they were leaving behind.

The S'hariens were, after all, "swords of the twilight," made in the style of the swords of the ancient Vulcan empires, by methods that no one but S'harien had been able to reconstruct. But those empires were long gone, and the planet was even now a far calmer place than it had been in those times of enormous ferocity and splendor. If Surak's teachings took hold, as all the Travelers now felt sure they would, then Vulcan would become quieter still. They would take the swords with them to remember the old Vulcan by—the energetic, angry, beautiful, whole Vulcan, all blood-green passion and joy that dared death, laughing. They took the swords though it was their enemy who gave them, and though the man who made them would sooner have seen them destroyed than in Rihannsu hands (or indeed any other). The sword became both the cause and the symbol of the Sundering. It was the sword that parted Vulcan. It was the sword that would eventually draw the two sundered parts together over the years, though neither side was to know that as *Rea's Helm* glided away from Vulcan and Charis, leaving its one stave behind it in the dark.

Perhaps those angry hearts in Meeting were right. Perhaps gifts do bind. Or perhaps, despite millennia, blood is enough.

Chapter Five

ARRHAE HAD NEVER before been so happy to be dismissed. Her thoughts were still in a whirl as she pattered downstairs more quickly than was proper, wondering, *What to do? What to do?* in a sort of frantic litany. Her hands were shaking and she couldn't make them stop, her heart was pounding far too fast, and for one horrible moment she thought that she was going to be sick right there and then.

The nausea passed without shaming her, and Arrhae leaned against the wall, pressing her head to the cool stone and feeling a droplet of sweat ooze clammily from her hairline. "Calm," she said. "Control." Then whimpered in sudden terror and clapped one of those shaking hands to her mouth, for the words had come out in Anglish.

This time she *was* sick, making it to the Elements-be-thanked 'fresher just in time. Arrhae sat for some minutes on the floor, shuddering and feeling wretched, before she felt capable of even turning on the disposal-sluices. *Poor tr'Aimne. If this is what he felt like in the flitter . . .*

That memory of ordinary everyday things, which seen now were neither, and never truly had been, helped to get her shocked mind back into some sort of coherent working order. Rinsing her face and her mouth with cold water, and feeling much better for it, Arrhae started to think of what had to be done. Not about McCoy the Federation officer—if that was truly what he was—but about Mak'khoi the prisoner, and where she was going to put him.

The storeroom, obviously—but had it been cleaned

yet? Aired? Heated? She had a sneaking suspicion that none of those things had been done, and why? Because she, *hru'hfe* of House Khellian, had preferred to gape at visitors like the lowliest scullery-slave rather than be about her proper business.

There, that feels more like it.

Arrhae's mouth quirked with annoyance. Half an hour ago she wouldn't have needed to consciously review her thoughts like that—and wouldn't have been thinking in Terran Anglish either! All of her acclimatization was ruined, and she had a feeling that she had already given herself away to the Terran—

—*No, his name's McCoy, and he's not a "Terran," he's one of my people . . . !*

—*But I'm Arrhae ir-Mnaeha t'Khellian, and he's one of the* enemies *of my people!*

"O Fire and Air and Earth," she moaned softly, sitting down again and wrapping her arms around the legs that were suddenly too weak to hold her up. Arrhae closed her eyes and rested her head on her knees, rocking backward and forward, backward and forward, no longer even sure of how to make her prayers. "Ohhh, God help me. . . ."

When it came, as come it must, the brief storm of weeping was shocking in its intensity and for a time left her drained of all emotion. That at least was good, for it meant that she could be cold and rational for a while, before her mind began to churn again and the terrors came flooding back. Arrhae washed her face a second time, straightened her rumpled clothing, and eyed herself critically in the burnished metal mirror.

"*Hha'hn, hru'hfe*," she told the reflection. *You'll do. For now, anyway.*

She channeled all of that pent-up nervous energy into organizing a scouring-squad for the new "secure quarters." The next half hour did nothing for Arrhae's popularity among the servants, but a great deal for her reputation as a maniacally efficient slave driver. Not that she shouted, or struck anyone. There was no need for such crude methods when her tongue and vocabulary seemed to acquire fresh cutting edges, new depths of subtlety, and new heights of eloquence. Even while they cursed her name and ancestry under their breath, more than one of the house-folk laboring with mops and cleaning rags were making mental note of some superbly original insult for their own later use. . . .

Arrhae had at first hoped she wouldn't be able to think of private matters if she allowed the fine fury of cleaning-supervision take her over, but she was wrong. There was always a voice tickling at the back of her mind, demanding that she attend to everything it had to say. Finally she switched over to automatic, at least where the cleanup was concerned, and began to listen in the hope that once heard, the words from her subconscious would go away.

"*. . . Please sit down, Lieutenant-Commander Haleakala . . .*"

"*. . . fed in the program parameters, and yours was one of the first names to come out.*"

Commodore Perry had been more than courteous in the hour or so since she'd been ushered into his office at Starfleet Intelligence Headquarters; the big man had been downright kindly, taking pains to disarm her nervousness—which had been more obvious than she liked to think—before starting to explain why she'd been pulled out of Xenosociology aboard *Excalibur* at such short notice.

"Romulans," she said. Just that. It was more than enough.

Perry nodded, touching the molecular fiche on the desk in front of him with one fingertip. It was tabbed with a data scrambler and the yellow/black/yellow-on-red of MOST SECRET, EYES ONLY information, almost the highest security level in Starfleet and certainly the highest that she'd ever shared a room with. "They call themselves *Rihannsu*. And that's just about the only reliable information that we have. Everything else"—he flipped one hand dismissively at the air—"is educated speculation at best and wild guesses at worst. We need to know more. Much more."

"'Know your enemy.' Is that it, sir?" *Oh, very bold, Terise. Tell him you disapprove of the word "enemy" now, why don't you?*

"In one way, yes. But not in such simplistic terms as you seem to be implying, Ms."

Ouch . . . ! "Noted, sir."

"There are a few agents already planted in the Romulan Empire; ninety-plus percent are Romulans themselves, and what information we glean from them is military—which would be all very well if we were planning war. If we were, say, Klingons. But what we want, and what the Federation needs, is a basis for *understanding* these people."

Perry glanced at something that flickered across the readout at one side of his desk, punched a couple of buttons to acknowledge it, and lifted one of the data chips that sat in an impeccably straight line beside their scanning-slot. "Vaebn tr'Lhoell," he said. "One of our Romulans, and a good, reliable agent. There's just one problem. The Romulan agents are too—too Romulan. They were born to and brought up with aspects of their culture that we can't begin to comprehend, and they can't explain them to an outsider any more than a bird could explain the sky. Only a deep-cover agent can do it, and physiology restricts us to either Terran or Vulcan. Even then, Romulan physiology is Vulcan rather than Terran; that much has been learned already. So where necessary, there'll have to be . . ." Perry's voice trailed off as he hunted for an appropriate term.

"'Cosmetic changes'?" Terise suggested. "And that's why"—with a sudden flash of brilliance—"my name came up in the personnel scan." Terise had a full name that sometimes felt yards long, a dusky complexion inherited from a Polynesian mother and an Italian father, and a facial bone-structure all her own that was sharp enough to split kindling. Several of her less lovable schoolfellows had called her "the Vulcan" because of it, although that had stopped once she graduated to Starfleet Academy and there were real Vulcans in the classes with her—as well as Andorians, Tellarites, and weirder species who departed from the bipedal hominid norm. Xenopathic screening of the student body also had something to do with it. Small use crewing a starship with half-a-dozen races and not making sure they wouldn't be at what passed for one another's throats before their first mission was a week old.

"Quite so. And you require fewer, er, changes than most. The ears, obviously, will need slight remodeling"—Perry cleared his throat noisily, now more ill at ease than she was, and Terise came very close to patting his hands in reassurance. "Hemoplasmic pigmentation tagging, primary craniofacial restructure . . . ? Who the hell wrote this? We're talking about people, not refitting a starship!"

"Commodore, I don't mind; truly I don't. If I'd been that thin-skinned, I'd never have survived high school. And sir, you've got at least one volunteer." All the words came out in a rush, the comforting inconsequential ones and the ones that might end up killing her. When it was done, Terise sat up very straight in her chair and swallowed, hard. That was such a cliché, but there came a time in everyone's life when only the tried and trusted gestures felt sufficiently adequate, and this was such a time right now.

"You do understand what you're letting yourself in for, Ms. Haleakala? Or is that Ms. LoBrutto? I've been presuming you don't use the hyphen, either. Excuse me. . . ."

"Yes and no, Commodore. Yes, I know what I'll be

going into, and the prospect terrifies me—but I'm a sociologist by profession and nobody trained in that discipline would ever pass up an opportunity like this." Terise hesitated over that sweeping statement, wondering if she should add *except the ones who want to live* and decided not to bother. Instead, she smiled wryly. "And no, it's neither LoBrutto nor hyphenated. You got it right first time."

"Thank you. For that and other matters. But I'm not logging your acceptance until after you've been briefed on the setup." Terise's eyebrows must have shot up involuntarily, because the Commodore looked at the security-blazoned fiche and then grinned at her. "Don't worry, Commander. What I'll tell you isn't anything like as confidential. Not at all. You won't be asked to sign anything in blood." He grinned again. "Not yet; not until it's green."

Terise made the sort of hollow laugh that would have sounded more genuine had she simply said "ha-ha" and been done with it.

"Quite so," said Perry. "But keep your sense of humor—you're going to need it." He dropped one of the data chips into its slot and keyed a string of characters. There was a momentary mosquito-whine, and sparkles of color sleeted across his desk readout as the monomolecular scanner kicked in.

"Authorization?" it said.

"Perry, Stephen C., Commodore, UFP Starfleet Intelligence Corps, CEG-0703-1960MS."

"Accepted. Data up and running."

"Good." Perry caught the "was that all?" look on Terise's face and nodded. "Yes, Commander, that's all—for this information at least. Getting at the other . . . Not so simple. Anyway, this is the game plan for this particular play, and I warn you right now, you won't like it. . . ."

". . . *like it?*"

"Eh?" Arrhae jolted back to the bad dream that was

real life, wondering who had been saying what. The *who* was S'anra, one of the scullery servants, and the *what?* had been repeated for Elements alone knew how many times.

"Hru'hfe, all here is finished—do you like it?"

She came back to awareness quickly enough after that, and glared around with the expression of someone expecting to find the work done poorly if at all. Instead, and to her unvoiced surprise, it had been done well. The floor, first brushed then scrubbed, had finally been polished brightly enough for Arrhae to see her quizzical face reflecting back from its tiled surface.

"Excellent," she said, genuinely pleased. "All of you have done well—and by that, done honor to our lord. My word as *hru'hfe* on it, I shall name all your names to him, and speak highly of them. S'anra, Ekkhae, Hanaj, you three attend to the furnishings—and, by my order, commandeer as many strong backs as you need to carry things. The colors and the patterns"—Arrhae hesitated, and made her hesitation plain. Only her decision was made plainer—"I leave to you." She smiled thinly at them, a lesser servant and two slaves entrusted with something she should attend to herself. "I may have to change things—but I would think well of you if I could leave all as I find it."

She looked around the storeroom while the servants filed past, confused by the warmth of her words but giving her profound reverences because of them, and she thought of how soon it would be a prison cell, and suppressed a shudder. Hangings of fur and textile relieved the starkness of the room's plain walls and gave a certain primitive splendor to the rough-hewn stones. Only the high-tech look of thermotropic heaters and incantube lighting made the place seem any different from the dungeons in the old tales of T'Eleijha and the Raven. Stories that Arrhae had loved to watch or hear, whenever she had the free time for either.

* * *

Stories that were no more than alien folklore to Lieutenant-Commander Terise Haleakala-LoBrutto.

Commodore Perry had been right. She didn't like it. Neither the plan, nor the execution of it. Had she not made a promise to herself before she volunteered that she wouldn't back out no matter what, Terise would have put in for an immediate transfer back to the *Excalibur* right after Perry told her what would be expected of her. No matter that the M-5 combat exercise didn't sound much fun, it didn't sound dangerous either.

This did.

Starfleet's basic plan was that she learn as much Romulan data and language as they had on file and then be seeded on one of their Romulan double agents as a sleeper, for fine-tuning before becoming an active deep-cover operative.

The realities behind the plan were less simple: for one thing, the language-tutoring would have to be a form of chemical-enhanced speed learning, and while that was highly efficient in its own small way, it was also the means to a three-day migraine headache that matched the Big Bang for intensity. Terise knew all about *that*, because to her lasting shame she had used it for illicit revision at college. Once . . . On all the other occasions she had done her assignments the way they were supposed to be done, and been thankful that any headaches earned had just been little ones.

But it was the prospect of sleeper-time that she really didn't like. Starfleet's knowledge of the Romulan language was restricted to what clipped military communications the Neutral Zone spy-satellites were able to monitor—and that wasn't anything like enough.

So she was going to be a slave. The ancient sold-into-bondage, chain-on-the-neck—"I gather it's been refined down to a sort of dog collar with the owner's name and address on it," Perry had told her in an attempt at comfort—sort of slave who was one degree up from the domestic animals because slaves *usually* didn't need to be told things more than once. . . .

Granted that her master was to be Vaebn tr'Lhoell or one of the other Romulans who would only pretend to treat her as property, the whole notion still made Terise feel twitchy. *What if anything goes wrong?* had been her first thought. After she had heard how she was to be "sold as unsatisfactory" to a more highly placed household once tr'Lhoell was certain that she could conduct herself as a native-born Rihanha, it had been her final thought as well.

How final that thought might turn out to be, Terise didn't like to consider. Certainly matters had proceeded apace once she had insisted that her acceptance of the mission be placed on record; almost as if somewhere high up in Starfleet there was a fear that she would back out if given enough peace to reconsider what she had done.

Terise was just a little bit uneasy at the speed with which she assimilated Romulan. She knew of the dangers confronting deep-cover operatives in hostile territory, and those dangers were not always a result of being caught. Sometimes the greatest hazards lay in *not* being detected, and in adapting too well to the role of an alternate personality. There was the standard cautionary tale of the longterm prisoner who tried to escape from jail by simulating madness, and who succeeded so completely that when he was released, it was into the care of an insane asylum. Such risks were not usual during an ordinary tour of duty in the lab of a starship, but this was no tour, and *nothing* about it was ordinary.

The name they gave her soon replaced her own—for the simple reason that no one at the Intelligence facility ever called her anything other than Arrhae ir-Mnaeha. Terise/Arrhae found the supposedly cumbersome Romulan names easy enough to manage, because only a few of them seemed to have more syllables than her own . . . or the name which had *been* her own and which was now fading away like a dream after waking. And they all had a meaning, which made the actual understanding of them a relatively simple thing once the language structure was shoehorned into her brain. But the shift in mindset necessary for that understanding, and for the many, many other things that Intelligence people had spent so long briefing her about?

That was something which she was certain that she would never accomplish. . . .

. . . Until she did.

"Madam, sirs, all is in readiness." Arrhae made the announcement from just inside the doorway, and was careful not to look directly at the man Mak'khoi. *McCoy,* her mind corrected. She ignored the correction. He was Federation—and that meant he was an enemy until the time when he could be proven otherwise. It made matters easier if she thought of him only as an abstract danger, like a venomous *nei'rrh* loose in an empty room. The sort of thing that she could walk softly around, in the knowledge that if she didn't disturb it, then she was safe. Always assuming, of course, that the *nei'rrh* in question wasn't feeling irritable, or pugnacious, or had had its feathers ruffled.

This one was suffering from all three. He knew not only what she had said, but all the substrata of meaning behind her simple declaration. That he was to be imprisoned; that a special place had been prepared for him; and that she was not going to reply to his signal. That, most of all, burned in his eyes as he stood up and Arrhae at last glanced toward him, knowing that not to do so would appear unnatural. Not a *nei'rrh* at all, she thought. A *thrai,* with all the memory for wrongs done him that *thraiin* were supposed to have. She tried to visualize Mak'khoi bearing such a grudge for years until the time was ripe for vengeance, like that old Klingon proverb people were so fond of quoting with a sneer, and found that she could not. There was a gentleness about the man that ran so deep it accorded ill with the hot rage he wore like a garment. As if he knew himself justified in his anger, but would as soon find reason to put it aside, even here, among his enemies.

"Soon enough, Doctor," she heard tr'Annhwi say. "When your trial is concluded and the sentence is in progress, think of my kinfolk as you howl."

Arrhae had heard threats uttered before; now and again, when in their cups, officers and other persons of sufficient rank to have had more sense would go so far as to make dueling challenges over H'daen tr'Khellian's dinner table, but what tr'Annhwi said, and the coarse, brutal way in which he said it to a prisoner with no means to respond, made Arrhae's hackles rise and her dislike of the Subcommander increase to detestation. She had many reasons, of which his behavior toward her in the hallway of her master's house was only the most personal. Arrhae ir-Mnaeha might have begun as a slave, but as her career advanced, so she associated with persons of good character and learned to comport herself in similar fashion. Such folk did not threaten the helpless, even when they were enemies; *mnhei'sahe* forbade it. Rather, they treated all, and especially their dearest enemies, as companions and equals worthy of respect and honor; *mnhei'sahe* required it.

Except that *mnhei'sahe* seemed to have become an outmoded concept. . . .

Except among people like her master and Commander t'Radaik, both of whom glared at tr'Annhwi in a way that wished him ill. "You will stay here, Subcommander," t'Radaik said. "And later, I think, we might discuss and clarify certain matters. The courtesy once considered part of Fleet rank, perhaps—or which rank is more appropriate to a lack of it? Sit down, and await me."

Tr'Annhwi stared at his superior for a few seconds, with the expression of a man not believing his own ears.

Not that he had never been disciplined before—very few in the Romulan military could make that claim—but to have it happen before civilians and an enemy . . .

He sat down with a jolt, mouth hanging open and eyes that had momentarily been wide with shock now narrowing with affront and fury. T'Radaik ignored his little performance, ignored *him*, as if he had ceased to exist. She turned instead, and pointedly, to Dr. McCoy, and gestured—Terranwise, with a crooking of all her fingers—that he should accompany her.

"Not all the Empire is so lacking in manners, Doctor," the Commander said, speaking Standard and choosing the correctness of her words with care. "Only most of it."

That was a perilous statement, and one which she dared not make in Rihannsu before so many witnesses. Only tr'Annhwi understood and might have proven dangerous—except that after his justly corrected rudeness, heard by all, any accusation that he could make would be seen only as spite.

Arrhae also understood, but was not so foolish as to make it known. She had very properly lowered her eyes while those of higher rank exchanged hard words; except in certain notorious Houses, servants were neither deaf nor expected to be, but they were expected to remain attentive while not *obviously* listening. At such times her facial muscles relaxed to an almost-Vulcan impassivity so that no matter what was said, she would not react to it. But for all her control and all her training in the hard school of slave to manager-of-servants, Arrhae's mouth still went dry at t'Radaik's next words. She tried to watch the Commander from under her brows while keeping her head bowed far enough to hide the expression which was surely plastered all over her face.

"Arrhae t'Khellian is *hru'hfe* to this House, Dr. Mak'khoi. She will attend you here, with"—a swift and winning smile was directed at H'daen—"her master's permission, of course."

H'daen gave his approval in the manner that he preferred over more modern things—such as saying *yes* and leaving it at that—with the elegant salute and half-bow that was so many years out-of-date. Even in the throes of early panic Arrhae wondered why the Commander had made a request instead of issuing the direct order which was more right and proper. And McCoy gazed at her, seeming no more than mildly curious. Then he merely nodded and walked past her without another glance, smiling thinly as captives do when hope recedes.

A gallows smile, like that which Vaebn tr'Lhoell had worn when they dragged him away with the food and the wine and the blood all smeared across his face and clothing. Arrhae shuddered and began to issue orders for the dining chamber to be cleared and cleaned.

Vaebn, she thought somberly. *Oh, Vaebn, what did you do wrong? And how do I avoid the same mistake . . . ?*

". . . if matters are well with you, Arrhae, then they are well with me also."

Though his verbal greeting was traditional, the handshake that followed it was not. Vaebn tr'Lhoell looked less like the Romulans of Terise's enhanced imagination than did several Vulcans of her immediate acquaintance. He was of only medium height, around her own meter and a half, and very slender, with that cool serenity which so many people associated with pure Vulcans and which she had encountered in so few at Intelligence Center. Oh, they had been calm and logical enough, but there was always an underlying tension about them when she was present, especially after the hemochromic tagging and the augmentation surgery. This man, this Rihanha who was to be her protector and her mentor and her master—*O-sensei,* suggested the part of her mind that came up with an appropriate word or phrase now and then, usually too late for it to be witty and worth saying anymore—was more in control of himself than all of them together.

Has to be, I guess, she thought in that garble of Romulan and Standard Anglish that her mind had been using of late, *because one false move and he's dead. And I'm dead with him! I wonder why he does it? Why any of them do it? Even me . . . ?*

The start of the mission was as dangerous as the rest seemed likely to be. A cloaked scoutship had seemed like a good idea while Commodore Perry had been bandying it about like an ace up his sleeve, but Terise had learned later that the cloaking device had been "acquired" from the Romulans themselves, and so recently that it was still throwing the occasional tantrum when fitted to Federation vessels. The three small ships run by Starfleet Intelligence for their clandestine missions were prototypes; laden with new technology, each had several untraced bugs to make their flights more interesting.

This particular scout had developed a small, irregularly recurring fault in—typically—its cloaking circuitry at a stage in the mission—also typically—where turnabout was out of the question. They had flipped out of cloak for two seconds while crossing the Neutral Zone perimeter, barely twenty thousand kilometers from the close-cordon patrol cruiser NCC-1843 *Nelson*, and those had been the longest two seconds of Terise's life. Because they hadn't been running an ID and had behaved—thanks to the malfunctioning cloaking device —like a Romulan vessel, they had been fired on, and had barely escaped with hull or hides intact.

It had given Terise an interesting demonstration of just how the ostensibly peaceful Federation military regarded Romulans, and never mind what Perry had said about cross-cultural education. She required no effort at all to guess how a notoriously belligerent warrior people might feel about the Federation, its personnel . . . and its spies.

She had been a "slave" in House Lhoell for fourteen standard months, and her "master" had tutored his stupidest possession exhaustively in the language, etiquette, and customs of the elevated society in which he moved. What the other slaves saw, and snickered over, was the new arrival spending a great deal of time in her lord's private chambers and seeming excessively tired as a consequence. Terise/Arrhae didn't let the coarse teasing worry her; some of her school "friends" had been just as cruel to a child far less able to cope than the Command-conditioned adult she had become.

She learned all the things that a native-born Rihanha was supposed to know, but the revelation of language came as she had been told it might: suddenly. Between one of Vaebn's sentences and the next, familiar things went strange and then snapped back to being more familiar than they had ever been before. Only their names had changed. Or not changed, been remembered correctly for the first time. After that, everything seemed to happen faster and faster, like a ball rolling down a hill.

A short time later Vaebn tr'Lhoell purchased himself a new slave. She was young and startlingly beautiful, and within days of her appearance—and nightly disappearances into Vaebn's private chambers—wagers were being laid among the other servants concerning how long Arrhae ir-Mnaeha would tolerate the situation. The staged fight when her patience "broke at last" surely provided gossip for months thereafter. Arrhae heard none of it. Her name, three-view image, listed abilities, and price were in the area computer's database before nightfall, and she was away from House Lhoell by late afternoon of the next day, as if Vaebn had sold her to the first bidder of a reasonable sum.

She knew differently. House Khellian had no connections to Starfleet Intelligence, Vaebn had warned her of that much, or indeed any connections to anywhere much. But it was an ideal base for an operative on such a mission as hers. Arrhae wondered, sometimes, just how the sale had been arranged. . . .

A House of good lineage fallen on hard times, Khellian was poorly served for the simple reason that its lord could afford to buy or employ no better than the dull slaves and sullen servants who misran the place. But Arrhae was aware of what Vaebn had told H'daen tr'Khellian about her capabilities and the true reason for her sudden sale. She had heard them laughing about it in H'daen's meeting room while she knelt on the floor outside in the proper submissive posture. Coarse masculine laughter at first, and then a softer, more thoughtful chuckling. H'daen had bidden his guest farewell, brought her to his study, struck a key on his personal computerpad, and then shown her what was on the screen. Her manumission, and her right to use his House-style as her own third name.

She had earned that freedom a hundred times over in the years that she had served House Khellian, scrabbling her way up the ladder of service until only Nnerhin tr'Hwersuil, *hru'hfe* of the household, held a higher rank. Nnerhin's death in that appalling traffic accident had left the way clear, and she was the obvious, indeed only, choice. But sometimes, lying awake in the darkness, Arrhae had wondered: *was that arranged as well . . . ?*

If there was an answer, she didn't want to know.

For a man who had just been verbally chastised by a senior officer, Subcommander tr'Annhwi looked improbably cheerful. He watched her as she bustled about, supervising the other servants and trying to keep herself so busy that she wouldn't have to think. She had labeled him as the sort of touchy, prideful man who balanced perpetually on the edge of anger, and who wouldn't tolerate any slight to his honor, and yet here he was, quite self-contained, sipping wine and smiling slightly at her every time their eyes met. That, most of all, made Arrhae uneasy.

He drained the winecup and waved away the servant who would have refilled it, pushed himself upright with only the slightest hint of sway in his posture, and made a quick military salute in her direction. "Too much wine already, *hru'hfe*. I should have drunk less at dinner. Then I wouldn't have . . . said what I did." He tugged at his uniform, straightening its half-cloak at his shoulder. "I shall make my apologies, and leave this house."

If a hnoiyika *looked contrite after it killed something,* thought Arrhae, *it would look something like you do now.*

"You think badly of me, too, don't you?"

"I . . . no, sir. Of course not. A gentleman may take wine with his fellows and—"

"That makes me glad." His smile widened and grew warmer. "Then I *can* visit you again?"

Arrhae felt as though someone had dropped a pound of ice into her guts. She had an overwhelming sense of having been maneuvered into a corner, because no matter what she said now would be either a self-contradiction or an insult—and she had no wish to insult *this* man. "You want to . . . visit me?" she managed at last, wondering what had prompted this and hoping that it was the wine.

"I do, and it would please me if you said yes. I was rude to you at first, but that was before I saw you properly."

Small excuse! And he talks like someone from a cheap play! There was only one problem; she had heard front-line Fleet officers, tough military men with only the merest veneer of culture, use exactly that sort of second-hand romantic speech to their ladies. It scared her. First Mak'khoi on her hands, with all that meant, and now this. She wasn't even sure what scared her most about it, that tr'Annhwi might need an ulterior motive to bring him back—or that he might be sincere.

"Uh, sir," she said, hunting for a way out that wouldn't sound like one, "I can make no such agreement without my lord's word on it."

"Then have no fear, lady, for I shall speak at once to H'daen tr'Khellian on this matter."

Lady . . . ? she thought wildly.

"And make"—for just an instant his smile became predatory—"suitably contrite apologies. Until we meet again, my lady." He bowed low with an easy playactor's grace and left Arrhae to her work and her confusion.

Oh, Powers, let H'daen be as angry as he seemed. . . . She blinked several times, and glared at the other servants who were staring at her and plainly on the point of tittering behind their hands. "This place," she said softly, "had better be clean when I come back. Or we'll see who'll be laughing then."

Chapter Six

Flight

REA'S HELM WAS the first ship to leave Vulcan, on 12 Ahhahr 140005. She spent three leisurely months accelerating out of Vulcan's solar system at nonrelativistic speeds, sending back close-flyby data from the nearby planets as she passed them. Behind her, in twos and threes, came the names still preserved in the Rihannsu fleets, both merchant and military, and never allowed to lie idle: *Warbird, Starcatcher, T'Hie, Pennon, Bloodwing* and *Corona, Lance* and *Gorget, Sunheart, Forge* and *Lost Road* and *Blacklight, Firestorm* and *Vengeance* and *Memory* and *Shield.* The ships stayed in communication via tightbeam laser and psilink. At first they tended not to stay too close to one another, in case some disaster might take several ships out at once. But the first ten years of the Journey broke them of this habit, as the sixteen ships forged outward and found interstellar space singularly uneventful, and close company a necessity.

There were numerous minor malfunctions aboard all the ships, as might be expected when technology has been custom-built for the first time and tested only as far as logic requires by a people both cautious and extremely impatient. But for those first ten years very few lives were lost: mostly results of maintenance-people's accidents while in vacuum, falls in high-gravity areas while ships were in acceleration phase, and so forth. There were several crop failures, mostly of non–survival-required crops like flatroot. When the wiltleaf blight struck the graminiformes on *Vengeance* and *Gorget,* the other ships were still able to supply them with surpluses of their own root production. (It is amusing to note that to this day, Rihannsu hailing from the south-continent areas settled from the populations of *Gorget* and *Vengeance* will tend to refuse to eat flatroot: those unfamiliar with finer points of their history will put this down to "religious tradition." But diary entries of that time are full of condemnation of "the wretched root," which was about all the two ships' people had to eat for nearly two years.) The Travelers were encouraged—if such minor problems were the worst they would have to contend with, they would do well indeed. It only remained to see what the universe itself had waiting for them in the way of planets.

The first star the ships reached, 88 Eri, was as we presently know it: a type K star with fifteen planets, all barren and too hot for even a Vulcan to appreciate them—there were lakes of molten lead on the closest planets. The ones farther out had long had their atmospheres burned off, and the Travelers had neither the equipment nor the patience for extended Vulcani-forming. They looped around 88 Eri and headed for 198 Eri, another of the K-type stars that had looked equally promising.

The cost of relativistic travel first began to be felt

here, though the Travelers had long been anticipating it. Their exploration of this first of many stars—acceleration, deceleration, in-system exploration, and assessment of planet viability—had taken them three years by ship time: on Vulcan, thirty years had passed.

The reestablishment of communication came as a shock for everyone involved. To begin with, while the Travelers were accelerating, and for most of the deceleration stage, psilink communication had naturally been disabled. To a sending mind on Vulcan, the thoughts of a mind moving at relativistic speeds were an unintelligibly slow growl; a receiving mind on one of the ships, when listening to a Vulcan mind, would hear nothing but another person living (it seemed) impossibly fast, too fast to make sense of. And even when the Travelers were nonrelativistic, there were other problems. Some of the linking groups, specially trained to be attuned to one another, had had deaths; some planetside teams had lost interest in the Travelers, being more concerned with occurrences on Vulcan. And indeed there was reason. Surak's teachings were spreading swiftly: there was some (carefully masked) dissatisfaction, even discontent, that energy should be wasted communicating with people who had disagreed violently enough with them to leave the planet. And Surak was no longer there to speak on their behalf in the planet's councils. He was dead, murdered by the Yhri faction with whom he had been dealing peace on behalf of those already united.

The news hit hard, though the Travelers had disowned him; there was mourning in the ships, and S'task was not seen for many days. There was a ship's council meeting scheduled during the period when he was missing, and the other councillors, S'task's neighbors, were too abashed by what they had heard about the depth of his grief to inquire of him whether he planned to attend. When they came together into the council chambers of *Rea's Helm*, they found S'task's chair empty, but laid across it was a sword, one of the

S'hariens that Surak had brought him. The councillors looked at it in silence and left it where it was. When S'task returned to council a month or so later, he would not comment, he simply found himself another chair to sit in. For many years thereafter, the sword remained in that chair, unmoved. After *Rea's Helm* made planetfall, and new chambers of government were established on ch'Rihan, the chair sat in them in the place of honor, behind senators and praetors and an abortive Emperor or two, reminding all lookers of the missing element in the Rihannsu equation: the silent force that had caused the Sundering, and still moved on the planet of their people's birth, though the man who gave it birth was gone. To touch the sword in the Empty Chair was nothing less than a man's death. Even naming it was dangerous—oaths sworn on it were kept, or the swearer died, sometimes with assistance.

The Journey went on, and had no need to turn homeward for its griefs: it found others. The second starfall, around 198 Eri, was disastrous. It was not quite as bad as it might have been, since numerous of the ships' councils had elected to have the ships accelerate at different rates, thereby stringing the ships out somewhat along their course. With psilinked communications, ships farther along the course could alert others of whether a star was viable or not, and the other accompanying ships could change course more quickly. The tactic was a sort of interstellar leapfrog, one that many other species working at relativistic speeds have found useful.

This might have worked out well enough, except that communications with Vulcan were again impossible. There was therefore no way that the Travelers could be warned of what Vulcan astronomers had detected in the neighborhood of 198 Eri with equipment newly augmented by improvements obtained from the Hamalki. Seven of eighteen ships were lost over the event horizon of a newly collapsed black hole. *Pennon, Starcatcher, Bloodwing, Forge, Lost Road, Lance,* and

Blacklight all came out of the boost phase of the psi-based "bootstrap" acceleration to find themselves falling down a "hole" through space in which time dilated and contracted wildly, and physical reality itself came undone around them. Even those ships that had warning were unable to pull out of the gravitational field of the singularity, though every jump-trained adept aboard the ships died trying to bootstrap them out again. The inhabitants of those ships spent long days looking through madness at the death that was inexorably sucking them in. No one knows to this day what the final fate of the people aboard the ships was—whether they died from the antithetical nature of "denatured" space itself, or whether the ships mercifully blew up first due to gravitational stress. Those from the surviving ships unlucky enough to be in mindlink with them succumbed to psychoses and died quickly, possibly in empathy, or slowly, raving to the end of their lives.

The tragedy slowed down the Journey immensely, as the ships approached 198 Eri and found its planets as hopeless as 88s had been. Every argument that could come up about the conduct of the Journey did so almost immediately, and the arguing continued for several years while the ships orbited 198 Eri and stored what stellar power they could. Should the Travelers turn back? Little use in that, some said. Vulcan might not want them back, and besides, what friends and families had been left behind were all old or dead now: relativity had taken its toll. Or keep going? Unwise, said others, when even empty-looking space turned out to be mined with deadly dangers you could not see until they were already in the process of killing you. Should they keep all the ships together (and risk having them all destroyed together)? Or should they spread them out (and risk not being able to come to one another's aid)? Should they stop using the bootstrap acceleration method, despite the fact that it used no fuel and conserved the ships' resources more completely than any other method? And the question was complicated by the fact that there was no more help available from Vulcan, even if any would have been offered them. The ships had recently passed the nine-point-five lightyear limit on unboosted telepathy. Even at nonrelativistic speeds, no adept heard anything but the mental analogue of four-centimeter noise, the sound of life in the universe breathing quietly to itself.

Three and a half years went by while the ships grieved, argued, and looked for answers. They found none, but once again will drove them outward: S'task had not come so far to turn back. Many in the ships were unwilling, but S'task carried the council of *Rea's Helm* and declared that his ship at least was going on: and the others would not let him go alone. Under conventional ramscoop drive at first, then using bootstrapping again as the memory of pain dulled a little, the ships headed for 4408A/B Trianguli, a promising "wide" binary with two possible stars.

4408B Tri is, of course, the star around which orbits the planet Iruh, and the Travelers could not have made a worse choice of a world to examine for colonization. If they had analyzed the Etoshan data more thoroughly, they might have avoided another disaster, but they did not. At one time the Inshai had cordoned off the system, but they were now long gone from those spaces, and all their warning buoys had been destroyed by the Etoshan pirates during their own ill-fated attempt to subdue the planet. So it was that the Travelers' ships came in cautiously, by ones and twos, and found 4408A surrounded by worlds covered in molten rock or liquid methane, and 4408B orbited by six planets, one of which registered on their instruments as a ninety-nine percent climactic match for Vulcan . . . and rich in metals, which Vulcan at its best had never been. The first two ships in, *T'Hie* and *Corona*, slipped into parking orbits and sent shuttles down to take more readings and assess the planet's climate and biochemistry. The shuttles did not come back, but long before

105

there was alarm about the issue, it was too late for the Travelers in orbit.

The Iruhe were doing as they had done with so many other travelers: they had sensed their minds from a distance and insinuated into their minds an image of Iruh as the perfect world, the one they were looking for. What use is an accurate instrument reading when the mind reading it is being influenced to inaccuracy? And not even Vulcans were capable of holding out against the influence of a species rated one of the most mentally powerful of the whole galaxy, with a reconstructed psi rating of nearly 160 (the most highly trained Vulcans rate about 30: most Terrans about 10). The crews of the shuttles served as an hors d'oeuvre for the Iruhe, and confirmed what had fallen into their toils, a phenomenal number of fiercely motivated, intelligent, mentally vigorous people. With false "reports" from the shuttles that seemed absolutely true, because the crewpeople seeing them were supplying familiar faces and details from their own minds, the Iruhe lured *Corona* and *T'Hie* into optimum range—close synchronous orbit—and proceeded to suck the life force out of the entire complement of both ships, over twelve thousand men, women, and children. Then they crashed the ships full of mindless, still-breathing husks into Iruh's methane seas, and waited eagerly for the rest of the feast, the other Travelers.

The torpor of a whole species of intellivores after a massive and unprecedented gorge was the only thing that saved the other ships. *Sunheart* coasted in next, and her navigations crew noticed with instant alarm that the ion trails of *T'Hie* and *Corona* stopped suddenly around Iruhe, and did not head out into space again. *Sunheart*'s command crew immediately made the wisest decisions possible under the circumstances: they ran. They veered off from the paradisial planet they saw, and warned off the other ships. In the hurry there were several mistakes made in navigations, and *Firestorm* and *Vengeance* fell out of contact with the other ships and only much later made the course corrections to find them again. But the hurry was necessary: there was no telling how long or short a grace period they would have had before the Iruhe "woke up" and noticed the rest of their dinner arriving.

The Travelers were, in any case, very fortunate. Few species had gotten off so lightly from encounters with Iruh: many more ships and several planets (after the Iruhe got in the habit of moving theirs around that arm of the Galaxy) were to fall victim to the insatiable mind-predators. Not until some seventeen hundred years later, when the Organians were asked to intervene, could anything effective be done about the Iruhe. And the irony is that no one knows to this day just what was "done." The planet is empty and quiet now, and there is a Federation research team there, sifting the ruined landmasses for what artifacts remain.

The courses of the Traveler ships still remaining become harder to trace from this point onward. *Firestorm* and *Vengeance* wandered for a long time, hunting the other ships, hearing the occasional psi-contact and using the vague directional sense from these to try to course-correct. The other ships meanwhile went through much the same experience—years and years of wandering among stars that turned out barren of planets, or among stars that had planets that were useless to them. The Travelers had thought that the odds of finding a habitable world, away from the aliens that troubled them so, were well in their favor. They found out otherwise, painfully. Here again, paying attention to the data from the Etoshans might have helped them. The Etoshans knew how poor in habitable worlds the Eridani-Trianguli spaces had been. It was one of the reasons they had been so surprised to find the Vulcans in the first place.

But might-have-beens were no use to the Travelers. They spent the next eighty-five standard years of relative time—nearly four hundred and fifty, out in the nonrelativistic universe—hunting desperately for a world, any world, that might suit them. Now they would be glad to Vulcaniform a planet, if they could only find one at all suitable, but most of the stars in deep Trianguli space were older Population I stars that had long before lost their planets, or were too unstable to have any to begin with. The planets they did find were uniformly gas giants or airless rocks that nothing could be done with in less than a couple of centuries.

The desperation was even worse because the ships had been built with hundred-year "viability envelopes." No one had expected the search for a new world to take much longer than fifty years, and their supplies, systems, and facilities had been designed with this timing in mind. Food was beginning to be scarce in some of the ships, systems were breaking down, and almost all the replacement parts were used up. *Warbird* was lost to a massive drive system malfunction; she had no adept left who could bootstrap her, and she fell into 114 Trianguli trying to slingshot around the star to pick up more boost. *Memory* went the same way, trying to use a black dwarf. The pulses from the small X-ray star produced after the collision are still reaching Earth.

The remaining ships—*Rea's Helm, Gorget, Sunheart, Vengeance,* and *Firestorm*—kept going as best they could. It was never easy. Odd diseases began to spring up in all the crews. There was speculation that radiation exposure was causing new mutagenic forms of diseases to which Vulcans were normally immune . . . since the symptoms for some of the "space fevers" resembled already-identified Vulcan diseases like lunglock fever, though they were more severe. The medical staff of all the ships had been attenuated by deaths from old age as well as from the diseases. They were able to do little, and before the epidemics began to taper off, from fifty to seventy percent of each ship's complement had died.

These diseases only aggravated—or, one might also

say, "ended"—a problem that had been worsening with the decay of the ships' viability envelopes. There were no more psitechs. Those that did not die bootstrapping the ships now died of disease, and there were no completely trained techs to replace them—partly because much of the oldstyle Vulcan psi-training required "circles" or groups of adepts to bring a psi-talented person to viability. There were no longer enough adepts to make up the necessary groups.

The documentation available—though quite complete—was also too objective: people who tried to teach themselves the mind techniques "by the book" never became more than talented amateurs. The direct "laying on of hands" was necessary to properly teach telepathy, mindmeld, and the other allied arts. So they died out as the Ships voyaged, and the sciences of the mind became the matter of legend. The Vulcans believe that present-day Rihannsu possess the raw ability to be trained in the mind sciences, but the actual experiment will doubtless not happen for quite a long while.

Meanwhile, the diseases took their toll everywhere. S'task's wife and children all perished within days of one another during *Rea*'s epidemic of mutagenic infectious pericarditis. S'task himself came very close to dying, and lay ill for months, not speaking, hardly eating. It was a very gaunt and shaky man who got up from his bed on the day *Rea*'s chief astronomer came to him to tell him that they thought they had found yet another star with planets.

The star they had found was 128 Trianguli, one of the group 123–128 Tri: a little rosette of dwarf K-type stars so far out in the arm as not to have been noticed by even the Etoshans. It would require *Rea* some ten years of acceleration—all their bootstrap adepts were now dead of old age or jump syndrome—and another ten to decelerate. This was the worst possible news: the period was well outside of *Rea*'s viability envelope.

"We may all be dead when we get there," said the chief astronomer to S'task.

"But we will have gotten there," said S'task. Still, he took the question to Council, and the surviving population of *Rea* agreed that they should take the chance and try to reach the star. The other surviving ships concurred.

They began the long acceleration. Other authors have covered in far more detail the crazed courage and dogged determination of these people as they bent their whole will to survival in ancient, cranky spacecraft that had no reason to be running any longer. But the spacecraft had, after all, been built by craftsmen, by Vulcans who loved their work and would rather have died than misplace a rivet out of laziness, and the workmanship, by and large, held. Nine years into deceleration they came within sensor range of 128 Tri and confirmed the astronomers' suspicions: the star had six planets, of which two were a "double planet" system like Earth and Earth's Moon . . . and both of the two were habitable within broad Vulcan parameters.

There were, of course, major differences to be dealt with. The two worlds had more water than Vulcan did, and their climates were respectively cooler. In fact, both planets had those things that the Vulcans had heard of from the Etoshan data but never seen, "oceans." Some people were nervous about the prospect of settling on worlds where water was such a commonplace. Others entertained the idea that in a place where water was so plentiful, one of the major causes of war might be eliminated. S'task, looking for the first time at the early telescopic images of the two green-golden worlds, and hearing one of his people mention this possibility, was silent for a few moments, then said, "Those who want war will find causes, no matter how many of them you take away." This proved to be true enough, later. With survival needs handled, the Rihannsu moved on to other concerns, matters of honor, and fought cheerfully about them for centuries. But that time was still far ahead of them. Right now they were merely desperately glad to find a world, two worlds, in fact, that looked like they would serve them as homes instead of the tired metal worlds that were rapidly losing their viability.

The year immediately following starfall was spent in cautious analysis of the worlds and how they should be best used by the Travelers. The larger of the two worlds had the biggest oceans, and three large landmasses, two with extensive "young" mountain ranges. The third was ninety percent desert, though its coastlines were fertile. The other planet, the one "frozen" in orbit around the larger body, again like Earth's Moon, had five continents, all mountainous and heavily forested. Both worlds revealed thousands of species of wildlife, a fact that astonished the Travelers: Vulcan has comparatively few, only three or four phyla with a spread of several hundred species, mostly plants.

The ships' scientists were fascinated by the fact that the species on both planets were quite similar, and there were several near-duplications. Arguments immediately began as to whether these planets had been colonized or visited by some other species in the past, or whether this astonishing parallel evolution had happened by itself. No artifacts suggestive of any other species' intervention or presence, however, were ever found. The question has never been satisfactorily answered, though there are possibilities: the 128 Tri system lies in the migratory path of the species known to Federation research as "the Builders," who played at "seeding" various planets with carbon-based life, predominantly hominid, some two million years ago. There is no ignoring the fact that ninety percent of the wildlife on the Two Worlds is compatible with Vulcan biochemistry, even if only by virtue of being carbohydrate. Levorotatory protein forms, common on almost every "nonseeded" planet, were almost completely absent in the ch'Rihan/ch'Havran biosystems.

Research went on, while the Travelers, eager to stop traveling, decided the questions of who should live where. No logical method could be approved by everyone, especially since there were several pieces of especially choice real estate that one or more groups had their eyes on. There was also concern that people should be sufficiently spread out so as not to overtax the resources of any one area in the long term. After several months of extremely acrimonious argument in ships' Meetings, S'task wearied of it all and suggested that the ships merely choose areas to live in by lottery. To his extreme surprise, the complements of the other ships agreed. Some ships preferred to go into the lottery as entire units, others divided up along family or clan lines, so that septs of clans scattered among the four surviving ships would all go to one area together.

The two planets were duly named ch'Rihan ("of the Declared") and ch'Havran ("of the Travelers"). It was rather odd that the results of the lottery left many of the more "reactionary," Vulcan-oriented houses living on ch'Havran, since the name more recalled the Journey than its end, as ch'Rihan did, and ch'Rihan became the home of the more "forward-looking," secessionist, revolutionary houses (S'task's own house was placed on ch'Rihan by the lottery). Notice was taken of this, perhaps more notice than was warranted, perhaps not. A people who have come to speak an artificial language will naturally be preoccupied with the meanings of words and names. The results of the lottery were taken as a sort of good omen, that the language fit the people, and vice versa, that this was indeed the place where they were supposed to be, the place to which they had been meant to come. Who the Rihannsu thought was doing the "meaning" is uncertain. Vulcan religion had changed considerably over the years of the Journey, and would change further.

It is also interesting to note that the "troublemaker" groups, those clans and tribes who had been pressured by one faction or another to make the Journey, almost all ended up on ch'Havran, and on its east continent—remote, rugged, and poorer in resources than the others. There have been suggestions among both Rihannsu and Federation historians that the lottery was rigged. There is no way to tell at this remote period in time. The computers in which the lottery data was stored and handled are long since dust.

If the lottery was, in fact, rigged to this effect, then evil would come of it later. The cultures that grew up unchecked on the East Continent, mostly out of contact with those on ch'Rihan and the other parts of ch'Havran, grew up savage, exploitative, and cruel, even by Rihannsu standards. Those East Continent factions would later instigate and finally openly provoke the Rihannsu's first war with the Federation, and the crews of ships from the Kihai and LLunih nations would commit atrocities that would adorn Federation propaganda tapes for years to come. It is mostly these nations that the Rihannsu have to thank for horrors like the abandonment and "evacuation" of Thieurrull (tr: "Hellguard") and the capture and rape of innocent Vulcans—atrocities that the Senate and Praetorate would have severely punished if they had known they were being planned and carried out by eastern-based and easterner-commanded ships, and secretly backed and funded by eastern praetors. Punishments there were, indeed, but much too late. The whole business was later taken, by people who believed that the lottery was rigged, as more evidence of the desperate correctness of Surak's statement that beginnings must be clean.

Other peculiarities set in as a result of the scattering of the populations of the many ships across two planets. Vulcan society has always had a distinctly matriarchal cast: this tendency came out strongly in several of the nations on ch'Havran, and most strongly in the Nn'-verian nation on the North Continent of ch'Rihan. It was the nation in which S'task came to live (the short while that he did), and by virtue of that the seat of government and the seat of the first and only Ruling Queen of the Two Worlds. T'Rehu (later Vriha t'Rehu) seized power and set her throne in the newly built Council Chambers, in front of the Empty Chair; she spilled the first blood in those chambers—regrettably, the first of much—and declared the rule of women (or at least woman) over men returned again. The Vulcans had tried this some thousands of years before, and had only indifferent success with it: women were generally not interested enough in war for the Vulcan nations of that time to support such rule for long. T'Rehu was cast down, and the council returned to power after ch'Rihan's first war. But from then until now women have held more than seventy percent of all positions in the government, and about sixty percent of those in the armed forces.

Another interesting thing happened over which sociologists are still arguing: Rihannsu women began to get interested in war. Many of the high-ranking East Continent officers responsible for the Hellguard atrocities were women. The etiology of this change, and the question of why it should happen so soon after the end of the Journey, is still a puzzle. Of the other "matriarchal" or female-oriented species in the galaxy (some seventy-five percent), only one other, the Bhvui, has done anything similar, and the histories of the two species are too different to make comparisons meaningful. But in any case, Rihanssu woman warriors have become almost as much of a legend as pre-Reformation Vulcan, and there are countless gossipy stories of "Romulan"-dominated worlds ruled by suave and sophisticated warrior princesses with harems full of good-looking men. The only thing to be said about these stories is, if they were true, the Rihannsu would not have had to enter into so many destructive deals with the Klingons to keep their economy afloat. They could have done quite nicely from the female tourist trade.

But again, these developments were in the future. The eighteen thousand remaining Travelers slowly left the ships over some three years, cautiously establishing support bases for themselves, until there were very few people still living in the ships. Some did choose to remain, mostly those people who had become agoraphobic over the long journey, or had been born in the ships and wanted nothing to do with open skies and planets. The Ship-Clans, as they came to be known, lived quite happily aboard their great echoing homes, looking down on the Two Worlds around which they coasted in asynchronous orbits.

The ships were resupplied and repaired over some years from planetary resources: people would return to the ships for holidays, out of nostalgia or curiosity. Over many more years this sort of thing came to an end, as the population turned over and there was no one left who had been born on Vulcan, or on shipboard during the Journey. The long run through interstellar night became something sung about, but not a thing anyone wanted to have experienced. Ch'Rihan and ch'Havran were the real worlds now, not those ancient ones with metal walls and skies that echoed.

Though they slowly dwindled, the Ship-Clans maintained the four ships of the Journey, and evening and morning they could be seen low above the planets' horizons, bright points in the sky. They did not stay there forever. Some hundreds of years later, due to neglect, government squabbles, economic troubles, and war, one at a time the stars fell: and the Two Worlds orbited Eisn, their "Homesun," cut off from the rest of the universe in the beginning of their long isolation. It was an unfortunate paradigm for the loss of sciences and technologies that began during that time and would continue for a thousand years to come. But the songs of the Rihannsu still recall the evening stars at sunset, and the breath of wind in trees, and the love of

115

starlight seen through evening rather than through the hard black of space. "The Journey is noble," said one bard's song, "and adventure and danger is sweet, but the wine by the fireside is sweeter, and knowing one's place."

Chapter Seven

H'DAEN TR'KHELLIAN WAS gazing out of the antechamber window when Arrhae came in to answer his summons. He didn't turn around, merely twisted somewhat and watched over his shoulder as she gave him the customary obeisance. He looked thoughtful and somewhat ill at ease.

"Fair day, *hru'hfirh*," she said as usual, straightening.

"After a poor night." H'daen looked her full in the face, as if searching for something that might give him an answer before he had to ask any questions aloud. Apparently he saw nothing, and shrugged. "Arrhae, is there truth in what I hear of you and Maiek tr'Annhwi?"

"My lord?" Arrhae had no need to pretend surprise. She knew that one of H'daen's body-servants was on intimate terms with Ekkhae, who had been among those cleaning the dining-chamber last night, but she hadn't expected the gossip to travel quite so fast as this. Nor had she expected anyone to give credence to it.

"The Subcommander sought me out before he left, and apologized at some length for his behavior. Then he asked if he was forgiven, if he would be permitted to enter my house again—and if I granted him the right to visit you. He told me that you wanted him to speak on this matter." H'daen crossed the room and sat down at his desk, pouring himself a cup of wine rather than asking her to do it. He had been drinking more of late, and earlier in the day, but with Eisn not yet clear of the horizon this cupful was more a continuation of last night's drinking than a new day's start. He swallowed perhaps half the cupful and refilled it before saying any more, and when he turned to face her again, his face was troubled. "It was my impression that you already visited with Lhaesl tr'Khev. Was I mistaken?"

Arrhae lowered her eyes uncomfortably. Lhaesl hadn't yet been officially snubbed, and was either too enamored or too dense to realize of his own accord that she had no interest in him. Granted that they were physically of an age, the differing metabolism of Rihannsu and Terran—no matter how accurately that Terran might be disguised—still meant that his twenty-eight and hers left him at a behavioral equivalent of fifteen. A pretty child, but a child for all that. "Tr'Khev visits me, lord. I do not encourage him; and though I should, I have not yet discouraged him in whatever way it needs for him to understand."

"Oh. Thank you. The situation becomes clearer, Arrhae. Then I was right in what I told tr'Annhwi."

"Told him . . . ?"

"That he could visit with you, that you were a free woman and one with a mind of your own, and that he would learn soon enough if he wasn't welcome."

Arrhae barely kept the strangulated squeak of horror in her throat, when what it really wanted to do was leap out as a full-fledged yell of *You old fool!!* Two days ago she wouldn't even have considered addressing the Head of House in any such fashion, but then, two days ago, she had almost forgotten who she was and what had brought her here. "And if I choose not to make him welcome, lord?" she wondered tentatively.

"I would prefer that you did, Arrhae."

"Prefer" indeed! That was an order. I wonder why? She watched him, but said nothing.

"House Annhwi is strong, wealthy, and well-placed—"

Question answered.

"—and the Subcommander's friendship would prove an asset to House Khellian. Arrhae, sit down. Fill my cup again and . . . and pour a cup for yourself."

The invitation was so out of place that Arrhae felt her face burn hot. "Lord, I am *hru'hfe* only, and—"

H'daen raised one finger and she was silent. "You are *hru'hfe* indeed, and a worthy ornament to this house, honored by its guests. Why wonder, then, that I bid you drink with me out of respect for that honor which reflects so well on me and on my House? Sit, Arrhae, and drink deep."

She sat down straight-backed, most uncomfortable with the situation but aware of being closely watched, and determinedly did as she was told. Expecting something rough as ale, Arrhae found the wine so much smoother and of better flavor that she put her mouthful down at a single gulp, then grimaced and felt tears prickle at her eyes as the liquid revealed itself correspondingly stronger—when the swallow had passed the point of no return.

H'daen smiled thinly but without any malice. "It takes everyone that way the first time they drink it. Even me. Now, again. It won't be such a shock; you might even start to like it."

He was right. Arrhae managed to down her second mouthful without spluttering, and actually enjoyed the small fusion furnace that came to life in the pit of her stomach. As for the rest of it, she set the cup down carefully and began to turn it around and around, watching the pretty sparkling of the reflec glaze. She would have watched moisture condense on glass, or paint dry—just so long as she didn't have to watch H'daen's eyes on her. At the back of her mind there was a suspicion, no matter how unfounded it might be, that H'daen might be trying to make her drunk in order to pry secrets from her. Only great caution would avoid that; she would appear to drink as she was expected to do, without absorbing any of the powerful toxins in the wine.

Yet H'daen himself was drinking without restraint, and the first and last rule of making someone drunk to loosen their tongue was not to get drunk first. He was on his third cupful now, and no matter how accustomed one might be to the potent liquor, immunity was a different matter. It wasn't as if he were drinking from another jug, either. Each pouring, his and hers, came from the same vessel. Arrhae caught him glancing in her direction once or twice, and the glances weren't furtive—she was used to those by now, and knew how to recognize them—but nervous. As if he were drinking to summon up enough courage to raise some delicate subject.

"McCoy," he said at last, and gave it Federation rather than Rihannsu inflection.

"He still sleeps, *hru'hfirh*," she said. "Or so I presume. I answered your summons before visiting his quarters." She made pretense of sipping more wine, barely allowing it to moisten her lips, even though she "swallowed" and made the appropriate small sigh of enjoyment.

"You grow accustomed faster than I did." H'daen swerved off on another tack as if frightened by the two syllables he had previously uttered, and he sounded almost envious.

"After drinking ale, lord, even coolant fluid becomes palatable." A dangerous thing to say, with its possible insult of his preferences in wine, but a joke if it were seen as such. It was; H'daen laughed quietly, forcing it so that it sounded more than it was, but genuinely amused for all that.

"Indeed so—especially if you drink it without water." There was a swift, small silence before he pushed both cup and jug aside halfway through yet another refill. "Enough of this. The Terrans call it *small talk*. Around and around like a bloodwing gathering its courage to settle on a dying *hlai*. Always around, and never to the point."

"And the point, lord, is Mak'khoi?"

"Yes. I . . . I have told you in the past that I trust you both with private words and with the honor of my House. That trust has not yet been misplaced." H'daen's stare was undisguised now, and he was trying to read her face as he might read charactery on a viewscreen. She met the stare for as long as seemed suitable, saying nothing, then demurely lowered her head in a bow of gratitude. "Now this Starfleet officer is given into my hands for safekeeping until the Senate brings him to trial." He pushed back from the desk, stood up, and began to pace.

"That Fleet Intelligence entrusted him to you is surely a great sign of favor in high places, lord."

"If it was widely known among my 'friends,'" H'daen said bitterly. "More probable that he was left here as the least likely place any rescuer would begin to look. You know how House Khellian fared when you came here. I owe you thanks, not as master to servant, but as one who appreciates the effort and effect of hard labor."

For all his dismissal of small talk, he was using it again, deferring the evil moment when he would have to say something that Arrhae was coming to expect might be treasonous. If it was, she didn't want to hear it; if it was spoken aloud under this roof, she wanted away from the house; and if it was spoken by H'daen, she would as soon be out of his employ and a beggar on the road before he said it. Surely he didn't think that Intelligence would leave so important a prize here and not leave some means of watching him . . . ?

Perhaps he did.

And perhaps this disdained old *thrai* was wilier than any gave him credit for, because he closed relays on his reader's keypad so that when the thing's viewscreen unfolded from the desk, it was already emitting a white-noise hum that set Arrhae's teeth on edge. And which would almost certainly make nonsense of any audio pickup hidden in the room. If a visual scan had been installed, H'daen played for its lenses by starting to work, in a most realistic fashion, with various electronic probes and fault-finders on the reader which had plainly "gone wrong." After a few minutes passed, he "gave up," sat down, and began to ponder about the problem—and his pondering seemed lost without at least two fingers and more usually a whole hand near or over his mouth. Only then did H'daen dare start to speak.

"There are those on ch'Rihan," he said, "who would pay more than a chain or two of cash to lay their hands on an officer of the Federation vessel *Enterprise*. And there are those who would look most highly on the man and the House who made such an acquisition possible."

"My lord . . . !" said Arrhae, shocked. "Commander t'Radaik—"

"Jaeih t'Radaik is of an ancient and noble House. To one like that, hardship and dishonor are words without meaning. Whereas to me . . ." He let the sentence hang, not needing to finish it.

"I—I understand, my lord."

"Yes, and disapprove. Good."

"My lord . . . ?"

"Do you think, Arrhae, that I would have taken you into my confidence where this plan is concerned if I suspected you were other than honorable? You're shocked, of course—but since mention of this would bring me, you, and the House you serve into still more disrepute, you'll say nothing and disapprove of me in private."

"But if Intelligence learned of what you have just told me, *hru'hfirh*?" It struck Arrhae even as she said it that the question was unnecessary, one with an obvious answer. She was even more right than she guessed.

"Then they could have learned from only one source,

121

and would also learn—from a similarly anonymous source—that my so-trusted *hru'hfe* is a spy for the Federation, suborned by her late last master tr'Lhoell," said H'daen silkily. "Tell me, whom would they believe?" Then he swore and scrambled to his feet with his hands reaching for her shoulders, for Arrhae's face had drained of color so fast and so completely that he thought she was about to faint. "Powers and Elements, Arrhae, it was a brutal answer to the question, but I didn't mean it!"

"No . . ." she whispered, waving him away, not wanting to be touched, not wanting him anywhere near her. In the single instant between H'daen's words and his realization that he had gone too far, all the suppressed horrors of her years undercover had run gibbering through her mind. Even now, knowing that he had threatened without knowledge of the truth made her feel no better. It was a reminder of too many things: of the Rihannsu paranoid fear of espionage, of her own delicately balanced position, of how the confession had been twisted out of Vaebn tr'Lhoell and what had been done to him afterward. Of the shattering of that which she had thought of as her life.

H'daen pushed her cup, refilled, across the desk and she drank eagerly, holding the cup in both hands but almost spilling it even so. "That was cruel, *hru'hfe* Arrhae. I ask pardon for it." She heard his voice as though from a great distance, saying unlikely things that no *hru'hfirh* ever said to a servant, no matter how senior or how favored. He was blaming himself and asking forgiveness. Wrong words, impossible words, that made her feel uncomfortable and wish that he would stop. But she knew what had provoked them, and it hadn't been the wine.

"You were frightened of what you had said, lord," she told him, coming straight out with it rather than trying to find some more acceptable substitute. He stared at her, unused to such plain speaking, and then shrugged. Arrhae took the shrug as approval, or at least as permission to continue. "And that made you say things that I know my own good lord would not have said. Yes, I disapprove of what you plan for Mak'khoi. Not only because Commander t'Radaik entrusted him to your keeping—but because you intend to sell him. I know what being sold is like, my lord, and *I* was sold only to work. He . . . would be going into the hands of those whose sole delight would be to prolong his death. Better to kill him now yourself. It would be a cleaner and more honorable thing to do."

"It seems that my *hru'hfe* is more than simply an efficient household manager," said H'daen, speaking in a flat, neutral tone that gave Arrhae nothing but the words it carried. She waited, her stomach fluttering, to learn if she had overreacted and said too much. He watched her for what felt like a long time, his face unreadable, then nodded. "It seems she is my conscience. Very well, Arrhae, carry my guilt if you must. But whatever happens, know this: if I or my House can benefit from this unlooked-for gift, then whatever must be done will be done—and the moral scruples of a servant will not get in my way. Do you understand?"

Arrhae pushed her winecup away with the tip of one index finger, knowing that the brief while when she and H'daen might drink together as equals was gone beyond recall. "Yes, lord," she said, standing up and making him an obeisance. "I understand perfectly. With my lord's permission, I will be about my duties now."

"Go—it's already late into the morning, and you have yet to attend Mak'khoi. By my word, treat him as a guest. How could he pass unnoticed if he tried to run, and where on ch'Rihan would he go?" H'daen shut down the whining viewscreen and folded it into his desk once more, remembering to play his role to its logical conclusion by slapping the monitor pettishly and muttering something about inadequate maintenance. But there was nothing pettish about the look he flicked at Arrhae; it was both a promise and a veiled threat.

"Remember," he said, and turned away.

So he was locked up again. So what? Leonard McCoy's only concern right now was about the woman he had seen. And about the way she moved. That first flinch when he came in had been all wrong, and he would stake—

McCoy recognized the bland comment that had been forming inside his head in the way that he could sometimes spot tired old medical phrases like "finish the course" and "not to be taken internally." Except that there was no longer anything bland about it. Staking his life on it was exactly what he was doing. If his briefing had been wrong, if planetfall had been wrong, if information had been wrong . . .

Then he was a dead man.

The door opened and his jailer came in. *Think of the devil . . .* McCoy suppressed a humorless smile and watched the young Romulan woman as she moved about his cramped quarters, straightening the recently vacated bed and unlocking the heavy window shutters. His intradermal had translated her title of *hru'hfe* as "servants'-manager," and it struck him that if she was doing the work that she would more normally have overseen, then she was probably the most trusted member of staff in the whole household. *Which might be a bad thing—or a very good one.*

"You're Arrhae," he said in Federation Standard.

She moved his pillow, a cylinder of stuffed leather as concession to Terran weakness instead of the smooth stone that a Rihanha used, and punched it to shape with unnecessary vigor before looking at him disdainfully down her hawk nose, rather as Spock might do. McCoy was half-expecting an eyebrow to go up. *"Ie,"* she replied. *"Arrhae. Hru'hfe i daise hfai s'Khellian. Hwiiy na th'ann Mak'khoi."*

"Is that my title: 'the prisoner McCoy'? I'd prefer

124

something else. Try 'Doctor'—though my friends call me 'Bones.'"

"*Hwiij th'ann-a—haei'n neth 'Mak'khoi,' neth 'D'okht'r,' neth 'Bohw'nns' nah'lai?*"

"No, it doesn't matter what you call me. But I'd prefer something other than a label, thank you very much. And try speaking Anglish!" He pitched her that one out of left field, watching for a reaction. Actually *hearing* one came as a surprise.

"If it would content you," she said. The Romulan accent was very thick and her intonation was heavy and oddly placed, making it hard for him to understand, but the words were Federation Standard. McCoy's eyebrows lifted and he was momentarily at a loss for anything to say, having considered every response that she might make—except this one. "But there is small need," the woman continued, and unless his ears deceived him, her accent was improving with every word. "You have a translit— trans*lator* and so understand Rihannsu. I am not a prisoner and have not need to understand *you*, Dr. Bones."

"Either Doctor or Bones, not both."

"Which? Choose."

"All right, Bones then. At least it'll *sound* as if there's a friend in the room." *And that, Dr. McCoy, was excessively waspish even for you.*

"So. Bones. Have you eaten firstmeal today, Bones?"

He shook his head. "Nor lastmeal yesterday. I haven't seen a hum—er, a soul since I was locked in here last night. Your Subcommander tr'Annhwi wasn't too keen on granting me any home comforts, and t'Radaik assumed and didn't think to ask."

Arrhae scowled and sucked in a sharp breath through her teeth. "Tr'Annhwi is not 'my' Subcommander, and never will be. No matter what he thinks. Doctor, you are already found guilty before your trial is convened, but for all that, do not judge all Rihannsu by that one's measure. This house is honorable, at least. You are a prisoner of the Imperium, but a guest under the roof of Khellian. Take comfort from that, at least."

"Your Anglish improves with practice, *hru'hfe*," said McCoy carefully. "Yet you didn't tell Commander t'Radaik that you spoke it. . . ."

Arrhae gave him what amounted to the Romulan version of an "old-fashioned look." "So that you have no cause to puzzle the matter, Bones, I shall explain. Privately, for your ears alone. My first master taught me the art, for his amusement, as one might teach *fvaiin* tricks." She turned away from him and busied herself with other things, talking all the while. "But he was a spy and a foul traitor, and met the fate that he deserved two farsuns past, and since that time I have had no cause to use the speech of my people's enemies. Nor would I—to learn one thing from a traitor might be to learn others, or so my present master might believe." Arrhae swung on him, doing nothing now but stare. "I advise you to forget. I shall not speak this speech to you otherwise, nor will I speak it either out of this room or in the company of any other person. Do you understand me?"

"Quite clearly." McCoy understood more clearly even than that; he knew the sound of something that had been carefully composed and then learned by heart. He stood up and glanced at the door that Arrhae had locked behind her. "Do you bring my food in here, or do you slide it under the door?"

"I have told you—you are a guest in House Khellian. My master H'daen has said it. Thus at night you will be here, and the door locked. By day you may walk freely in the house, and in the gardens around the house." She glanced out of the window, then back at McCoy. "Betray this trust and you spend all your time here. Try to run and you will go to a military detention cell—if someone with kin lost to the Federation Starfleet does not take out your entrails first. On ch'Rihan, you are not difficult to identify."

"And who was—"

Arrhae, on her way to the door, stopped and looked at him with a mixture of amusement and impatience. "Doctor, do you wish to eat, or to talk? If talk, then stay here and do it yourself. *I* am hungry."

Nothing was said during their brief meal, eaten under the curious gaze of many eyes. Arrhae conducted herself with the same faultless manners and distant courtesy that she had seen H'daen employ when he disapproved of one person or another, making it plain to those watching eyes—any pair of which could be reporting directly back to Intelligence—that she resented being made to feel like the keeper of some performing animal. From the look of him, McCoy knew what she was thinking. And didn't like it.

"You wear a translator, Mak'khoi?" Arrhae said as the dishes were being cleared away, using Rihannsu and speaking for the benefit of whatever ears went with spying eyes. The man nodded, still far from pleased with her if his face was anything to go by. "So know this, Lord H'daen tr'Khellian grants you guestright to walk as you please. . . ."

The brief lecture and its veiled warning done, she pushed back from the table and stood up, turning in time to see three heads peering in from the kitchen. They jerked back out of sight, but Arrhae compressed her lips into a thin line and stalked toward the door, working out something suitably irritable to say. McCoy was still in his chair, watching her. The man wasn't smiling—they both knew he was in too dangerous a position for that—but her renewed acquaintance with Terran facial expressions told Arrhae that the glint in his eye had something to do with sardonic humor. He understood exactly what she was about, and approved of it.

"I'm for taking a stroll in the gardens, Arrhae," he said.

She looked back at the sound of his voice. "Ridiculous," she said, annoyed. Then to him, more loudly, "Don't waste time making noises that I can't understand, Mak'khoi. Can you show me by signs?" He snorted at that, then gestured at the open window, tapped his chest, and made walking movements with two fingers on the table. "Oh. I see. Yes, go. But this could so easily become an embarrassment. I shall ask the lord for some kind of translating unit, Mak'khoi. Until then, keep your needs simple. Go *on,* I said. I have my work to do. . . ."

That work was much as it had always been, despite the secret upheaval in Arrhae's life. Making her disapproval of eavesdroppers quite plain to the kitchen staff was a break in the routine, but the rest of it was mostly another attempt to get the accounts sorted out when documents and receipts said one thing but the expenditure tally in the household computer said something else entirely.

Once in a while she wondered what McCoy was doing with his time. There was no point in trying to escape on foot from the Khellian estate, because it was quite simply too big. For all H'daen's straitened circumstances, that was only where money was concerned; his true wealth was in land, and if he would only sell some of it to the developer-contractors in i'Ramnau. . . . Arrhae had once, very diffidently, made the suggestion, and had sparked a tirade of startling intensity for daring to presume that "a few dirty chains of cash" could buy the property that his ancestors had enriched with their blood. It had been the only time that Arrhae had ever seen her lord lose his composure and shout at her. Strange that pride and honor would keep him poor in the midst of potential plenty and that same honor-created poverty would make him contemplate something so dishonorable—and so dangerous—as betraying Commander t'Radaik's trust. Imperial Fleet Intelligence was not likely to forgive what he had in mind for

McCoy if he went through with it. Whatever H'daen was paid, he wouldn't have much time to enjoy being rich before he became dead. . . .

Arrhae tapped another string of figures into the computer and stared at the screen without really seeing it, her brain so dulled by the boredom of the repetitious task and the confusion of the past day that it was several seconds before the meaning of the readout sank in. And she began to laugh.

Chief cook tr'Aimne, heading for the coolroom with a basket of prepared meatrolls, paused in her office doorway to look at her as if she had lost her mind. "I got it right," Arrhae told him, fighting to get coherence through her giggles. "Five days at this damned-to-Areinnye keyboard, and I got it right at last!"

Tr'Aimne stared, and Arrhae guessed that this frantic laughter had little to do with her successful computing and a great deal to do with what she had been going through. Concealing this, pretending not to know that, being controlled and calm at all times . . .

"Well done, *hru'hfe,*" said tr'Aimne in a deadly monotone. He plainly still hadn't forgiven her for that flitter ride into i'Ramnau, and he wasn't getting excited over any of *her* successes, no indeed. At least his undisguised dislike helped Arrhae get some sort of leash on what was too near hysteria for her liking.

"Thank you, Chief Cook," she said, equally flat. "I'm so very glad you're pleased. Now—get those to the coolroom and stop wasting time." He glared at her as the status quo restored itself with a thud, then whisked disdainfully away with his nose in the air.

"'Find a man who's a good cook, learn what he knows—then lose him,'" Arrhae quoted softly to herself. She glanced sidelong at the computer-screen and grinned a bit, hit SAVE and PRINT with a finger-fork in one quick motion, and caught the sheets as they emerged, then stood up, flexing her shoulders luxuriously. "Time off for good behavior," she said. *Time off spent doing your extra duties. Take a walk and find out what he's up to.*

She had walked almost around the mansion before she saw McCoy. He was sitting on top of one of the ornamental rock arrangements in the greater garden, and Arrhae was pleased to see that he had taken care not to disturb the mosses that surrounded and enhanced the pattern of the rocks. His back was toward her and he was hunched forward so that his elbows rested on his knees. She hesitated; every line of his body indicated gloom and depression and—by the sound of it—he was muttering to himself. *Hardly surprising,* Arrhae thought, wondering if she should leave him to be miserable in peace.

Then, even though she had made no noise, he straightened and snapped around at the waist, suddenly enough to make Arrhae jump. "Yes?" he said, staring at her.

"I wondered where you were."

"Not far away. Where could I go? You said that much yourself." He sounded bitter, and that wasn't surprising either. "And should we be talking anyway, since you 'don't understand me'? Or have you suddenly remembered again?"

Stubborn, prideful . . . ! "Doctor, what I said inside —about a translator—I meant it. Then we *can* talk, without needing one eye in our backs for every word." Arrhae saw his brows go up. "For my back, anyway. If they thought I was a spy . . ."

"I understand," said McCoy, and all the anger had left his voice. "At least, I begin to understand."

Arrhae turned away, studying the mosses with apparent interest while she tried to decide what *that* might mean. Nothing much, most likely. It was merely proof of what she had thought at the very beginning; McCoy would sooner be amiable than angry, and his gruffness was no more than a mannerism, like H'daen's preference for gestures over words. "Thank you for making

130

the attempt anyway," she said in an effort to be graceful over the business and restore something of her own crumpled honor. "Your translator: could you read a Rihanha book, perhaps?"

Small talk, Arrhae, small talk. Do you want to hear a Terran voice so much that you'll indulge in pointless chatter with a Fleet prisoner? The answer to that, despite the danger, was an unequivocal *yes*.

McCoy looked at her strangely, and shook his head. "It only operates on received speech. But thanks for asking, anyway." He tapped the heel of one boot thoughtfully against the surface of the rocks and glanced first toward the house and then back to her. "I was wondering—which is my room? That one?"

"No, that." She pointed Romulan-fashion with a jerk of her chin. "At the corner. You can see the storage-access doors; inside, they're behind an embroid—" Arrhae broke off short. "You're not a fool, Dr. Bones McCoy. Neither am I. You knew which room it was all the time. Why ask me?"

"Curiosity, nothing more. I wasn't sure. And I don't have an escape planned, if that's what's wrong. Everyone keeps telling me what a waste of time it is."

"You should come in."

"I'd as soon stay here for—"

"Doctor, I was not asking you, I was *telling* you."

McCoy got to his feet and brushed a little dust off the seat of his pants, then shrugged ostentatiously at her and sauntered back to the house.

Chapter Eight

Force and Power

THE CH'RIHAN OF the four morning and evening stars, the ch'Rihan of song, is a fair place. Wetter than Vulcan ever was, rich with seasons whose change could be perceived, full of game and food, full of noble land on which noble houses were built, green under a green-golden sky, wide-horizoned, soft-breezed, altogether a paradise. Looking back at those songs, it is sobering to consider that of the eighteen thousand surviving Travelers, perhaps six thousand died in the first ten years of their settlement.

Relatively few of these died from privation, lack of supplies, or any of the other problems common to pioneer planets far from their colonizing worlds. Most of them died from war: civil wars, international, intertribal, and interclan wars. They died in small skirmishes, epic battles, ritual murders, massacres, ambushes, pogroms, purges, and dynastic feuds. So many people died that the gene pool was almost unable to sufficiently establish itself. When the mutated lunglock virus spread around the planet and to ch'Havran fifty years after the Settlement, the population dropped to a nearly unviable nine thousand. Only through the vigorous, almost obsessive increase of the population over the following several hundred years—through multiple-birth "forcing," creche techniques, and some cloning—did the Rihannsu manage to survive at all.

The later Rihannsu historians have almost unanimously joined in condemning Lai i-Ramnau tr'Ehhelih for suggesting that the Rihannsu brought this devastating result on themselves by leaving Vulcan in the first place, and thus "running away from the problem" that should have been solved as a whole planet before they left. "They brought their wars with them in the ships," he said in Vehe'rrIhlan, the "Non-Apology." "Their aggression, which they fought so hard to keep, was their silent passenger, their smuggled-on stowaway, the one voice not raised at Meeting. But for all its silence, they knew it was there. They brought their problem with them when they fled it, as all do who part company with a trouble before it is completely resolved. Change of place is not solution of problem, change of persons is not solution of problem, but they threw even this shred of logic away when they left Vulcan. They attempted to become a new culture, but they went about this mostly by turning their backs on the old one. One who follows such a course is still following nothing but the old programming in reverse, or twisted—as if a computer programmer turned over a punch card and ran it backward. The results may look new, but the card is the same, and the program is the same, and sooner or later terribly familiar results will follow. The Travelers fought for the freedom to fight. They won the freedom, but they also won the fighting. . . ."

They killed Lai tr'Ehhelih some years after he wrote those words, and his works were expunged in many kingdoms and councillories. In others, mostly Eastern strongholds on ch'Havran, they were carefully hidden and preserved, which is fortunate. Otherwise we should know nothing of this hated, feared, angry little man, who told the truth as he saw it, and was so universally condemned. In retrospect, there may have been something to the truth he told. The Two Worlds have never been at peace with each other or themselves, and the first thousand years of their settlement were a broil of violence. The warfare led finally to unity and a sort of power, but the union was uneasy, and the power passed frequently from one hand to another, and never rested easy in any.

The government of ch'Rihan and ch'Havran, as

mentioned before, began as extensions both of the civil structure of the ships and the governmental structure on Vulcan. Unfortunately, the first of these proved more divisive than inclusive, and the settlement scheme for the Two Worlds began to interfere almost immediately with the second.

Originally there was supposed to be in the Two Worlds: one Councillory—consisting of the Grand Council of the planet (to which each local clan, tribe, or city sent one or more representatives) and the High Council (consisting of the thirty most senior councillors from the Grand Council, and ten of the most junior). By choice, people had been widely scattered in settlement, so as not to overtax natural resources. But not every family had its flitter anymore. The Rihannsu had brought maybe a thousand small vehicles with them among the surviving ships, and every trip in every one of them was grudged. Most of them were solar-powered, true, but there was the matter of spare parts, wear and tear, and so forth. For those first years, status was often reckoned not in land (of which many people had a great deal) but transportation.

With mobility so decreased, it was no longer a matter of simply calling a Grand Council meeting and having people flit in casually from all over the planet, every week or so. There had to be fewer meetings. It was a logistical problem getting everyone together, especially in the years before the communications networks were completely settled in place. With fewer meetings, more problems piled up to be handled, and the meetings had to be long—a problem, since pre-Reformation Vulcans were no fonder than the post-Reformation ones of spending endless hours in pursuit of bureaucracy. Less got done in Council meetings, both the Grand Council and the High one. The High Council in particular suffered from quick turnover in the early years, as many of the oldest councillors were in extreme old age, and there was less continuity of experience than was usual. More misunderstandings and mismanagements cropped up than had done at home on Vulcan, and people at home were often dissatisfied with the results.

In addition, there were more things to fight about than there had been in the old days . . . both more concrete problems and more abstract ones. Not only were there the familiar divisions, but blocs that voted with what ship they had been in. These "ship-blocs" often disastrously divided votes on important matters. Land—its boundaries and use of its resources—often became an issue, and there could be as many as fifteen or twenty factions—subdivisions of clans, tribes, or ship-blocs—fighting over who would get what. Here again, tr'Ehhelih may have told the right truth: even in the midst of plenty the Rihannsu could not get the context of the ancient scarcity of good land out of their minds, or their hearts. The squabbles, raids, and annexations were endless.

Government was slowed down by both these sets of problems at times when it could hardly afford to be, during the first half-century of the Settlement. Its ill function caused its collapse, an abrupt one, and the Ruling Queen's rise.

The most obvious trigger of the bloody events was the terrible famine in the South Continent on ch'Havran, during which almost half of the fifteen hundred people scattered across it died of starvation in the seventy-eighth year after the Settlement. But it could be said that the system had already been staggering under a burden of distances increased beyond management, and reduced logistical and technological support. It was bound to fall soon, and perhaps the sooner the better. However, the Councils fell badly, and the toll in lives and resources—and honor—was high.

The Ruling Queen's rise is paradoxical to this day, even among Rihannsu. She was one of those people with that inexplicable quality that Terrans call "charisma" and Rihannsu "nuhirrien," "look-toward." People would listen to her, gladly give her things they could hardly spare, forgive her terrible deeds. Her power was astonishing, and unaccountable. She was not a great physical beauty, or a very mighty warrior, or marvelously persuasive, or any of the other things people normally find attractive. She simply had that quality, like Earth's Hitler, like (at the other end of the spectrum) Surak, of being followed. Some have used the word "sociopath" to describe her, but the term loses some of its meaning in Rihannsu culture, where one is expected to reach out one's hand and take what one wants . . . as the Travelers did.

T'Rehu was a North-Continent Grand Councillor's daughter who succeeded her father in office after his death. (Rihannsu political offices to this day change hands by birth succession rather than election, except when relatives are lacking or there is dishonor involved. A senator whom his district considers substandard cannot be voted out of office, but his senatoriate can send him their swords by way of suggestion that he use them on himself. Very rarely is the suggestion ignored.)

At first there seemed nothing special about her. She was capable enough, and her councillory (Elheu district, in the ship-bloc nation called Nn'Verih) prospered, and its clans with it. As time went on, however, others looked at their prosperity and became suspicious of it, noticing that the neighbors of Elheu were dying off, or being killed in inexplicable feuds, and ceding their lands—choice ones—to Elheu. No one quite had the nerve to suggest treachery, but all the same, puppets of T'Rehu's house or members of her family were soon sitting in the council chairs of more and more Nn'Verih districts. And there were disturbing reports of armed raids, House-burnings, forced marriages, and mind-betrothals, forced conceptions and births so that children related to T'Rehu's House would inherit councillories and (after suitable training in her house) dance to her lyre.

Not all of these reports were true, of course. But it seems true enough that T'Rehu was vastly dissatisfied with the way the council system worked. Numerous families of her district had, in her youth, suffered from terrible lack of the basic needs: food in that part of the continent was scarce, there were famines and plagues, good medical help was hard to come by. No one knows whether the story is true that T'Rehu lost a lover to lunglock fever because the council "could not afford" to send a healer out with the vaccine, newly developed and very expensive. It may be propaganda generated by one of T'Rehu's people. But even if it is, the story was probably truth somewhere else, painfully indicative of the kind of suffering that went on in the Two Worlds during their early days.

Time passed and the problem grew too slowly, perhaps, for either the Grand Council or High Council to perceive it clearly in their busy and infrequent meetings. The population increased in Nn'Verih, and most especially in Elheu, increased almost fifty percent over twenty years. Scientists were welcome in Nn'Verih, especially if they specialized in fertility or cloning. The place got a great name for research, though where the money for it was coming from, and the facilities, was often in question. The usual explanation was that Elheu had political connections with the Ship-Clans. People who looked too closely into the question tended to stop abruptly, either out of seeming choice or because they were suddenly nowhere to be found.

And rather suddenly, about sixty years after the Settlement, Elheu had an army. Oddly enough, this came as a surprise. For all its warfare, Vulcan was never very good at organizing it: there had been no standing armies. A leader with a cause would raise what force he could by spreading the news around as to why one should fight: if you convinced people well enough, you would have a larger army than your enemy, and you would have a chance to beat them. Then after your victory (Elements granting you won), everyone would do what looting and spoiling they felt was necessary, and take the booty home to their own clans and tribes. For these reasons, alliances were never considered to have any more permanence than a pattern of dust on a windy day: you could not keep the force that had made you worth allying with. A standing army would have been considered an outrageous expense. Where would you keep them? And more important, where would they get food and water?

This situation was probably fortunate: if Vulcan had supported the standing-army concept, there would probably be nothing there now but sand, burying the tallest spires of the last-standing cities. What was unfortunate was that ch'Rihan did have enough resources of local food and water to support large organized groups of people. T'Rehu had made the conceptual jump, and invented the standing army. She did not sit around thinking of things to do with it for more time than was absolutely necessary.

She did wait a while, however. She waited until it was perfectly obvious to both the Grand Council and High Council what she was likely to do if anyone crossed her. Between the years 60 and 72 A.S. she made pointed examples of a few small territories not far from Elheu. She massed troops on their border (only a matter of a couple of thousand, but in those days, those were numbers to be reckoned with) and then had them sent false intelligence that, for political purposes, she was bluffing them. Predictably, to look bold before the other Houses, they defied her. T'Rehu then came down on them—little pieces of the world, county-sized by Earth standards, full of gentleman farmers busy scratching their livings out of a still-protesting planet—and she burned their crops and houses and killed those who resisted, and captured those who did not. If they entered her service willingly, well. If they did not, she turned her adepts loose on the captives and had them mindchanged, so that they went into her service anyway. If the mindchange didn't work, the captives in question were never seen again.

The Grand Council immediately convened and went into uproar. T'Rehu went among them, utterly cool—as well she might have been, with her bodyguard about her. Very nearly she swept the Sword off the Empty Chair and took it for herself, but at the last moment prudence or fear prevented her. She had her guards overturn the Master Councillor's chair, with him in it, and sat down there herself with her S'harien across her lap, unsheathed—one of the few of the great swords that Surak did not put aboard the ships himself. There she stayed for a noisy half hour, and let them rave about honor and outrage. "Say what you like, and do what you like," she said at last, "I am your mistress now. Idiots and old men shall not run my land anymore, nor any other I can get my hands on."

This panicked the Council, as well it might have. Perhaps a hundred of the three hundred twelve of them had lands that bordered on T'Rehu's . . . or might later, at the rate she was going. Councillors from the other continents were scornful. Granted that the woman had outstepped her bounds on the North Continent, and should be punished, but how could she hope to transport an army across the seas, or to ch'Havran?

She merely smiled and reminded them of her friendship with the Ship-Clans. Many hearts went cold in their owners' sides as they remembered the mass transports lying in hangar-bays in the Four Ships, each transport capable of handling five hundred people at a time. There were more than enough transports to manage a smallish army . . . or a largish one.

They did the only thing they could think of, they

offered her the Master Councillory, the lordship of the Grand Council, if she would hold her hand. S'task stood up at that and walked out of Council, which he had been attending by courtesy (High Councillors might, though they had to ask permission of the Grandees). "I did not give you leave to go," the imperious voice rang out behind him.

"I have no need to ask it, of you especially," said S'task. His voice was not so firm as it had been once: he was very old, even by Vulcan standards, and troubled with circulatory and bone-marrow problems that may have been caused by cumulative radiation exposure on the Journey. But he was as fierce as he had ever been, and few dared to cross his mild voice when it was raised in either Council.

"I shall kill you if you do not ask leave," said T'Rehu, standing up with the S'harien in her hand.

He turned to her, and the carefully preserved Council tape records, for all that they have been copied hundreds of times, still clearly show the cool scorn in his eyes. It might have been Surak dealing with some childish flaw in logic. "You may do so," he said. "That is the prerogative of force. But I give no honor to force. Power, yes. But you have no power, none that I recognize. I ask no leave of you." And he walked out of chambers, while T'Rehu stood behind him with the sword shaking in her hand.

"You will not do that twice!" she cried, and then found her composure again, and was seated, while the chamber stirred and murmured in fear at the terrible audacity of the woman who would challenge the authority of the father of the Two Worlds, the leader of the Journey. Their fear became too much for them. Possibly had they united against her then, they might have stopped her. There might have been a war, but it would have been a small one.

They did not unite against her. They gave T'Rehu the Grand Councillorship, and for a while it held her quiet as she played with the politics of the "lower house" and amused herself. But it did not hold her long, and the thought of her rebuff in front of the Grandees still rankled. She waited for an excuse, and one presented itself.

There are several theories for the cause of the famine in the South Continent in 78 A.S. The accusation that T'Rehu started it herself is probably baseless: Rihannsu biotechnology was not far enough along to make germ warfare at all likely. As far as anyone can tell from the records remaining, the weather was quite enough to do it—one of those paradoxical years that happens in many a temperate climate, when winter simply refuses to let go, and temperatures remain subnormal all year long. Freak weather killed most of the imported cultivated graminiformes, and the South Continent people were short of other staples. They would not plant "the wretched root," and so had none when it might have saved their lives. Help was marshaled and sent from other continents and nations, but not quickly enough to save a thousand lives. Part of this (though T'Rehu did all she could to conceal the fact) was the sheer stubbornness of the southerners: they had a tradition of bearing suffering without complaint as they had in *Gorget* and *Vengeance*. And without complaint they died, by hundreds. The help arrived too late.

To T'Rehu, it was a gift from the Elements. She swept into the Grand Council and delivered them a long diatribe, berating them for not doing better for the people in their care. (Carefully she avoided any line of reasoning that might have indicated she, as Master Councillor, was at all responsible for "her" governing body's failures.) "It will not be allowed to happen again," she said, and the next day she informed the High Council that the Master Councillor required them to meet.

They sent back to say that the "request" was incorrectly made, but nonetheless they would accommodate her. What the Forty had not been expecting was to find her waiting in Chambers for them the next morning, with five cohorts of a hundred warriors each standing outside (and many of them inside that crowded little room as well). T'Rehu told them that their rule was ineffective. Others better suited to handling the affairs of two great worlds would now assume it.

The Forty, to their credit, did not freeze as completely as the Grand Council had. They had suspected something of T'Rehu's intent, and had come armed; they defied her. But her eye was not on them. She was watching S'task. He rose up, and slowly and carefully turned his back on her, and headed toward the chamber doors.

"I have not given you leave," she said, and this time her voice was heard to be shaking in the hush that had fallen on the room.

S'task said never a word.

She signed to her guard, and one of them threw a dart-spear at S'task, and it pierced his side and his heart, and that was the end of him. Only he lifted up his head as he lay there bleeding out his life in the uproar and the massacre that followed, and he said to T'Rehu, "The beginning is contaminated, and force will not avail you, or it."

So he died there, two hundred forty-eight years old, in the building whose cornerstone he had laid, as he had laid the cornerstone of the Journey itself. Not many missed the irony that it was the old "Vulcan," the way of kings and queens and unbridled passions and wars, for which he had fought, that had killed S'task at last.

It killed the High Council, too, and some members of the Grand Council as well fell victim to T'Rehu as she purged the "corrupt" government of ch'Rihan and ch'Havran and set herself as Ruling Queen in its place, taking as her model the Ruling Queens of Kh'reitekh in northern Vulcan in the ancient days. Her accession was a gaudy affair, and well attended, though it might seem strange from our end of time that people would turn out peaceably to see the murderess of S'task take up the spear of royalty. The truth was that most of the attendees were local people, some of whom had been ordered to attend or their families would suffer, and S'task's popularity had been quietly waning for some years, as if now that the Journey was done, most people had no more need for him. Perhaps the citizenry had been looking, as the governed sometimes will, for something, anything, to replace a government that bores them. For eighteen years the Rihannsu got one that was not at all boring . . . and that was about all that could be said for it.

Eighteen years is a short term in any office by Vulcan or Rihannsu reckoning. T'Rehu took the title-name *Vriha,* "highest," and conducted her court in the old high-handed fashion, handing out life and death as it pleased her. She did not have time to do much harm to the Two Worlds, she was by and large too busy gratifying her own desires, mostly for bigger palaces, more luxuries for her favorites, and more money to pay her soldiers. She had the vigorous love of pleasure of a Terran Elizabeth I, without either the sense of responsibility or the high intelligence that drove that monarch. At first she made a great show of being a "just ruler," sending help to the famine-struck South continent (and the help did no more good than that previously sent by the Councils—most of the people were already dead). But eventually "her people" came to concern her only insofar as they gave her money or bowed before her.

T'Rehu had the old Council chambers razed and built new ones, bigger and grander, with a throne for her, one ostentatiously blocking the Empty Chair from view . . . though she did not quite dare to get rid of it or the sword. She chose new councillors, one of them from each continent, totaling twelve in all, mostly women. She made each of them responsible for their whole landmass, and if things went ill there, there was no use pleading for mercy. The floors were marble, and easily washed clean. She went through a fair number of councillors this way, and no one dared chide her for it. They might be next.

She was not mad enough to let all her political connections lapse when she came into power. She enriched the Ship-Clans considerably, delaying for a little the beginning of their decline. In return she demanded a great deal of application of Shipside technology to the problems of ch'Rihan and ch'Havran, particularly the transportation and communication problems. Naturally these were for the benefit of her throne—it being difficult to control two worlds properly without quick communication and widespread swift transportation—but accidentally these measures did the Rihannsu people some good as well. The first factories for communications hardware and small transport were set up under her aegis, and by 96 A.S. a tolerable videotelephone system was in operation, and at least one House in every five had its own flitter, or could afford one.

But her rule could not last long, simply because it would occur for other people to do what she had done as well. The East-Continent factions on ch'Havran smarted under her rule—since their continent was poor, she paid little notice to them—and they decided to do something about it. By themselves, without assistance from the fertility experts, without cloning, they doubled their continental population during T'Rehu's reign and they quietly raised and trained their own young army in philosophies that the Spartans would have recognized instantly. Ruthless hatred of the enemy, self-sacrifice, instant obedience, and the nation above all—not the state. In this case, that was T'Rehu. They made their own arrangements with the Ship-Clans as well, for one thing their rugged hills had that T'Rehu did not know about—mines with some of the largest optical-grade rubies ever seen on any world, perfect for generating large-scale laser light.

The Easterners descended on T'Rehu in the eighteenth year of her reign, brought her (unwillingly) to battle with twice her forces' numbers, and killed her on the plains of Aihai outside the capital city of Ra'tleihfi, which she was still completing. There was not so much rejoicing at this in the Two Worlds as confusion. The Easterners might have moved into the power vacuum and set themselves up as kings, but to their credit, they did not. They wanted a return to a quieter sort of government, one in which tyranny would have difficulty going for such a long time uncorrected.

From this victory in ch'Rihan's first war, after some squabbling among various continents for supremacy, came the Praetorial and Senatorial structure that we know today, a resurrection of the councillories crossed with the Queen's Twelve. Our Federation Standard terms are, of course, worn-down Latin cognates: "Praetor" for the Rihannsu *Fvillha,* "landmaster," and "Senator" for *deihu,* "elder." The Rihannsu functions are fairly close in some ways to the Roman ones: the Senate passing and vetoing legislation (in the Rihannsu version, one half of the Senate being assigned the business of doing nothing but veto, probably as a reaction to T'Rehu's tyranny): the Praetorate wielding judicial and executive power for whole continents, implementing the laws passed . . . and sometimes getting laws passed for which they feel the need. The Senate is counted as two houses, so that all the governing bodies taken together are *seiHehllirh,* the "Tricameron." Together the Three (or Two) Houses have weathered many troubles, and even the occasional Emperor or Empress . . . very occasional. History has shown the Rihannsu to have little trust in "single rulers." They have long seemed to prefer them in groups, feeling perhaps that there is safety in numbers. If one gets out of hand, the others will pull him or her down. And indeed the doings of the Praetorate sometimes look, to an outsider, like nothing so much as the minute-to-minute business of a bucket of crabs—each trying to climb out on the others' backs, the ones underneath unfailingly pulling off balance the ones climbing on them.

It proved to be a form of government not very stable in the short term: a never-ending swirl of alliances, betrayals, whisperings, veiled allusions, matters of honor shadowy and open, machinations, string-pulling, and arguments forever. Yet despite this, the Rihannsu governmental system proved perfect for the people they were in the process of becoming, and stable in the long run, for people wanted no more T'Rehus. The Tricameron survived through the loss of the Ships and the loss of spaceflight technology, through the rediscovery of the sciences and the flowering of the Rihannsu arts, through several more wars and several surprisingly long periods of peace, through the first Rihannsu contact with an alien species and the intertwining of the Two Worlds' affairs, willy-nilly, with those of the Klingons and the Federation. It survives yet, the crabs climbing up and pulling down as of old. And if the Rihannsu have their way, it will go on for as long as their worlds have people on them. "Certain it is and sure," says the song, "love burns, ale burns, fire burns, politics burns. But cold were life without them."

Chapter Nine

THERE WERE FEWER people in i'Ramnau than at the same time last week. Fewer people, and poorer produce. Arrhae was grateful for the one, but annoyed about the other. And wary all the time. Nobody *looked* unfriendly; but then, that was the problem. Any of the other shoppers who passed her by could be—and probably were—Intelligence operatives watching the person responsible for their latest and most important catch.

There was no way in which she could forget about McCoy, not with the translator device belted around her waist that bumped her hipbone most uncomfortably every time she moved. H'daen had presented it to her only yesterday, with some ceremony and an interminable list of do's and don'ts. *Be careful with it, it's expensive Fleet property; don't lose it; don't play with the control settings; and above all, keep it out of McCoy's hands.* H'daen was simply passing on instructions that he didn't understand, and that one most of all. Arrhae ir-Mnaeha wouldn't have understood it either—but Lieutenant-Commander Haleakala did. Unless Romulan translators were vastly different from the Federation hand-trans units that she was used to, the internal duotronic transtator circuitry could be converted, with a lot of knowledge and a little work, into a small, crude, but very nasty form of primitive blaster.

Terise thought about that, and about what would become of her otherself if anything of the sort should happen, and strapped it on at once. It hadn't been farther than an arm's length away ever since.

147

McCoy was the principal reason for her being here anyway. After the translator had arrived, and she had been able to talk to him for the "first time"—without a lengthy explanation of her sudden linguistic ability— she had tried to find out what an unenhanced Terran metabolism could, and more important, couldn't digest. Not only was it important for his jailer to keep her prisoner well and healthy, but more personal reasons could see that the man had enough trouble already without a dose of *llhrei'sian*. "The Titanian two-step," McCoy had called it, and at the old, old Starfleet slang Arrhae/Terise had laughed out loud for the first time since he came into the house.

Most of the goods for the house were being delivered, and that left only McCoy's own provisions to be bought and carried about the town. Shopping for what were largely unusual items, Arrhae managed to forget her troubles, at least for a while. Most especially when she was bargaining stallholders up from their excessively honorable—and excessively low—first prices toward something that the honor and status of House Khellian required her to pay. It amused her that a people who had attained warpflight and who had learned how to cloak something the size of a battlecruiser still couldn't buy meat and vegetables without haggling like the feudal societies she had studied in college.

And then she saw him again.

It was the fourth time now that he had been standing off to one side, watching her. A small man, darkly good-looking—and not really paying attention to the goods he was about to buy. Arrhae was unaccustomed to being looked at by young men on Earth, but here—well, Lhaesl tr'Khev, bless him, had been far from subtle in his compliments, and though she had never dared admit it, even to herself, the small, sharp, high-boned features that hadn't drawn a second glance at home went beyond pretty into what Romulans regarded as classic beauty. Except that this man didn't have the speculative, appraising, or just plain appreciative expression that she was used to. Instead, he was looking at her with the intensity of someone trying to remember a name or where they had last seen a face. On an arrest-sheet, perhaps . . .

Arrhae felt her mouth become dry and metallic-tasting. She turned away quickly, as if not looking at the man could banish him to some distant place, and began to scoop parceled *hlai*-filets from the countertop. At least this meat was the final item on her list of purchases; everything else—another quick glance side-ways confirmed that her shadow was still where she had last seen him—was going to wait until another day, and she was ready, willing, and able to face down anybody, including H'daen himself, in defense of her decision. Or Chief Cook tr'Aimne, who for a blessing wasn't with her today even though—or perhaps because—H'daen, pleased that she had brought the Varrhan flitter back undamaged, had given her the use of it again. At least there was a quick way out of the city and back home. Bidding the meat-vendor a fair day in a voice that trembled only very slightly, she made off with as much haste as dignity and a full load of groceries permitted, leaving the man holding uncollected change from five full chains of cash and wondering what had happened to so suddenly increase House Khellian's opinion of its own honor.

Two armored constables sauntered past her, local men, exchanging cheerful comments with shoppers and salespeople alike, and Arrhae wondered if she dared. . . . A swift look behind gave her the answer to that, because her pursuer was no longer in sight and without him what could she say? *Nothing,* she thought savagely, and hurried past them in the general direction of the flitpark.

She didn't go straight there, but followed a twisty, convoluted course through the greater and lesser streets of i'Ramnau, with much doubling back and breathless pausing in doorways. No sign. . . . Even the park was almost deserted, flitters in less than a quarter

of its bays on a day when it was usually filled to
capacity, and she began to smile at her own fears.
Lhaesl tr'Khev wasn't the only young man who needed
a lesson in manners when it came to the admiring of
ladies. Dropping her packs beside the Varrhan, she
leaned one hand on its warm hull and reached out with
the other to pop its cargo-bay—then jumped backward
and almost screamed aloud when a hand came from the
vehicle's interior and grabbed her firmly by the wrist.

"Hru'hfe s'Khellian?"

Arrhae tugged once, uselessly. *"Ie,"* she said in a
defeated voice.

"Good."

The young man who had followed her—probably
from her first arrival in the flitpark if she but knew the
whole of it—eased himself out of the prime-chair and
straightened up with a little sigh of relief. "Hot in there
without the 'cyclers running," he said. "Then your
name would be Arrhae ir-Mnaeha?" He still hadn't let
go of her arm.

"Yes."

"Good." And this time he let her go.

Arrhae rubbed at her wrist more for something to do
than because it pained her; the man hadn't been brutal,
just most decisive. She glanced around the park for a
potential rescuer if one should become necessary, and
then back at him. "Why good?" she said, while inside
her otherself Terise speculated on how she could take
him out with a minimum of noise and disturbance.
"Why were you following me?"

"Mnhei'sahe," he said quietly.

Arrhae shivered at the word, and Terise went far, far
away into her subconscious. *Mnhei'sahe* was controlled
more by circumstances than by definition. It could
mean lifelong friendship or unremitting hatred, but the
friendship did not always mean long life or the hatred
sudden death. The word was as slippery as a *nei'rrh*,
and often as deadly, and the Rihanha that was Arrhae
wondered what its meaning might be this time. She

tried to remember who she might have offended in the past; who might have decided that this was a good time to take revenge for real or imagined slights. She looked nervously at the young man and wondered if, concealed somewhere, he carried the edged steel that was considered appropriate for honorable murder.

As far as she could see, he was unarmed; and he was smiling. It was one of the weakest smiles that she had seen in her life, a poor somber apology of a thing, but at least the grimness was turned inward rather than directed at her.

"Nveid tr'AAnikh," he said with a little bow of introduction. The name meant nothing to Arrhae, and it seemed likely that her expression told Nveid as much. He looked around, then gestured at the flitter. "Could we get inside please, and drive?"

"Where?" Arrhae said coldly. She had recovered from her fright, and anger was starting to replace it, because if this was an arrest, it was the strangest she had ever heard of; and such a recovery was inevitable anyway, she was getting so much practice at being scared and hiding the fact from various people. Either that or just give up and take refuge in madness.

"Wherever you like. I'm afraid they might have had me watched."

"Who?" Another irritable monosyllable from Arrhae, who once again was smelling the unpleasant aroma of intrigue and wanted nothing more to do with it.

"My family," he said. "They don't approve of my attitude."

Arrhae managed a very good hollow laugh. This man was neither her master nor anyone of such importance as Commander t'Radaik. For the first time in long enough, she was confronted by someone whose requests she could refuse. "Because you accost other people's servants about their lawful business? Are you surprised, tr'AAnikh?"

"It isn't that. It's because of my brother."

She brushed past him and dropped her parcels into the Varrhan's cargo-space, then made to get inside. His arm was braced across the doorway, and Arrhae looked at it with disapproval while Terise Haleakala gazed calmly through the same eyes and noted wrong-way striking angles directed against the locked elbow joint. "Are you fond of using that arm, Nveid tr'AAnikh," she said gently.

He looked right back at her, paler now than he had been, and said, "McCoy."

Arrhae took a single step backward, her facial muscles already frozen and expressionless. "Get in," she snapped. "You know how, invited or not."

Nveid scrambled inside with the quick, economical movements of someone who had spent time in the cramped confines of a Fleet Warbird. "You should lock the doors," he said, smiling.

"Why bother? Without the drive codes you wouldn't have gone anywhere." She slid into the prime-seat, strapped herself in, and punched in the activator program, noticing absently as she fed in a manual override to her logged routeplans that he was right, it *was* hot without the 'cyclers running. They cut in even as she thought about them, as the flitter's systems came to life and she lifted it clear of the parkbay in a smooth, tight 3-G arc that squashed tr'AAnikh back into the padded seat.

"You drive like Nniol used to," he said when he had the breath to do it.

Arrhae glanced at him, confirmed that the overrides were up and running, and took the flitter out toward open country at a speed just below city-traffic limits. "What about McCoy?" she said, not interested in who or how she drove like. "And what does *mnhei'sahe* have to do with all this?"

"Return to auto," said Nveid.

Arrhae laughed scornfully. "Can't take the thought of a woman at the controls, eh?"

"I've seen how you react to a shock, and I don't intend to die because of it."

That stopped her laughing, and an instant later persuaded her to let the flitter's onboards take over. "Very amusing, tr'AAnikh," she said quietly. "Why shouldn't I be proud and haughty and throw you out right now?"

"Because you want to hear me."

"Then talk to me, man, and hope I don't throw you out anyway. . . ."

"I doubt it." Nveid looked confident enough, almost too confident for Arrhae's liking, though she pushed that thought back until it became important again. "I told you before: it concerns my brother Nniol, and *mnhei'sahe*, and Dr. McCoy of the Federation vessel *Enterprise*." He paused as a thought struck him. "That *is* the man held at H'daen tr'Khellian's mansion? Not some other of the same name?"

"McCoy of the *Enterprise*," Arrhae confirmed. "So?"

"My brother Nniol served aboard Ael t'Rllaillieu's *Bloodwing*, and my sister aboard *Javelin* under LLunih tr'Raedheol. I don't know all the details—nobody does outside High Command—but there was some treason involving *Bloodwing* and *Enterprise* and . . . *Javelin* was destroyed."

"Your brother killed his own sister . . . ?"

"Who knows? *Bloodwing* will never return to ch'Rihan, and *Javelin*'s dust can tell no tale. But my family decided. They formally disowned Nniol. His name was written and burned. . . . I displease them because I speak about him still and because I say that *mnhei'sahe* required him to do what . . . what he did."

"Oh. That one. All duty and obligation goes to your Commander, not to your family?"

"Always. We are an honorable house, and my sister would have done the same. As would I. On board ship the Commander becomes *hru'hfirh*, although some are more deserving of the courtesy than others. Ael t'Rllaillieu may be a traitor now, but in her time she was the best Captain that my brother had the honor to obey."

"And McCoy? Where does he fit in? Do you want to kill him in requital for your brother and sister . . . ?" Nveid stared at her, shocked. "Isn't that what your honor requires?" Arrhae was beginning to doubt it somehow; this man wasn't like tr'Annhwi, or, if he was, he hid it well.

"No, it isn't." He sat back in the seat, relaxing a little. *"Hru'hfe,* there are entire Houses who think that way—but there are also entire Houses who think as I do, that their bloodkin acted with *mnhei'sahe* in this sad business. One of them would have spoken with you— maybe s'Khnialmnae—except that every one of them is under close observation by Fleet Intelligence. I need only worry about my immediate family. . . ."

"Then what do you and these other Houses want to do with McCoy?" The impatient edge in Arrhae's voice—adopted from one of the Fleet officers who visited House Khellian—cut through Nveid's reminisc- ing and brought him bolt upright. He blinked and stared at her with the injured air of a man who'd heard that tone from his superiors and hadn't thought to get it here as well.

"We want to help him escape."

Arrhae knew that this youngster had been quite right to insist she put the flitter back on automatics before surprising her like that—otherwise she would probably have crashed it into the side of a hill right here and now. At least she managed not to show it this time. Practice, probably. Why did people keep saying things like this to her? Why couldn't she just go back to being a full-time servants' manager and a very part-time deep-cover spy? What had gone wrong with her life? "Oh, is that all?" she said, very controlled. "Nothing else? Why not the Sword from the Empty Chair as a parting gift, perhaps?"

154

Nveid laughed softly. "You're as cool as a Vulcan," he said. "I hadn't expected it—but then, that's why Fleet put McCoy in your hands, I suppose. We'll make it worthwhile, of course, and nobody will know you were ever involved."

"You do know the Senate punishment for treason?"

"Of course." Nveid's voice went harsh. "The Justiciary Praetor read sentence on Nniol's name. If he's ever caught, they'll carry it out. All of it. The penalty for espionage is much the same, except they start with eyes and ears instead of tongue and hands. And *that* they've planned for McCoy, sometime in the next tenday. The Houses I represent aren't going to allow it. There is still such a thing as—"

"—honor on ch'Rihan, yes. How did I guess you'd say something like that? And Nveid, I don't know what value you and your friends put on 'worthwhile,' but there isn't enough money on ch'Rihan to match the value I put on my skin."

"But I told you, nobody will know—"

"Until somebody does, and where would that leave me? Being slowly shredded on the public-broadcast channel, like they did to Vaebn tr'Lhoell. I'm sure he thought nobody would ever know about him, either."

"You could consider our proposal, at least."

Arrhae brought the flitter onto a course back to i'Ramnau and locked into the traffic-grid before she turned to look at Nveid. "You heard me consider. You heard my conclusion. Listen to me. You found out where McCoy was being held, and I—doubtless to my regret, if it ever comes out—confirmed that the man in House Khellian was indeed the one that you and your friends suspected. I want nothing more to do with it. You will get out of this flitter when I get back to the park, and you will go away, and you will leave me alone or I swear that I'll report the lot of you just to make sure that I'm safe!"

Her voice had risen to a near-shriek during the tirade, so that Nveid was watching her now with wide, shocked eyes and a plainly visible doubt that this woman would have been of any use at all. That was as Arrhae wished. She had no desire to be made use of again; it was already happening far too much for her liking. The flitter settled into its recently vacated bay with a jarring thump that almost certainly took paint off the A-G housings, but she was past caring about such details, and past worrying whether H'daen saw the damage and forbade her to go anywhere near i'Ramnau ever again. The way she felt now, that wouldn't be a punishment.

She hit the canopy control-tab and watched as Nveid tr'AAnikh climbed out. He moved more slowly than she had seen him do before, and the look he directed back at her was more regretful than anything else. "Reconsider," he said.

"No. What do you expect from a servant, man? We leave the concerns of honor to those with free time to worry about them."

"Then that's your last—"

"I said, *yes!*" Arrhae snapped the canopy shut on whatever else he was trying to say, and lifted the flitter clear with enough violence to trigger a stress-warning alarm. *Last time you'll get clearance for this,* she thought grimly. *And I think it's time I had another talk with the good doctor. Otherwise things are going to get right out of hand. If they haven't already . . .*

Outside, it began to rain.

Arrhae disabled the autos and took the flitter into its garage on manual. It was a simple test; either she was back in control of herself and could handle the vehicle safely, or she would crash it and kill herself. Sometimes that seemed preferable. Certainly it would be less complicated. She sat for a long while in the quiet, after the engine noise had died away, and listened to the pattering of rain on the roof, wondering what to do next. *Unload the shopping,* she thought. *And then go see McCoy.*

S'anra met her in the corridor as she left the garage area, summoned most likely by the door-chime as the flitter came in. "You're back!" she began excitedly. "There's someone here to see you, and—"

"Take these to the kitchen and store them." Arrhae pushed the parcels into S'anra's arms. They were caught by no more than automatic reflex, and a bundle of vegetable tubers fell off the unstable pile. She picked it off the floor and slapped it emphatically back on top of the heap of packages. "And tell whoever it is that I'm busy."

"But Arrhae . . ."

That drew a disapproving glare. Junior servants and slaves were not permitted to call their superiors by name, only by rank or title. "Mind your manners—and don't contradict me. I have work to do, so I'll be along in a while. Go say so."

S'anra gaped like a landed fish for a second or two—because of her mistake maybe, or because Arrhae was being unusually tetchy, or for some other reason restricted to scullery slaves—then scurried away with the groceries. Arrhae watched her go, thinking back to when she had been no more than a slave herself, with a slave's small concerns and worries. And with only the problems of learning several thousand years of cultural history hanging overhead. She smiled thinly, and went to find McCoy.

He wasn't in his room, and Arrhae had a momentary fit of the horrors while she imagined all the things that might have happened while she was away. *While you were away—as if your being here would have made any difference if a squad of Fleet troopers came for him. . . .* Then she began thinking, more sensibly again, of all the places that McCoy had grown fond of during the past tenday.

First and foremost was the garden. *In* this *downpour?* Arrhae thought dubiously, looking out at the lowering gray sky. *Well, why not. The quicker you go out to see, the quicker you can get back indoors. . . .*

And, of course, that was where he was. She found McCoy as she had seen him so many times before, sitting on top of the rocks in the garden, talking to himself. Arrhae could hear the soft mumble of his voice as she approached, and he most certainly heard her splashy footfalls, for he climbed down and came to meet her. "Do you really like this weather so much?" she demanded, feeling a rivulet of chilly water starting to wander down inside her supposedly rainproof over-robe. "Look at you, man; why didn't you ask for a coat! You're soaked to the skin!"

McCoy shook raindrops from his hair. "Yes, in fact I do like it. I can't see the house through the rain, and that way I don't have to think about being locked up all night. And I couldn't ask for a coat because nobody here speaks Anglish and the only translator in the area had been taken shopping. But I wanted some fresh air, so I came out anyway. I knew you wouldn't mind."

"Dammit, McCoy, you're impossible!" she yelled. And then realized that the words were idiomatic Anglish and had come out in a voice untainted by any trace of a Rihannsu accent.

Oh, no. O Elements. I am betrayed. And by myself . . .

"Good," McCoy said, exactly as Nveid tr'AAnikh had done. Then he smiled the small smile of someone whose theories have been conclusively proven. "But you're right. I am impossible. And it's getting wetter out here than even I like, so shouldn't we go indoors now?" Since McCoy's clothing was already so water-logged that it had stopped soaking up the rain, his remark was more to give her an out than because he was concerned.

Arrhae took it as gracefully as she could, though she pointedly refused to say anything to him either in Anglish or translated Rihannsu. She had an unpleasant feeling, justified or not, that he had laid a trap for her—and the even more unpleasant feeling of having walked right into it. After eight years of cautiously avoiding the attention of Imperial Intelligence, it irked her to realize that this drowned rat of a medical officer had maneuvered her into a position that would mean unpleasant death if anyone else had overheard her words. All her intentions of talking to him were evaporating fast, and yet there were things that he had to be told.

"Be more careful in future," she said at last, speaking low and letting her accent do whatever it wanted to—which in this instance was to slur and jump most alarmingly. "Not that you have much of it. Your trial's been set for sometime soon, and the sentence has already been agreed."

"Death, of course."

"Of course. But it seems, Doctor, that you're very popular among . . . certain groups. That popularity spread to me, briefly, and I didn't like it—but I think you can expect visitors after dark."

"Oh, wonderful." McCoy didn't sound impressed. "It should relieve the boredom of being locked in all night." He passed her, squelching, rather, on the wet ground, and looked back briefly. This time he wasn't smiling. "And Arrhae, I think we should have some sort of talk soon, about languages, and history, and people who aren't what they seem." McCoy waited for a reaction, saw none, shrugged, and walked back toward the house, leaving Arrhae to the rain and to her own thoughts.

"Where were you, *hru'hfe?*" Ekkhae pounced on her as she stamped irritably into the house, quailed from the glower that the question provoked, but continued determinedly for all that. "Master H'daen has been waiting for you since you came back from the city. In the antechamber. He has a guest. . . ."

"Another one? Who is it this time?"

"A visitor." Ekkhae came down hard on the word, as

if it had some special significance, and smiled oddly as she said it.

Arrhae took off the sopping overrobe and tossed it at the little slave. Despite being suddenly encumbered by a swathe of clammy fabric, Ekkhae's smile grew wider and more peculiar. "What's wrong with you?" Arrhae snapped. "Your teeth hurt?"

"No, *hru'hfe.*"

"Then put that away—and drape it properly; I don't want creases."

"No, *hru'hfe.* I mean yes, *hru'hfe.* That is, I—"

"Just do it," said Arrhae wearily, thinking *yes, hru'hfe,* and saying it under her breath as Ekkhae bustled away. She wasn't ready for an afternoon of fending off Lhaesl tr'Khev, and by the sound of it, that was who awaited her. She could almost feel sorry for H'daen, being forced to play the host until she arrived to rescue him. Lhaesl was an amiable fool—with the emphasis on *fool.*

Except that it was tr'Annhwi instead.

The Subcommander set his winecup down and stood up as she came into the room, smiling as pleasantly as he was able—which wasn't very. "I told you that I would come to visit you," he said, making his usual theatrical bow.

Arrhae groaned inwardly. There was only one way out of this, and with H'daen sitting on the other side of the table, that way would make a fool out of him and a liar out of her. "I . . . I hadn't thought my lord H'daen would have granted permission after—"

"After what happened? Your lord forgave me. He is a generous man." Again the smile. "You will find me generous too."

"But Lhaesl . . ."

"What?" H'daen's winecup thumped against the surface of the table and, overfull as usual, immediately spilled. Powers alone knew what he had said about their conversation of last week, but by the sound of it

he had said enough to wish that Arrhae had kept her mouth tight shut. It was too late now; the damage had plainly been done and all H'daen could do was try to extricate himself with as much dignity—and as much speed—as he could muster. The look on his face boded ill for the next conversation with his *hru'hfe,* but Arrhae felt that she could weather that storm more easily than spending an evening with tr'Annhwi.

Who was looking remarkably unconcerned. "I regret this misunderstanding, *hru'hfirh,*" he said without the anger Arrhae might have expected from a man whose passions seemed to run so high. When he looked at her, there was no longer any more interest in his face than when anyone looked at a servant. "Your lord's wine is spilled, woman." Tr'Annhwi's voice was cold now, drained of the warmth that she guessed had been false all along. "Clean up this mess and refill his cup."

H'daen said nothing to confirm or deny that she should obey. He didn't even look in her direction. Instead, he inclined his head to tr'Annhwi, as if inviting him to continue with something he had been saying before Arrhae came in. "You mentioned something about Mak'khoi, Subcommander," he said, ignoring Arrhae's efforts to tidy his desk as he might ignore a piece of furniture, and thus not seeing the brief glance of shock she directed at him. "About handing him over to you. You said that you would make it worth my while. Tell me: what amount of money are we talking about . . . ?"

Chapter Ten

Flowering

"RIHANNSU ARE CONSERVATIVES," Lai tr'Ehhelih said once in another of his more unpopular books, "though they would die rather than admit it. No revolutionary who has come many lightyears through terrible privation and suffering would want to admit in public that he secretly misses the conditions he left behind. It makes fascinating viewing, from the sociological standpoint, to watch them decrying the 'corrupt customs' of the Old World, and then settling into just slightly different versions of those customs, with the greatest self-congratulation and smugness. When change happens on ch'Rihan, it happens by chance, or the boredom of the Elements. No one here ever set out to change anything, not on purpose."

Tr'Ehhelih was being bitter, as usual, but also as usual there were elements of truth in his words. There were areas in which the Rihannsu were truly innovative —some sciences and arts—but somehow the energy always seemed to start seeping out of those areas after a while. Innovation would slowly drop off, the whole matter would fall gradually into tradition, and a generation later no one would ever know that there had been invention or different ways of doing something. There would be one way, and that way "the way it's always been done."

Spaceflight was one of these areas of accomplishment, and perhaps the most tragic. The body of engineering talent that built the Ships was one of the most astonishing collections of determined genius ever gathered on Vulcan, and the Travelers tried hard to preserve the fruits of that genius. All the Ships' libraries were crammed full of technical information in every field known to the Vulcans. The Ships' librarians were aware that they were stocking "time capsules." Each of the Ships duplicated information found in all the others, and no one grudged the redundancy, which, considering the history of the Journey, was wise.

But the one thing they could not stock the Ships with, with any certainty, was talent and incentive to use the information preserved there. The brilliant minds that designed the Ships' systems, for the most part, went along on the Journey. But many of them died, in the various tragedies that befell the Travelers, or later on of old age. More specialists in navigations, space science, and astronautical engineering were trained in the process of the Journey, of course, but there is no forcing a person to be brilliant at a science—especially one that the children of the time tended to think of (in the early years) as something of a nuisance. They either remembered Vulcan, and were ambivalent about having been forced to leave it, or they were born on the Journey and were full of stories about the wonders of living on a planet, in the open air. Some of them were understandably bored or annoyed with the whole issue of Ships.

This, unfortunately, was the generation that finally landed on ch'Rihan, and knowingly or unknowingly went about setting the course of the planet's civilization for the next thousand years or so. The government that came into power after the accession of the Ruling Queen acted, by inaction, for the whole generation. Their general feeling was that they were still getting the world on its feet, and had no time to start designing new starships, or (worse yet) devoting the then-scarce cash or venture capital of the planet to large building efforts. That they *did* find fairly large amounts sometime later to spend on wars in the South Continent and in the East on ch'Havran was a fact pointed out to the Senate on several occasions. But very few voices made this complaint, and little notice was taken. The majority of people in the Two Worlds felt that they had thought enough about space for a while. The past two hundred years had been devoted to it. It was time to settle down, get some crops yielding properly, and find out who their neighbors were, and their enemies. If anyone needed to worry about it, let it be the Ship-Clans.

Unfortunately, the Ship-Clans had problems of their own. They were dwindling. The Travelers in general had little interest in keeping up the populations of the Ships, with a new world underfoot to live in, and there were defections from the Ship-Clans as time went on—people who saw no particular reason to stay inship, among metal walls, while there was green grass to walk on and green-gold sky to walk under for the first time in almost a hundred years.

There were other problems. At first funding and material support from ch'Rihan were fairly munificent: but after the reorganization of the Praetorate and Senate, the assistance began to taper off slowly as the loyal voices in the government became preoccupied with other concerns, or died out and were replaced by people who cared less. The hydroponics gardens on the Ships were the first to go, then data storage and processing, as valuable spare parts were shipped on-planet, and no replacements made. There had been agreements that a priority of manufacture, once it got going, would be semiconductor and transtator technology to support both the Ships' needs and those of the telecommunication and defense networks that would have to be built. But for the first century and a half these needs were almost completely ignored in favor of farm manufactures—agricultural machinery, fertilizer, and food-processing equipment. It was ironic that the gardens of ch'Rihan and ch'Havran flourished as never before, while the vast Shipborne flats that had kept so many Vulcan plants alive to see the new world now lay barren, and the computers that had so successfully calculated what species could fit in where in the new ecosystem were down now half the time and uncertain of operation the rest of it.

What it all added up to was a slow slide in space technology, so that by around 250 A.S. the Rihannsu would not have had the ability to get quickly off-planet if they had needed to. True, there seemed to be no need. By accident (if there are such things, which Rihannsu religion generally doubts), they had found the one good spot in a backwater, an area of the galaxy ignored as a "desert" by most of the spacefaring species in the area. It would be some seventeen hundred years before the Klingons and the Federation found them, which was just as well, for they were woefully unprepared. Other than the Ships, only a few heavy transports were built to handle food shipments from ch'Havran (whose drier climate proved more conducive to the Vulcan grains they had brought with them; the North and Northwest Continents of ch'Havran became the "breadbasket" of the Two Worlds). Once the transports were built, there was very little further interest in space, and one by one the Ships were allowed to fall. They were obsolete, it was said. Something better and newer could be built. There was no need for them anymore—there were no signs of alien presence out this far. The few voices lifted in protest, the people who said the Ships should be kept at least for history's sake, were ignored. Never has the classical Rihannsu character flaw, that of deadly practicality, proved more fatal. The Ship-Clans slowly left the ships as their engines were shut down and their orbits began to decay. Between 300 and 400 A.S. they all fell.

The Rihannsu at least decided to build a planetary "defense" system—though critics pointed out that if the system noticed anything coming at the planet, it would not be able to carry the battle to it. What kind of defense was that? But this, too, fell on deaf ears, especially since several key Praetors of this period had significant political and financial involvements with the guilds building the defense systems.

To do them justice, the network they prepared to build to warn them of incoming alien craft was an ambitious and forward-looking design, and would have been an effective one had it not been scaled down to almost nothing over later years by Praetors filching the funds dedicated to it for "more important" pet projects. When it was finished in 508 A.S., it consisted of a network of chemically fueled and solar-powered defense satellite/platforms armed with particle-beam weapons and solar-output lasers connected to an outer "warning network" of twelve satellites in long hyperbolic orbits around the Eisn system. The coverage of the warning satellites was incomplete—by rights there should have been about fifty of them—and because not enough money was spent on the code for the computers running the inner defense satellites, they had a nasty habit of firing at the few friendly craft that used local space. The original outer satellites are still there, their atomic batteries and cesium clocks ticking faithfully away though their computers have long crashed. The close orbital platforms have fallen into ch'Rihan's atmosphere and burned up, except for the one preserved as a museum. For the next fifteen hundred years or so, no one would much care. Later, they would care a great deal indeed, and Houses would rise and fall because of money "reappropriated" into private pockets for hunting lodges, banquets, and the occasional murder. But in the meantime, the Rihannsu, rich and poor alike, settled down each after his or her own manner to cultivate their fields, their families, and the arts.

War was counted as an art, perhaps the chief of them. The mindset of the Rihannsu at that point regarding war was that it (and, in its turn, peace) should be practiced *in extremis*. The simple delights of home and household, and the greatest luxury available according to one's means, should be shared with friends and enemies alike in time of peace. War, when it was needed, should be brutal, swift, fierce, and *enjoyable*. Noble pleasures should accompany the army into the field. There should be fine food and excellent wine and discussions of epic poetry the night before the battle. In the morning there should be blood in green rivers, and single combats of note between both champions and the lesser knights: no pity or quarter granted save to the properly prostrated foe—to him or her, courtesy, honor, and the extraction of a fat ransom after the victory dinner.

Honor was the heart of it all, and grew more to the heart of Rihannsu culture as time went by. In war was often its best example, since there more than elsewhere the Rihannsu (as other species) had an "excuse" to forget about it in the heat of the moment. To their credit, they did not often forget. The given word was kept. They still sing of besieged Ihhliae, that great city, ringed around with the troops from neighboring Rhehiv'je, and how the Senator from the city came out and begged the Rhehiv'jen to have mercy on her starving people. The answer was no surprise, especially since the Rhehiv'jen had been there since the beginning of the year, in the foulest weather in memory, and it was now high summer, and their crops not in. The Ihhliae were told that there was no help for it—all their men were going to be put to the sword. But as a courtesy to the ladies of the city (it was one of the very few regions where women did not fight), they would be allowed to come out the next morning, and to leave with whatever they could carry that was of value to them. There was chagrin and considerable surprise when the women came out the next morning, each carrying her husband on her back. But the word had been given, and when the men came back and besieged Rhehiv'je the next year, it was all taken in good part.

Arts of other sorts were also practiced. Few species

have been so fond of the pleasures of the table, without turning entirely into gluttons or food critics, than the Rihannsu. Ch'Rihan in particular was rich in foods that they could adapt. There were several hundred species of fowl, numerous flightless lizards, and several flying ones that made very tasty roasts, as well as various large herd beasts that could feed whole Houses for days, and endless fruits and grains.

There was also ale, and wine. Vulcans knew about wine—the pre-Reform joke was that it was discovered just before the very first war, and caused it when the first man pointed at the second, drunk, and laughed at him. But the poor dry fruits of Vulcan were no match for the *lehe'jhme* of ch'Rihan, that grew in rich rose-colored clusters on trees three hundred feet high, in unbelievable abundance. The first Rihannsu saw the herds of wild *hlai* staggering and croaking their way across the southern veldts like a mass migration of sozzled giant ostriches, and they knew they were onto a good thing. They followed the herds in the deeps of summer, through the blue and emerald grass, and found that they had been drinking from waterholes into which the *lehe'jhme* had fallen in great numbers and fermented. From the drinking-holes, courtesy of the inebriated *hlai* of past centuries, come the more than five thousand Rihannsu wines that are coddled, blended, and smiled over around the planet today.

Ale was another story, a "poor man's drink" (or Northern ch'Havranha's drink—most fruits do not grow there) coerced out of roasted Vulcan *keh* grain and "malted" native ch'Havranssu breadmake, the whole first brewed and fermented for a month or so, then distilled and recarbonated. People drink Rihannsu ale for the same reason they drink Saurian brandy—to prove they *can*.

There were other arts than eating and drinking. The "plastic arts" were always highly developed on Vulcan. Their abstract sculpture and painting were particularly fine. During the Journey (with its scarcity of materials to work in), the pictorial and sculptorial arts became more concrete, not less—an unexpected development. Or perhaps not, in a situation where people in general and artists in particular were looking most definitely forward into a future they hoped would be better than the past they had—and looking with equal intensity at a present which they had created themselves and which they were, to put it mildly, stuck with.

The stark, clean, conceptually advanced, mathematically derived concepts and images formerly reserved for "high art" in the old days began to turn up everywhere—on clothing, in furniture and hangings, personal effects, sprayed or painted on walls of the Ships. Later, on ch'Rihan and ch'Havran, they expanded to cover whole mountainsides (e.g. the Mural Chain in West-Continent ch'Rihan). No home, however poor, was complete without "pictures" of one kind or another. Everybody made them, and most of them were stunning, and the tradition has continued unchanged for fifteen hundred years. Rihannsu art, especially the painted, sculpted, and woven, is treasured all over the worlds for its vitality, tenderness, ferocity, clarity, and sheer style—often imitated, but the spirit of it rarely if ever caught, and only approached in a cool manner by the Vulcans. The Rihannsu culture has the highest artist-per-capita ratio in the known galaxy. No one knows why. "Perhaps," tr'Ehhelih said, "giving up your world enables you to *see* the one you finally wind up with."

The nonphysical arts and humanities did as well. They had fifteen hundred long and comfortable years to mold themselves, and the changes in philosophy, religion, literature, and poetry were greater than tr'Ehhelih would have liked to admit.

Vulcan religion before the Flight was, to put it mildly, haphazard. Most worlds have two or three or five major religions, sometimes mutually exclusive, sometimes not, which arise over a millennium or so and then contend genteelly (or not so genteelly) with one another for almost the rest of the planet's existence. Vulcan had about six hundred religions pre-Reformation: a vivid, noisy, energetic, violent sprawl and squabble of gods, demigods, *animae,* geniuses, demons, angels, golems, powers, principalities, forces, *noeses,* and other hypersomatic beings of types too difficult to explain to Earth people, who, by and large, are spoiled by the ridiculous simplicity of their own beliefs. The phrase "the one God" would have brought the average Vulcan-in-the-street to a standstill and caused him to ask, *"Which* 'One'?" since there were about ninety deities, protodeities, holy creatures, and other contenders for the title. Some planets never discover Immanence: Vulcan was littered with it.

The Travelers came of a wild assortment of religions, but one "major" professed faith began slowly to sort itself out among them as the Journey progressed. Perhaps at first it was not so much a religion as a fad or a joke. "Matter as God," that was where the idea started, with some nameless Traveler in *Gorget* who left a dissertation on the subject in the message section of the ship's computer net.

"Things," she said, "notice." It did, in fact, begin as a joke, one that other species share. Have you noticed, she said, that when you really need something—the key to your quarters, a favorite piece of clothing—you can't find it? You search everywhere, and there's no result. But any other time, when there's no need, the thing in question is always under your hand. This, said the nameless Contributor, is a proof that the Universe is sentient, or at least borderline-sentient: it craves attention, like a small child, and responds to it depending on how *you* treat it—with affection, or annoyance. For further proof, she suggested that a person looking for something under these circumstances should walk around their quarters, calling the thing in question by its name. It always turns up. (Before the reader laughs, by the way, s/he is advised to try this on the next thing s/he loses. The technique has its moments.)

The initial letters in the Contribution were naturally humorous ones, but the tone grew increasingly serious (though never somber: jokes were always part of it). There was something about this philosophy that seemed to work peculiarly well for the Travelers, who had "made" their own worlds and their own language, and had come to exercise a measure of control over their own lives that few planetbound people do, or ever become conscious of. The "selfness" of matter became an issue for these people: the (to us) seemingly mundane observation that the physical universe had *existence*, had weight, hard edges, "the dignity of existence," as one Contributor called it. Things *existed* and so had a right to nobility, a right to be honored and appreciated, as much as more sentient things that walked around and demanded the honor themselves. Things had a right to names: when named, and called by those names, of course they would respond positively—for the universe wants to be ordered, wants to be cared for, and has nothing to fulfill this function (said another Contributor) but us. Or (said a third person) if there are indeed gods, we're *their* tool toward this purpose. This is our chance to be gods, on the physical level, the caretakers and orderers of the "less sentient" kinds of life.

More than nine thousand people, from *Gorget* and other Ships, added to this written tradition as time went by: they wrote letters, dissertations, essays, critiques, poems, songs, prose, satire. It was the longest-running conversation on one subject in the history of that net. The Contribution started two years after the departure from Vulcan, and continued without a missed day until seventy-eight years thereafter, the day the core of the computer in question crashed fatally, killing the database. However, numerous people among the remaining ships had hardcopy, and over a thousand of the Travelers contributed to restoring the database. It was as if it were something that mattered profoundly enough to them that their precious private time—for everyone worked on the Ships—was still worth contributing to the preservation of the Thread.

Names became a great issue for these people. Many of them already had *rehei*, "nicknames" (like the "handles" of Earth's early nets) in the computer network. Many of them adopted these as "fourth names," thus identifying themselves as people participating in the Contributors' Net. Over several hundred more years, fourth names became commonplace, then slowly began to be kept private, shared only with one's family or most intimate friends. A fourth name was not given you by someone else: you found it in yourself—it was inherent in you, as a "proper" name was inherent in a well-named physical object. You just had to look for it, and if you looked carefully enough, you would find the "right" name. It is perhaps because of this tradition, exercised on things as well as people, that the names given places, animals, vegetables, and minerals on ch'Rihan when the Travelers arrived have rarely been surpassed for vigor, humor, appropriateness, and a sort of affectionate quality. It was as if the Travelers were naming children. And by and large, the Two Worlds were kind enough to their colonists.

In addition, the types of matter themselves became an issue. This part of the discussion was at the start more clearly a joke than any other. There was a long and cheerful side-thread on how many "elemental" kinds of matter there were, some people holding out for four—earth, air, fire, and water, as on many another planet—others opting for five (add "plasma") or six (add "collapsed matter"). But the reckoning finally settled down to four, and people would converse learnedly (though only about half-seriously) about the "attributes" and "tendencies" of different kinds of matter: the impetuosity, ravenousness, and light-contributing nature of Fire, the malleability and passiveness of Water, and so forth. Slowly, in this tradition, the Elements became as it were embodiments of themselves, personifications (for want of a better word) of "arch-matter," which when invoked might aid the invoker, but only if the aid flowed both ways. "Be kind to the world, and the world will be kind to you," seems to have been the philosophy. People, too, were judged by their temperaments as to which Element they had most affinity to. In later years such sayings became very commonplace: "She has too much Fire in her, she'll eat you alive." "He's all Earth and no Air: he'll never move an inch." Almost certainly people sometimes perceive themselves as "having the traits" of certain Elements, and so the joke came full circle and began to be taken seriously.

S'task knew perfectly well about this growing tradition, for he himself was one of the Contributors, though a rare one. He watched with some amusement, during the late part of his life, as these traditions settled into "the way things have always been," and other older religions and beliefs slipped away, gently, without alarums or excursions. For his own part he was what an Earth person would consider an agnostic. "I am unsure of everything," he remarked in one message, "except of the fact that I am certain to remain unsure." But to the "Elemental" school of thought—especially the part about treating the universe kindly—he gave a certain grudging acceptance. He would not admit publicly, of course, that this had anything to do with Surak, and the voice saying to him long ago, "The universe is concerned with means, not ends. . . ."

"Surely there is no harm in taking care of the universe," wrote S'task in the Contribution, "for parts of it certainly seem to need it. If it craves order, so do human beings, and we have common cause; if (as it appears) it delights in diversity, we should cast out fear and help it be diverse, and learn to do so ourselves. If we must move through the worlds and change things, let us then be kindly caretakers: let us be toward matter as we would have the forces that move our own lives be toward us. It is no guarantee of preferential treatment by Things. But we will at least know we acted with magnanimity and honor, and if the universe sometimes seems insensible to this, let us keep acting that way until it notices."

Some people listened to him, some did not. Ch'Rihan and ch'Havran were never united about anything, and they would have been bored with life, one suspects, if they had been. The Two Worlds spent a relatively happy fifteen hundred years taming their worlds, living in them, enjoying them, untroubled by anything but their own wars and (sometimes) their own peace. But the end of the Golden Age came at last, too soon, the day the failing defense net woke up and reported something approaching the system, decelerating rapidly from the speed of light. All that happened after that, in the past hundred years, makes a terrible tale, but most terrible to the Rihannsu, who feel that their tranquil "childhood" as a people was stolen from them when two of the most driven species in the galaxy stumbled over their paradise. "Perhaps," said one rueful commentator of the time, "we have not been as kind to the Elements as we thought. . . ."

Chapter Eleven

McCoy SAT DOWN on the hard bed and cursed under his breath. The business in the garden had been a near-perfect chance to open proper communications with Terise Haleakala, and like a fool he had let it slip. Well, maybe not quite so badly as all that; they had reached a certain understanding now. At least he was certain that this "Arrhae"—damn Starfleet Intelligence for picking such a common name!—was the deep-cover operative who was at the center of this clandestine mission. The beginning of the mission, just as he was the end of it. How final that end might be depended on so many variables that his head began to pound just in anticipation, and he had to lie back with his eyes shut for some minutes until the throbbing receded back to its usual dull ache in his temples.

"All right," he muttered, "tomorrow. Like it or not." Despite all his experience in medical and psychiatric practice, he had never been comfortable with this sort of thing. How do you tell a woman who's spent eight years doing a job you couldn't handle for a week that Starfleet isn't sure about her mental health anymore? Come straight out and ask her? "Excuse the question, Lieutenant-Commander, but we haven't had a report from you in two years. So tell us—are you still a Terran agent, or would you prefer to be a Romulan . . . ?" Not the sort of subtle approach that might be expected from a man who was "the best we've got."

That was what Steve Perry had called him, anyway. Except that if being bait for a Romulan frigate and its rabidly xenophobic Subcommander was what compliments from Starfleet's Chief of Intelligence led to, then he'd stick to Spock's insults and be glad of them, thanks very much. Except that Chief Medical Officers—even when they were "the best"—didn't talk that way to Admirals. They took what was said to them with the best grace that they could muster, and when they were asked to jump, their only question was supposed to be "how high?"

Or "where to . . . ?"

He had sat on the far side of Perry's desk, flanked by Jim Kirk and Spock, listening while the Admiral outlined a plan as complex and dangerous as the cloaking-device theft of eight years ago. There were only two advantages: he knew more about Romulans now than he had done then, and—most important of all—he was being told about it in advance. That was where being "the best" came in.

Specializations in xenopsychology and -psychiatry, and longterm experience as CMO of the *Enterprise*—thus an acquaintance with what amounted to a gestalt life form, for that defined the multi-racial, multi-species environment aboard the starship more accurately than simply crew. All of it added up to why he had been selected and then approached for this mission over the heads of other, perhaps equally talented, officers. It had been an unnerving hour for McCoy, sitting there watching his future being measured out in very small doses. For although the intricacies of the plot had been laid long and deep, using sleepers and double agents on both sides of the Neutral Zone, still, when it came to the crunch, his life or death was going to depend on timing.

And he had volunteered for it. Not at first, but after several refusals that nobody, particularly Kirk and Spock, had seen for other than his habitual grumbling. There had never been any question of conscription, not for him, not for anybody—not for a mission like this one. As soon conscript a spy and then expect the reports to be other than cautious, shallow, and lacking in any form of detail, if any reports ever came back at all. That was another thing: the spy—Perry preferred the term "deep-cover agent" to the older, more traditional word, but McCoy knew a spy when one was described to him—who had provided such excellent data for six years and then fallen silent in the past two. Last reports had shown her as a high-ranked servant in a poor but respectable Romulan noble house, and there had been nothing to indicate her activities—acquiring sociological background information rather than military or governmental secrets—had attracted anyone's attention.

McCoy had been given a chance to read through the nonclassified sections of her dossier, and after what amounted to a high-level intercession at Command level—Admiral Perry looked after his own, even when they only worked for him part-time—he was cleared to see all of it. The MOST SECRET stuff made fascinating reading. . . .

But that was all by the way; he had already made his feelings known on various matters, including the leaking of his (prearranged, naturally) traveling plans to Romulan agents, both those who were already known and, as a form of test, to several suspects. That same data, accurately provided by Federation double agents in the Empire, would serve to improve the reputation of any whose past reports had been of dubious quality, and hopefully make their future survival more secure.

Except for one problem: that the Romulans might not fall in with the theory behind all the other machinations, that if opportunity arose, they would want to capture a member of the *Enterprise* command crew—notorious war criminals all—and bring them back to ch'Rihan for trial. Their outrage over the Levaeri V debacle might run so high, even after the passage of a standard year, that instead of taking the offered bait as a prisoner, they might send a hunter-killer ship to blow the proposed captive into plasma. . . .

That was a risk they had all debated, and finally set aside as unlikely. So many highly placed Romulans had grudges to settle with the USS *Enterprise* that an anonymous, impersonal photon torpedo wouldn't satisfy them. The Romulan psyche was such that any punishment would have to be protracted, degrading, and painful—and administered after due process of their elaborate legal codes.

Listening to that particular part of the discussion had given McCoy a nasty crawling feeling at the nape of his neck, but at least the plan had worked. So far.

The storage-access doors at the back of his room rattled a bit, and he sat up. There was a small click as one door opened, revealing a vertical slice of the rainy Romulan night, and a vague, low outline entered the room, closing the door neatly—if a little awkwardly—behind it.

McCoy put his eyebrows up . . . and smiled.

"If mere money is all you want for him, then name your price." Subcommander tr'Annhwi gazed equably at the man across the table, reading him like an open book. He knew avarice when he saw it; but he could also recognize hope, and in this instance that was something he could play on to even better effect. "As I told that"—his narrow eyes flicked briefly toward Arrhae and then away again—"I am a generous man. But I can offer you much more than that: privileges, and the recognition of your House as a power in the Senate. I can offer you the restoration of everything that you have seen slip away from s'Khellian in these past years. H'daen, I can give you back your honor."

"In exchange for this one man?" Tr'Khellian plainly couldn't believe what he was hearing, and equally, wanted to believe it as much as anything he had ever heard in his life. "But why so much for so little—for a single Federation prisoner?"

"I told you before." Impatience and a hint of what lay beneath his bland exterior lent an ugly edge to tr'Annhwi's words before he recovered himself and twisted his mouth into an expression that approximated a smile. "There are too many factors, but most concern *mnhei'sahe,* my personal honor and that of my own House. That one represents a tiny portion of the blood-debt owed the Imperium by the Federation, which policy"—tr'Annhwi sneered the word—"forbids us to collect. But *mnhei'sahe* transcends policy, as you well know, and McCoy is a Command officer of the ship which owes blood-debt to many Houses. All will gain a morsel of contentment when sentence is executed on him, but I want all of it, for the honor of House Annhwi—and for my own satisfaction."

"What will you . . . ?" H'daen didn't complete his question. There was no need for it, or an answer, and he was a squeamish man at best.

"Cause him pain in whatever fashion pleases me," said tr'Annhwi. "For as long as pleases me. And then—eventually—I shall kill him."

"But Commander t'Radaik left him with me," H'daen said, as if reminding himself rather than the uncaring man across the table. "How will you explain the"—he swallowed, looking unwell—"the state of his body?"

"What body?" Tr'Annhwi drew the sidearm he wore as part of his uniform and laid it with a dull metallic clank beside his winecup. "A phaser set to disrupt doesn't leave one. At least"—he favored H'daen with an ugly, feral grin—"not one with enough molecular integrity to show what it looked like before it died. And you need have no worries about t'Radaik blaming you; prisoners are always being shot while escaping, and she'll never know it didn't happen this time. . . ." He picked up the phaser again and bounced it once or twice on the palm of his hand as if it were a toy, smiling indulgently.

H'daen stared at it with the horrified fascination of a man unfamiliar with weapons and uneasy in their presence. He was visibly relieved when tr'Annhwi tucked the phaser back into its holster and instead withdrew a small rectangle of plastic from the pouch on his belt. It wasn't quite so noisy as the phaser when he flipped it onto the table, but it carried just as much impact in H'daen's eyes.

"Prime-transfer authority," tr'Annhwi said—unnecessarily, because H'daen knew perfectly well what it was.

And what it meant. His guest might have come to the house with some romantic notion in the back of his mind, but the appearance of this thing made it clear that romance was not the Subcommander's first concern. Nobody carried transfer authorities for any longer than their business required, because each card represented enormous wealth in cash or securities, deposited somewhere for exchange once the card itself was exchanged and a deal completed. Even upside down, H'daen could see the amount of data with which it was imprinted. This one small card could buy half the city of i'Ramnau—and the half worth buying, at that.

He sat quite still for a moment, just looking at it, then held out the winecup in his hand toward the empty air. Arrhae, commanded to clean the anteroom and not daring to stop until the order was countermanded, darted immediately to fill it, met her lord's eyes, and saw not the greed that tr'Annhwi had read there, but a terrible confused indecision. It was as if all that H'daen had thought was right and proper about his world had suddenly been dashed to fragments about his feet. Arrhae recognized that expression more readily than most, for something much the same had stared out of her mirror on several mornings since McCoy arrived to complicate the house.

"My lord," she said, "there is a matter from i'Ramnau that needs your attention."

"Not now, Arrhae. . . ."

There was no certainty in the way he said it, or she would never have dared to persist; not with tr'Annhwi's suspicious eyes on her. "It would be best dealt with at once, *hru'hfirh;* then you can return to your other business without further interruptions."

"Get about your duties, servant!" snapped

tr'Annhwi, and his glare should have killed her on the spot.

He knows—or at least guesses—what I might say, she thought, flinching from the promise of pain in the Subcommander's cold face. *O Powers and Elements, let H'daen hear me!*

He heard something at least, the same thing that had caused no reaction less than a quarter-hour before. Before certain things about his guest had come to light. But now . . .

"Subcommander, Arrhae ir-Mnaeha is *hru'hfe* to this house, and no mere servant for all and any to command." There was a strength and dignity about H'daen's voice that Arrhae had not heard for many months; it came from an awareness of the Naming of his House, which if it had fallen into poverty and insignificance was at least decent and worthy of the fair-speaking that many higher Houses had forfeited these past few years.

Tr'Annhwi opened his mouth to say something—insulting, by the twist of his lips—then remembered where he was and shut it again without uttering a sound. No matter how wealthy or how powerful he might be elsewhere, right now he was only a Fleet Subcommander guesting under the roof of an Imperial Praetor, and not merely courtesy but caution dictated his behavior.

"Arrhae," said H'daen, getting to his feet, "come with me." He turned from the table, not without a long, thoughtful look at the prime-transfer card, and walked out of the room with Arrhae at his heels. Once the door was shut behind them, with tr'Annhwi on the far side of it, he turned on her. "You had best have a fine explanation for this, girl, or I shall—"

"My lord, your worst punishment would be better than the kindnesses of that one," she said, and looked him in the eye as she said it. "I am *hru'hfe* to the house, and you were pleased to call me your conscience. These are not moral scruples now, but my own fears for your honor. You know me. You know I speak what I perceive as truth," Arrhae paused, watching him, and smiled quickly, "so far as manners permit."

"This also is truth. Speak more of it, Arrhae. I will hear you."

"There is little more, lord, and I speak as a servant ignorant of the policies within a noble House—but how can the Powers favor any House, when honor is set aside and the brief regard of men can be only attained by breaking trust and selling a helpless man as though he were a beast? There is guest-right on Mak'khoi, and your word on that right. Only your word can betray it. . . ."

H'daen stood where he was for a brief time, very still, looking with blank eyes at something only he could see. Then that dull gaze focused on Arrhae. "Have you no duties of your own, that you must interfere in my private affairs? Go—do something of use to earn your keep, and leave me be!" He turned away from her and went back inside the antechamber, and the sound of its door closing was like the lid of a coffin coming down. She took three slow steps in the direction of McCoy's room, hoping against hope that H'daen would summon her back with a change of mind, but there was no other sound.

On her fourth step, Arrhae began to run.

McCoy heard the footsteps pattering along the corridor a bare two seconds before someone began to fumble with the lock. He glanced around his room and at the companion who had slipped into it half an hour before, and realized that there was nowhere and no time to hide.

No time at all. The door burst open, slammed shut as quickly—and Arrhae, his jailer, went sprawling as she tripped over something that hadn't been there before. He picked her up, brushed her down, muttered softly when he saw the grazes running from knee to ankle along both shins, and waited for the questions to start.

He didn't have to wait long, only enough for the woman to recover the breath that the fall had knocked out of her. There was a very brief wince as skinned legs made their presence felt, and then a mental hiccup that reflected clearly in her eyes, as everything she had been intending to say when she came through the door was suddenly replaced by a lot of things she hadn't expected to say at all. The first one was fairly obvious.

"What's this rock doing in here?"

Less obvious, at least to Arrhae, was the possibility of an answer from the rock itself. She got one all the same.

"I was speaking to Dr. McCoy, ma'am," it said in a courteous if rather grating voice that came from an unmistakable Starfleet voder on its back, marked with equally unmistakable Lieutenant's stripes. "I hope you didn't hurt yourself."

Arrhae gave a startled squeak and took a hasty step backward, this time almost tripping over the low table that was one of McCoy's few pieces of furniture. Though she caught herself from falling, she sat down on it hard enough to jolt the wind out of her yet again. She stared, wide-eyed and gasping, while the rock shuffled around to "face" her with the sound of one large slab of granite dragging over another. At least, so she presumed, because the rank insignia on the voder was now right side up and she had the definite feeling of being looked at—except that there was nothing that corresponded to eyes on the crusted, sparkling surface.

McCoy had eyes, though, and they were glittering with wicked amusement at Arrhae's discomfiture. He was grinning at her, and she didn't like it. "What goes on here?" she demanded. Shock, confusion, fear, and now more shock hadn't made for a particularly good evening so far, and she had the nasty feeling that it would start to go downhill rapidly once her questions were answered. Always assuming that it hadn't happened already.

"Commander Haleakala," said McCoy, "allow me to

introduce Lieutenant Naraht, USS *Enterprise,* on temporary assignment to Starfleet Intelligence. He's acting as my backup."

"He . . . ? But it's a rock—isn't it?"

"No. A Horta." McCoy grinned quickly as he realized something important. "Of course, you were landed on ch'Rihan before we—Commander, the Hortas are native to Janus VI; silicon-based life forms that live in rock, burrow through it, and eat it."

"You're joking. . . ."

"They're also highly intelligent, and good-humored to a fault—which is just as well, otherwise Naraht would be very tired of hearing comments like that. Why say I'm joking when the proof's right there in front of you."

"I'm sorry. Excuse me, Lieutenant, I didn't know people like you existed."

"My mother thought the same about"—Naraht shuffled the shaggy sensory fringe that edged his body, seeming slightly embarrassed—"about carbon-based people. Like you and the doctor. No offense taken, Commander."

"Um, quite so." Terise looked at Naraht somewhat oddly. "What I don't understand is why you're not on fire." McCoy looked up at her quizzically. "Well, I mean," she said, "an oxygen atmosphere is the equivalent of a reducing atmosphere to a silicon-based creature. Or they always told us in xenobiology that it would be, if silicon-based life was ever discovered. How is he able to walk around without doing the equivalent of burning, or rusting?"

McCoy smiled, and if it was a look of pure triumph, then it was justified. The solution to the problem was his, and had indirectly made the introduction of Hortas into Starfleet possible. "He's been sprayed with Teflon on his top layers and his tentacular fringe," he said. "It seals the oxygen in our atmosphere away from his silicon, and doesn't react itself to either the silicon or his ambient acids—since Teflon is less chemically reactive than even glass. His bottom layer doesn't need it: it's made of a natural Teflon analogue anyway, to protect it from the acid he secretes."

"He sometimes secretes," said Naraht gently. "I'm not such a glutton that I need to eat every time I move."

"Well, I'm not sure you eat enough as it is," McCoy said. "Boy your age should be half again your size. I've never been sure that starship food agrees with you. Wretched synthesized rock, it's not the same as the real thing. Not enough minerals."

Arrhae shook her head, still bemused. "But Mr. Naraht, how did you get planetside without being captured?"

"Meteorite-style." Naraht might have had no face, but his voice smiled. "My carapace has a higher ablative rating than tempered ceramic or glasteel. Once we were in orbit over ch'Rihan, I arranged an explosion in the *Vega*'s hold and bailed out . . . and went down in free fall."

McCoy nodded. "He's a good navigator—could have worked out the accelerations and ephemera himself, the boy's got a calculator in his head, like most of his people. But the Romulans obliged by putting us in a holding pattern up there." He jerked a thumb a couple of times at the ceiling, then let the hand drop and grinned some more. "Congratulations," he said.

"Why?"

"On the way you're taking all this."

"Dr. McCoy—"

"Bones, please."

"Bones, there's a saying here: 'If the sword shatters, take its fragments to a forge.' I've had a long time to put a lot of pieces back together, and I'm getting good at it."

"'If life hands you a lemon, make lemonade.'"

"I prefer the Romulan version."

"Do you now?" McCoy looked at her very thoughtfully, but didn't enlarge on his comment.

"It has more dignity. . . ."

"Of course."

"Now, why do you keep calling me Commander? What sort of ship is *Vega,* and how were you captured? What brought you to this house? And don't deny that you were expecting to find me here! And tr'Annhwi's back, trying to buy you from H'daen. . . ."

McCoy had been smiling a bit indulgently at the stream of questions, but that last took the last traces of smile right off his face. "Perry didn't reckon on that," he muttered, knowing that he should have realized the possibility himself, after seeing at close range what Romulans were capable of doing when it came to honor-based grudges.

"Perry??"

"The Service," McCoy said with some asperity, "takes care of its own. . . . Look, Terise—oh, you were promoted, don't look at me like that—look, never mind the personal aspect, but I can't be the subject of a personal vendetta just now. I'm supposed to appear before the Senate and . . ."

"I tried, Bones. I really tried. I thought that what I said, and the way I said it, would have made H'daen tr'Khellian throw the whole dirty notion out, but he—well, it's his only chance to do something for the reputation of his House, to lift it out of the gutter, and I think—" She stopped, and cocked her head to one side, listening. "Get Naraht out of here! We're going to have company. . . ."

Her ears were more attuned to sounds in the house, but after the noise of Naraht's departure had faded—and McCoy was still amazed at how fast the Horta could move when he was in a hurry—the angry voices were distant but distinct. And the heavy slam of the frontmost door was completely audible. Silence fell briefly, and was broken after a little while by footsteps in the corridor outside. McCoy stayed where he was, sitting on the single low chair that was all his room could boast, but Arrhae rose from the table and took up a wary position in front of the storage door with its neatly, almost invisibly snapped lock.

And H'daen tr'Khellian came in. There was the print of an open hand across one side of his face, already greening into a bruise, and he looked crumpled, but not crushed. "I thought that I would find you here," he said to Arrhae, and bowed greeting to McCoy with a stiffness that looked more a consequence of pain than of reserve.

"Yes, my lord," she said, carefully noncommittal.

"I considered tr'Annhwi's offer. And refused it, to his displeasure—as you might surmise from my appearance. But I decided that if his was an example of the honor of young and wealthy Rihannsu, then I would rather remain part of the old and poor. Here. A keepsake for you. The price of one alien, soon to die—or half the city of i'Ramnau." He extended one hand and poured the snapped quarters of the prime-transfer card from his palm to hers, smiling as thinly and ironically as the indignity of a fast-puffing lip would let him. "It still isn't enough to buy honor, not the old-fashioned kind."

Arrhae closed her fist on the broken card and felt a sudden, ridiculous sting of tears fill her eyes. It had nothing to do with the small pain as sharp corners pricked her skin and drew small beads of emerald blood, nothing to do with that at all. She glanced at McCoy, wondering if he understood, or would ever understand, just what had been done for him. "Lord," she said then, and doubled over to give H'daen the deep, deep bow that was his due as Head of House, and that she gave him now for the first time because she wanted to and because he deserved such respect rather than because it was something that went with her role.

McCoy did understand, and was annoyed that there was no way he could show some form of respectful thanks without giving too many secrets away. He had to sit unconcernedly, "not knowing" what was being said until Arrhae thought to activate her translator, and hoping that H'daen didn't notice they had already been talking without it.

"Since you seem likely to tell Mak'khoi what has happened whether I give permission or not," H'daen said quietly, "I allow it. Tell him also . . . Tell him that he will be tried before the Senate in six days. That the sentence has already been agreed upon. And that it is not the way I would interpret our ancient laws. And Arrhae . . . ?"

"My lord?"

"I intend to sleep late tomorrow. Very late indeed. This has been a tiring day." He smiled crookedly. "But educational. Very." He closed the door behind him as he left.

"Now, that," said McCoy, "is a Romulan gentleman of the old school. Like a lady I once knew. Here. Wipe your eyes."

Arrhae took the proffered handkerchief, only a big layered sheet of soft paper from the supply she had instructed should be put in here, but very welcome for all that. She hadn't expected to cry into them herself. She hadn't expected to cry about anything much, least of all H'daen. After a little while she felt better, apart from an inclination to sniffle, and managed a damp smile for McCoy's benefit.

"You're bearing up well, Terise," he said. "I'm glad of that. We were worried about you. Seriously worried. No reports from you for two years, even though other operatives were able to tell us where you were and what you were doing."

"You thought I'd gone over. Turned Romulan."

"It was a possibility. One of the chances that were taken when you went out in the first place. I'm glad we were wrong. Now, Terise, I'm authorized to ask you this: when I'm pulled out, do you want to be pulled as well?"

"Pulled out? Taken out, you mean. In case you didn't understand H'daen, or the meaning wasn't clear, you're going for trial in six days. But you've been sentenced already. Bones, you're dead!"

To her astonishment he smiled. "I've been pronounced dead by people far more qualified to do it than you, Terise, and people far more certain of what they were saying. Yet here I am."

"You thought that I might have gone native, or gone schizophrenic, or gone mad—have you ever thought of looking at yourself that way?"

He looked at her with ironic astonishment, and a little wickedness. "Don't be silly," he said. "I'm the psychiatrist here. I have paperwork that says I'm sane."

From her expression it was plain that Terise had her doubts. "Doctor," she said very slowly, as if speaking to someone with a hearing impairment, or an impairment somewhere more vital, "don't you understand it? Your trial is nothing but a formality. They're going to pull you to pieces, and they're going to make an entertainment of it!—if you even make it that far. If someone else doesn't come in here and make H'daen an offer he can't refuse . . . or just come in and take you by force. You have to get out while you can!"

McCoy shook his head slowly. He was beginning to feel sorrier for this woman than he felt for himself, at this stage of the game, no mean accomplishment. "I have things to do," he said. "Anyway, I'm not going to leave this planet without seeing the sights. The Senate Chambers. The Council of Praetors."

"The scenic execution pits!!"

McCoy put one eyebrow up at her and grinned, a wicked look. "Think I'll just give that last spot a miss. Don't you worry about it. Meantime, I've got things to take care of, and I'd guess you do too. Why don't you go take care of them."

She looked at him rather helplessly. "Do you always hedge like this with your friends? What are you planning? How am I supposed to help you if you won't tell me?!"

He sighed, and smiled again, a little ruefully. "You're not supposed to help me . . . yet. You go on, Terise. Take care of things. You won't be able to be any help to me if they fire you or something."

She nodded, looking at him with extreme irritation that nonetheless had a sort of edge of affection and grudging admiration on it. It was a look he had seen from many a patient in his time, the "you won't let me run things my way, dammit!" expression. McCoy was pleased. There was hope for her after all, and he could relax a little, as much as anyone can relax who has most of two planets out for his blood.

"All right," she said. "Good night to you, Bones."

"Good night," he said. Then he remembered something. "Oh, and Arrhae?" he said to her back as she headed toward the door.

"Yes?"

"I'm told the soil in the back garden needs lime."

He leaned back on his couch and smiled, hearing the sound of laughter go down the hall, laughter that was not hysterical at all.

Chapter Twelve

Empires

"WE WERE EXCITED," said the captain of the Federation vessel USS *Carrizal* during the postmission debriefing following its return from the Trianguli stars, a little more than a hundred years ago. "It was the first hit we'd had in nine months of scouring that sector. A hominid culture, obviously highly developed, a large population, it was everything we had hoped for. Better yet, the same people were on *two* worlds . . . an Earth-Moon configuration. Mike Maliani, our astrogator, suggested Romus and Remus as nicknames for the planets until we found out their real names from the people who lived there. After the twin brothers in an ancient Italian myth." On the debriefing tape, Captain Dini smiles rather ruefully. "I was never a specialist in the classics: I wish I were. Mike's misspelling of 'Romulus' is going to haunt me to the grave. But at that point I thought he knew what he was talking about."

A pause. "Anyway, we were really excited. You know how few spacefaring species there are: the standing orders are to closely examine any we find. But we weren't so excited that we went in without the proper protocols. We gave them everything we had: the classic first-contact series—atomic ratios, binary counting, pictures. You name it. There was never any answer, even though we're sure they knew we were there. They had an outer cordon of defense satellites that noticed us, and after the messages from the satellites were received on the planets, the message traffic on the bigger planet increased by about a thousand percent. But there was nothing we could do with it by way of translation—after that first message there was silence, and everything that came later was encoded—some kind of closed-satchel code, very sophisticated, and no way to break it in anything short of a decade, without a supercomp or the code key."

There is a long silence on the tape as Captain Dini shakes his head and looks puzzled. "We never came any closer to their planet than two orbits out," he says, "right beyond the fifth planet in the system. We never came near them. We just observed, and took readings, and went away quietly. I'll never understand what happened."

What happened was the First Romulan War, as the Federation later called it. What it looked like, from the Federation side, was a long, bloody conflict started without provocation by the Romulans. From the other side it wore a different aspect.

The appearance of *Carrizal* caused such a panic as the Rihannsu had never known since they became Rihannsu. In terms of a Rihanha's lifetime, it was thirty generations and more since the Settlement, and the actual records of the appearance of aliens on Vulcan, all those many years ago, were not so much lost as largely ignored. People *knew* through the history they were taught in the academies what had happened on Vulcan in the old days . . . and the history had bent and changed, what with telling and retelling, and neglecting to go back to the original source material. Not that that would have helped much. The source material itself had been altered in the Journey, but very few—scholars and historians—knew this, or cared. What the Rihannsu knew about this incursion into their space was that it closely matched the pattern followed by the Etoshans so long ago: quiet observation coupled with or followed by proffers of peaceful contact. They were not going to be had *that* way again.

Ch'Rihan and ch'Havran had, over sixteen hundred years, become superbly industrialized. The Rihannsu have always had a way with machines: and this, coupled with their great concern for taking care of the worlds they found after such Journey and suffering, produced two planets that were technologically most advanced at manufacture, without looking that way. Few factories were visible from the atmosphere, let alone from space. Aesthetics required that they be either pleasant to look at, or completely concealed. Many factories were underground. Release of waste products into the ambient environment, even waste so seemingly innocuous as steam or hot water, was forbidden by Praetorial indict, and a capital crime. A starship passing through, even one looking carefully, as *Carrizal* did, would see two pastoral-looking worlds, unspoiled, quiet. One would hardly suspect the frenetic manufacture that was to start after *Carrizal*'s departure.

There was frantic action elsewhere as well. In the Praetorate and the Senate some heads rolled, and the survivors scrambled to start working on the defense of the planet—or to otherwise take advantage of the situation. The defense satellites had not been approached closely enough by the invading ship to trigger their weaponry. Cannily, it had stayed out of range. There was no way to tell if the Two Worlds could be defended against the ship that had appeared there, no telling what kind of weaponry it had. But from their experience in air combat (almost every nation of each planet had its own air force, which they used liberally for both friendly and unfriendly skirmishes), the Rihannsu military specialists knew that even a heavily armed ship should not be able to do much against overwhelming numbers.

They got busy, digging frantically through ancient computer memories and printouts and film and metal media for the forgotten space technology they needed. Had the Ships been spared, even one of them—had their data been preserved in one place rather than scattered all over two worlds—the Federation's boundaries might be much different now. But even what remained was useful, and the Rihannsu were frightened. It is unwise to frighten a Rihanha. Within a year after *Carrizal*'s visit, ch'Rihan's numerous nations had built, among them, some three *thousand* spacecraft armed with particle-beam weapons and the beginnings of defensive shields. Ch'Havran had built four thousand. They were crude little craft, and their cylindrical shapes recalled those of the Ships, though there was no need for them to spin for gravity: artificial gravity had been mastered a century or so earlier.

It was three more years before the next ship came. The unlucky *Balboa* came in broadcasting messages of peace and friendship, and was blown to bits by the massed particle beams of a squadron of fifty. After that the Rihannsu grew a little bolder, and went hunting: a task force caught *Stone Mountain,* to which *Balboa* had sent a distress call, and captured her by carefully using high-powered lasers to explosively decompress the crew compartments. They towed *Stone Mountain* home, took her apart, and shortly thereafter added warp drive to their little cruisers.

The Federation considers the War to have begun with the destruction of *Balboa*. In the twenty-five years of warfare that followed, no less than forty-six Federation task forces of ever-increasing size and firepower went into Rihannsu space to deal with the aggression against them, and even with vastly superior firepower, most of them suffered heavy damage if not annihilation. "I can't understand it," says one fleet Admiral in a debriefing. "Their ships are junk. We should be able to shoot them down like clay pigeons." But the huge numbers of the Rihannsu craft made them impossible to profitably engage; even "smart" photon torpedoes could target only one vessel at a time. When there were twelve more climbing up your tail, the situation became impossible. Starfleet kept trying with bigger and better weapons—until two things happened at once: there was a change of administration, and the Vulcans joined the Federation.

The only indication of what the Rihannsu looked like had come from a very few burned and decompressed bodies picked up in space. When Vulcan was discovered, and after negotiation entered the Federation, their High Council was pointedly asked whether it knew anything about these people. The Vulcans, all logic—and selective truth—told the Federation that they were not sure who these people were. There had indeed been some attempts to colonize other worlds, they admitted, but those ships had been out of touch with Vulcan for some seventeen hundred years. The first Vulcan Ambassador, a grimly handsome gentleman who had just been posted to Earth, made this statement to the Admirals of Starfleet in such a way that they immediately found it politic to drop the subject. But through the ambassador, the Vulcan High Council gave the Federation a piece of good advice. "Make peace with them," Sarek told the Admirals, "and close the door. Stop fighting. You will probably never beat them. But you can stop your ships being destroyed."

The advice went down hard, and Starfleet tried to do it their own way for several years more. But finally, as Vulcan's increasing displeasure became plainer, Fleet acquiesced. The War ended with the Treaty of Alpha Trianguli, probably the first treaty in Federation history to have been negotiated entirely by data upload. No representatives of the two sides ever met. The Rihannsu had no interest in letting their enemies find out any more about them than could be revealed by autopsy. They might be back someday.

The treaty established what came to be called the Romulan Neutral Zone, an egg-shaped area of space about ninety lightyears long and forty wide, with 128 Trianguli at its center. The Zone itself was the "shell" of the egg, a buffer area all the way around, one lightyear thick, marked and guarded by defense/monitoring satellites of both sides. Everything inside the Zone was considered "the Romulan Star Empire," even though there was as yet no such thing. The Federation was not exactly hurt by this treaty: as far as they were concerned, there were no strategically promising planets in the area. Perhaps they were not looking hard enough. Later some Federation officials would kick themselves when finding out about Rhei'llhne, a planet just barely inside the Neutral Zone in Rihannsu space, and almost richer in dilithium than Direidi.

So the war ended, and as far as the Federation was concerned, for fifty years nothing came out of the Zone, not a signal, not a ship. Perhaps, some thought, the people in there had gotten sick of fighting. Wiser heads, or those who thought they knew what stock the "Romulans" had sprung from, suspected otherwise.

The Rihannsu had stopped fighting indeed, but as for being tired of it, this was unlikely. There was a matter of honor, *mnhei'sahe*, still to be resolved. So much of the Two Worlds' economies were poured into starship weapons research that they still have not recovered entirely from the austerity it caused the contributing nations. They rebuilt the defense satellite system to hundreds of times its former strength, and trained some of the best star pilots ever seen in any species anywhere.

They also decided not to make the mistake their forefathers had made with the Etoshans. The Rihannsu scientists spent literally years translating the complete contents of the reference computers of the Federation ships they had so far managed to capture. They realized from what they found that they were one small pair of planets caught between two Empires, and that to survive, they were going to have to have an Empire themselves.

So began the "expansionist" period of Rihannsu history, in which they tackled planetary colonization with the same ferocious desperation they had used to build a fleet out of nothing. They needed better ships to do this, of course. They wound up reconstructing numerous large people-carriers along the Ship model, though, of course, with warp drive these craft did not need generation capability. Twenty planets were settled in eighteen years, and population-increase technology was used of the sort that had made ch'Rihan and ch'Havran themselves so rapidly viable. Not all the settlements were successful, nor are they now; Hellguard was one glaring example.

During this period the Rihannsu also developed the Warbird-class starship, acknowledged by everyone, including the Klingons and the Federation, to be one of the finest, solidest, most maneuverable warp-capable craft ever designed. If it had a flaw, it was that it was small; but its weaponry was redoubtable, and the plasma-based molecular implosion field that Warbirds carried had problems only with ships that could outrun the field. Another allied invention was the cloaking device, which tantalized everyone who saw it, particularly the Klingons.

The Klingons didn't get it until much later than the Federation did. The Klingons got other things, mostly defense contracts.

The relationship was a strange one from the first. The Rihannsu economy began to be in serious trouble, despite the beginning inflow of goods and capital from the tributary worlds, because of all the funds being diverted to military research. There was also a question as to whether the research was, in fact, doing any good: a Warbird out on a mission to test the security of the Neutral Zone ran into a starship called *Enterprise* and never came back again. At the same time, the Klingon Empire was beginning to encroach on the far side of the Neutral Zone, and the first two or three interstellar engagements left both sides looking at each other and wishing there were some way to forestall the all-out war that was certainly coming. Rather cleverly, the Klingons made overtures to the Rihannsu based on their own enmity with the Federation, and offered to sell them ships and "more advanced technology," some of it Federation. Everyone, they claimed, stood to benefit from this arrangement. The Neutral Zone border on their side would be "secure," and the Klingon economy (also in trouble) would benefit from the extra capital and goods.

The deal turned out to be of dubious worth. For one thing, the Rihannsu buying ships from the Klingons was comparable to Rolls-Royce buying parts from Ford. The Klingon ships were built by the lowest bidder, and performed as such. Also, most of the Federation technology the Klingons had to offer was obsolete. But the treaty suited the aims of the expansionist lobbies in Praetorate and Senate, and so was ratified, much to the Rihannsu's eventual regret. In the meantime, the Rihannsu shipwrights (and some of the ship captains) muttered over the needlessly high cost of Klingon replacement parts, and did their best to tinker the ships into something better than nominal performance. Mostly it was a losing battle. Klingons build good weaponry, but their greatest interest in spacecraft tends to be in blowing them up.

Meanwhile other forces were stirring. The Federation sent the only ship that had been successful with Romulans to see if it could get its hands on the cloaking device. It did, and *Enterprise,* merely an annoying name before, became a matter for curses and vengeance. How some of those curses turned out, and what form the vengeance took, other chroniclers have recently covered more completely in the press.

In terms of policy, matters have changed little from that point, some few years ago, to the present day. The Rihannsu lie inside their protected Zone, while their Praetorate and Senate hatch plots, count the incoming funds from the tributary worlds, and look for ways to regain an honor which they never truly lost. Some people in the computer nets (still cherished as a quaint but much-loved relic of the Ship days) have ventured the opinion that some kind of overture toward peace should be made. The Federation at least builds decent starships. And, some have said, if the Federation truly wanted to destroy the Rihannsu, why haven't they come and done it in force? Their resources are presently huge enough to crush the Two Worlds as the little ships swarmed over *Balboa,* by sheer strength of numbers.

But so many only reply to this line of thought with ridicule. "Cowardice," they say. Others point out that the Rihannsu, however hostile they may be to the United Federation of Planets, also serve as the Federation's buffer between them and the Klingons. Annex the Rihannsu spaces (even if they could) and suddenly Federation and Klingon policies come into direct conflict. It makes more sense to let the Rihannsu take the brunt. This argument generates more bitterness among Rihannsu than even the first. Fear of the Rihannsu—that a Rihanha can understand, though he loathes it. But being ignored, or taken for granted, that is the unforgivable. For those who ignore the power of the Two Worlds, no hate will ever be sufficient.

The voices still speak quietly of the old ways here and there: of peace, and nobility, and perhaps even *rapprochement* with the Vulcans. But that turn of mind has a long time to wait before it comes into vogue in the Praetorate. The Rihannsu in power now are the children of the twenty-five years of blood: their memories are long, and the fear that awoke when *Carrizal* arrived is still cold in their stomachs at night. Perhaps a hundred years from now, perhaps two hundred, children will be born who will sleep sounder, and think more wisely by day. Until then, the Two Worlds are alone in the long night. Nothing has changed since the Ships: the Worlds still have walls.

Hope is not dead, of course. Every now and then some one hand reaches out—not necessarily the hand of a great general or statesman—and hits the wall, and a bit of stonework falls down. Perhaps the hands of the little do less than the hands of the great. But there are many more of them, and they tend not to squabble among themselves as much as the great do, nor are they terminally embarrassed by statements like the one heard for so many years on both sides of the Zone, "I don't understand. . . ." They are the ones likely to work to understand: to find answers, and to share them. As long as this goes on, there is always a chance: and if the small ever manage to teach this art to the great, the Elements Themselves will not contain all the unfolding possibilities, as the walls come down at last.

Chapter Thirteen

McCoy PUSHED THE reader-screen aside and rubbed both hands over his face. Romulan law was one of the most stultifying subjects that he had ever studied, and despite the amount of persuasion he had employed to get a logic-solid reader with an onboard visual translator, there were times—usually deep into the pontifications of some long-dead Senator—when he had the feeling that he would be better employed doing something else, like watching the grass grow. It was intricate, and the older legal terms sometimes refused to translate into even the stilted Federation Standard that the reader produced. There was no such thing as an out, anyway; even the Right of Statement, a standard clause in capital crimes—of which there were an excessive number—was no more than an opportunity to explain or defend the offense for which the speaker would afterward be executed.

At least the implant was giving him no problems other than those anticipated. McCoy had expected a headache, had almost hoped for one, just a little one, something that he could grouse about to Intelligence and say *I told you so* when he got back. Turning a man into a living data recorder—it wasn't proper. But at least it worked. When the microsolid buried in his cortex memory centers was in operation, his normally excellent memory was enhanced out to auditory and visual eidesis. He remembered *everything*. And until he mastered the neural impulses that switched the blasted thing on and off, he had to leaf through a mass of data equivalent to the *Index XenoMedicalis* to find the scribbled margin note that said "socks are in boots, under bed."

There was information locked into it already, supplied by *Bloodwing*'s surgeon, t'Hrienteh. Names and faces, the workings of the Senate—t'Hrienteh's family were highly placed—medical background on Romulan psychiatry and body kinesics. All the things that would make his task on ch'Rihan easier, or at least more straightforward. That was why he had to stay on-planet for long enough to be taken before the Senate and the Praetorate, so that he could interpret what he saw and heard in the light of what he knew. A delicate business at best, and already very dangerous.

McCoy's chief interest in the Romulan law books was an attempt to find out how long espionage trials might be expected to last, how much time he had to play with before the legal system began to play with him. Using knives . . .

Arrhae took a step backward from the door, and stared at the two men who had evidently rung the chime a few seconds before. After their parting in i'Ramnau, Nveid tr'AAnikh was the last person on ch'Rihan that she expected to see. "What are *you* doing here?" she wanted to know. "And who is this?"

Nveid's companion was a little taller and a little fairer, but the most obvious difference was that while Nveid wore civilian clothing, the other man was in Fleet uniform. "Llhran tr'Khnialmnae," he said, saluting her. His gaze shifted from her face to the hall behind her, checking that it was empty. "Nveid has spoken to you already about—certain matters. My sister Aidoann was third-in-command of *Bloodwing*."

"Llhran is taking a great risk in coming here," Nveid said. "I told you of the families who supported the action of their kinfolk aboard *Bloodwing;* House Khnialmnae is one of the more outspoken. Their respect for honor is very high."

"And what," Arrhae said through her teeth, "of their respect for the peace and the lives of those who want no part of this madness? I want you to let me alone. And alone is not standing two by two with a surveillance subject on the steps of my master's house. Go away."

"*Hru'hfe*, we should like to speak with H'daen tr'Khellian." Llhran spoke now in a more formal phase of language, one that made quite clear the difference between a Senior Centurion and a senior servant. "It is a matter concerning the prisoner Mak'khoi."

"And how much do you two want to offer me . . . ?" H'daen looked down at them from the balcony above the door, his face weary and his voice totally disinterested. "Or are you just taking him away at long last?"

"My lord . . . ?" Nveid was confused, and it showed. Whatever had brought him here, it was nothing to do with helping McCoy to escape. Not yet, anyway. "We wanted to speak to the Federation officer held captive here."

"Do it. Do whatever you want. Just don't ask me to get involved again." He touched his cheekbone just beneath the right eye, where a blue-brown bruise mottled the skin. "Involvement hurts too much."

"My lord, you are a Praetor, and we—"

"I am a make-weight," H'daen responded with all the savagery of a man who had too recently discovered that his place in the scheme of things was far lower than he had believed. "The only Praetors you need ask permission of are the young *hnoiyikar* who believe that wealth and the freedom to employ brutality are all that honor means." He turned away from them and went indoors.

"So . . . ?" Nveid was watching Arrhae closely, more closely than she liked, and she shrugged dismissively.

"I'll take you to him and leave you a translator. After that, say what you want out of my hearing. And leave quickly."

Llhran looked at her, then at Nveid. "Servants have better manners where I come from," he said pointedly, and Arrhae blushed.

"Sir, I doubt that servants are so frightened where you come from," she said, and ushered the pair indoors before either man could think of a suitably cutting response. "If you would follow me, I shall take you to Mak'khoi. And then I have work of my own that needs attention. Evidently"—and she watched Nveid carefully—"the Senatorial Judiciary have decided that their prisoner would feel more comfortable with a familiar face beside him—so before we go to the trial in Ra'tleihfi I must deal with everything that won't be done while I'm away. . . ."

"You are going to the capital?" Llhran clearly didn't believe what he was hearing. "A servant?"

"Hru'hfe of an old House, Llhe'," Nveid said. "Different places, different customs. She's rather more than just 'a servant.'"

"Oh." He didn't sound convinced.

Not that Arrhae was concerned; she was past worrying about anybody's opinions other than McCoy's and her own. "In here," she said. "That is, if he isn't in the garden"—and she smiled—"communing with nature. . . ."

McCoy wasn't, although he probably wished that he were. Instead, he was sitting with his head in his hands, mumbling legal phrases and looking very like a man with a sore head. Which was entirely accurate. Right now, never mind all his other troubles, what Leonard McCoy wanted in all the world was a twenty-mil ampule of Aerosal and a spray hypo. Dammit, he'd settle for three aspirin and a glass of water. He looked at his visitors without much interest, automatically registering their body language—both of them were extremely apprehensive about something or other, and trying not to show it, and the man in uniform had the air of someone whose opinions had been gently but firmly squelched—before turning his attention to their faces. Young faces, closed and wary, but inquisitive for all that. He summoned up a smile and nodded to them, began to shut down the reader's input-output systems, shutting down his own "onboard" circuitry as he did so. At least that was getting easier. McCoy added the last data-solid to the stack that already filled his little table to overflowing, and wondered if the two Romulans had ever seen a Terran face before. He doubted it.

Arrhae introduced them to him as if to her lord, then made herself scarce and closed the door as she went out. McCoy wondered who had been giving her a hard time, and put his money on the Centurion. That young man didn't have the hardness of another tr'Annhwi, but there was a determination about him that suggested he wasn't open for any sort of nonsense from his subordinates. The sort of mindset that would have put a lad who looked about eighteen into a Senior Centurion's uniform. Or maybe he was just somebody's sister's kid. . . .

"I recognize your House-names," McCoy said, switching on the boxy Romulan-issue translator and trying to find somewhere to set it down. It balanced rather precariously on top of the smallest heap of computer junk, and he cocked a wary eye at it before he let it go. "Your kin on *Bloodwing* were in good health last time I saw them. Take a seat, both of you—if you can find one."

"Thank you, Doctor," said Nveid, offering him the ghost of a bow. Llhran began to salute, thought better of it in the presence of an enemy officer, and nodded his head fractionally instead. Once they were both seated side by side on the bed, very straight-backed and looking far from comfortable, Nveid cleared his throat significantly. It amused McCoy to find that sound used in exactly the same way as it was back home. "Sir," the Romulan began, "did the *hru'hfe* tell you that I spoke with her in i'Ramnau yesterday?"

McCoy shook his head. "The *hru'hfe* regards me as an unnecessary disturbance of the peace in this household. She'll be glad to see me gone."

Nveid frowned and muttered something to Llhran.

Though he spoke too softly for either the translator or McCoy's ears to catch the words, his tone sounded irritable. *Good,* McCoy thought with a touch of satisfaction, *that should give Terise a bit more cover.*

"What was the subject of the conversation?" asked McCoy, wondering if this was what Arrhae meant about him becoming overly popular, and whether that was a good or a bad thing. Nveid cleared his throat again, a mannerism that McCoy had decided was mostly nervousness, mixed with just a bit of affectation.

"You were."

"Oh? In what sense? Good, bad, or indifferent?"

"You may find it good, I trust." Nveid took a long breath and glanced at Llhran tr'Khnialmnae, who nodded quickly. "Sir, there are many Houses on ch'Rihan who . . ."

". . . and both duty and the obligations of honor therefore require that we do other than stand by while you are condemned and killed."

"And what form would this 'other' take, Nveid tr'AAnikh?"

"We would endeavor to help you escape from ch'Rihan and from Imperial space, and return you across the Neutral Zone to your own people. The starliner *Vega* was released yesterday, after repairs to her hull were completed, and . . . well, we have supporters everywhere, those of us who have no love for the pirates who would try to run this Empire as the accursed Klingons run theirs. Several of our people are seeded among the traffic-control nets." McCoy grinned suddenly. "They 'acquired' all of this tenday's access codes for the inner-system approaches."

"Even through the planetary defenses?" said McCoy, grinning even harder.

"Of course—all of the weapon-platforms run by automatics anyway."

"Then bear it in mind for later."

"Later . . . ?"

"Yes. After I've been to the Senate Chambers and

had a chance to study how the Praetorate runs this particular show."

"*Study* them?" Llhran was halfway to his feet, shocked out of his military composure by McCoy's declaration. "Doctor, they want you dead. Get out while you can!"

"Calmly, son, calmly. I know what I'm doing, and I've got my orders to back them up. Standard procedure: if a suitably qualified officer is in a position to obtain new social understanding of another intelligent people, it is incumbent upon him to gather such information as he deems useful to that end. Failing to comply, Centurion tr'Khnialmnae, would place my honor as a Starfleet officer in jeopardy, instead of just my life."

"Ah." Llhran subsided, understanding that particular argument as he might not have understood something with no parallel among the Rihannsu. Personal honor, especially among military personnel from the noble Houses, was a currency more widely used than any other.

"So what *can* we do to help you, Doctor?"

McCoy smiled a little to himself at Nveid's eagerness to do anything at all, and do it at once. There was something about the young Romulan's earnest enthusiasm that reminded him of Naraht when the Horta was a newly graduated ensign. When he had referred to the youngster as a "space cadet" he hadn't been making fun. Nveid tr'AAnikh was a little like that except that he was a Romulan and therefore most likely susceptible to the use of violence in discussion. Any people that used suicide, whether genuine or enforced, as an instrument of political policy could aspire only to benevolence on their better days, and on most of the other days needed watching.

"Try this," he said, choosing his words with care. "If your traffic-control system is anything like ours, there'll be regular tests of the communications network—so have one of your people transmit a test signal of a standard geometric progression based on the first three prime numbers." McCoy closed his eyes briefly and when they opened again they were staring intently at something only he could see. "Exactly one standard Romulan day after that, send a tight-beam tachyon squirt on a decohesive packet frequency of 5-18-54 to coordinates GalLat 177D 48.210M, GalLong +6D 14.335M, DistArbGalCore 24015 L.Y. No repetition, no acknowledgment. That should do it."

When his eyes slid back into focus, they met the suspicious stares of two Romulans who were plainly beginning to wonder whether the requirements of honor weren't getting them into something more than they had bargained for. "Doctor," said Llhran, speaking, McCoy guessed, with the full weight of his centurionate training behind him, "what will receive that signal?"

"Not an invasion force, Centurion. A single ship, and not even a Federation warship at that."

"But cloaked with the device stolen from us by your Captain Kirk."

"Ah, well. That's history, isn't it? Anyway, the ship'll come in, pluck me from the very jaws of imminent dissolution, and whisk me away before the Imperial fleet is any the wiser."

"So you say. Can we trust you?"

"Or I you?" McCoy's shoulders lifted in a dismissive shrug. "'Trust' isn't a word much used between the Federation and the Imperium. I think starting to use it is long overdue. Instead of taking the chance you offer me now, I'll do what honor dictates and trust that when I'm on trial, you'll have done your part to get me safely away. If you don't trust me after I trust you, then I'll die—I presume unpleasantly—and where does that leave the *mnhei'sahe* you mentioned so often?"

He sat back while the two Romulans muttered softly to each other, not trying to overhear what they said since he would be told their verdict soon enough. His hands were sweating. Not unusual. They sweated before he undertook any sort of surgery, and this excision of mistrust was one of the hardest operations he had ever performed.

Nveid and Llhran came out of their huddle, and McCoy was startled to see how much color both men had lost. Putting their own lives on the line was evidently one thing, but making a decision that might well be laying their homeworld open to attack was another matter entirely. "Very well, Dr. McCoy," said Nveid. "Trust it shall be. If anything goes wrong, then Elements and Powers all witness that we acted as we thought best for all, now and in the future."

"Come along, Doctor," said Commander t'Radaik. "You have had quite enough time to set your affairs here in order." She stood in the doorway of his room with armed and helmeted guards at her back and watched as McCoy bundled the few possessions he had accumulated into a grab-bag.

Enough time? he thought, nervous even though he hoped it wouldn't show. *No. There's never anything like enough, not when there's a trial and an execution in the offing.* He was determined, however, not to resort to the black humor that was such a cliché on occasions like this. Granted that few of his psych patients had ever been in the gallows situation for real, but—

"Doctor . . ."

Now, that was the voice of a Romulan Intelligence officer whose patience was finally at an end. McCoy glanced quickly around the room, hoping that he had overlooked nothing of importance, then lifted his small bagful of property and took the first step of the last mile.

It was rather farther than a mile, and he wasn't going to be walking it. The Senate Chambers in Ra'tleihfi were more than three hundred kilometers due north of H'daen's mansion, an hour's ride in an ordinary flitter, rather longer in the heavy military vehicle squatting like a gray-armored toad in front of the house.

Arrhae was standing beside it, looking ill at ease in the company of so many soldiers, and McCoy managed to summon up a smile for her especial benefit. The expression she gave back might have been a smile—it might equally have been the facial spasm of someone with indigestion.

"In," ordered t'Radaik. They got in, surrounded by disruptor-armed guards; there wasn't a lot of choice in the matter. McCoy looked back toward the house and saw H'daen tr'Khellian watching them. The man looked as uneasy as both of them, and McCoy thought about what H'daen had said five nights before. Something about this not being the way Romulan law should be interpreted. Well, just recently he had read enough of that same law to know that H'daen was being optimistic. Trials weren't a nice, civilized judge and jury, with mannered arguments and reasoning from defense and prosecution, even in cases where the verdict and sentence hadn't already been settled well in advance. The onus of proof was on the accused rather than on the accuser. "Guilty until proven innocent," and God help you if the court decided that all they needed was a confession. Romulan judiciary inquisitors were supposedly so skillful that they could not only get blood out of the proverbial stone, they could also force the stone to admit that it was spying for the Federation.

McCoy thought of Naraht, young Lieutenant Rock, and put that line of reasoning as far out of his mind as it would go. . . .

The flitter's rearmost hatch rose with a hiss and whine of heavy-gauge hydraulics, settling into its hermetic slots and shutting off all light until the vehicle's internal systems were switched on from the control compartment. After that it was only a matter of minutes before the flitter rumbled into the air and whisked off north toward Ra'tleihfi. Toward the Senate, and the Praetorate, and those scenic execution pits that Arrhae had mentioned.

Arrhae leaned over him, offering a small flask that by

the scent contained good-quality wine. "Naraht?" With an appropriate lifting of the flask, she made the word sound like an invitation to take a drink.

McCoy accepted, taking a single careful swig of the liquor before handing it back. "Later," he said. "In the city. When I really need it." He hoped that the Horta could burrow to Ra'tleihfi as fast as Naraht had claimed he could, homing on the logic-solid buried in McCoy's brain. Between Naraht and the as yet unconfirmed rescue ship all using him as a beacon, and Intelligence using him as an ambulatory information-gathering system, what McCoy most looked forward to about completing this mission and getting home safe was to lie down on a nice friendly neurosurgery table and let Johnny Russell take the hardware out of his head. Of course, if things went wrong, some Romulan would take it out—but McCoy doubted he would appreciate that surgery quite as much.

The four Romulan guards glanced at their charges, shrugged expressively, and since nobody was offering wine their way, they resorted instead to the ale-and-water mixture in their issue canteens.

The flitter reached Ra'tleihfi before noon, traveling through the high-level zones reserved for priority traffic. Even with the starships back on maneuvers in his stomach, McCoy had enough curiosity to open the shielding on one of the armored viewports and peer out at the Rihannsu capital city nearly a mile below. It was smaller than he had imagined; at the back of his mind had been an image of something like L.A.Plex, a sprawling metropolis that went on for miles. Instead, he saw a place that was more like New York Old City: clustered spikes of tall buildings crammed together into the smallest groundspace possible, all steel and glass and plastic, a strangely pleasing hybrid that was hi-tech out of Art Deco and a style of classic severity like that of the antique Doric order.

Scattered here and there among the towering crystalline columns were buildings antique in their own right, rather than through any similarity to an Old-Earth school of architecture. McCoy knew, because Arrhae had told him, that the Senate Chamber and the Praetorate building had both been dedicated directly following the tyranny of the Ruling Queen. That meant they had been standing in the same place, and had been in continuous turbulent use for more than a millennium. No building now standing on Earth could boast such a history.

The flitter settled ponderously into a reinforced bay at the rear of the Senate Chamber, crouched buglike on its landers for a few seconds, then slid underground. If the procedure was meant to unsettle prisoners, it worked. For prisoners who were unsettled already, it worked even better.

"Leonard Edward McCoy." The Judiciary Praetor read his name with a passable Anglish pronunciation. McCoy watched her and wondered why every courtroom charge-sheet across the galaxy managed to look like every other charge-sheet, no matter how much they differed in form and style and material. The Praetor was reciting biographical information about the soon-to-be-accused, in considerable—and accurate—detail. McCoy wondered how many of the personnel at Starfleet Command were Romulan and Klingon equivalents of Arrhae/Terise.

He looked down at his wrists, snugged close together by a fine silk ribbon. It looked like no more than a token binder, more symbolic of his position in this court than of any practical use. Except that he had seen how it had been heat-sealed, not the band of gray silk, but the monofilament running through the center of its weave. Token binding indeed. *Honorable if honorably worn,* the Security chief had said as it was put on. *Don't test it and it won't hurt you. Pull, and . . .* He hadn't bothered to say, but McCoy knew quite well enough without explanations. Any pressure on a strand one molecule thick—far too fine for the naked eye to see—would insinuate it between any other molecules it came in contact with. Pull, and both your hands fall off.

"Charges," said the Praetor, her voice echoing through the marble chamber that had heard the same word God—or the Elements—alone knew how many times since it was built. With the marble floor that was so easily washed clean . . . McCoy began to pay attention, more through curiosity than real interest.

"Espionage. Sabotage. Conspiracy. Aiding and abetting the theft of military secrets. Damage to Imperial installations. Complicity in the impersonation of a Rihannsu officer. Actions prejudicial to the security of the Imperium and the public good. The sentence of this tribunal, duly considering all evidence laid before it, is that the prisoner is guilty of all charges and shall die by the penalty prescribed. . . ."

Chapter Fourteen

McCoy SWALLOWED. ANTICIPATING something like this, no matter how accurate that anticipation might have been, hadn't really prepared him for hearing his own sentence of death read out in open court. For maybe fifteen seconds he sat there sweating, with his guts in an upheaval that reminded him with acidic immediacy that he hadn't eaten so far today. And then the feeling went away as a twinge of discomfort shot through a very certain filling in his rearmost right molar.

Phantom pain was one thing, tracking-sensor feedback was quite another. His equanimity reasserted itself somewhat. *You're the one with the stacked deck*, he thought, *don't panic now. Besides, we all die sooner or later. . . .* Not that he would not rather put off the "evil day." He wiped his hands briskly on his pants legs, squelched the highly inappropriate smug smile that was threatening to take over his face, and got to his feet. Immediately he was the focus of attention, and the aiming-point for the phasers which by rights his guards were not supposed to carry within the Senate Chamber lest they dishonor the Sword in the Empty Chair. McCoy looked at them, and at the leveled weapons, then dismissed them all with a lift of disdainful eyebrows, and turned his attention to other matters. "Ladies and gentlemen—"

The Judiciary Praetor glared at him. "The condemned will sit down and be silent!"

"Why should I?" McCoy snapped back, then took a deep breath. "When I demand the Right of Statement."

There was immediate and noisy uproar in the House, and McCoy smiled thinly as he observed that for the first time in several years, the Tricameron was unanimous in a proposal—that he, Leonard E. McCoy, be suppressed severely and at once. He reviewed the mental-neural protocols that cut in on the analysis-solid, felt reality waver for an instant, and then with his enhanced awareness of the situation, realized just what a large splash his demand had made in the otherwise-tranquil pool of poison that was the Rihannsu executive. He wondered what "suppression" meant, and had a sudden vision of being put into a bag and sat on, like an Alice-in-Wonderland guinea pig. Except, of course, that someone was far more likely to yell "Off with his head!" in the comforting knowledge that it would be done.

Indeed, the Judiciary Praetor would be more than willing to do the deed herself, and was entirely capable of it. One of the most important pieces of acquired information in the logic-solid was a names-and-faces list of the Praetors and the most notable Senators, and while he hadn't been aware of her rank, he knew— uncomfortably—that this hawk-faced woman was

Hloal t'Illialhlae, wife of *Battlequeen*'s late Commander and a most appropriate consort for that vicious gentleman. The information in the solid was that this woman had turned into a regular harpy since her husband's death in the Levaeri V incident. Understandable. But McCoy wasn't going to let it move him at the moment.

"Well?" he said stubbornly. "What about it? If you're subjecting me to the full rigors of the law, you'd better realize that it cuts both ways. Otherwise, why bother with this farce at all?"

The Praetor ignored him for a moment. "Disable those monitor cameras," she commanded, "and black out all transmissions on the public channel!" Once it was done and confirmed, Hloal turned her attention back to McCoy. Her smile was predatory. "Yes, indeed, Doctor. Why bother?"

"Let him talk, t'Illialhlae," called someone from the Senate benches. "It might be fun."

McCoy glanced at the woman who spoke. She was in uniform, her hair worn up in a braid and her face marred by a scar running from one ear to the corner of her mouth so that she smiled constantly on that side. *Eviess t'Tei*, the memory told him. *Senator, regional governor, noted duelist.* And someone whose suggestions aren't ignored more than once. For a few seconds Hloal matched stares with Eviess, while McCoy watched in fascination; then Eviess traced the length of that shocking scar with one fingertip and smiled sweetly, as if she remembered the original wound and reveled in the memory.

"If the House so desires . . . ?" asked Hloal abruptly. It was most interesting to see her back down in front of the entire assembly, trying all the while not to seem ruffled by her defeat. "All those in favor of the Right of Statement, so indicate." Most of the men and women in the chamber came to their feet, paused to check their number, and sat down again with an air of collective satisfaction. "Against?" Many fewer this time; McCoy spotted more "familiar" faces, most of them people he had been warned about.

"The proposal is carried by majority vote," said Hloal, speaking as if the admission tasted bad. "The Right of Statement is granted. Unbind him." She gazed at McCoy and he saw calm return slowly to her as she remembered that he was the loser no matter what small victory he won right now. "There is no time limit to the Right of Statement, Dr. McCoy; you may talk for as long as you like." Equanimity became amusement. "Indeed, you may talk for as long as you can. And when you are no longer able to talk, sentence will be carried out. It would be more dignified if you accepted the inevitable."

"I requested the Right," said McCoy stubbornly. "I stand by it."

"As you wish. The honorable members of the House may come and go as they please," she said clearly enough for the Praetors and Senators to hear, "but so far as you are concerned, there will be no recesses or meal breaks in this particular Senate session. And no, ah, relief breaks either. There you are, and there you stay. No matter what." Hloal smiled faintly. "So I suggest you make yourself comfortable. It will be a long, long, day."

McCoy knew what Hloal and the rest thought that they were seeing: a coward trying to hold on to his life for just a little longer. Maybe, their faces said, when the torturers came for him at last, they would have to drag him to the execution pits, pausing now and then to humorously pry his fingers free of whatever he had clung to in an attempt to slow his progress.

He smiled, and saw her eyebrows lift, for despite its grimness the smile had nothing of the usual false bravado about it. *The day's going to be longer than you think, dear. You've never heard a good ol' southern filibuster before. I hope your seat cushion's a soft one. . . .*

"Mak'khoi!" Eviess t'Tei was on her feet, looking

disturbingly enthusiastic. "With or without the option?"

"Option?" he echoed, not understanding her.

"Of single combat. To give you the chance of an honorable death."

"You presume, madam. What if *I* win?"

Eviess didn't actually laugh in his face, but there was a twitchy smile on her lips that suggested she was humoring him by even considering the possibility. "If you win, then you fight another representative of the court. And, if necessary, another. The end will be the same, sooner or later. But cleaner and less protracted."

"That," said a voice McCoy remembered without resorting to the data-solid, "depends on who your opponent is. Eviess t'Tei, I claim first fight."

"Subcommander Maiek tr'Annhwi," said t'Tei. "But then, who else? Your manners still need mending. . . ."

Of course tr'Annhwi was here. He wouldn't miss this trial—or the execution afterward—for all the wealth of the Two Worlds, and if there was any way in which he could make his presence more personally felt, he would do it. If McCoy let him. Except that playing d'Artagnan to the Subcommander's Jussac wasn't high on his list of Important Things to Do.

Instead, he smiled at tr'Annhwi and all the others, put one forearm across his stomach and the other across his back, and offered them a ludicrous dancing-school bow that impressed nobody and—as intended—affronted many. But at least they quieted down. It took a moment for the silence to suit him.

"Praetors, and ladies and gentlemen of the jury—wherever they are—unaccustomed as I am to public speaking, I should like to take this opportunity to thank all of you for your consideration in not wearying me with such unnecessary details as a fair trial. No matter that this is a common practice amongst civilized peoples —like the Klingons—" As the first uproar of the session echoed through the Senate Chamber, McCoy's smile

got even wider. He always had loved a good
audience. . . .

Arrhae listened first with disbelief at his audacity,
and then with slowly mounting admiration for the
man's stamina and invention.

He had talked about everything, beginning relevant-
ly enough with a discussion of the Romulan legal
system as it pertained to espionage and the preservation of fleeting military secrets, and then progressed
outward as though in concentric circles, touching briefly on war as an exercise in honor and then dwelling for a
considerable time on treachery as an entertainment, a
hobby, and an art form. Names were named, and
members of the Senate could be seen blushing and
shifting uncomfortably on their benches as certain of
their ancestors were used as examples of notably shady
behavior.

After that, McCoy's subjects had grown steadily
more diverse, and he had given each the attention it
deserved no matter how little it might have had to do
with the Right of Statement as laid down in legislation.
There had been the monologue—there was no other
word to describe it—on the correct preparation of
"Tex-Mex chili" ("whatever that is," Arrhae heard
from the Praetorate benches behind her), together with
a vituperative diatribe against those heretics ("ah,
religious schism . . .") who recommended the use of
beans ("whatever *they* are . . .") in the pot instead of
as fixin's on the side. ("'Fix' means to repair," said
someone sagely, "therefore this *t'shllei* is without doubt
a medication." "Why?" There was a pause for near-
audible thought while Arrhae fought down her giggles.
"Well"—conclusively—"he *is* a doctor—though Federation medical practice sounds a little primitive to
me. . . .")

Although none present could make the connection
between crude medicines and food, he then proceeded
to recall in impassioned detail the eating-houses of New

York Old City and the dishes served there. Shortly afterward a technician was summoned to adjust and retune the translator circuitry, but without success. At one stage it was throwing out three words in five as untranslatable or meaningless: neither *pii'tsa, blo'hnii,* or *t'su-hshi* had any comparable term in Rihannsu, and *fvhonn'du,* rather than a food, seemed an analogue of a torture technique—now fallen from favor—in which parts of the subject's body were immersed in heated oil. . . .

He was playing for time, of course—although what Naraht could do all by himself, she didn't know. McCoy probably did, but he hadn't had an opportunity to tell her yet, and by the sound of things, wouldn't have the time for hours yet. Then he coughed, cleared his throat, and coughed again, a harsh racking noise that sounded to Arrhae like a death rattle. She saw many of the Praetors and Senators who had been half-asleep with boredom jerk suddenly awake and lean forward like a pack of *thraiin* whose prey has faltered at long last. And as if in a dream she felt herself rise from the bench she had been assigned, lift water, ale, and a cup from the nearest of the many refreshment trays set about the chamber, and, greatly daring, take them to McCoy. . . .

Holding forth on the War Between the States—or the Late Great Unpleasantness, depending on company— was difficult enough when the listener was another southern gentleman, and downright awkward in the vicinity of a damn'Yankee, but during a Rihannsu Right of Statement it became well-nigh impossible. McCoy's throat was parched and gritty, and his entire jawbone hummed with feedback subharmonics. He had seldom been so glad to see a drink as when Arrhae held out the cup of neat ale to him, and didn't give her time to cut the vivid blue liquid with water before he gulped it down.

And spent the next few seconds wondering if the brain implant had gone into overload. After the first fine flurry of spluttering, gasping, and wiping his eyes, McCoy hem-hemmed experimentally to make sure that his gullet was still where he had felt it last—and then held out the cup for a refill.

"If you people ferried some of this across the Neutral Zone, you'd all be rich," he said. "Though personally I'd use it only for medicinal purposes. Rubbing on sprained joints, sterilizing instruments, taking the enamel off teeth. . . . That sort of thing. I can tell you, it wouldn't make a mint julep. For that you need Kentucky bourbon, and you need fresh mint—and you can't grow proper mint unless . . ."

And he was off again. Arrhae looked at him without smiling, wondering how long this could last before the voice tired.

What's he waiting for? she wondered. It all made no sense, not as a mere exhibition of bravado. Sooner or later his invention would run out. True, he was waiting for Naraht—but McCoy acted as if—

—*as if he really thought he was going to get out of here*— Off the planet. Out of the system. Home. To the Federation . . .

She heard his voice twice: once, here and now, raspy, saying something about bourbon and the size to which ice should be shaved, and how a glass should be properly chilled: once, clear, calm and a little tired, in her head. *I'm authorized to ask you this: when I'm pulled out, do you want to be pulled as well?*

Home?

Arrhae paled. Terise was staggered. Home . . .

But this is home! part of her cried . . . and the worst of it was, she couldn't tell which part.

Eight years here. Working, learning Rihannsu in all its subtlety, learning customs, reading, learning a people, its troubles and joys. She knew the Rihannsu now better than she had known any Earth people, and understood life here far better than she had understood life on Earth. *Who comes to their own life, after all,* she thought, *and studies it as if it were a strange thing, something completely alien to them? Perhaps more people should—*

But her problem wasn't what other people should do. McCoy's question hung fire in her mind, tantalizing her. She had never given him an answer.

Starfleet again. To give up constant fear, and drudgery—being *hru'hfe* was never easy—and to go back to freedom, the stars, other worlds, other people. To see how her old friends on Earth and Mars were doing. To bleed *red*.

She shuddered. Abruptly it seemed an odd color to bleed.

McCoy might be doing it right here, very shortly, if whatever he was planning didn't work out. And she didn't know how to help him.

You don't have to help me. Not yet.

She shuddered again.

I'm authorized to ask you this. . . .

Arrhae wished he had not.

And she felt a little tremor in the floor, as if someone had dropped something.

Arrhae looked around. No sound. No one had dropped anything, it had to have been her imagination. McCoy was going on at length about cocktail shakers.

The tremor repeated itself, more strongly this time. Arrhae glanced quickly from side to side, wondering if anyone else had noticed or if it was indeed just a trick of her overwrought mind. It had to be; all the members of the Senate and the Praetorate were settling back into their attitudes of boredom and McCoy was preaching the virtues of first melting the sugar for a julep in a little hot water.

But just as he began to describe how some of the mint leaves should be bruised and others left intact, he stopped talking. Hloal t'Illialhlae and Subcommander tr'Annhwi were on their feet almost simultaneously, grinning. And then the grins were wiped from both their faces as a crack appeared in the middle of the floor, right before the Empty Chair itself.

The crack widened with a small, crisp *snap* that echoed astonishingly in the silence that had filled the Senate Chamber. Then it exploded wide open with a hiss as of strong reagents and a nostril-tingling scent of acid, and a *thing* reared up out of the Earth to begin rumbling across the floor, leaving a track in its wake that was eroded into the very marble slabs themselves.

What happened to him? she thought, for Lieutenant Naraht was twice the size that he had been when Arrhae tripped over him only six days ago, and his rank-marked voder now looked like a badge rather than a piece of electronics. Whether Hortas had some sort of silicon-based late-adolescent growth spurt, or whether he'd just followed doctor's orders and indulged in a bit of feeding-up between H'daen's house and here, she didn't know. It was enough that he had arrived, and arrived in such a way as to create the maximum amount of confusion. There was plenty of it, what with normally staid persons of rank running about like *hlai* with their heads cut off, and screaming, and the air sharp with acid fumes, and the shouting of orders that no one heeded. . . .

Terise began to suspect that McCoy just might manage to pull this off after all.

For McCoy, it all made a most satisfying parallel to the scene on *Vega*'s bridge after her holds were blown open. A phaser whined shrilly, almost at his elbow, as one of the four guards drew his illegally carried sidearm and sent a bolt of disruptor-level energy crackling into Naraht's side. The Horta didn't even notice, but the Rihannsu guard did briefly, before McCoy shifted his stance on the podium and jabbed that so-convenient elbow backward into the man's throat. *One thing about being a medic,* he thought as he dived to scoop up the fallen phaser, *you know which parts to aim for.* Then thoughts of anything other than survival got pushed aside as more phaser fire ionized the acid-heavy air and blew the podium to jagged fragments. . . .

He was lucky; apart from that one attempt to dust him, they kept stubbornly shooting at Naraht despite the fact that it was clear they were wasting their time and ammunition-charges. But when a living Representative of the Elements moved among mortals, those mortals could scarcely be blamed for throwing rational behavior to the winds. Naraht wasn't being damaged, but he was angry, confronted with ludicrously imbalanced odds and doing whatever had to be done moment by moment, whether that meant barging about like a sentient tank, breaking things and people with the brisk efficiency he brought to everything. "Took you long enough to get here!" McCoy shouted at him across the room,

"Doctor," Naraht said, ramming a firing guard into the wall, "let's see *you* burrow through two hundred fifty-three miles of rock that fast."

"And another thing," McCoy shouted, "what happened to you? You're twice your size!"

Naraht laughed, a sound so bizarre that several Rihannsu who had been about to concentrate their fire on him broke and ran away. "You're the one who's always twitting me about needing to put on some weight! So I snacked on the way. Besides"—and the artificial voice got unusually cheerful—"the granite here is *very* good."

Several other people concentrated phaser fire on Naraht, three beams together. It must have stung: Naraht charged them. One of them did not get out of the way fast enough, holding his stance and firing. Then the man tried to scream and didn't finish it before Naraht lunged over him and left a shriveled, flattened, acid-eaten lump behind. Very few corpses looked as dead as those left by a Horta. . . .

McCoy took a chance to do some pouncing of his own, out from behind a sheltering bench that was neither high enough nor thick enough for his liking, to grab Arrhae by the arm and drag her under cover. She tried to wrench free, and lashed out at him before realizing who it was, which was just as well since it made her look just as he wanted, a hostage seized by an armed and desperate man. A hostage, moreover, who was *hru'hfe* of a House presently riding high in the favor of Imperial Intelligence. With his captured phaser pressed to the side of her head, it looked as though McCoy was uttering warnings and threats, and thanks to Naraht's rampage, no one was close enough to know any different.

"The ship's on its way down, Terise," he said, using her real name quietly despite the noise and violence only a score of feet away. "Not long now—then we can go home."

She twisted away from him, far enough to turn and see his face, almost far enough—McCoy dragged her back a bit—to put herself at risk again, and took a quick breath of the smoky, smelly air, and said, "You go. I'm staying."

He looked at her carefully. "You must have expected it, Bones," she said. "Surely you must. If I go home, I'm just another sociologist with her nose buried in a stack of books, more memories than some, but that's all. No family, no ties, nothing. Here—here I'm unique. I'm of some use. And I've grown used to ch'Rihan, used to the people and the customs, I . . . Oh, Elements, Bones, I *love* this place!"

He glanced away from her for several seconds. When he looked back, he was smiling slightly. "Do the job, Terise. Do the job and do it well." He took a moment to stick his head up and snap off two quick shots, then ducked behind the bench again, staring expectantly at the Senate Chamber ceiling. "We'll have to find another outside contact," he said. "There's no one to pass your reports through anymore."

"I'll work something out. A *hru'hfe* has a *little* pull." And she evidently had a thought, for her eyebrows went up in the Rihannsu version of a suppressed smile.

"Maybe in goods shipments," she said. "There *is* some clandestine trade across the Neutral Zone. You could order some ale. . . ."

"I already have," McCoy said, and laughed under his breath. "Listen. You take the phaser and make a break for it, I'll go after you and grab you. You throw me and go for Naraht. I have a confession to make—" He cocked an eye at her, feeling slightly sheepish. "I second-guessed you and told Naraht you'd probably want to stay. He won't hurt you too much. Keep your eyes closed. The acid is pretty strong up close when he's busy. Your people'll be convinced whose side you're on."

She took his hand, neither squeezing nor shaking it but simply holding it. "Leaving my adopted family would hurt more," she said softly.

"Prosper, then," McCoy said as quietly. "Stick with them. And if you can, if they'll listen . . . tell them that the rest of the family is waiting for them to come home and join the rest of us."

Arrhae nodded. Then her grip tightened and the balance of her crouch changed, and McCoy yelped as she bit him in the hand he was trying to keep over her mouth. The phaser was ripped out of his hand, and he was slammed sideways into the bench so hard his head spun. . . .

Arrhae ir-Mnaeha tr'Khellian broke free of her captor in the sight of many present, stole the phaser right out of his fingers, and fled before he could seize her again. If there had been more phasers in the chamber, or if she hadn't been so frightened that she forgot to use it, he could have easily been killed or struck down by a stun-charge so that the various penalties could have been executed after all. Instead, she ran from him and was attacked at once by the Earth-monster that had ravaged the Senate, injuring or killing many. Senators and Praetors, people of note and substance, saw Arrhae stand her ground as many of military Houses had not, and shoot her phaser at the monster while it bore down on her and brushed her aside as if she did not exist. . . .

Arrhae sprawled on the ground, gasping with the pain of a collarbone that had snapped like a stick when Naraht's fast-moving bulk had slammed into her braced shooting-arm. Her entire left side throbbed and tingled both with the impact and the heavy-sunburn sensation of mild acid burns. McCoy had been right, it did hurt. But she had been right too . . . and sometimes that fact could make a marvelous painkiller.

Home. Home by choice. At last.

Arrhae took that thought with her to the shadows. . . .

Someone was yelling for more guards—none of whom had yet answered the summons—and was adding demands for heavy weapons. *Come on, what are you waiting for?* he thought . . . and as if on cue, a fine plume of dust started spiraling down out of nowhere, adding its powdery texture to the cocktail of suspended solids in the air. Other plumes joined it quickly, and a wedge of stucco popped out of the frieze that ran between walls and ceiling proper.

Then the whole roof and ceiling structure shuddered as some vast weight settled on them, and moaned with intolerable anguish at the strain. It was a horrifying thing to hear a stone building seem to groan with pain, and inside the Senate Chamber all had become as quiet as when they saw the first crack in the floor. Someone went to the great double doors and pulled them open, looked out—and refused to cross the threshold. He turned very slowly and walked back to his place on the veto side of the House with his face the color of new cheese and his eyes seeming sunk back into his head. Only when he was seated again did he look his fellows in the face. "The building is ringed with soldiers," he said to all and none of them. "They are not Rihannsu. And there is a starship on the roof."

Nobody laughed.

A column of crimson sparkle came alive in the middle of the floor as somebody beamed in from the "starship on the roof," and still nobody spoke or moved. As the transporter-dazzle faded, McCoy got off the floor, dusted himself down, and endeavored without much success to put right the ravages of the past few minutes' activity. *The cavalry's arrived*, he thought. But he didn't say it aloud.

Ael i-Mhiessan t'Rllaillieu stood there surveying the Senate Chamber of Ra'tleihfi on ch'Rihan, and said nothing. She looked much as she had when McCoy had seen her last: a little, straight, slender woman who came about up to his collarbone, with long dark hair neatly braided and coiled around her head—a woman whose face looked fierce even when it was quiet, a lady whose eyes were always alert and intelligent, sometimes wicked, often merry.

Right now the eyes were very alert indeed, but not so merry. To McCoy she had the look of a woman briefly possessed by memories. She had a right to be. From what she had told him, the last time she had stood here she had seen her niece, the young "Romulan" Commander whom McCoy and Kirk had known, formally stripped of House-name and exiled. It had been a little death for everyone involved, McCoy thought. *And Rihannsu rarely leave death unavenged. She not only has them where she wants them, she has you there, too, Leonard, my boy. What if she decided on a whim to get rid of you as well? In her eyes, way back when, when we first met, you were as culpable for the Commander's trial and exile as Jim Kirk was.* . . .

He brushed the thought aside as a result of all this physical exertion. The tension of it made him a little paranoid sometimes. Ael was simply standing and looking around the place, not so much at people but at the building itself. Many of the ancient sigils hanging here and there now had blastholes in them, and the white marble of the place was all burn-scorched and spattered with the viridian of blood.

She moved at last. Her boots crunched on broken stone and other, grimmer remnants as she walked slowly forward, her eyes moving, always moving, from face to face, from floor to walls to ceiling. Their gaze rested a moment on the smashed body of one of McCoy's guards, a phaser still clutched in one hand even though the arm lay feet from where it should have been. "Weapons," she said softly. "Indeed." The silence in the room became profound. The holster at her own belt was conspicuously empty.

Ael picked her way carefully across the torn paving. *"Bloodwing* roosts on the roof," she said conversationally, "and her phasers have stunned all for a kilometer around this building. No use in waiting for your guards. Or for any small patrol-craft foolish enough to try anything. The phasers are no longer set to merely stun."

She came to a stand beside the Empty Chair, looking thoughtfully at what lay in it. "Poor thing," she said to the Sword. "For a millennium and a half no other weapon less noble has been permitted under this roof for any cause, not even for blood feud. Now they bring in blasters wholesale to guard one poor weak Terran. Or simply to terrify him for their pleasure."

People shifted where they stood. She ignored them, smiling a terrible smile at the Sword. "It seems nobility is gone from this place . . . among other things. The kept word . . . the paid debt. Honor."

"Traitress!" someone shouted. "You, to speak of honor!"

She turned slowly, and McCoy was glad the look in her eyes was not turned on him. "When I helped the Federation attack and destroy Levaeri V," she said clearly, "the only thing I betrayed was a government that would have used the technology being developed there to destroy the last nobilities and freedoms of the people it was sworn to guard. I would do the same again. Beware, for if you give me reason, I *shall* do so again. Only respect for this old place that S'task built keeps me from putting a photon torpedo into it to keep you all company." She grinned, and that wicked look was back. "I have always wondered how one of those would go off in atmosphere."

She turned again to the Chair. "This is no place for you," she said. The Sword lay there, a long silent curve of black metal sheath, black jade hilt, so perfectly made that there was no telling where one began and the other left off except for the slight difference in the quality of their sheen. Ael put out her hand and picked up the Sword by its sheath.

The silence that fell was profound. "You have sold honor for power," she said to the Senate and the Praetors. "You have sold what a Rihannsu used to be, to what a Klingon thinks a Rihannsu *ought* to. You have sold your names, you have sold everything that mattered about this world—the nobility, the striving to be something *right*—for the sake of being feared in nearby spaces. You have sold the open dealing of your noble ancestors for plots and intrigues that cannot stand the light of day, and sold your courage for expediency. Your foremothers would put their burned bones back together and come haunting you if they could. But they cannot. So I have."

She hefted the Sword in her hand. "I have come paying a debt, to show you how it is done . . . in case you have forgotten. And meanwhile, my worthies, I shall take the Sword, and if you want it back, well, perhaps you might ask your friends the Klingons to send a fleet to find me. Or perhaps they would laugh and show you how to truly run this Empire as they run theirs, by sending that fleet here instead. They half-own you as it is. You might still change that . . . but I see little chance of it. Cowardice is a habit hard to break. Still, I wish that you might . . . and I will gladly serve the Empire again, when it *is* an Empire again . . . the one our fathers and mothers of long ago crossed the night to build."

And Ael turned her back disdainfully on the entire Tricameron of the Romulan Empire, and looked at McCoy.

"Doctor," she said very calmly, as if they had met under more peaceful circumstances, "my business here is done. Are there other matters needing your attention, or shall we take our leave?"

"I'm done here," he said. "And so's Naraht."

"Ensign Rock—or Lieutenant now, I see." McCoy had a definite feeling that Ael was deliberately "not noticing" things unless they were of some importance to her at a given moment. Passing Naraht by unnoticed was all very well in a garden rock arrangement, but on what had been a flat, bare floor—and which was still reasonably clean, so far as skirmish sites went—he was hard to miss. "You've grown, sir."

Naraht shuffled and rumbled a bit before replying, the Hortan equivalent of a blush. "Madam," he said, "you are more beautiful than I remembered."

McCoy put an eyebrow up in mild surprise, then smiled slightly. "Must be the ears," he said to Ael. "His mother always did have a soft spot for them."

"Soft spot?" said Naraht. "*My* mother?"

Ael smiled, and bowed slightly to Naraht. "I make no judgment as to that," she said. "But as regards beauty, if that is your perception, may I remain so. May we all." She glanced back at the others in the chamber, and her amusement diluted somewhat as she flipped open a communicator. "In any case, I would as soon not overstay my welcome here, and I suspect I did that within the first second of my standing on the floor. *Bloodwing*, three to beam up. These coordinates. Energize. . . ."

Arrhae drifted in and out of consciousness as she lay on the floor, aching. She had seen moments of Ael t'Rllaillieu's visit to the Senate Chamber, but each of those moments had faded to black before anything of interest happened. She opened her eyes again just as Ael, McCoy, and Naraht dissolved in a whirl of transporter effect, and heard Ael's final words before the beam whisked words and speaker both away. *"Bloodwing* is the only ship of any size here, so we—"

As the darkness rose around her mind again, Arrhae thought she heard the chirp of another communicator opening, unless it was just a memory of the first. The voice that spoke into it was no more than a susurrant mumble, like waves on the seashore, and she wasn't able to concentrate on who it was or what they said. Her arm hurt, and she was so tired.

"Avenger, this is tr'Annhwi . . ."

So tired . . .

"Beam me up! Emergency alert . . . !"

So . . .

"Go to battle stations. . . ."

. . . tired . . .

Chapter Fifteen

McCoy HAD BEEN aboard a Rihannsu warship before, but that had been a Klingon-built *Akif*-class battlecruiser, and it had at least been roomy. *Bloodwing* was nothing of the sort. None of his kinesic-analysis studies of viewscreen recordings that showed Warbird bridges had prepared him for the reality of just how *cramped* the rest of the ship might be. Not that it caused him to stoop or anything so obvious; there was just a lot less free space than he was used to on the *Enterprise,* and if Naraht had indulged his appetite any further, the Horta would have been in real trouble.

He recognized familiar faces among the small group

waiting for them in the transporter room. With the implant running, they would have been as well known to him as the crew of the *Enterprise,* and even now their names came back like those of old friends: Khoal and Ejiul and T'maekh, big Dhiemn and little N'alae, and his fellow protoplaser-wielder, Chief Surgeon t'Hrienteh. She at least looked pleased to see him there, but the rest had eyes only for their Commander, and for what she carried cradled like a child in the crook of one arm. Not a one of them spoke as Ael stepped down from the transporter platform, looking for all the world like a queen—or the Ruling Queen herself.

"Now *there* is a tale for the evenings," said someone softly and reverently.

Ael smiled a bit and reversed the Sword so that its scabbard-chape grounded with a small, neat click against the deck. "A long tale for many evenings, my children. But not just now. Are the landing party up and safe?"

"All up, Commander," Ejiul said, checking a read-out for confirmation. "They came up by cargo elevator through the rear hangar-bay. Since we had landed, more or less, it was quicker than using the transporter."

"Excellent." Ael toggled the wall-mounted intercom and said, "Bridge, all secure. Lift ship."

"Vectors on line, up and running."

McCoy recognized the voice as that of Aidoann t'Khnialmnae, and wondered with a little shudder whether Nniol tr'AAnikh was aboard as well. There were thanks he had to make at second hand, and not waste too much time about doing it.

Then Aidoann's voice came back sounding more concerned than before. *"Commander, we have detected another beam-up from the Senate Chambers. This wasn't anything to do with us."*

"Tr'Annhwi," said McCoy to the air. He suddenly remembered that despite not wearing a weapon with his uniform—tr'Annhwi respected that tradition at least—the Subcommander had been wearing an equipment belt. That meant a communicator. And *that* meant he could get back to *Avenger,* which if its captain was on-planet, had to be in orbit waiting for him.

"You know one of House s'Annhwi, Doctor?" asked Ael as she made for the door and the turbolift beyond. "Then my compliments on the quality of your enemies."

If he had thought the transporter room was cramped, that was nothing to being inside a turbolift with a Rihannsu Commander and a noticeably oversized Horta. Getting out onto *Bloodwing*'s little bridge was almost a relief—though once Naraht rumbled after them, the situation became much as before. Nobody looked up to stare, even though the news of their arrival with the Sword had probably run through the ship in the few seconds that they were in the lift, and nobody moved from their seat while their commander was on the bridge. Or almost nobody.

None of Ael's people wore Rihannsu Fleet uniform now, even though they were still dressed in a distinctly military style, but the young man who kick-swiveled his station chair around and then left it in a single springy bounce wore neither Romulan nor makeshift. He was Terran-human, in a Federation Starfleet Command-gold shirt, and he was grinning as he reached out to shake the doctor's hand.

"Well, Dr. McCoy!" he said, shaking as vigorously as someone priming an old-style water pump, "I'm glad to see you're not dead yet!" And grinned even wider as McCoy gaped in confusion. This was an elaboration he hadn't expected. "Luks, sir. Ensign Ron Luks, of Starfleet Intelligence."

"Ah." Everything became suddenly clear. "So Admiral Perry sent you to hold the old man's hand. On the wrist, or off it?"

Luks stopping shaking hands and went a little pink.

Then he grinned again. "I acted as courier for the access codes on our side of the Neutral Zone, sir—and I *was* hoping to see some action," he said, "but so far it's just been a flitter-ride."

"A very long flitter-ride," said Ael, sitting down in her Command chair. "Or perhaps it only seemed that way. Starfleet's ensigns, Doctor, seem to vie with one another in the display of enthusiasm. But I think we've found the action that you wanted so badly. Tactical." Schematics came up on the main screen, showing their position near the surface of ch'Rihan and that of *Avenger* in a high geosynchronous orbit.

"This is more like it," said Ensign Luks, pointing at the screen. The blue triangle representing the frigate was underscored by a rapidly scrolling column of data, and McCoy suspected he knew what it meant.

Aidoann confirmed it. "*Avenger* was in orbital shutdown until a matter of seconds ago, Commander," she said, enhancing the image so that more information filled it. "They've just gone over to active status, while we are lifting clear . . . *now.*"

The ship jolted somewhat under McCoy's feet and the viewer image reformatted, putting the schematic display up into a screen window overlaid on an exterior scan of Ra'tleihfi as the city dropped away beneath them. There were several columns of smoke crawling skyward, last traces presumably of those patrol-craft Ael had mentioned so scornfully. For all that he had to admire the courage of anybody who would attack something the size of a Warbird with no more than a lightly armed atmosphere shuttle. It was very much more the traditional image of Romulan behavior than that which he had learned in the past days, and he wondered if it was typical because of the tradition, or traditional because it was a typical character trait. Whichever, it seemed entirely in accordance with the old custom of honorable suicide. . . .

Bloodwing's people began bustling about in the way

that McCoy had seen so many times on the *Enterprise*, with the same quiet determination—and the same pre-combat nerves that were more or less well hidden.

"This could be fun," said Luks, grinning again. McCoy snorted. He sat down at an empty station, closed the antiroll arms across his thighs in anticipation of a rough ride, and waited for the "fun" to start. Luks watched him for a second or two, then decided that there might be something to the precaution after all and followed suit.

"Power availability?" Ael said quietly.

"Minimal, Commander. Maneuvering on thrusters, no more. We can't use impulse power in atmosphere, and the lift tubes—"

"Noted—but hurry it up. Photon torpedoes?"

"Armed. All tubes charged and ready."

"Phaser banks . . . ?"

"Locked on target. Standing by."

"Shields?"

"Raised."

"Screens?"

"Maximum deflection."

"Bloodwing, this is Ael. Battle stations, battle stations. Secure for combat maneuvers. Success to you, and *mnhei'sahe.* Ael out." She turned around and gazed with dry amusement at Ensign Luks, who had followed everything with the expression of someone whose dreams were coming true. "This is the 'fun' part, Ensign," she said, lecturing him gently. "We are down here. *Avenger,* a more modern and more powerful ship, is up there, blocking our escape route. We must therefore dodge and feint until an opening presents itself, without getting blown up in the process, and without taking too long about it in case somebody recodes or overrides the defensive-satellite chain so that they'll be waiting for us too. Enough fun for you?"

Luks had gone a little pale during Ael's recitation, but he recovered fast. "You'll run?" he said, plainly not expecting such behavior from Rihannsu, even renegade ones.

"Of course. Starting now." Ael returned her attention to the tactical display, where *Avenger* was running at nominal capability. McCoy watched her, and saw irritation in every line of her body as she sat bolt-upright in her Command chair, refusing to make use of its comfortably padded back.

The two ships were engaged in a slow-motion race for viable in-atmosphere power, and the first to get it would win. Normally starships with a landing capability could ascend from or descend to their landing fields only out of parking orbit, but the maneuvering thrusters for attitude control in zero-G dock could be adapted from normal configuration. Ael seemed to be silently cursing herself for not having it done earlier—or perhaps for not firing on *Avenger* when she first had the chance.

Except that doing so was not the Romulan way. Or, at least, not Ael's way . . .

"Master Engineer tr'Keirianh, Commander: We have power . . . !"

McCoy saw Ael's left hand relax from its fist as *Bloodwing*'s Engineer made his jubilant report, then saw it clench tight an instant later as she looked at the screen and realized that *Avenger*'s Engineer was probably saying exactly the same words. The schematic flipped out to fill the screen again, and more figures began to flicker across it in pursuit of the tiny ship-silhouettes. Then *Bloodwing* jolted as if she had hit something—or something had hit her.

"Phaser fire, atmosphere attenuated." Aidoann, at the helm station, transferred the screen to visual again; below was a gray-green-brown blur of land, and above, in the gray sky, were the fading bluestreak traces of hard radiation sleeting from the track of *Avenger*'s phaser beams. "Returning fire—"

"No!" Ael was most decisive, and although a lesser

captain might in very truth have struck fist against seat arm, she allowed her voice to do that work. "Not until we reach space," she said. "I will not take that responsibility—"

This time *Bloodwing* bucked like a high-spirited horse with spurs struck into its flanks, and McCoy felt the familiar sensation of being pitched in three dimensions at once. For just one instant he thought that he could hear the thunderclap roar of some huge explosion, although that might have been the tinnitus brought on by the implant in his brain. Or he might indeed have heard the sound of a photon torpedo detonating in sound-bearing atmosphere.

"Tr'Annhwi's mad," said Ael flatly. "O Elements, to use a torpedo so close to ch'Rihan . . ." She glanced back at McCoy and Ensign Luks, spared a smile for Naraht, and tightened the smile to a ferocious grin. "Enough. If he was obeying the rules of war, it might be worthwhile to keep running, but he's thrown out the rules of common sense as well. Take us up!"

Bloodwing leaped for space with Aidoann and Hvaid performing a two-part chant of countdown before cutting in the impulse drive. It was a fine-spun line they traveled, for using impulse power in atmosphere would not only shatter windows over hundreds of hectares, it would probably cause widespread molecular disruption of the planet's ozone layer. That was the sort of thing which tr'Annhwi's casual use of heavy weapons might have caused already—there was no way to be certain, and only one sure way to stop it from happening again.

"Confirming: phasers locked. Firing."

Needles of fire spat from the Warbird as *Avenger*'s vulture shape swelled ever larger on the screen—superimposed now with gunnery and targeting data—and the long, lean, wide-winged shape vanished behind expanding globes of incandescent energy before slashing through them with her shields barely affected and delivering not one but a salvo of photon torpedoes straight at *Bloodwing*.

"Evasive," snapped Ael. It was already engaged, if speed of response was anything to go by, and McCoy felt the gravity grids flutter along a 3-G variant curve during the maneuver stresses, and then cut out completely for a long half-second when the volley of proximity-fused torpedoes exploded beneath and behind them, flinging out enough wild energy for the screen to black out completely as it filtered the glare. *Bloodwing*'s phasers opened up again as *Avenger* twisted past at .25*c* less than eight klicks away, an impossible point-blank full-deflection shot that still succeeded in bracketing the other ship.

Avenger flipped over, belly-up like a dead shark, and for an instant it seemed that she was beginning the long tumble that would end only when a scratch of brilliant light flared and faded across the Romulan night sky. Then she completed the roll and corrected the plunge planetward, skipping across the outer envelope of atmosphere with a flare of friction-heated particles dragging in her wake, opened momentarily to full impulse power, and came back at *Bloodwing* yet again.

"These damned Klingon gunnery augmentation circuits should be—" Ael said fiercely, and didn't bother completing the curse.

McCoy watched from his seat, listening and trying to remain as detached about this as he had been about the death sentence in the Senate Chamber. It was difficult; space battles, even this unfamiliar dogfighting at low impulse speeds, were situations in which familiarity did not breed contempt so much as terror. Evidently some Klingon-built improvement to *Bloodwing*'s phasers was proving ineffective against *Avenger*, a latest-generation warship built by those same Klingons.

For an instant the high-mag image of tr'Annhwi's ship ran head-on toward *Bloodwing*, wingtip phaser conduits glaring intolerably bright as they spat destructive energy. The screen became a Bosch vision of Hell seen through a stained-glass window in the nanosecond before it filtered down to impenetrable black, and

Bloodwing shuddered under the flail of sequential direct hits.

"Commander," said Aidoann calmly, "shields four and five are now reduced to sixty-five percent efficiency, and the progression curve indicates failure after three more strikes."

Ael nodded. "What about *Avenger*'s present status?"

"Sensors indicate a shift in energy consumption; they're channeling more power through the weapons systems. Shields are holding at . . . eighty percent of standard."

"Oh. I see. Typical of him. And in that Klingon scow too. Well, let's see it catch us when we go into warp and—"

A communicator whistle interrupted her. *"Engineering, this is tr'Keirianh. Can you give me seven standard minutes to put this mess back together?"*

Ael looked at the speaker/mike with an offended, betrayed expression, and McCoy looked at her. She was not a lady who liked her words suddenly made hollow before they were fully spoken, even by a Chief Engineer whose problems and requests sounded very familiar.

"Do what you can, Giellun," she said after a glance at the tactical repeaters, "but I can't promise you so much as seven seconds. . . ." And then she turned right around, as did McCoy, to stare at movement where right now no movement should have been.

Ensign Luks was standing by his chair, looking confident, eager, determined—and scared stiff. *Oh, God,* thought McCoy, *another space cadet!* "Sit down, son," he said aloud. "This isn't your affair any more than it's mine." Luks stayed where he was, and gave no sign of even having heard McCoy. All his attention was directed at Ael.

"If you need seven minutes, then you also need a diversion," he said. "Clear the cutter for takeoff."

There might have been surprise in Ael's mind, or confusion, or disbelief, or scorn. "You're going to die," she said matter-of-factly.

Luks shrugged at that, then grinned broadly. "Maybe—most everyone I know will too. But not right now. Not me. I'm the best you've got."

"Son," said McCoy, "did you take the *Kobayashi Maru* test?"

"Yeah, I did, sir." Another grin. "Tried it once, and didn't like it. It's such a downer."

"But worth remembering."

"Not for me—I like something a bit more cheerful. Catch you in ten minutes or so, Doc. You can buy me a drink." Luks grinned some more, until McCoy wondered whether some muscle rictus was at work. "But don't leave without me on that account."

He headed off with Hvaid, whistling some catchy tune or other that McCoy couldn't place. *Bloodwing* shuddered again, and orange warning lights began to flash on the ship's-schematic board. Evidently tr'Annhwi's scanner officer, that overly keen Subcenturion tr'Hwaehrai, had noticed the weakness in *Bloodwing*'s shields, because those last shots had hit fair and square on the damaged sectors and reduced them to barely forty percent effective.

"He's away!"

Bloodwing's screen flickered to a new image as Luks's cutter shot from the rearmost hangar-bay and darted straight at *Avenger* like a mouse attacking a lion. *Avenger* sheered off with enough violence to threaten her nacelle integrity, though whether it was because of the incongruity, or the unexpectedness, or the ferocious salvo of fire from the cutter's single phaser mounting—or because it was so very definitely a Federation cutter—nobody on *Bloodwing* knew.

Luks *was* the best, McCoy decided—or if he wasn't, he would do until the best arrived. He flung his little vessel about the combat area, raking *Avenger* with insignificant but probably infuriating blasts, and then disobligingly evading the response. And he was having fun, which was more than McCoy could say about his own part of the mission. *Well, that's what he wanted, isn't it?*

"Engineering, report. How go the repairs?" Despite her coolness while he was here, Ael watched Luks's gadfly attacks on the screen and nipped the tip of one finger between her teeth. Since the cutter was launched, *Bloodwing* had gone unscathed as her opponent concentrated planet-cracking firepower against a ship no bigger than one of its warpdrive nacelles. "Engineering . . . ?"

"Two more minutes—maybe less."

"One. That's all. This . . . performance . . . can't last much longer."

There was a silence at the other end of the channel, but it still had the unmistakable hiss of an open carrier. Ael stared at it, her finger poised over the recall button on her personal comm board. Then tr'Keirianh came back, coughing and breathless but sounding very pleased with himself.

"The mains are back on line, Commander. Up to warp four at your discretion."

"Not enough—but it'll have to do. Bring that young fool back in here and—" Her words stopped short when a phaser beam as thick as the cutter's hull clipped Luks's ship and split it open. "Oh, *no!*"

McCoy was on his feet, fingers gripping the padded arms of the station chair so tightly that they had sunk through the skinning and into the foam beneath, watching fragments of metal and plastic sparkle in the light of Eisn. *Avenger* cruised disdainfully through the cloud of glittering slivers, and swung with ominous deliberation back on *Bloodwing*'s trail. *He knew the risks.* That was the only coherent thought his mind could form right now, and it was totally inadequate for—

"Bloodwing . . . ?" Luks's voice was weak, and not just because of a poor transmission signal. McCoy had

heard too many mortally injured men not to recognize one now. "Bloodwing, *you still there . . . ?*"

"This is Ael, Ensign. Yes, we're still here. We shall use a tractor beam and—"

"*—and nothing! Get out of here before that . . .*" His voice trailed off and there was silence for so long that Ael leaned forward to cut the connection. *Avenger* was forgotten just for these few seconds. By *Bloodwing*'s people, anyway. Not by Luks. "*I'd as soon not . . . be their guest,*" he managed to say. "*And you folks deserve some peace. . . .*"

There was a click as he cut the connection, and everyone's eyes went to the main viewscreen, dominated by the predatory outline of tr'Annhwi's *Avenger.* The brief flash of an attitude thruster was noticeable only because it took place in the warship's shadow, but the consequence of Ensign Luks's decision was going to be enough to cast shadows of its own as far away as ch'Rihan.

His crippled cutter drove like a piloted torpedo straight into the nearest of *Avenger*'s nacelle pods and cracked it wide open, letting in space. The matter and antimatter of two warp-capable ships combined, uncontrolled. A blink later there was nothing but a single globular spasm of destruction as furiously radiant as a nova. It expanded, pure white light, impossible to look at. It would not fade for hours.

On board *Bloodwing* the main viewscreen swung away from the blinding light to the cool starfields that surrounded 128 Trianguli. Nobody said a word to McCoy for what felt to him like a very long time, until Ael touched her communicator gently. "Damage reports?" she said.

"*The shields took all of it—whatever* it *was, Commander.*"

"Good. Prepare for warpspeed. Aidoann, you know the course, through the Federation Neutral Zone, and . . . and he left his codes programmed into the navigator's station. Implement warp four on my command." Ael sat back and closed her eyes, looking very tired. When she opened them again, it was to gaze steadily at McCoy, who gazed as steadily back.

"Well," he said.

"Or ill. But his choice. Our peoples have more in common than either of them choose to see. You're the doctor. Tell me, how long to cure the blindness?"

"I don't have that answer for you, Ael," he said softly.

"I thought not. Too long for my lifetime, at least. Or if they listen to your little Arrhae, maybe not so long after all. Aidoann, Hvaid, warp four. Take us away home."

Epilogue

"THEY WILL BE convinced, Doctor," said Ael. "Rest assured of that. I saw what Lieutenant Rock left of two or three who stood up to him"—Naraht shuffled and rumbled, plainly not proud of himself—"and any who faced him with that knowledge in mind would surely be either heroic or insane. From what you say, Arrhae ir-Mnaeha is a most self-possessed young woman. She will have them dueling for the privilege of lacing up her sandals."

"Um." McCoy rolled neat ale around in a chunky crystal glass, staring at its color and feeling pretty blue himself. "I keep thinking about her. And about Luks . . ."

The postmortem on the day's events had run on long into ship's night, without really getting anywhere but back to the beginning again. Food had been prepared, toyed with, and nibbled at, but for the most part ignored in favor of wine and ale. Lots of both.

"He was all fire, that one," Ael said quietly, "they burn bright, and burn out. He knew what he did, and he did well. Leave him his brightness. The Elements did not mind doing so."

The Sword lay on Ael's side of the wardroom table, a reminder of events past and events yet to come, but more cutting even than the Sword's edge was another empty chair where Ensign Luks was meant to sit. "Turn down an empty glass," McCoy said, drained his, and did.

"Knowing *that* one, he would rather you filled it and drank," she said, "but you've done enough of that for any three Terrans. I think"—and she pulled the ale bottle and the winejug across the table and out of his reach—"that *these* belong where you can't get at them. This is not medical advice. This is the owner of the drinks-cabinet speaking."

Very, very slowly he began to smile. "You sound like my ex-wife," he said.

Ael considered that. "I'll assume you meant that as a compliment. Don't correct me if I'm wrong."

"Correct a lady? Never."

"At least not on her own ship. Come, then, enough of you, all Earth and tears . . . a walking mud puddle. We are all heroes here, and deserve to make ourselves better cheer. Tell me about Arrhae. Why did she stay behind? I confess to fascination, because given the chance to go home myself . . ."

He looked at her speculatively. "She wanted to stay with her family."

Ael made a Spock-eyebrow at him. "Indeed. How strange it is: we feel closer to the kin we adopt than to the ones we're born to. A perceptive young woman, I would say."

She sat back and looked at the Sword. "And you?" McCoy said. "Whom have *you* adopted lately?"

"Ah," Ael said. "The paid debt. I wondered when that would come up to be handled."

"But, Ael, you don't owe me anything. Or the Federation, or even Jim."

A slight smile tugged at her lips. "Jim. No, of course not. So much the more reason to pay the debt back. Or forward."

McCoy scowled. "Bloody *mnhei'sahe* again. Not even the implant does anything about that word."

Ael smiled. "Only people can do anything about it. And the day you understand it," she said, "that day our wars are done. Meantime . . . we must still translate for others. By actions, not words. I have an Empire to rehabilitate. You have your own worlds to save, I shouldn't wonder."

He looked at her and saw no mockery. He had none for her either. "All of them," he said.

She stood up and stretched. "A heroic goal, befitting a hero. But even heroes must start small. And for me, that means a ship to run. For you, a liter of ale to sleep off. Drink less next time . . . but dream well now. We're going home."

"Not to yours."

"Someday," she said from outside the door.

Arrhae i-Khellian t'Llhweiir stood in the dark silence of the garden and looked up at the aurora curtain hanging in the night sky. It was fading now—which was to say that it was no longer bright enough to be seen during daylight hours—but it still rippled and crackled wonderfully as it ran through its random color-shifts. Arrhae watched as the blue-green background glow became suffused with an astonishing chrome yellow shot with incandescent red, and the whole fragile structure seemed to billow like a drapery of finest silk. Scores of cameras had been pointed skyward and hundreds upon hundreds of recreational tapes had been made, regardless of what had been the cause of the phenomenon.

The public channels had claimed that brave and noble Fleet warships had brought the "pirate" vessel to battle just beyond ch'Rihan's atmosphere, demonstrating with many and various models, diagrams, and computer-simulated animations the manner in which it had been englobed and blown apart as it tried frantically to flee from the engagement. . . .

However, Senators knew differently.

It was probably unheard of in the long history of the Rihannsu for any House, no matter how noble, to be served both willingly and well by a *hru'hfe* with her own entirely independent House-name, much less one who held a seat in the Senate Chambers, though that was a nominal matter for the present, since the actual building was still closed for extensive reconstruction and, until another had been built, Arrhae could have held her assigned seat—or its fragments—in her two cupped hands.

The image of what that august body would have said and done had they known the true provenance of their latest member was one over which Arrhae preferred to draw a veil. . . .

Once the dust had settled and various outraged persons had been mollified by the execution, suicide, or banishment of various others, Arrhae had found herself a hero. And after her collarbone had been set, regenerated, and, most important, had stopped hurting, she began to enjoy herself. It was rare behavior nowadays, but in the past the elevation of a trusted servant to a position of nobility had been a common reward for services beyond that normally expected. In her case, someone had spent a long time rummaging through the records to find sufficient authority for her promotion to the Senate.

Then there had been the interview with Commander t'Radaik's replacement, which had become a sort of drunken picnic in the garden after the Intelligence officer had arrived at House Khellian with enough food and alcohol for the entire household and had begged time off for everyone. Arrhae remembered that quite fondly, because the man had been *very* handsome— and, more to the point, had gone away entirely satisfied that nobody here had known anything about the shocking debacle at the last espionage trial but one.

Khre'Riov or not, Intelligence or not, he hadn't found it easy to get by H'daen tr'Khellian, who had promoted himself to honorary uncle, father figure, and, for all Arrhae knew, representative agent. The reprehensible behavior of the late Subcommander tr'Annhwi had soured him against his old practice of cultivating any and all who seemed likely to be of use; and with a Senator working under his own roof, he no longer needed such doubtful patronage anyway.

When that Senator was also a hero who had the good fortune to be a beautiful young woman and unmarried besides, what H'daen was finding he did need was a stick to beat the suitors away from his front door. . . .

She looked up at the sky, at the aurora and at the stars beyond. . . . *If they'll listen . . . tell them that the rest of the family is waiting.* . . . "They're not ready to listen to *me*, Bones," Arrhae said softly to the night and the darkness. "Not just yet. But they'll be ready sooner than they think, and when they are, I'll be ready too. I . . . or my children."

She smiled at the notion, and because she had dared to say it aloud even to herself; then she turned from the stars and walked back into her House: her home.

Glossary

Translator's Note:

This glossary is not intended to be exhaustive, but rather merely a general guide to various terms of interest. In many places translations are approximate due to inadequate equivalents in the translating language.

aefvadh—"Be welcome."

aehallh—monster-ghost. An illusory creature: cognate to "nightmare" in Terran tradition, a creature that "rides" the dreamer to his perdition. Also, the "image" or illusion that one being has of another; as opposed to the true nature of the being in question.

Ael—proper name, fairly common on ch'Havran. "Winged." In other usage an adjective with connotations indicating a creature that moves quickly, gives one little time to make out details.

afw'ein—reason, as in use of one's faculties, rather than as the "excuse" one contrives to explain one's behavior.

Aidoann—proper name, uncommon. "Moon."

aihai—plains, plain country. Flatlands: cognomen "prairie."

aihr—"this is." Indicative noun prefix or infix.

Arrhae—proper name, der. "arrhe", q.v.

arrhe—worth-in-cash. Originally derogatory (a servant who performed the duties of slaves below his/her rank; modified to be "a servant more worthy of higher position than those awarded it").

au'e—"Oh yes." (Emphatic form "oh *yes!*")

auethn—advise me—answer a query.

ch'Havran—(planet) "of the Travelers."

ch'Havranha, ch'Havranssu—native(s) of the planet.

ch'Rihan—(planet) "of the Declared."

daise—prefix; chief, principal, senior, foremost (etc.).

daisemi'in—chief among several (choices, candidates).

deihu—"elder"; a member of the Senate; regarded as an equivalent to the Terran "Senator": cf. Latin "senex."

Eisn—"homesun." The G9 star 128 Trianguli.

Eitreih'hveinn—the Farmers' Festival.

enarrain—senior centurion; colonel of infantry, commodore of Fleet forces. Minimum rank at which the officer may command more than his own vessel.

erei'riov—subcommander; captain of infantry, lieutenant-commander of Fleet—usual rank for a First Officer.

erein—antecenturion/subcenturion (translation sources vary); officer-cadet of infantry, ensign of Fleet forces.

fvai, fvaiin—child's riding-beast and house-pet (in larger houses) analogous to the Terran Oligocene-period *Mesohippus* in size—that of the Holocene-period *C. familiaris inostranzewi* (Great Dane)—though only approximate appearance.

fvillha—Rihannsu analogue to Terran "praetor": originally a judicial-level official with some executive powers (now much expanded). Cf. *fvillhaih*, "Praetorate."

galae—fleet; most specifically, space-fleet, since the battles of Rihannsu history were principally land-based. However, there was a later, enthusiastic adoption of massed airpower in both the offensive and defensive modes, and it is here, rather than in naval tradition, that the term has its origins.

haerh, haerht—cargo space, cargo hold.

haudet'—fr. *haud,* writing, and *etrehh,* machine. Computer printout: sometimes, screen dump as well. Cf. *hnhaudr,* "data transfer": direct protocol transfer from one computer to another.

Hellguard—872 Trianguli V, a failed colony planet hastily and incompletely evacuated after "the Second Federation Encroachment."

hfai, hfehan—bond-servant; one earning a wage but without the liberty of changing employers at will.

hfihar, hfihrnn—House(s); noble families, not dwellings.

hlai, hlaiin—large flightless birds farmed for their meat; similar to the Terran ostrich, *Struthio camelus.* The very largest ones are also sometimes tamed for children to ride. This, however, renders their meat unusable.

hlai'hwy, hlai'vna—"held" and "loose" *hlai;* domesticated and wild (game) birds.

hna'h—activation-imperative suffix: e.g. "Fire!" "Energize!" "Go!"

hnafirh—"see," but not an active verb: passive with an implication that someone else must cooperate in the act by imparting or sharing information. Cf. *hnafirh'rau,* "Let me/us see it."

hnafiv—"hear," as above: *hnavif'rau,* "let me/us hear it."

hnoiyika, hnoiyikar—predator, similar to the Terran weasel *mustela frenata*—but 4 feet long, excluding tail, and 3 feet tall at the shoulder. Notorious for their vicious habits and insatiable appetites.

hrrau—at/on/in: a general locative particle or infix.

hru'hfe—Head-of-Household. The senior servant among domestic staff, appointed as overseer and servants' manager.

hru'hfirh—Head-of-House, euph. "The Lord." Most senior member of a noble family.

h'ta-fvau—"To last-place, immediate-return!" (Come back here!)

hteij—transporter, transmat. Not considered as a reliable form of travel, most of the time (possibly understandable, considering that the technology is purchased second-hand from the Klingons).

hwaveyiir—"command-executive center"; the flight bridge of a ship, as opposed to the combat-control area. (See *oira*.)

hwiiy—"You are": sometimes imperative.

ie'yyak-hnah—"Fire phasers!"

iehyyak—"multiple" rather than "several" phasers, especially in reference to shipboard phaser-banks.

khellian—arch. "hunter"; also the name of a minor Praetorial house.

khoi—"switch off," "cease," "finish."

khre'riov—commander-general; equivalent to a colonel of infantry or a commodore of Fleet forces.

kllhe—the annelid worm, introduced to domestic *hlai*-pens, which ingests the acidic dung and thus processes it to usable fertilizer. Also an insult.

kll'inghann—the Klingon people. (However, see *lloannen'mhrahel*.)

Levaeri V—fifth planet of the Levaeri system (identified with 113 Tri): site of an orbital station at which various biological researches were conducted until the destruction of the base by Federation forces and the renegade ship *Bloodwing*.

lhhei—"Madam."

llaekh-ae'rl—"laughing-murder"; the practice or *kata* forms of a common Rihannsu unarmed combat technique. Provenance of the name is uncertain.

llhrei'sian—diarrhea as a result of mild food-poisoning; a term exactly equivalent to "the runs," "the Titanian two-step," "the (any number of edible objects) revenge."

llilla'hu—that will do, "that's just enough": barely adequate, sufficient.

lloann'mhrahel—the United Federation of Planets; however, the word translates most accurately as "Them, from There" (as opposed to "Us, from Here"). The Klingons, once encountered, were promptly named *khell'oann-mhehorael* (More of Them, from Somewhere Else).

lloann'na—catchall title for a UFP member, translating exactly as "a/the Fed."

lloannen'galae—Federation fleet, battlegroup, task force; the word has aggressive connotations which do not differentiate between warships and unarmed civilian vessels, but then the Rihannsu have seldom seen the need to regard other ships than theirs as other than potential enemies.

mnek'nra, mnekha—"well, good, correct, satisfactory." Inferior-superior and superior-inferior modes, respectively.

mnhei'sahe—the Ruling Passion: a concept or concept-complex which rules most of Rihannsu life in terms of honor. *Mnhei'sahe* is primarily occupied with courtesy to the people around one: this courtesy, depending on circumstances, may require killing a person to do him honor, or severely disadvantaging oneself on his behalf. There are many ramifications too involved to go into, but generally *mnhei'sahe* is satisfied if all the parties to an agreement or situation feel that their "face" or honor is intact after a social (or other) transaction. NB: The concept has occasionally been mistranslated as implying that a given action is done "for another person's good." This is incorrect: such a concept literally does not exist in Rihannsu. One does things for one's own good—or rather, the good of one's honor—and if properly carried out, the actions in question will have benefited the other parties in the transaction as well.

nei'rrh—small birds, similar in size and flight characteristics to the Terran hummingbirds (fam. Trochilidae), with a poison-secreting spur on the upper mandible of the beak. Also an insult, referring to a person annoying or dangerous out of all proportion to their size, status, or (usually) worth.

neth . . . nah'lai—either . . . or.

nuhirrien—"look-toward"; the quality of charisma or mass attractiveness.

oal'lhlih—"announce the presence/the arrival."

oira—"battle-control"; aboard Warbird-class and smaller ships this is the same bridge-deck (see *hwaveyiir*) as the standard flight-control area, although rigged for combat; but on the larger, Klingon-built *Akif* and *K't'inga*-class vessels the word refers to a separate, heavily armored area deep in the command prow.

qiuu, qiuu'n (oaii)—all, everything, "the lot."

Ra'kholh—Avenger. A popular ship-name in the Rihannsu Fleet.

rekkhai—"sir"; inferior-superior high-phase mode.

rha, rh'e—"indeed," "is that so" (colloq. vulg. "oh yeah?").

rrh-thanai—hostage-fostering. Sometimes the making of peace by the exchange of children, each to be brought up in the other's tradition to further understanding and harmony; sometimes the exchange is to simply provide leverage and a surety of good behavior: "Don't do this, or your son/daughter will die." Fosterings often start in one context and wind up in another.

S'harien—lit. "pierceblood"; the name, in Old Vulcan, chosen by pre-Sundering Vulcan's most famous swordsmith as a reaction against the teachings of Surak: the name was also given to his swords.

siuren—"minutes"; or at least, the Rihannsu equivalent, actually equal to 50.5 seconds.

sseikea—a scavenger, analogous to the Terran hyena *Crocuta crocuta* and employed as an insult in the same way.

ssuaj-ha—"Understood!" (Inferior-superior mode.)

ssuej-d'ifv—"Do you understand?" (Superior-inferior mode.)

sthea'hwill—"I request (an action) be done at once." (Superior-inferior, courteous mode.)

ta krenn—"Look here, look at this."

ta'khoi—"Screen off." Usage for voice-activation equipment and (if used to another person) very explicit superiority.

ta'rhae—"Screen on." (See above.)

th'ann, th'ann-a—"a/the prisoner."

thrai, thraiin—predator, analogous to the Terran wolverine *Gulo luscus;* and possessed of similar legendary traits for persistence, vengeful stubbornness, and ferocity.

tlhei—"my word"; occasionally as in "my (given) Word" but more usually "my command/order/bidding."

urru—"go to . . ." A non-mode imperative, which (if circumstances permit) can be used from low to high as well as the more usual vice versa.

vaed'rae—"Hear me/attend me." More imperative than "listen," and more formal.

vah-udt—"What rank?" "Who are you (to be asking/doing this)?"

vriha—highest, most superior.

yhfi-ss'ue—"travel-tubes"; the public transport system, of five rail-mounted cars, powered by electromagnetic linear motors, carrying 20 persons in an enclosed weatherproof tube.

THE

STAR TREK
PHENOMENON

Hands shaking, Mia sprayed the water vigorously, but there was simply not enough flow to combat the hungry fire.

She retreated to the front porch, skin stinging from the poisonous air.

Dallas appeared at the upstairs window. He shouted something to Mia, but she could not understand. The fire was nearly upon her, heat scalded her face and hands, smoke filling her lungs. She backed farther away, praying the fire engine would arrive soon to douse the flames.

Finally, Dallas came out carrying Cora and led her away from the burning house.

Mia put her mouth to the woman's cheek, praying for a reassuring puff of air. Panic swirled through her veins as she felt nothing at all. Starting CPR, she pressed her hands to Cora's chest.

"Come on, Cora," she said. "You're not going to leave me now."

Dallas dropped to his knees and performed the rescue breaths at the end of her compression cycles. After a full minute, Dallas checked her pulse.

He shook his head.

Tears trickled down Mia's cheeks as she began the next cycle.

Books by Dana Mentink

Love Inspired Suspense

  Killer Cargo
  Flashover
  Race to Rescue
  Endless Night
  Betrayal in the Badlands
  Turbulence
  Buried Truth
  Escape from the Badlands
  Lost Legacy
  Dangerous Melody
  Final Resort
  †*Shock Wave*
  †*Force of Nature*
  Race for the Gold
  †*Flood Zone*

  *Treasure Seekers
  †Stormswept

DANA MENTINK

is an award-winning author of Christian fiction. Her novel *Betrayal in the Badlands* won a 2010 RT Reviewer's Choice Award, and she was pleased to win the 2013 Carol Award for *Lost Legacy*. She has authored more than a dozen Love Inspired Suspense novels. Dana loves feedback from her readers. Contact her via her website at www.danamentink.com.

FLOOD ZONE
DANA MENTINK

⟨H⟩ HARLEQUIN® LOVE INSPIRED® SUSPENSE

Recycling programs
for this product may
not exist in your area.

™ LOVE INSPIRED BOOKS

ISBN-13: 978-0-373-67619-4

FLOOD ZONE

Copyright © 2014 by Dana Mentink

www.Harlequin.com

Printed in U.S.A.

Trust in the Lord with all your heart;
do not depend on your own understanding.
Seek his will in all you do,
and he will show you which path to take.
—*Proverbs* 3:5–6

To my Mike,
who is always there through the floods.

ONE

Forget meeting tonight. Must speak to you and Dallas now. URGENT.

Mia risked another peek at the cell phone screen as she guided her battered Toyota up the steep mountain grade to Cora's country house just after six in the evening. She'd thought Cora's proposed after-hours meeting at the medical clinic where they both worked was odd in the first place. Now the message to cancel. Stranger still. But Cora had been acting oddly, excusing herself to take phone calls, peeping into file folders squirreled away in her desk for weeks. On this particular day, Cora had left at lunch time. Strange.

Her gaze darted to the rearview mirror. Dallas Black drove his truck behind her. Something about the tall, tousle-headed rebel made her stomach flip, no matter how sternly she chided herself.

Look what the last dark-eyed charmer did to you, Mia.

Stuffing that uncomfortable thought back down into the secret place where she kept all her worries, Mia focused on navigating the winding, wet road, finally pulling onto Cora's graveled drive. Dallas got out, long and lean in jeans and a T-shirt, a couple of months overdue for a haircut. Somehow, the hair spidering across his face suited him, refusing to play nicely.

She knew he'd finished patching Cora's roof only the day before, while on break from teaching Search and Rescue classes. He'd been there every weekend for the past month or two working when the rain let up. While Dallas banged on the roof, Mia and her young daughter, Gracie, helped Cora organize closets. Cora insisted the little group take a long dinner break together every evening during which even Juno, Dallas's German Shepherd, got his share of fragrant stew. What Dallas got out of the deal, besides some pocket change and women chatter, she had no clue. Surely, he didn't need the money that badly. *Maybe he's just a nice guy, Mia. Maybe,* her suspicious heart echoed mockingly. *Yeah, and maybe you were happy to see him every weekend just to admire his roofing skills.* Never mind. They were almost done organizing closets, and then she could put Dallas safely out of her thoughts.

The residence was at the back of a large property, a good acre of shrubland screened it from the road. It was cool, the May rain puddling the already saturated ground. It was to be a bad storm season in Colorado, talk of floods coming. It made her long for Florida's mild climate, but she'd never return there. *Ever.*

Juno hopped out, nose twitching.

"Stay out of the mud, dog," Dallas advised.

Mia joined him.

"Ideas regarding what Cora needs to talk about?" he asked.

"No." Mia shook her head. "She's been secretive lately, spending extra hours at the clinic. I almost got the feeling she might be lying to me about something."

They looked at Juno who had busied himself snuffling through the underbrush until he froze. Mia thought at first that he'd caught the scent of a bird or groundhog. Then she got it, too. The acrid tang of smoke as she took a few steps toward the house.

Dallas sprinted up the drive with Mia right behind him. They cleared the thickly clustered cottonwood trees in time to hear the whoosh of breaking glass when the lower story window exploded. Mia nearly skidded into him as the shards rained down on the muddy ground.

Her mind struggled to process what was happening. He gripped her arms, and she saw the tiny reflected flames burning in his chocolate irises. "Call for help. Keep Juno out."

Mia's hands shook so badly she could barely

manage to hold on to both the phone and Juno's collar. The dog was barking furiously, yanking against her restraining arm in an effort to get to his owner. Nearly eighty pounds of muscle, Juno was determined, and he definitely did not see her as the boss.

Frantically, she dialed the emergency number. Tears started in her eyes as she realized she was not getting a signal. The tall Colorado mountain peaks in the distance interfered. She would have to move and see if she could find another spot that would work. Dragging Juno with one hand, she made her way back toward the car. They'd only gotten about ten feet when Juno broke loose from her grasp and ran straight for the burning house.

"Juno, stop!" she yelled. The smoke was now roiling through the downstairs, and she'd lost sight of Dallas. There was no choice but to keep trying to find a place to make the call. Three times she tried before she got a signal.

"Please help," she rasped. "Cora Graham's house on Stick Pine Road is on fire."

The dispatcher gave her a fifteen minute ETA.

Her heart sank. They could both be dead in fifteen minutes. She stowed the phone in her pocket and ran to the front porch where she remembered there was a hose Cora used to water her patches of brilliant snapdragons. The wood of the old house crackled violently, letting loose with a spark every now and then that burned little holes through the fabric of her jacket. One started to smolder, and she slapped a hand to snuff it out. Flames flashed out the first-floor windows. Juno barked furiously, dashing in helpless fits and starts, unsure how to get to his master.

She cranked the hose and squirted the water at the open front door. *Where are you, Dallas?* Inside, the flames had spread through the sitting room, enveloping the oak furniture in crackling orange and yellow. She climbed up the porch steps, dousing the wood with water and forcing her way into the entry, past the spurts of flame.

She sprayed the water vigorously, but there was simply not enough flow to combat the hungry fire. She retreated to the front porch, skin stinging from the poisonous air.

Dallas appeared at the upstairs window. He shouted something to Mia, but she could not understand. The fire was nearly upon her, heat scalded her face and hands, smoke filling her lungs. She backed farther away, praying the fire engine would arrive soon to douse the flames.

There was no welcoming wail of sirens.

She scanned the upper story and once again caught sight of Dallas. He was batting at the flaming curtains with a blanket. She saw a way she could help. Climbing a few feet up an ivy-covered trellis allowed her to stretch the hose far enough that she could train the water on the burning fabric. Dallas jerked in surprise and then disappeared back inside, returning a moment later with Cora in his arms and stepping onto the roof. Mia's heart lodged in her throat as she watched Dallas walking on the precariously pitched shingles with his precious burden.

His feet skidded, and he fell on his back, somehow stopping his slide before he fell over the edge. Mia jumped off the trellis and cast the hose aside. "Here, lower her down to me."

It was an awkward process, but Dallas managed to ease Cora low enough that Mia could grab her around the waist. Staggering under the weight, she tottered backwards until Dallas jumped down and they both carried Cora away from the burning house. Juno raced behind them to a flat spot of grass where they laid the old woman. Dallas ordered the dog to stay.

Mia brushed sooty hair away from Cora's forehead. Her sparkling blue eyes were closed, her mouth, slack. She put her cheek to Cora's mouth, praying for a reassuring puff of air. Panic swirled through her veins as she felt nothing at all. Starting CPR, she pressed her hands to Cora's chest.

"Come on, Cora," she said. "You're not going to leave me now."

Dallas dropped to his knees and performed the rescue breaths at the end of her compression cycles. After a full minute, Dallas checked her pulse.

He shook his head.

Tears trickled down Mia's cheeks as she began the next cycle. "You haven't finished learning Italian," she said to Cora. "You're only on lesson three, and that's not going to be enough if you want to go to Rome." Another set of compressions and rescue breaths.

This time she didn't allow herself to look at Dallas. Cora was going to live. Shoulders aching she pressed with renewed vigor. "And your nephew is happily married in Seattle. He's not going to want to come and take care of this sprawling old place, isn't that what you always said, Cora?"

Sirens pierced the air and a fire truck appeared through the smoke, rumbling up the grade, followed by an ambulance. Mia did not slow her efforts.

"You wake up right now, do you hear me? I mean it. I told you over and over not to keep those silly scented candles in your bedroom. They did not keep away the mosquitos, no matter what you say. You wake up so I can chew you out properly." Tears dripped from her face and cleared spots of black from Cora's forehead.

The medics ran over, but stopped short when Juno barked at them until Dallas quieted him. They pushed forward, eyeing the big dog suspiciously, and edged Mia out of the way.

"I have to stay with her," she pleaded.

Dallas drew her back, his voice oddly soft. "They've got it, Mia. Let them work."

"But…"

He gently, but firmly, took her arm and moved her several yards distant from the paramedics.

She breathed in and out, forcing herself to stop crying. "I'm okay, I'm okay," she repeated, waving him away when he came close.

Dallas stood there, long muscled arms black with soot, the edges of his hair singed at the tips, looking at her until she couldn't stand it anymore. "What is it? What are you thinking?"

Dallas didn't answer.

"Please tell me." She moved closer, the dark pools of his eyes not giving away anything.

Dallas considered. "I wasn't sure what type of service dog Juno would be. Before I trained him in Search and Rescue, a buddy of mine had a go at making him a drug-sniffing dog, but Juno doesn't obey anyone but me, so he flunked out. Mastered only the first lesson."

"What are you saying?"

He pulled a plastic pill bottle from his pocket. "These were on the bedside table. Do you know what she takes them for?"

Mia took the bottle and held it up to the light from the engines. "It's her blood pressure medication. I pick up her prescriptions myself."

Dallas frowned.

Mia felt the seeds of dread take hold deep down.

She put her hands on Dallas's unyielding chest. "Dallas, please tell me what you're thinking."

"The first lesson, the only one that Juno mastered…"

She found she was holding her breath as he finished.

"Was alerting on drugs…like cocaine."

Dallas mentally berated himself for mentioning Juno's behavior at that moment. Mia was already trembling as the shock of what had happened settled in.

Should've waited. How many times had he said that to himself?

This time he did not allow her to pull away when he folded her in a smoky embrace. She was so small, so slight in his arms, and he resisted the urge to run his hands along her shoulders. He thought of all the things he should say, the comforts he could whisper in her ear, but everything fled, driven away by the feel of her. She stiffened suddenly, and he wondered if she'd been hurt in the fire.

"There," Mia gasped, pointing behind the house.

He turned in time to see a woman with a wild tangle of red hair framed by the trees that backed the property. She stood frozen for a moment, eyes wide and face soot-stained and then she bolted into the woods.

"Stop," Dallas called, and he and Juno took off into the trees, Mia stumbling along behind.

"Who was that?" she asked, panting.

He didn't know.

"I thought I saw her outside the clinic one time, talking to Cora, but I'm not sure," Mia said.

A cursory search yielded nothing, though the falling rain and smoke didn't help. After a short time, they left off looking to follow the ambulance to the hospital.

In the waiting room, Mia sat on a hard-backed chair, and Dallas paced as much as the narrow hallway would allow until the doctor delivered his news. "I'm sorry. She didn't make it."

Dallas watched the spirit leak out of Mia as she put her head in her hands. Something cut at him, something deeper than the grief at Cora's death. He swallowed hard and stepped aside with the doctor. "Do you have a cause of death?"

The physician, whose name tag read Dr. Carp, hesitated. "She was dead upon arrival, but we called the police immediately after you told us about the pills. They took possession of them. Autopsy will be later this week." That much Dallas already knew as he and Mia had told their story to a young uniformed cop named Brownley.

The doctor left and Dallas sat next to Mia. He didn't speak. There was nothing to say anyway. Best to wait until she could articulate the thoughts that rolled across her face like wind sweeping through grass. Finally, he took her hand, hoping she would not yank it away. She didn't.

"Cora wanted to tell us something, something important," Mia said, her voice wobbling as she clutched his fingers. "Can you guess anything at all about what it was?"

Dallas shook his head. "No."

"I'm sure Juno was wrong about the pills," she said, a tiny pleading note to her voice. "Those were for her blood pressure. I delivered them to her myself. They couldn't have hurt her. Could they?"

He covered her hand with his palm. "Whatever this is, however it went down, was not your fault."

"That woman... Who was she?" Her brown eyes were haunted. "Dallas..." she whispered. "I'm scared."

He pulled her to her feet then and embraced her because he did not know the words to say. He never did, probably never would. "I'm taking you home."

A short, balding man with a thick, silvered mustache came close. "In a minute. I'm Detective Stiving, Ms. Verde, and I need to ask you some questions."

Dallas felt his gut tighten. Stiving. Perfect.

He and Stiving had been oil and water since Dallas had butted in on a missing-person's case and found a teen lost near Rockglen Creek whom Stiving had insisted was a runaway.

"Kid's a loose cannon," Stiving had insisted. "Drinks and parties like his father."

Runaway or lost, Dallas and Juno found the kid named Farley who'd fallen into a ravine, and the press was there to catch it. Since then, Dallas had gotten a bogus speeding ticket and been stopped twice by Stiving for no particular reason. Not good, but in a small town like Spanish Canyon, Stiving was it.

"Doc says you're making allegations about drugs," Stiving said, holding up the bottle of pills nestled in an evidence bag. "Looking to get some more publicity for yourself?"

"Juno alerted on that pill bottle."

"Juno is a drug-sniffing flunk-out, from what I've heard. I thought his forte was tracking down idiots who get lost in the woods."

Mia wiped her sleeve across her cheeks. "What kind of talk is that for a law enforcement officer?" she said indignantly. "Cora is…was a long-time resident of this town. I should think you'd want to be thorough investigating her death."

His blue eyes narrowed, face blotching with color. "Yes, Ms. Verde, I will. I started by running a check on you. It made for interesting reading. Since you've had such a long and storied history with law enforcement, I guess you'd know that I'll be contacting you for follow up information as soon as I get this to the lab."

Mia went white and then red.

Dallas clenched his jaw. *Don't mouth off to the cops, Dallas.* "We saw a woman with red hair running away from the house."

Stiving blinked. "Really? Did you recognize her?"

Mia shook her head. "She might have come to the clinic to talk to Cora, but I'm not sure. I only saw her for a moment."

"And you?"

Dallas shrugged.

"Right. Well, we'll investigate that while we're checking into things." The detective's phone rang, and he walked away to answer it and then left abruptly.

Mia put a hand on Dallas's wrist, her fingers ice cold. "I have to go. Tina needs to get home, and I want to read Gracie a story before bed." She looked at her soiled clothes. "It will take some explaining about why I look like this." Her lip trembled. "I'll need to tell Gracie about Cora."

He wondered how a woman with filthy hair, torn clothes and a grief-stained face could look so beautiful, like Whistler's painting of the woman in white he'd seen in his mother's art books decades ago. Would she be so trusting if she knew the truth about what brought him to town? Dallas had been many things in his life, a gang member, a wanderer and a drinker. He'd never been a liar, not until now, with her. It tightened something deep in his gut.

He had to remind himself he had good reasons for the subterfuge.

He'd been hired by Antonia, Mia's sister, to keep watch over her due to the prevalence of Mia's ex-husband Hector Sandoval's many enemies. Cora, a friend of Antonia's new husband, was in on the whole thing. An accomplice, he thought ruefully, who'd arranged for Dallas to hang out on her property just as often as the stubborn and ferociously independent Mia did.

He returned to the truck where Juno was sound asleep and waited until Mia got into her car. Following her home, he ran things over in his mind. Cora was obviously disturbed when she messaged both Dallas and Mia. How coincidental was it that her house burned down and she lost her life on the very same night Mia spotted some mystery woman fleeing the scene? Very coincidental, and Dallas Black did not believe in coincidence any more than he believed that Elvis still strolled planet Earth.

He walked Mia to her front door and waited while she stepped into the tiny front room.

Four-year-old Gracie came flying down the hall, short bob of hair bouncing around her, eyes alight with pleasure at the sight of him. They'd encountered each other many times at Cora's house while he was on the roof and she was digging holes around the property. When rain interrupted the roofing, they built card houses together, impressed with their creations until Juno knocked them over with a jerk of his tail.

"Did you come to play?" She took in his appearance and laughed. "You need a shower, Mr. Dallas."

He laughed, too, and Mia tried to draw Gracie away.

"Can he come in for a snack?" the child asked. "I've got Goldfish."

Dallas got down on one knee. "You eat goldfish? Don't the fins get stuck in your teeth?"

She giggled. "They're cracker fish. Juno will like them."

"Juno can't have Goldfish tonight, but we'll come another time."

She frowned. "Okay, but what if I don't have Goldfish then? Mommy eats them sometimes when I'm asleep and she's off her diet."

Mia's face flushed, and Dallas hid a grin.

"Tell you what, Goldfish girl. Next time I come with Juno, I'll bring some Goldfish along. How's that?"

She nodded, finally trotting off into the kitchen.

"You don't have to make good on that promise," Mia whispered as she let Dallas out. "As a matter of fact, I'd rather you didn't promise her things at all. I know you'd never mean to disappoint, but Gracie's been let down in a big way by her father."

"No sweat," he said. Something flickered in her face, something thoughtful. "You're not planning to go to the clinic, right?"

Mia jerked. "How did you know I was thinking about that?"

"Call it a knack. Don't go there by yourself, just in case whatever she was looking into has something to do with the fire."

She stayed silent.

"If you do have to go, I'll go with you."

She offered a courteous smile. "Thanks, Dallas. I appreciate it."

But you'll never allow it. He understood. He recognized the shadows that danced in her eyes for what they were. Fear. A desperate, ponderous weight of fear that she did not want to expose to anyone. Who would? He'd known that, tasted that when he was being beaten within an inch of his life during his gang days. That fear was hideous and bred on itself, multiplying exponentially the longer it was kept in the dark, like a poisonous fungus. He wished he could tell her. There is only one antidote, One who could defeat that fear. Instead, he remained silent until he heard the sound of the lock turning.

Juno and Dallas made one more stop on the way home, purchasing a bone for Juno and a handful of hot peppers for himself. With some help from the store clerk, he also secured five bags of Goldfish crackers, which he stowed in the back of his truck. Who knew Goldfish came in so many flavors? Dallas smiled to himself. Gracie knew, and that was enough.

TWO

The parking lot was empty, quiet, save for the patter of a cold rain and the scuff of Mia's shoes as she made her way to the darkened clinic hours later. She was grateful that Tina offered to stay late. It was almost eight by the time Mia embarked on her mission. She knew she should have called Dallas, but the only thing that scared her more than what had happened to Cora was the thought of losing herself to another man who would betray her and Gracie. She realized her hands were in her pockets, hidden away, a habit she'd developed after she'd stabbed her husband.

The horror lapped at her afresh. Her own hands had lashed out with that knife, powered by terror that Hector would kill her and take Gracie away into his corrupt world. She would never have done it, but she believed, heart and soul, that Hector meant to end her life. After Mia's arrest, she'd endured six months of jail time, knowing Gracie was with Hector, near people both ruthless and greed-driven, the worst being her own husband. After her release, she'd fled with

Gracie, unaware that Hector would soon concoct a plot to outwit his enemies that involved kidnapping her sister, Antonia. While her sister fought for her life on a hurricane-ravaged island, Mia hid out like a frightened rabbit.

Sometimes her mind told her it was a dream, a nightmare, but she still remembered the feel of that knife in her hand and how her life had almost ended because she trusted the wrong man in spite of her father's warnings, Antonia's pleadings. In spite of her own troubled intuition.

Never again. Better to go it alone. A quick stop at the clinic. See if by chance Cora had left anything there that might be of help. In and out. Something wheeled along by her feet, and she gasped. Just a leaf, torn loose by the storm.

She bit back a wave of self-disgust at finding herself scuttling along, cringing at every leaf. She was an office clerk at the Spanish Canyon Clinic after all, and Cora was, had been, a volunteer. All perfectly aboveboard. But why had Cora originally insisted they wait until long after closing time to meet?

Her throat ached when she thought of her friend. Had she suffered? Had she known her house was burning around her?

Quickening her pace she sought shelter from the spring rain under the awning, keys ready in her hand, heart beating a little too hard, too erratically. Cora's nightmarish death came on a date that already held terrible memories, her wedding anniversary.

An annual reminder of the worst mistake of her life. But Hector had been so gentle when they'd first met, even professing to be a Christian, until he'd begun to worship another kind of God, the god of money, power and excitement, when he'd gotten involved in the drug trade. It was long over. Hector was jailed on new charges, the divorce finalized two years before, but Hector did not want to accept his losses, so she lived as anonymous a life as she could manage.

With teeth gritted, she wondered—Had Hector found her again?

His reach hadn't extended to Spanish Canyon, Colorado. Not this time.

Wind carried a cold spray of rain onto her face that trickled down the back of her neck. She wished there was someone else around, the janitor, a late working nurse, anyone. They might be parked in the underground garage, she thought hopefully. With a surge of relief she saw the lights on in the back of the building where she and Cora shared a desk.

Jamming her key in the lock, she left the rain behind and headed down the silent corridor to the rear of the building. She did not know what she hoped to accomplish. Maybe it was all just a way to keep busy.

Cora's desk was bare, save for a paperweight rock engraved with the words *Be Still*. An impossible task, it seemed, for the nearly eighty-year-old woman who had recently decided to learn Italian and tour Europe. Her eyes were drawn to her own desk. Shadows must be deceiving. Silhouetted in the lamplight was a vase full of long-stemmed roses. Trancelike, she moved closer and turned on her own work light. Yellow roses, which had once been her favorite. A gilt-edged card.

I'm sorry. I love you and we can be a family again. Hector.

Sweat beaded on her forehead. It was as if he was there, right there, standing in the shadows. Fear turned into hatred for the man who had stripped away her belief in herself.

Hector didn't strip it away. You handed it over, wrapped in a bow.

The floor creaked, and she spun around with a scream.

"I'm sorry," Dr. Elias said with an apologetic smile. "I didn't mean to scare you. I was working late and noticed the florist had been here. Nice roses. Curiosity won out, and I checked the card." He raised an apologetic eyebrow, the fiftysomething face calm and serene. "My wife says I'm incurably nosey, and I hate to admit that she's got me pegged."

Mia forced out a calming breath. "I'm surprised to see you here so late."

"Insomnia. It usually sends me to the computer to play solitaire, but I get tired of beating myself, so I come here sometimes."

"Did you…did you hear about Cora?"

He nodded, mournfully. "Tragic. Cora was an excellent lady and a noble spirit." He shook his head. "Why do the good die before their time?"

It was a question she'd asked many times to a God who'd never given her a straight answer.

Dr. Elias cleared his throat. "Anyway, I'm glad you came so you could get your flowers, but why so late? Insomnia trouble for you also?"

She was about to tell him about the prearranged meeting with Cora, but something stopped her. "I just wanted to clean up Cora's desk."

"Looks clean already." Something in his inflection made her wonder if he'd been looking through Cora's belongings. Ridiculous. Crazy suspicion.

He surveyed the ceiling for a long moment. "It's good, actually, that we have a private moment so we can talk. I feel as though I have treated you well, hired you on in spite of your criminal record."

She winced. "Yes, you have. I appreciate that."

"It was Cora who went to bat for you, you know. She felt passionately that you would be an asset to this clinic. I was reluctant, I'll admit."

Mia started. She hadn't even known Cora when she moved to Spanish Canyon. She'd been following a lead on a job that her sister had dug up. Close to nursing school. Quiet town where nobody knew her.

"So I'm loathe to ask it, Mia, but when were you going to mention the truth about your criminal husband?"

She kept her chin high, even though at five three she barely reached his shoulder. Her phone vibrated in her pocket. "Ex-husband."

He blinked, his smooth complexion bordered by a distinguished head of gray hair that went well with his stature as head of the town's largest general medicine clinic. "I knew he was abusive, you were arrested for stabbing him I realize, but you didn't quite tell me the whole story. The flowers got me curious and I did a little checking. Nosey, just like my wife says. He wasn't just an abusive spouse. He's a Miami drug kingpin with powerful friends." His pale gray eyes locked on hers. "You didn't feel like you should mention that?"

Mention it? She was too busy trying to forget it.

"Is that why you don't use your married name? Sandoval?"

"It's not my name because I'm not married anymore. I haven't been for years. Simple as that."

He looked at the ceiling again while he talked. "Not really so simple. I've tried to support you here, to give you the hours you need to get you through nursing school and help you earn some money to keep food on the table for Gracie."

She didn't like it when he said Gracie's name, for some reason that she could not articulate. Did she feel the swell of distrust when she looked at him because he had the same self-assured manner as Hector? The doctor had been nothing but gracious.

"I would do anything for my own kids, as you know. It hasn't always been easy to afford everything times two, but that's the price of having twins. Jake and Renee are both in private high school now, so I understand wanting the best for your kids. But why lie? Especially to me."

"I never lied. You asked about my ex-husband, and I told you the reason I was sent to jail."

"You neglected to mention your husband is a Miami drug lord. You thought you'd pulled the wool over my eyes, didn't you? Simple country doctor. Easy to do, you figured?"

"No, nothing like that, really," she said.

The phone buzzed again.

Something sparked in his eyes. "Omissions are lies, and I'm afraid I'm going to have to ask you to leave." His brow furrowed. "It pains me to do it, it really does, but I have a professional obligation, no matter what my personal feelings are. My patients have to have absolute trust in me and my staff, and if you're still getting flowers from a drug kingpin, I can't risk having you here."

Mia would not let him see her cry. Head high, she nodded. "I'll be out of here in fifteen minutes."

She went to the desk in the corner of the Spanish Canyon Clinic and shoved the picture of Gracie into a bag along with a collection of notepads. Cora's *Learn Italian Today* book was on her desk, under a box of tissue, and she scooped it up as well. She'd never dropped a phone call, never misplaced a file or been anything but pleasant to everyone and even that wasn't enough to overshadow her disastrous marriage.

Blinking to keep the tears at bay, her mind ran wild. No job. How would she finish school? Would it be the end of her dreams to finally give Gracie a stable, normal life? Her phone demanded her attention again and this time she yanked it from her pocket. It was a text from Dallas.

Ok?

Was she?

Dr. Elias still stood there, filling the doorway with his blocky shoulders, a look of indecision on his face. "This husband, Hector. He's tracked you everywhere, hasn't he?"

One of the notepads sliced into her finger giving her a paper cut. She shook off the sting angrily.

"Hector must be jealous." The lamplight etched Dr. Elias in tight shadow. "Have you given him reason?"

She froze. "What?"

"The tough guy with the dog. I've seen him talking to you. Hector can't be happy about this."

Seen Dallas? Something cold trickled through her. Why had Dr. Elias noticed whom she'd been talking to?

He flicked a glance into her bag. "You're not taking any clinic information, are you?"

She burned. "No, Doctor. I would not behave unethically, even after I've been wrongly terminated."

A glimmer of a smile lit his face. "I always liked your spunk, Mia Verde Sandoval. Too bad."

Mia grabbed her bag and purse and went to the door, but he barred her path.

He didn't move, just watched her as if he was weighing something in his mind. He reached out a hand to touch her forearm, but she recoiled.

"Hold on. I can see the truth now. You didn't lie to deceive, you lied because you're afraid."

Her breath caught and she shook her head.

"Yes, that's it, isn't it? You're afraid that Hector will find you." He stared closely at her. "No, you're afraid that you can't trust yourself, your choices, your judgments." He took her arm.

The fingers felt cold there against her skin, her own feet rooted to the floor. It was as if he'd stepped inside her, peered into the cold dark place in her heart where she herself dared not go.

"I know what it's like to be lied to. I'm so sorry, Mia," he said, pupils glittering in the dimly lit office.

He leaned toward her and lowered his voice to a whisper. "I'm dense, sometimes. I didn't realize. I can help you."

Standing this close she realized how strong he looked. Her fingers clutched her car keys, and she raised them in front of her.

"I want to leave. Now."

He laughed and moved a step closer. She was acutely aware of how empty the clinic was, how dark the outer corridors. "You're a beautiful woman, you know that?" His gaze flickered up and down her body. "You deserve more. I can help you get your life back."

She pressed back until she bumped into the file cabinets, a metal handle digging into her spine. He put his hands out, kneading her shoulders.

She jerked away from his grasp. "I want to go," she whispered, gripping the keys. "I will scream the place down if you touch me again."

He chuckled. "You came here after hours, almost as if you were looking for me."

The implication was clear. *Who do you think they'll believe?*

She gripped the keys, palms clammy, readying herself to gouge and bite and kick. Unsure.

"You're not seeing things clearly, Mia. You don't know what's right and wrong anymore, do you?" The words were almost a whisper, his mouth curved in a soft smile. "You need help."

Help? Was that what he offered? Her gut told her to run. Should she trust that instinct?

From somewhere far away, she heard herself say, "I want to go. Now."

"Maybe you don't know what you want," he said, eyes glittering.

"Yes, she does," said a low voice. The doctor was jerked back and dumped in an unceremonious pile on the floor. Dallas Black looked down at Elias, his dark eyes blending with the shadows.

She realized Dallas must have been expecting her to act stupidly and visit the clinic and her cheeks burned, but relief overrode any other sensation.

"I was just fired," Mia announced. "And now I'm going to leave."

Dallas didn't move. "Good. Doesn't pay to work for dirtbags."

"Trespassing and assault," Dr. Elias snapped at Dallas, scrambling to his feet. "I will have you arrested."

Dallas ignored the comment completely. "Ready to go?" he said to her.

"Get off my property," Dr. Elias snarled. Gone was the genial smile, any vestiges of warmth, fire blazed in his eyes.

Mia gripped her bag and walked to the door on shaky legs, grateful to have Dallas looking over her shoulder at the doctor. She was desperate to end the situation. Dallas had a complete disregard for rules and she wanted to finish the whole confrontation before anything worse happened.

"You are turning away from someone who wants to help you, Mia," Dr. Elias said, nostrils flared. "And look what you're walking into."

"Goodbye, Dr. Elias," Mia said.

"Don't forget your flowers," he yelled.

"Keep them," she said.

Dallas's truck was parked at the curb, and Juno sat next to it. When he saw her his tail went into overtime, and he whined until she gave him a cursory pat. He licked her face.

"If a man approached my ride, Juno would bark up a storm, but with you he'd hand over the keys," Dallas said. *Smart dog.*

Juno was once an aggressive shelter resident after having been beaten and starved by a cruel owner. Dallas had spent six months tracking down that negligent owner on his own dime, until the man was charged with animal cruelty and subjected to hefty fines. It wasn't enough in Dallas's view.

Mia straightened in spite of Juno's disappointment and gave him a tight smile. "He must know I'm a cat person and he's trying to help me see the light." She paused. "I would have handled the situation, you know. No one will keep me from Gracie."

"No doubt. I'm just glad I was in the neighborhood." In truth he'd been driving around town, too restless to stay home, checking the clinic lot every so often in case Mia showed up like he suspected she'd do. "I'm not sure…" She bit her lip. "I don't know if Dr. Elias was going to hurt me. He said he wanted to help."

Help? That wasn't what Dallas had heard in the good doctor's tone when he put his hands on Mia. "What did your gut tell you?"

"To leave."

"Then you did the right thing." Dallas clamped down on the anger that ticked at his insides. His own instincts told him Dr. Elias was interested in much more than Mia's well-being. He despised the thought of Elias being anywhere near Mia. Or touching her. Or looking in her general direction.

Overprotective, Black.

Overprotective? How could that be when she kept him at arm's length and he wasn't interested in a relationship anyway? Whatever the reason, something about her, her strength perhaps, stayed in his mind like a lingering fragrance.

It made him pretty sure that if she knew the real reason he'd come to Spanish Canyon, to protect her without her consent, she'd let him have it with both barrels, but the roses on her desk indicated there was ample cause for him to keep an eye on her.

He'd met Mia at the wedding of her sister, Antonia, to Hector's brother Reuben Sandoval after the two barely survived a hurricane. Oddly, he'd befriended

Antonia three years prior in the wake of a massive earthquake that struck San Francisco where he assisted his brother, Trey, in rescuing Antonia and Sage Harrington, now Trey's wife. At least Antonia and Trey had both found love matches in the midst of disaster. A memory from that wedding stayed sharp in his mind. Mia's face torn with sorrow, or was it guilt, cradling Gracie in her arms. Hemingway said people healed stronger where they were broken. Mia, though she didn't ever discuss her past, was like that, he figured. *Sometimes it takes more strength to ask for help than to go it alone, Mia.*

He snapped out of his reverie when she sighed heavily. "Go ahead and say it. I was dumb to come here, after hours, in light of all that's happened."

He considered. "Yeah."

"I have good reasons for doing things my own way."

"Don't we all." He tried to catch her eye, but she avoided his gaze. "You okay?"

"Yes."

"Sure?"

"I'm perfectly fine," she said with a little too much bravado. He caught the tremble of her lips in spite of the dim light. It made his stomach tighten.

"I'll follow you home again."

"I'm fine. There's no reason."

"It's dark, weather's bad and you were harassed. That's three reasons." He opened the door for her.

She rolled her eyes and started to get into the car when the bag slipped from her hands. She snatched it up but not before Cora's Italian book plopped out. It fell open, and she saw something stuck inside. Picking it up hastily, she said, "What's this?"

From between the pages she pulled out a four-by-six photo, and Dallas shone his penlight on it.

"We've seen this woman before," she said grimly.

Dallas felt a stir of foreboding flow through his belly. "Running away from Cora's burning house."

THREE

Sleep eluded Mia. Though she felt like throwing herself on the floor and sobbing at the loss of her dear friend, she would not allow Gracie to witness such an outburst. The best thing she could offer now was a heavy dose of mothering in between scouring the want ads and internet sites for employment opportunities. A breakfast of scrambled eggs, toast cut into a heart shape, and a half dozen stories later, and Gracie was content to go into the soggy backyard and hunt for snails. Unless the snails had teeny scuba suits, Mia didn't think she'd have much luck.

She sat on the couch and considered the facts.

The little house they now occupied was rented. Cora had helped her find the place, and though she received a settlement when she divorced Hector, she steadfastly refused to take any child-support money. Dr. Elias was right. Hector Sandoval was involved in the drug trade, and she did not want a single penny of tainted money to find its way to Gracie.

Hector claimed in every letter that he'd repented,

but she did not believe him or any other man for that matter. The most important person in her life was Gracie, and Mia would not fail her. So how could she tell her daughter about Cora? Images of the fire raced through her memory, especially the moment when the red-haired woman had appeared through the smoke. Whoever she was, she had answers. Hopefully, the police chief could help ferret out the truth, though he'd not been able to grant her an audience until the following day. Dallas had advised her to bypass Stiving, and she'd agreed. It was best to talk to the chief. For now, the picture was tucked safely in an envelope in the back of the top desk drawer.

The doorbell rang.

Tina stepped inside, chewing madly on a piece of pink gum with a stack of books under her arm to be perused during Gracie's nap time. Mia greeted her warmly. The stick-thin college sophomore babysat for Mia during the day and took community classes at night. Since Mia's nursing school was off due to a semester break, she'd been logging as many hours at Dr. Elias's clinic as she could and Tina had been invaluable. The two exchanged a quiet talk about Cora's death, news of which had already spread all over the quiet mountain community.

"Have you told her yet?" Tina asked, discarding her gum into a wrapper and snatching a leftover piece of toast.

"No." Mia sighed, eyes misting. "I haven't had the courage."

Tina gave her a hug which almost loosed the flood gates of emotion until Mia stepped back. "I'm glad you could come today. I've got to find another job."

"Yeah? What happened to the gig at the clinic?"

"I was…let go last night."

Tina swallowed the last bit of toast. "Oh, bummer. What are you going to do now?"

"Go into town and beat the bushes if I have to. Anything to make the rent."

"That's the spirit."

Mia nodded. "There's got to be somebody looking for a hard-working gal like me."

"We are women, hear us roar," Tina cried, pumping a fist. "Go get 'em!"

Wishing she could share some of Tina's enthusiasm, she grabbed her bag. After they'd made arrangements for Tina to deliver Gracie to Mia in the late afternoon, she headed for the car.

"Time to hit it," she murmured to herself. "Hear me roar."

Fearing that her roar was more like a pitiful mew at the moment, she headed to town.

After a full day of walking the main streets of Spanish Canyon, Mia had nothing to show for it but sore feet and a rumbling belly. She'd already gobbled her peanut butter and marshmallow fluff sandwich, and at a little past three, her stomach was demanding attention, as it seemed to do no matter what diet she was doing her best to adhere to. Besides, a sign on Sam's Sammies advertised for "help wanted."

I'm a master of the peanut butter and fluff, she reminded herself as she entered and introduced herself to the owner.

Sam Shepherd, a massive man with sprigs of white hair sprouting from the top of his head met her inquiry with enthusiasm. "Sure thing. Why don't you fill out an application?" He pushed over a greasy piece of paper affixed to a clipboard. "Say, I was sure sorry to hear about Cora."

She nodded. "Me, too."

"You know her well?"

Mia only managed a quick yes.

He raised a bristly eyebrow. "Heard talk that it wasn't an accident."

She hadn't noticed Detective Stiving sitting in the corner booth until he spoke up. "Looking more and more like that's the case," he said.

A moment later, Dallas strolled in, surveying the group with quiet amusement and causing Mia to wonder about the timing.

"Well, Sam, seems like business is picking up," Dallas said.

Stiving chewed a pickle spear. "What do you want?"

Dallas arched an eyebrow. "A sandwich. Isn't that

why you're here?" He smiled at Sam. "The usual, my good man."

"Vegetarian with extra mustard and no eggplant, heavy on the jalapenos," Sam rattled off.

Dallas slouched into a chair, long legs extended. "Don't let me interrupt."

Mia felt the twin pangs of affection and irritation at seeing Dallas there. She wanted the man out of her life, yet why did something inside her warm up whenever he appeared? Was he keeping tabs on her? The thought both infuriated and tantalized her. *Focus, would you?* "I'll just fill this out," she said to Sam, making her way to a chair well away from Dallas.

Stiving followed her. "You might not want to take a new job, just yet."

Something about the gleam in his eye worried her. "Why?"

"Because it seems you're an heiress."

She blinked. "What are you talking about?"

"Just got word that Cora left her house and property to you. Of course, the house is pretty messed up, but the twenty acres of property, well that's worth a nice tidy sum, I'll bet."

Mia realized her mouth was hanging open. "Cora left her property to me?"

"Does that surprise you?"

"Of course it does. I had no idea."

"That right?" He wiped his thick fingers on a

paper napkin. Graying chest hair puffed out at the top of his uniform shirt. "No idea at all?"

"None. What are you implying?"

"Cops, you know, look at these things called motives. Inheriting a nice chunk of land is motive."

"For what?" Mia managed to squeak out.

"For murder," he said with a smile.

Dallas moved closer when it seemed as though Mia was unable to marshal a response. "What do you have that points in that direction?"

Stiving leveled a derisive look at him. "Not that it's your business, but the coroner's initial take is that Cora didn't die from the fire."

Mia let out a little cry, her face gone deadly pale. Dallas tensed. "Cause?"

Stiving stretched against the upholstered booth. "That's as much as I'm going to say right now. You all have a great day. I'll be in touch. Soon."

He left. Dallas realized that Sam had been standing just behind them holding a sandwich on a plastic plate. "Uh, well, I'm real sorry and all that, Mia, but maybe Stiving is right. With everything going on, it doesn't seem like a good time to have you start working here."

He shoved the plate at Dallas and waddled back to the kitchen.

Dallas dropped money on the counter, no tip, and left the sandwich on the table. By the time he'd finished, Mia had made her way outside, sinking onto a brick planter, oblivious to Juno, who had been watching through the window the whole time, swabbing an eager tongue over her hand.

Dallas sat next to her. Dark clouds overhead promised more rain and dulled the soft brown of her eyes. Or maybe it was the shock that did it. What to say to comfort her in the present situation eluded him, so he went with his gut.

"They don't have any proof. He's trying to rattle you."

The words seemed to startle her. "He thinks she was poisoned with the pills I got for her."

"Speculation and proof are two different things."

"Juno knew there was something in those pills."

"Doesn't mean you put it there."

She pressed shaking hands to her mouth. "I can't believe it. He wants to put me in jail. I can't go to jail, Dallas."

Her voice broke and it killed him. "You won't."

"But my past…isn't lily white."

"Whose is?" He wanted to smooth away the furrow between her brows, the agony in her expression. "It was self-defense before. Totally different. Your ex admits that now."

Her eyes rounded. "Have you been studying my past?"

Smooth, Dallas. Why don't you explain how you

know every detail of her life? He went for casual. "Heard it somewhere."

She was too upset to think more about it. "Maybe I should leave here," she whispered. "Go back to Florida."

His pulse accelerated the tiniest bit. He said as gently as he could, "Thought you wanted a fresh start."

"Away from the Sandoval name," she finished. "I do, but my past seems to have followed me here."

And did her husband's past have anything to do with her current situation? He did not see how it could, but it was his job to find out. He'd made a promise. "There was someone else at Cora's house who could have tampered with the pills. We just have to figure out who the woman in the photo is."

Mia chewed her lip. "This is a nightmare."

"We'll fix it."

Her eyes flickered at the pronoun.

We? When had loner Dallas Black begun to think of them as partners? The only partner he'd ever really trusted was the kind covered with fur and with a tendency to slobber. "Look who's just hit town," he said as Gracie broke away from Tina and ran to them, splashing through the puddles on the sidewalk.

"Hi, Mr. Dallas. Hi, Mommy. I'm here," she announced, heading straight for Juno to give him an ear rub. "Tina said we could get ice cream."

Mia recovered herself to give Tina a stern look.

The girl shrugged. "Sorry. I can't say no to those dimples."

"I can," Mia said, her mouth twisting in sadness. "But I won't. I think I could use a scoop, too."

"Mr. Dallas, come on," Gracie said, tugging on his hand. "We can get some for Juno."

Mia's look was enough to discourage him. "I've got to go right now, Gracie. Maybe another time."

Mia's slight nod affirmed he'd made the right choice, so why did his heart tell him otherwise? He moved close to Mia, talking low in her ear and trying not to breathe in a lungful of her shampoo-scented hair. "I've got a friend who works at the police department. I'll go see what I can find out."

She put a hand on his biceps. "I don't want to ask you to do that for me."

"You didn't ask."

He heard her sigh, sad as the sound of a blues song, as she led Gracie away without looking back, her shoulders hunched against the storm-washed sky.

Mia tried to keep Gracie occupied with the ice cream parlor and the park, but all the while her mind was racing. The police thought she'd killed her dearest friend. How could it be happening? And to inherit when Cora had blood relatives to whom she could pass her estate? The only spot of comfort was Dallas, and she had to steel herself against any connection, no matter how much she craved it. Still, she thought she could remember the feel of his hard muscled arm under her fingers—strong, solid, the steady warmth in his eyes.

You've seen eyes like those before, remember, Mia?

Rain began to fall a little after five, and she zipped Gracie's jacket and insisted they return to the car where a nasty surprise awaited her. Her rear tire was flat all the way to the rim.

"Great. I must have driven over a screw or something." With a heavy sigh, she gave her purse to Gracie to hold and got the jack and lug wrench from the trunk. Two gentlemen and a young couple out walking their dog stopped and offered help, but Mia waved with a cheer she did not feel and finished the job herself. The effort took much longer than it should have and it was nearly sundown when she cleansed her grease-stained hands with one of her endless supply of disinfectant wipes and took the road toward home.

Gracie sang "Where Does the Ladybug Live?" as the miles went by and Mia even joined in for a while, but, as darkness fell, her stress returned. No job, no way to pay the rent and now a replacement tire needed to be purchased.

Gritting her teeth, she forced the worry down deep.

"I'm hungry," Gracie announced as they pulled into the garage.

"How can you be hungry when you ate two scoops of ice cream?"

Gracie twisted a strand of hair while she thought about it. "Dunno, but I am."

"Mac and cheese?"

The little girl nodded as she helped Mia unbuckle her car seat straps.

Mia mentally inventoried the pantry cupboard, hard to keep stocked with a voracious babysitter and child. Fortunately, there was one box left of nature's most perfect food. She helped Gracie from the car and hit the button to close the garage door.

Mia noted the interior door was unlocked, probably because Tina simply could not be induced to lock it. Mia sighed. Oh, to be an innocent eighteen-year-old again. Gracie pulled out her step stool and disappeared into the pantry.

Suddenly, the burdens of the day crashed in on Mia and she felt much older than her twenty-eight years. And why shouldn't she as the ex-wife of a drug runner and now the object of suspicion for her friend's death? *Murder, murder,* the word crawled through her mind. Tears threatened, but she would not allow them, not for a moment. Mothers did not have the luxury of folding up like tents. A shower. A quick five minute shower would wash off the grime from the day.

Hanging her purse on the kitchen hook and plugging in her cell phone to charge, she headed for the bedroom, removing her jacket. Finger poised on the light switch, she froze. A shadow was silhouetted in front of the window, just for a second before it slithered behind the cover of the drapes. Someone was in her bedroom.

Fear rushed hot into her gut, firing her nerves as she ran down the hallway. Behind her she could hear the swish of fabric as the intruder detached from the curtains. Feet thudded across the carpeted floor, her own clattering madly on the wood planked hallway as she raced for the kitchen, sweeping up her purse and grabbing Gracie who was shaking the box of macaroni and singing.

She seized her daughter with such force she heard the breath whoosh out of her, but Mia paid no heed. The man was in the hallway now, only a few feet behind her. Mia burst into the garage, hit the button and dove into the driver's side, shoving Gracie over onto the passenger seat and cranking the ignition.

The interior garage door opened, and the man appeared—thin, white, crew cut. She saw him reach for the button to stop the door from opening. She would be trapped, she and Gracie, at the mercy of this stranger.

No, she thought savagely, flipping the brights on. He flinched, throwing a hand over his eyes. The door was nearly half open now. Only a few more inches and she could get out.

Terror squeezed her insides as she saw him recover and reach for the button again.

Hurry, hurry, she commanded the groaning metal gears.

This time when he reached for the button, he succeeded and the door stopped its upward progress.

He pressed it again and it began to slide down, sealing off their escape.

FOUR

Dallas listened to the rain pounding down on the metal roof of the twenty-nine-foot trailer he rented. It was a gem of a unit as far as he was concerned, far enough away from the other trailer park residents that he enjoyed the illusion of solitude. That and the fact that the river just at the edge of the property had already persuaded many folks to temporarily relocate to another trailer park on higher ground. He wasn't completely familiar with Colorado weather patterns, but he'd give it a good couple of days before he needed to grab his pack and head for another spot.

Dallas sprawled on his back on the narrow bunk, Juno snoring on his mat on the floor. His thoughts wandered back to Mia and the fire. His police contact hadn't been able to tell him much, but he knew that circumstantial evidence could convict a person in the eyes of the law and the community.

Motive and means. Mia had both.

He got to his feet and took up his guitar from the closet. Juno burrowed deeper into his mat as Dallas strummed out a few chords on the instrument that was a gift from his brother, Trey. So, indirectly, was Dallas's damaged spleen and knee, but he did not hold that against his brother anymore. Dallas got into gang life to emulate Trey, but no one had forced him.

He'd gone in willingly and come out so damaged he would never realize his dream of being a Marine like their father.

He tried to remember his sixteen-year-old self, armed and patrolling the ten-block territory as a sentinel of sorts, a lookout for Uncle, the older leader of the gang who pedaled dope, which kept the wheels rolling. He'd admired Uncle, feared him even, yet watched him hand out new shoes and Fourth of July fireworks to the kids who couldn't afford either. They were the same kids who would be members one day, looking for that combination of belonging and protection that Uncle provided. Sixteen years old, carrying a gun, drinking and protecting a hoodlum's drug business. He cringed at the memory. What an idiot. What a coward.

How many trailers had he stayed in over the years? How many apartments or cabins had he called home until people got to know him a little too well and he felt that restless urge to move on? Was he still looking for that place to belong?

Or was it more cowardice? Probably, God forgive him. It was safer not to get to know people and to prevent them from knowing him. Safe…with a helping of sin mixed in. His grandfather's favorite base-ball player, Mickey Mantle, said gangs were where cowards went to hide. Maybe they sometimes went to trailer parks, too. He fought the rising tide of self-recrimination with a muttered prayer.

The clock reminded him he hadn't eaten dinner. The fridge didn't offer much so he grabbed a rainbow of hot peppers and an onion. Armed with a perfectly balanced knife, he allowed himself to be soothed by the precision of the slices as they fell away onto the cutting board.

Juno surged to his feet, ears cocked.

Company.

So late? And in the throes of a pounding rain? He put down the knife and sidled to the window, peering through the blinds. Nothing. No cars visible, but then his windows faced the tree-lined creek so he wouldn't see one anyway. Juno was standing in front of the door, staring with laser-like precision, ears swiveling, as if he could see beyond the metal if he just worked hard enough at it. With hearing four times greater than a human's, Juno was not often wrong about what he heard.

Dallas tried to peer through the blinds again, but the angle was wrong. Still no one knocked. Juno maintained his ferocious intensity, which told Dallas someone was out there. The slightest sound or scent telegraphed to a dog just as strongly as a stiff-knuckled rap on the door.

Okay. Let's play. Dallas gripped the door handle. Juno's whiskers quivered, body trembling, sensing a game in the offing. Juno, like every great SAR dog, had an intense play drive that never wound down.

Dallas did a slow count to three and yanked the handle.

Wind barreled in along with a gust of rain, and Juno charged down the metal stairs onto the wooden porch. He turned in circles looking for something that wasn't there.

Dallas kept his fists ready and gave the dog the moment he needed to get his bearings. Moisture-laden air confused Juno's senses, but not for long.

The dog shoved his head in the gap under the trailer and began to bark for all he was worth, tail whirling.

A woman's scream cut through the storm.

"Sit," Dallas yelled to Juno, who complied with a reluctant whine.

"Whoever you are under the trailer, come out."

No answer.

"If you don't come out, the dog is coming in."

Now there was movement, a raspy breathing, a set of slender fingers wrapping around the edge of the trailer, the impression of a face.

"He'll bite me."

Dallas called Juno to him and held the dog by the collar, more to assure the woman than out of fear that Juno would disobey. Juno didn't bite people. He was more interested in getting them to throw a ball for him to fetch. "Come out."

She emerged, soggy and mud streaked, her hair plastered in coils against her face. Red hair.

"You were there at the fire."

She didn't answer, trembling in the falling rain.

"Come inside. We'll talk."

She didn't move. "Are you a friend of Cora's?"

"Are you?" He could see the thoughts racing through her mind as she chewed her lip without answering. "All I can tell you is I won't hurt you."

"How do I know I can trust you?" she said through chattering teeth.

"Guess you can't. You came here to find me and here I am. If you want to talk, we do it inside. Don't want the dog to catch cold."

After another long look at Juno, the woman ran up the steps.

He tossed her a towel, which she wrapped around her shoulders before she sank onto the kitchen chair. Juno did his thing, sniffing her muddy shoes and the hem of her sodden linen pants.

Dallas studied her while he heated water in the microwave and flung in a tea bag which had come with the trailer. Some sort of fruity herbal stuff. Her clothes had been nice at one point, ruined now. A light jacket was not up to the task of keeping her dry from the pummeling rain. No purse.

"Who are you?" he asked as he handed her the tea.

She clutched it between her shaking hands, her knuckles white.

"Susan." She swallowed. "I was going to meet Cora, and I saw the house burning. I tried to get inside to help her."

Nice story. "Why were you meeting her?"

"She was…looking into something for me." She locked eyes on his, hers a pale gray. "Is she all right?"

Dallas considered. Time to find out if Susan really was a friend to Cora. "Dead." He gauged her reaction.

The woman did not move, as if the words were lost in the steam from the mug she held to her lips. "Dead."

"So why were you going to see her?"

She gazed into the tea. "How did the fire start?"

"Maybe I should be asking you that."

She jerked. "You think I set it?"

"So far I've seen you running away from a fire and sneaking outside my trailer. Puts your character in question."

A glimmer of a smile lifted her lips, but there was something under the trailing wet hair, behind the gaunt lines of her mouth that revealed a hardness he hadn't seen at first. "So you're wondering if you can trust me?" she said.

"Not wondering. I'm not going to trust you, not until you give me the truth."

"You're a hard man."

He sat opposite her. "I've got peppers to sauté. What are you here for?"

She held his eyes with hers, a slight lift to her chin. "Justice."

"Not easy to find."

"I know. But I'm going to have it. I'm going to get back what belongs to me." The last words came out as a hiss.

"What were you doing at Cora's?"

"Meeting her there. She was trying to help me unmask a villain, so to speak."

"Who?"

"It's private."

He rapped a hand on the table. "We're wasting time. Cora was likely murdered and you were there at the scene."

"If I was going to kill someone, or burn a house in this town," she said, after drinking deeply of the tea, "that's not the one I would have picked. And by the way, you were there, too, at the scene. Did you have something to do with Cora's death?"

Dallas resisted the urge to raise his voice. "If you thought I did, a quick phone call to the police would take care of it. You came here for another reason."

"I wanted to know about Cora, and I'm not asking the police for personal reasons."

Very personal, judging from the flicker of emotion that pinched the corners of her mouth. Impasse. They'd gotten there, he could tell. Whatever her motives, he wasn't going to pry them out of her. Women didn't work that way, he'd learned. Instead he sat back in the chair and waited.

Mia's mouth went dry as the garage door stopped with a groan, halfway up. The man hopped off the step and ran to the car. He was coming to drag her out. The old car had no automatic locks so she slammed the button down and realized in a hot wave of panic that he was not headed to her side, but Gracie's.

"Lock the door, Gracie," Mia shouted.

Gracie sat frozen, staring at her mother.

Mia dove across her and hammered the lock, the back door, as well. The man banged his palms against the glass.

Gracie screamed. "Stop, stop!"

Mia nearly screamed too until the man stepped away suddenly. He picked up a metal bucket and swung it hard at the passenger window with a deafening crash until the glass was etched through with cracks.

"Get down onto the floor," Mia yelled to Gracie, "and cover your head with your hands."

She yanked the car into Reverse. After one quick breath, she stomped on the gas. The car shot backwards into the garage door. There was a terrible moment when the roof met the unyielding mass and she thought she had made a fatal error. Groaning metal, the sound of breaking glass and then quite without warning the car punched through, shearing the garage door into a crumpled mess, exploding onto the rain-slicked driveway.

Mia was oblivious to the damage. Only two facts remained, her car was still functioning and they were free from the garage. She reversed down the slope, cranked the car into Drive and sped off down the road, putting as much distance between the man and Gracie as she possibly could. One mile, two, her stomach remained in a tight knot, fingers clenched around the steering wheel.

She forced several breaths in and out before she could coax her voice into action. "Gracie Louise, are you hurt?"

Gracie's tiny voice floated up from the floor. "Scary."

"You're right," she said, relief making her voice thick. "But it's okay now. You can climb back on the seat. Be careful of the glass."

Gracie emerged like a hare having narrowly escaped the fox. Her lips were parted, eyes wide and wet. "Mommy, that was a bad man."

Mia gave a shaky laugh and took her daughter's hand. "Yes, he was."

"Why was he in our house?"

She swallowed. "I don't know, but we'll go someplace safe until we find out, okay?"

"Where?"

The million dollar question. The nearest hotel was an hour away, and they didn't have the money to stay in one for long anyway. Rain splattered through the side window that had broken when it impacted the garage door. She felt the bitter tide of anger rise as she contemplated her own helplessness. Mia risked a quick stop, engine running, to move Gracie to the backseat and buckle her into her booster. She kissed her and caressed her daughter's plump cheeks. "I'm going to figure out something, okay?"

Gracie nodded, shaking the box of macaroni she still clung to. "But I'm hungry."

Mia smiled as she climbed back into the driver's seat, but worry soon overwhelmed her. She didn't even have a cell phone to call the police. The storm intensified as she drove along, rattling the sides of the car. If she could call her sister for advice...

Your sister who is busy with her new husband and her new life. They were tight now, together again after all the anguish Mia had caused, but still there remained in the shadows between them, a heavy weight of guilt. It stemmed from the fact that her sister had been right about Hector when Mia refused to hear a bad word about him, a feeling that burgeoned during her time in jail with all its horrors. Because of Hector, Antonia was almost killed and there was nobody to blame for bringing him into their lives but Mia. No, she would not call Antonia.

"Why not call Hector?" her derisive thoughts

chided her. He was sitting around in prison with nothing much to do and a reach that seemed to exceed the metal walls that caged him. She could grovel even more and throw herself on Dr. Elias's mercy. Was there any pride left to salvage? Self-pity gave way to a hot flood of determination.

Stand on your own two feet, for once in your life.

Mile after mile gave her no clarity, no better sense of what to do. Only the instinct to keep going, to get away from whoever had violated their home, kept her pressing the car forward. She'd made up her mind to stop at the next town she came to and call the police when she realized where she was, at the entrance to the trailer park where Dallas lived. She'd given him a lift there once when his truck had engine trouble.

She saw the silhouette of his vehicle, and she pulled her car next to it, motor still running.

"Where are we?" Gracie said, unbuckling her strap.

"Nowhere, I was just stopping to rest my eyes for a minute." What was she doing? She would not go to Dallas for help, the man who already seemed to have a strange influence over her pulse. An image of long-stemmed yellow roses floated into her mind. It was followed by a vision of Hector, the man whom she'd loved desperately, blindly, the husband who lied to her from the first kiss and right on until his arrest for drug dealing and later for the attempted abduction of her sister. *Fool, fool, fool.* Tears brimmed, captive in her eyes.

She swallowed hard. "Put your seat belt back on, we're not stopping here."

"But there's Juno," Gracie gabbled, shoving open the door and hopping out.

"Get back in the car right now, Gracie Louise," Mia said, noting the spill of light from Dallas's door as he emerged onto the trailer steps, peering into the darkness.

"Hi, Dallas," Gracie called. "Can you make me some mac and cheese?"

Mia sighed. God could not lead her to another dark-haired man who would prove her a fool again. If that was His plan, Mia was going to make one of her own. Jaw tense, she stepped out of the car and went to retrieve her daughter.

FIVE

"Sorry to bother you," Mia said, forcing a light tone, as Dallas bent to talk to Gracie, Juno dancing on eager paws beside him.

"Someone broke into our house," Gracie said. "I think it was the Boogeyman. He wanted this." She thrust the box of mac and cheese up in the rain.

Dallas's face was a picture of confusion. "Huh?" he finally managed.

Mia squished up to him, feet sinking into the grass. "We had a break-in. We're going to the next town to call the cops."

It was hard to read his expression through the sheeting rain. "Come inside."

Gracie hooted her approval and headed for the trailer.

"No," Mia said too quickly. "I mean, we don't want to involve you. I can handle it." She wished her teeth had not begun to chatter madly at that moment.

"You can handle it inside, out of the rain."

"I appreciate the offer."

"Inside then." And that was that. Dallas turned his back and ushered Gracie and Juno up the steps, politely holding the door for Mia, his muscled forearm gleaming wetly. And what was a woman on the edge of desperation supposed to do about that?

Just a phone call. A quick stop to rest and then out. She squelched up the trailer steps and inside, stopping abruptly in the doorway until he came up behind and pushed her gently through.

"I'll leave puddles."

His gaze flickered around the tidy interior. "You won't be the first one." He sighed. "Gone."

"Who?"

"The redhead from the fire. Name's Susan. She came here."

Mia gasped. "What did she want? Who is she?"

He shrugged. "Not the chatty type. Only got that she was meeting Cora and she has some big trust issues. She was sitting at the table when I heard you pull up. She must have snuck out." He leveled a look at Juno. "Aren't you supposed to alert me to people sneaking around, dog?"

Juno shook water from his thick coat and hurled himself on the floor to offer his belly to Gracie for scratching.

Mia giggled.

Dallas did not, but she thought there was a slight quirk on his lips. Mia made one more trip into the rain to fetch the bag of spare clothes she kept in the car. In a few moments, Gracie was wearing faded jeans and a T-shirt, one size too small but dry.

"Can you make this?" Gracie said, shaking the box of macaroni at Dallas.

"What is it?"

The child blinked. "It's mac and cheese. Don'tcha eat that?"

"No," Dallas said.

"Well, what do you eat?" she demanded.

"Spicy food that makes you sweat. But I can probably manage mac and cheese."

"No need," Mia said.

Dallas pointed to the tiny bathroom. "There's a sweatshirt hanging on a hook in there. It's ugly, but dry."

"We're not staying."

"I got that. Go put on something dry anyway. I don't think I can enjoy eating this mac stuff while you're dripping all over the floor." He turned to Gracie. "How do you cook it? The label's blurry from the rain."

"Dump the stuff in bubbling water," Gracie sang out as Mia headed to the bathroom.

"Don't get too close to Juno," she warned Gracie. "He'll get mad if you pester him."

Dallas quirked an eyebrow. "He's never mad at kids, but I'll watch them anyway."

Mia walked into the bathroom and leaned her head against the door. *Safe. You're safe for the moment, and so is Gracie.* She wanted to whisper a prayer, but something hardened the words in her throat. *You got yourself out of that jam, Mia, and you can handle whatever comes next. All by yourself.*

She squeezed the water out of her hair and slicked it down straight as best she could. Rolling up her sodden shirt, she pulled on the soft gray sweatshirt that went down past her knees. It felt warm against her skin.

She emerged to find Dallas in deep discussion with Gracie as she stared at the pile of jigsaw puzzle pieces set out on a piece of plywood that served as a table.

"I don't know what it's going to be," Dallas said.

Gracie blinked. "But what's the picture on the box?"

"A mouse chewed the box, so I put the pieces in a plastic bag. Can't remember what the picture is."

She touched a piece with one soft fingertip. "You haven't gotten many pieces together."

He nodded, staring ruefully at the corner where a half dozen pieces were connected. "I move a lot. Gotta put it away each time."

"How long have you been working on it?" Mia asked.

He squinted. "Going on twelve years now."

She wasn't sure whether to gasp or laugh. "Really?"

"Well, I think it's going to be a dog puzzle," Gracie said.

"Could be. My mother gave it to me for my fifteenth birthday. She can't remember what the picture was, either." He sniffed. "Is mac and cheese supposed to smell like that?"

They looked at the pot which was bubbling madly on the stove. Mia grabbed a potholder and took it off the heat. There were bits of packaging swirling through the noodles and grainy orange tinted water. "Uh-oh. You dumped in the cheese envelope."

"The what?"

"I forgot to tell him," Gracie wailed. "You're not 'posed to put the cheese envelope in the water."

Mia put the mess into the sink. "I'm afraid it's ruined."

Dallas sighed. "I should have paid better attention while I was dumping. Who puts cheese in an envelope anyway?"

Gracie sat forlornly next to Juno. "Awww, rats."

"Hang on," Dallas said, wrenching open the cupboard. "I just remembered something." He held a bag of Goldfish triumphantly in the air. "How about some of these?"

Gracie cheered, and Mia had to laugh as he handed Gracie the crackers with all the solemnity of a professor awarding a diploma. "Just don't feed too many to the dog," he said.

After a moment of hesitation, he said to Mia, "I'm making tofu and peppers. Share them with me?" She had not shared a private meal with a man since her disastrous marriage. Sweat popped out on her forehead.

"Oh, I couldn't."

"There's no meat, but I've got plenty." His black eyes fastened on her.

Mia was a committed carnivore, but how could she say no to the man whose sweatshirt she was wearing and who had massacred a box of mac and cheese in an effort to feed her child?

"Yes," she said humbly. "That would be very nice."

"Here's a phone to call the cops. Then you can tell me about what happened."

She sank down at the table. "You're not going to believe me."

"Try…" His words trailed off as he scanned the kitchen counter.

"What's wrong?"

"Before she took off, Susan helped herself."

"To your dinner?"

"No," he said, voice low and deep. "To my knife."

Dallas kept the words low so Gracie wouldn't hear, but he needn't have worried. She was deep in conversation with Juno about the merits of some or other Goldfish flavor over the rest.

He selected another knife from the block and began slicing peppers, while Mia phoned the police. There was no way to avoid listening in and that was fine since he was itching to know the details of what sent Mia and Gracie out into the night. To him.

Was she really there in his trailer, rolling her damp hair into a ponytail? He nearly nicked his finger trying to take a sideways glance at her.

Mia explained the break-in to the dispatcher and gave Dallas's cell number as a contact before hanging up.

"They'll send a unit when they can, but the levee is failing just north of town." She laughed, a bitter sound. "They may need to evacuate my neighborhood anyway. It's true what they say, when it rains, it pours."

He dumped the peppers into sizzling olive oil and applied himself to neatly cubing the silken tofu. "It's not a coincidence. Guy was looking for something, maybe."

"Or looking to..." Her voice trailed away.

He stirred the pan with a wooden spoon. "I think he was searching and you surprised him. You said you had a flat. My guess is he made that happen to buy some time so he could search."

"For what? Why?" Her lips parted in exasperation, dark eyes flashing. He found his own mouth had gone dry.

"Could it be connected to the fire?" Mia pressed her hands to her forehead. "I don't even know what Cora was looking into. She didn't give me the slightest clue."

"Yes, she did," he said, sliding a plate in front of her.

Mia gasped. "The photo. It's in a file drawer. I have to go back and get it."

"In the morning. Sleep here. Juno and I will find an empty unit, and you can have this one."

"No, we couldn't displace you."

He sat on a chair across from her. "You're tired, and Gracie needs a safe place to sleep."

He could see the struggle unfold across her face in magnificent waves. "Mia, I'm not pressuring you to do anything. I'm just offering a safe place to sleep until morning. That's all."

She bit her lip.

He took her hand, the delicate fingers cool in his own. "Let's pray." He closed his eyes and thanked the Lord for keeping Gracie and Mia safe and for the provision of food and shelter. When he straightened, he thought he could see a million thoughts, a cascading river of emotions rolling through her eyes.

"I wouldn't guess you to be the kind to pray."

"Yeah? Because I'm a troublemaker?"

"No, no, of course not." She laughed. "Well, maybe a little."

"Troublemakers need God more than most." He picked up his fork and started to eat.

She did the same. "Wow, hot." She panted, reaching for a glass of water.

"Sorry." He handed her a piece of bread. "Water

doesn't really help much. I've done a lot of backpacking. Spicy adds flavor to camping food." He considered the contents of the fridge. "I have some eggs. I'll scramble you some."

He started to rise, but she stopped him with a touch on his arm that seemed to ignite an odd flicker of nerves all the way up to his shoulder.

"This is fine." She swallowed. "Hector…loved spicy food, too, I just haven't had it in a while. Thank you for cooking it for me."

He should have gone with the eggs. "Do you worry about what he'll do when he's out?"

She swallowed and wiped her mouth with a paper napkin. "He already knows too much about my life, even from prison."

And Hector's enemies did, too. He had squirreled away money, so the rumor went, a hefty sum extorted or swindled from his competitors, including the ferocious Garza family. Garza wanted it back and he'd sent out feelers to discover if Mia knew the whereabouts of the jackpot. Could be the guy who broke into her house wasn't searching for the photo, but the money.

A friendly DEA agent had alerted Reuben and Antonia to Garza's interest. And Antonia had hired Dallas to keep tabs on Mia. Dallas was good at watching people, finding the lost—fighting—if necessary, and skirting rules when they did not serve. He had no home, no ties. He was the perfect man for the job.

And Mia would despise him when she found out. He speared another slice of pepper.

For now, he would allow himself to savor the relative closeness between them, a feeling he had not experienced in a very long time. It was a shame that staring was bad manners, because all he really wanted to do was sit motionless and drink her in.

Her gaze was soft as she watched Gracie play with Juno, feeding him way more Goldfish than any dog should consume. When a gust of rain hammered on the metal roof with such force that it boomed through the trailer, Gracie ran to her mother's arms.

"It's okay, baby," Mia crooned. "Just the rain."

"Where's the bad man?"

Mia exchanged a quick look with Dallas.

"Bad man isn't going to come here," Dallas said.

"Why?"

"Because Juno is big and scary, and so am I."

Gracie smiled and hopped in his lap. He was so startled he didn't know what to do, sitting there as if he had a live grenade on his knees. Should he stand up? Give her a pat? Instead he sat rigid, hands raised, like a complete dork.

She grabbed him around the neck and pasted a cheesy kiss on his cheek. "I'm glad we came here."

So am I, his heart supplied, much to the surprise of his mind, but he was still relieved when she vacated his lap.

He saw to the details as best he could, thinking his

mother would have played the job of host much better than he. Extra blankets for Mia and Gracie, heater turned on to a low hum to ward off the chill. Couple of clean towels in case anybody needed showering. Was there something else? Antacids, to cure any hot pepper damage. And magazines? *Wilderness Survival*. Did women like that sort of thing? He stood awkwardly in the doorway.

"Keep my phone here." He pulled out a spare he always had handy and programmed his cell into the one he gave Mia. "Call if you need anything. Use the laptop if you want. You can sign on as a guest."

Gracie crimped her lips. "What if the bad man comes while you're gone?" she whispered.

He considered telling her about the trailer he would sleep in across the way which gave him a direct line of sight that he intended to monitor on a regular basis. There were other things he could share, but he did not. "You want Juno to stay with you?"

"Yes." Gracie nodded, hopping from foot to foot. "Juno will watch me sleep."

"Actually, he'll sleep, too."

Mia shot him a look that indicated he probably should have kept that fact to himself. How was someone supposed to know what to divulge to a kid and what not to? Was there some kind of instruction manual?

"Juno will sleep, but he hears things that you can't."

"Like bad men?"

Dallas nodded.

"If he hears me, how will he know I'm not bad?"

"He just knows."

"Like God?"

Dallas took in the little bow of a mouth, the sweet innocence in that sober gaze and something moved inside him. "Yes, Gracie. God made dogs smart that way."

"My daddy's bad," Gracie whispered, so low he almost didn't hear it.

He heard Mia gasp, her lips pressed together. He swallowed and sent up a little prayer that he wouldn't say something stupid and took a knee. "Your daddy made mistakes. If he's sorry, God will help him be a good man again."

"God can do that?" she said, eyebrow raised.

"Yes, He can."

"How do you know?"

Dallas blew out a breath. "Because I was a bad man, and God helped me to be good again." Gracie gave him a long, serious look, then hugged him.

Mia wrapped her arms around herself. Had he made things better? Or worse? He could not tell from the expression on her face. Without another word that might tip the balance to one side or the other, he let himself out into the rain.

SIX

The night droned on. Rain hammered down and thoughts thundered through Mia's mind, three words pinching uncomfortably at her heart.

My daddy's bad.

Hector had done terrible things. He was bad, in some ways, but he had nearly died trying to save her sister from the trap he'd set for her on the island. He'd gone to prison, professing he would come out a better man. They had no future together, nothing that should stir her toward forgiveness. She would never love him again. The rage and hatred inside her would stay forever, she feared, blackening and staining her whole life. If Hector was bad, unforgivable, unredeemable, what did that mean for the child he had fathered? Or the wife who'd made so many mistakes herself?

And what of Dallas? She knew only a small bit about his troubled youth, but without question she was also certain Dallas Black was a good man. Then again, she'd thought Hector was, too.

Mia felt the soft rise and fall of Gracie's breathing, her back curled against Mia's stomach on the narrow bunk bed. How small she was, this little girl who looked to Mia to show her who God was, a god of forgiveness. It was something Mia could say with her mouth, but not embrace in her soul.

If he's sorry, God will help him be a good man again.

She wondered afresh about the strange and straightforward Dallas Black. The troublemaker with a certainty about himself and God that she could no longer deny attracted her. She itched to soothe her restlessness with movement. Careful not to wake Gracie, Mia crept from the bed, earning an intense look from Juno who was stationed on the floor.

He stared at her, pupils two glimmers in the dimness. Dogs were strange to her, galumphing creatures who made messes and were prone to biting. The big lumbering animal scared her a bit, but he undeniably enchanted Gracie for some reason. Slobbery tongue, muddy paws, sharp teeth.

And a friend, to a child who had no others.

She crouched down next to the animal. "Thank you, Juno," she whispered.

The dog swiveled his ears, considering, and then laid his head back on his paws and assumed his watchful rest.

She clicked on the small light above the kitchen

table and powered up Dallas's laptop, navigating to her inbox. While the computer booted up, she peered out the blinds into the unceasing rain. Across the way, a dim yellow light gleamed from the window of Dallas's trailer. It made her feel better to know he was there and at the same time grateful there was a safe distance between them.

The previous day played back in her mind like a bad movie. Cora gone and so was her job. Dr. Elias's face flashed in her memory. Had she misread the whole situation? Had he really been offering help? Trust your instincts, Dallas told her. But she trusted nothing about herself anymore, especially where men were concerned.

Pulling her attention back to the laptop, she opened her inbox. A message from her sister.

How are you? Hurricane cleanup continues here. Reuben is confident that he can start replanting the orchard soon. The man lives, eats and breathes oranges. How did I get fixed up with a guy who loves oranges more than me?

Mia smiled. Reuben loved his orchard, but they both knew that the man was desperately in love with Antonia. She felt the pang of envy. Hector had loved her, too, in his own way, but he'd loved power and money more.

I hear there is flooding in your area. Come to visit us in Florida. Aside from the odd hurricane, we've got perfect weather. We'll put you to work, but you'll be above water. I'd feel better if I could keep my eyes on you.

Antonia knew that Hector tracked Mia everywhere. And Hector's enemies? The people he'd cheated and double-crossed? Did they track her everywhere, too? A shiver rippled up her spine and she read the remainder of the message.

I know you don't want me to do the protective big sister thing. I'll try to be good, I promise. Reuben wants you here, too. He misses Gracie, and he wants to see her climb a tree. Waiting for your reply. A

Mia's fingers stiffened over the keyboard. See Gracie climb a tree? How did her sister know Gracie had managed to clamber up the old cottonwood tree in the backyard of their rented house a few days prior? The child was bursting with pride, even though Dallas had to get a ladder to fetch her down, and reported the accomplishment to everyone who crossed their path in the small town. Was Antonia having someone spy on her? Teeth gritted, she forced out several measured breaths.

She was turning into a nutcase. Reuben's life was

trees. Of course he'd want to see Gracie climb one. She read the email again. The tree-climbing reference was purely coincidental, and her paranoia was turning her against the one person she knew was completely on her side. Hitting Reply, she contemplated how to put into words all that had happened the past two days.

Cora is dead. I am under suspicion for the murder. An intruder broke into our house. I'm staying in Dallas's trailer. I'm scared, worried, alone.

She perused the words that would send her sister into a panic. The sister who had been right all along. The woman who deserved above everyone else to enjoy the start of a marriage to the man she'd loved and lost and found again.

Backspace. Delete.

Blinking back tears she typed instead:

Gracie's growing like mad. She checks her teeth every day to see if they are loose, so desperate to use the special tooth box you sent. So busy here with work and school. Will write soon. Love you and Reuben. M

The inbox was cluttered with ads and offers from every company she'd ordered from recently using a credit card with her maiden name. It was a very tiny victory, but she took comfort in the fact that she had been able to provide the bare bones necessities with her very own hard-earned cash. Thanks to a secondhand store in town, she'd even managed a plastic wading pool that had gotten them through the hot months. It was light-years from the expensive toys and top-of-the-line clothes Gracie had when she was a baby in Hector's home, but it was bought with honest money. Gracie didn't seem to realize they were living perilously close to the poverty line. Not yet, anyway.

Clearing out the junk brought her to the last email. Her heart hammered. It could not be. The sender's name, *c.graham,* did not change no matter how hard she blinked. Cora Graham had sent her an email at four-thirty on the day she'd died, shortly after she'd sent the text summoning them to her house.

Panic squeezed Mia's stomach, and for a moment, she was too terrified to click open the email. Finally, with fingers gone cold, she did.

Find P. Finnigan. He knows the truth. I can't...

The message ended abruptly. Mia's heart pounded. Cora had sent the message when? As the smoke overcame her? As the poison paralyzed her body and she realized she could not escape?

Sobs wrenched through Mia. She clapped a hand over her mouth to keep from waking Gracie and staggered to the porch, stepping outside, grateful that the rain had momentarily slowed to a trickle. Sucking in deep breaths, she tried to rein in her stampeding emotions. It should not have surprised her to hear Dallas's door open. In a moment, he was next to her, peering into her face.

"Tell me," he said softly.

She couldn't answer over the grief that welled up inside.

With arms both strong and gentle, he pulled her close, not offering any more words, but the warmth and solace of his body pressed to hers.

With her head tucked under his chin, he let the mist dance lightly against his face, finding himself oddly relaxed with her in his arms. It was as if she molded naturally into his embrace, a perfect fit with a man who never fit in anywhere. He pressed his cheek against her hair and wondered if there was something he should be saying.

He went with silence. She would tell him what made her cry, or not. He would do everything in his power to help. That was all there was to it. So instead he relished the feel of her there, until the mist turned to drizzle and he guided her back into the trailer.

She wiped her face and sat at the kitchen table. He slid in across from her.

"I'm sorry," she said. "I slipped into hysteria there for a minute."

"No sweat."

"It was because of this." She turned the laptop to face him. "It's from Cora."

He read it. "Do you know a P. Finnigan?"

She shook her head, eyes huge in the near darkness. "Should we tell the police?"

"Yes. When you meet with them tomorrow. I'll work on it."

"How?"

"Let me worry about it. Get some sleep."

She offered an exasperated look. "Easy for you to say. You don't seem to need any sleep. Were you keeping watch on us all this time?"

I haven't been able to take my eyes off you since the day I met you, his fickle heart supplied. Fortunately, his mouth was still in charge. "Don't need much sleep."

"Or much furniture?"

He shrugged.

"Or a TV?"

"Too noisy." He won a smile with that one.

She rested her chin on her hand. "What do you need?"

The question surprised him. "Simple stuff. Backpack. Hot shower. Dog kibble."

That got a giggle that faded rapidly. "I mean, you move around all the time, like you're looking for something. What is it?"

How did he get himself into this sticky conversation? The silence stretched into awkward so he broke down and told her. "Ever hear that verse from Proverbs? Starts with 'trust in the Lord' and ends with 'Seek his will in all you do, and he will show you which path to take?'"

She nodded solemnly.

"Well, I tried to take my own path plenty of times, and it got me in jail and beaten badly and deep into gang life." He watched carefully to see if she would recoil. Most women did when he got around to his sorry life history. Those brown eyes stayed riveted to his face.

"Why a gang?"

"My dad died when I was a teen, and I went nuts. Joined a gang, figured it made me a man, cool, like my brother."

"But he got out, didn't he?"

"Yeah. He's smarter than me. Military straightened him out. He tried to get me out, too, but I'm hardheaded. Took the beating to do that. I woke up handcuffed to the bed, and the first thing I thought of was, had I killed someone?"

She stayed quiet.

"I hadn't. God spared me from that, but I could have." His voice hitched a little. "Oh, how easily I could have done it."

"You wanted to go into the military, didn't you? Your brother told me, I think." Her voice was soft and soothing, like water over river stones.

He sighed. "My whole life I wanted to be a Marine

like my father. My choices ruined that for me. They don't take people with damaged legs and gang histories." It still hurt to say it, but somehow, telling it to her, it was more of a dull ache than a ripping pain.

"I'm sorry."

"I'm not. Oh, I wish I could have done it some other way, but destroying my life brought me to the edge of ruin and that's where I finally found God. From then on, I figured I'd let Him show me where to go and I guess He brought me here for a while."

"Until it's time to go again?"

"Dunno. He'll thump me on the head when He wants me to put down some roots." He paused. "What about you? What do you need?"

She laughed, but there was no joy in the sound. "I need a place to call home, where I can put down roots so deep Gracie and I will never be uprooted again, but I'm never going to get that."

"No?"

"No, because Hector will never leave us alone, and everywhere we go his bad choices follow us." She closed her eyes for a moment and breathed out a sigh. "No, our bad choices. I've…" She swallowed. "I've been to jail, too, and now it looks as if I might be going there again." Her face paled. "What have we done to Gracie? Two people who were supposed to love and protect her? What have we done?"

Tears sparkled there in her eyes, but she would not let them fall. *Good girl, Mia.*

He took her hands and squeezed hard. "Gracie is happy and loved. Even I can tell that, and kids are like space aliens to me."

Small smile.

"Not one person on this Earth has no regrets."

Juno thrashed in his sleep.

"Except dogs."

"That's probably true." He fell into the warmth of those eyes. "I'll help you find a place to put down roots." Dumb. The moment he said it she pulled away. Way to go, Dallas Foot-in-Mouth Black.

Her tone became careful, formal. "Thank you, but I'm going to take care of us. That's a lesson I learned the hard way. I can only count on myself."

Wrong lesson. No bigger disappointment than one-self. "Sure. I didn't mean anything by it." He looked outside. "Sun's almost up. I'll follow you into town so you can talk to the cops."

He headed for the door, not at a run but close to it. "There are some eggs, like I said, and maybe cheese somewhere. Will Gracie eat that?"

She nodded, face still tight. "Yes, thank you. I'll replace it all when I can."

He let her have that, if it was what she needed to feel in control.

"Good night, Mia."

Two hours later he followed her bashed up car to-ward town. Ominous signs of disaster preparation were visible as they drove along the main street. Shop owners were filling burlap bags with sand to be piled along the embankment that would optimistically stem the flood. Mia decided to stop and retrieve the photo before meeting with the police chief, so they drove along rain-drenched streets toward the lower lying valley where she rented a home. His gut tightened as a dark-colored SUV trailed behind them along the main drag and onto the narrow two-lane road. Not cause for alarm, per se, but he thought it just might be the same SUV he'd noticed parked on the side of the road several miles back. Colorado plates. Might be a rental.

Dallas slowed and so did the SUV. Not good. Keeping a distance. Nothing to be done to lose the guy at this point. Besides, in one of his stay-up-all-night reading frenzies, hadn't he read some sage advice from a Chinese general in 400 BC about keeping your friends close and your enemies closer?

"All right," he whispered, earning an interested look from Juno in the passenger seat. He maintained a steady pace, and the car dropped back just enough to preserve the gap between them.

He braked hard when Mia stopped abruptly. In a moment, he understood. The road dipped down, following the slope of the valley, only now the asphalt had disappeared under several feet of water. The surface was muddy and rippled, speckled with leaves and broken branches. She got out, hands on hips turning to give him an exasperated look that almost made him smile.

He joined her, noting that the SUV had pulled over a half mile behind them.

"Can your truck make it across?"

"Might, but I'm not going to risk anyone's safety. There's a bridge back a ways. We'll double back."

She groaned. "That will take us another half hour."

"Better late than drowned."

She looked as though she didn't appreciate his pearls of wisdom, but she acquiesced.

Juno sniffed disinterestedly at the water, stopping a moment to eye the car behind them on the road.

A look of fear flashed across her face. "Who is that?"

"Dunno, but I'll find out in a minute. Let's head for the bridge."

Mia gave the SUV a second look. He knew she wanted to ask more questions, but instead she got behind the wheel and turned around. Dallas fell in behind her and by the time they were rolling, the SUV had disappeared. Not for long. As he predicted, it picked them up again some five miles in, once again hanging back just enough.

The bridge was of sturdy steel construction, spanning the river that was normally well below its concrete piers. Now the water lapped considerably above that mark, but not enough to leave the structure impassable.

Yet.

Dallas decided it was time to get a better handle on the situation.

Mia drove over the bridge, and when she was safely across, he followed suit. A couple of feet in, he stomped on the brakes, bringing his vehicle to a dead stop.

"Time to come clean," he muttered, looking into the rearview as the SUV made the approach to the bridge. He stopped abruptly, too.

If their shadow was there for purely innocent reasons, he'd wait patiently, figuring there was some obstruction, maybe even honk after a bit, or try to pass. Certainly he'd get out of the car to investigate why Dallas was stopped, blocking the road.

Instead, the driver backed rapidly off the bridge, did a jerky three-point turn and took off in the other direction.

Dallas almost smiled for the second time that morning. He rolled down the window and called to Mia who had stopped and stuck her head out the window to question him.

"Go on. I'll be there soon."

Her eyes widened, quarter-size. "What are you doing?"

"Just making friends," he called out the window.

SEVEN

Dallas let the SUV outdistance him until it sped around a sharp bend in the shrub-lined road. He slowed and turned up a rough stretch which was probably more a trail than a road, but a way Dallas and Juno had explored many times in their backpacking travels. He stopped for only a moment to call a friend and give him the plate number.

"You know I got things to do 'sides hack info for you, right?" Farley said.

Dallas laughed. "Gonna help me or not?"

Farley snorted. "If you and Fido hadn't saved my life, I'd be in the bottom of a ravine with vultures using my bones for toothpicks."

"Vultures don't have teeth. Staying sober?"

"Yeah, man. Prayed myself through the last real bad stretch."

Dallas had prayed right along with him. And picked Farley up when he hadn't made it through, cleaned him up, filled him with coffee and nearly hog-tied the kid to get him to a meeting. "Gotta win, every day."

"I know, Mother, I know. Stop nagging and let me get to work."

"While you're at it, can you see if there's a P. Finnigan living in the area?"

"All right. See ya." Farley clicked off.

Dallas pushed the truck along, rocks pinging into the bottom, irritating Juno who barked just once.

"Half a mile more." Dallas squeezed the truck by a narrow section of path, branches scraping the sides, until he'd looped back out to the main road. A recent rock slide took out a bend of the highway, leaving the section blocked with a mess of boulders and only one lane passable. It was marked with cones and caution signs. Handy. He rolled down the window and listened to learn if he'd guessed correctly.

The sound of the SUV's approach told him he had. He edged past the rockfall and pulled the truck across the road. SUV guy would pass the blockage, encounter the truck and have to stop and back, which would slow him down enough for Dallas to get a good look. Risky, but with Mia's situation worsening by the minute, he needed some intel. Keep your enemies close…

The SUV was taking an unhurried pace. Dallas got out of the truck and he and Juno took a position behind a pile of rocks. Juno gave him the "you're probably crazy but I'm happy to participate in your insanity" look. They waited less than five minutes.

The SUV made the turn, stopped so fast the tires skidded a few inches. Dallas crouched low, peering over a granite lip of rock to identify the driver. To his surprise, the man shoved open the door and got out. Dallas took a picture with his cell phone.

Not much to him, but strength had nothing to do with size. Fair skin, buzz-cut hair. Tight skinny jeans and a shiny jacket that was probably fashionable somewhere in the world where Dallas hoped he never found himself.

The guy looked slowly around, hands loose at his sides. "We gonna talk?" he called out, voice higher pitched than Dallas guessed.

Dallas climbed out from behind the rock, and Juno scampered over to the man. He gave him a careful circling before he settled on sniffing his sneakers. "You're following Mia. Why? Who are you?"

The kid had to be no more than twenty. "Archie. How do you know I'm not following you?"

Dallas considered. "I'm not worth following. Did you break into her house?"

Archie crouched slowly and offered an outstretched hand to Juno. "I love dogs. Miss mine. He's some sort of lab and husky mix. Chews my shoes when I don't walk him enough and leaves them on the bed for me to find."

Dallas waited, watching to make sure Archie

didn't reach for any kind of weapon in his ridiculous excuse for a jacket. "I asked you a question."

"My boss sent me here. I do what I'm told."

"Who's your boss?"

Archie straightened. "Guy who wants his property back."

Dallas's pulse sped up a fraction. "Do you work for Hector?"

Archie laughed. "Good one. I like to be on the winning team." He checked his watch. "You're a roadblock, in more ways than one. You need to step aside."

"Not if you're after Mia."

"She has something that belongs to my boss. He wants it back. No need for any pain. Just a simple negotiation."

"She doesn't have anything, and if you hurt her, it will be the last thing you ever do." He had not raised his voice, but the intensity made Juno return to his side and sit, rigid with expectation.

"All right," Archie said, pulling out a switchblade and flicking it open. "This is as good a place to kill you as any, but I don't want to hurt the dog. Tell him not to attack."

Juno wasn't an attack dog. In fact, he was the perfect Search and Rescue dog because he was passionately interested in people, but they also had a bond that surpassed owner and worker.

"All right," Dallas said calmly. "I'll send him to

fetch and then you and I can get down to business. May I?" He gestured to a stick on the ground a few feet away and Archie nodded.

Dallas bent over to get the stick and while he was at it, grabbed a palm full of gravel loosed from the earlier slide.

"Okay, Juno. Ready to fetch?"

Juno shot to his feet as Dallas tossed the stick into the trees and then turned to fire the handful of gravel at Archie who instinctively raised an arm to cover his face. It was enough. Dallas aimed for Archie's arm and threw himself on top of the man, bringing him to the ground.

Juno returned and danced in crazy circles around the two, barking at a deafening volume.

Dallas used all his strength to slam Archie's knife hand into the ground, but the kid held fast. He dealt Dallas a blow with his free fist that got him in the back of the head, sending stars shooting across his vision. A flash of fire across his forearm rocked Dallas back as Archie rolled away. Dallas scrambled to his feet, a line of red dripping from the wound on his arm.

Archie was already standing, eyeing the dog who continued to bark, uncertain, taking darting hops toward Archie and Dallas. "What happened to fetch?"

"He fetches people, not sticks, and he's not an attack dog, so don't hurt him."

"No," Archie said. "I guess I won't. Nice moves. Heard you were in a gang back in the day."

Dallas did not react to Archie's knowledge. Kid had done some research. "Not anymore."

"You can never get out of that world."

"Yes, you can. I did."

"You're gonna be in my face if I let you leave."

"If you're after Mia, then you're right. I will."

"Why? You into her or something?"

"Just a friend."

Archie gave him a look. "Uh-huh. Sure." He straightened. "Short on time, so I'm gonna end it here, but I'll take care of the dog for you."

"Appreciate that." Dallas went into a ready stance, learned not in a karate studio or a self-defense class, but from adrenaline-fueled fights with other lost young men bent on self-destruction. To defend their brotherhood, what had been his brotherhood, his family, or so he'd fooled himself into believing. All for Uncle, for the territory. He did not want to fight, but if it would free Mia, then he would do it. Juno whined, big torso heaving with confusion. A finder, not a fighter. Dallas wished he had spent his life doing the same.

Self-recrimination later, he told himself. There was no effective way to defend against a knife attack and he had the scars to prove it. Only one alternative that wouldn't get him killed and he took it. When Archie lunged forward, Dallas jerked aside and aimed a crushing kick at Archie's knee.

Archie's grunt of pain told Dallas he'd hit the target. He stumbled and Dallas aimed another kick at the knife hand which sent the switchblade spiraling into the bushes as Archie fell stomach-first onto the wet ground.

Dallas immediately knelt on his back, knee between the shoulder blades, shushing the furiously barking Juno.

Dallas's heart was pounding, the pulse hammering so loudly in his ears he did not at first hear the chug of a heavy vehicle approaching from the other side of the rock slide.

"Someone's coming. Moving fast," Archie puffed. "What are you gonna do? You don't move your truck, whoever that is could slam right into it and go over the cliff."

He was right, but the second he released Archie, the guy would bolt or find his switchblade and have another go at Dallas. The pop of gravel sounded louder now.

No choice. He couldn't risk causing an accident.

He leaned closer to Archie. "Stay away from Mia."

Archie answered with a laugh. Dallas released his hold and ran to the truck, cranked the engine as Juno leapt in and got the truck out of the way with a screech of tires. He made it just far enough to pull off onto the narrow shoulder when Archie flashed by in his SUV, snapping off a salute to Dallas. A moment more passed before an emergency vehicle swept by, no sirens going, but lights flashing.

They, too, had to take the roundabout way to Mia's neighborhood since the main road was underwater. The driver gave Dallas a wave, thanking him for pulling off the road.

He settled in behind, trying not to crowd the responders. Should he worry more that the situation ahead had turned into an emergency? Or that he'd let Archie, the guy with a switchblade, get that much closer to Mia and Gracie?

Hands gripping the wheel, Mia answered Gracie's myriad questions mechanically, not realizing what she was agreeing to.

"I can have ice cream for breakfast? Super duper," Gracie said. "You never let me have that before. Not even Tina lets me have ice cream for breakfast, only cookies."

Mia blinked. "What? No of course you can't have ice cream for breakfast. I was thinking about something else, and Tina should not give you cookies for breakfast, either."

In truth, she was trying to squash down the concern that washed through her belly. Dallas had taken off after a stranger to do what? Confront him? Follow the car? She hit the brakes as a roadblock appeared.

A police volunteer in an orange vest approached her open window.

"What is it? What's going on?"

"Levee failed. Town's flooded. We're evacuating now."

"But I've got to get to my house. I need to…" Retrieve a picture of a woman who was at the scene of a murder? That seemed too fantastic a tale to drop on the harried-looking volunteer who was already wet to the skin, though it had stopped raining. "I have to get something. It's important."

"Sorry, ma'am. It's not safe to drive in. You can see from the road there, where everyone is gathered. No farther than that."

She dutifully pulled the car off the road, turned off the engine and helped Gracie out. They skirted giant puddles and slogged through patches of grass until they came to a gathering of a half dozen people wearing emergency vests who were peering at clipboards along with the volunteer firefighters. It was a sort of makeshift emergency center with a pop-up canopy to keep off the rain. With Gracie bundled close, Mia drew to the edge of the bluff, gazing down at what had been her home.

The house she rented was one of only a half dozen, scattered in between with thickly clustered trees. Now the quiet, country road was a river, water lapping the middle of the doorways. At first she couldn't locate her house, until she saw the weathervane turning lazily in the breeze.

Gracie pulled at her mother's hand. "Where's our house?"

Mia breathed out a long sigh. She had not yet even managed to tell Gracie the hard truth about Cora, but there was no way to shield her child from this. "The levee couldn't hold all the water. It spilled over and flooded our house."

They stood for a moment in silence.

"When will the water go away?"

Great question, and she'd give her eye teeth to know the answer. "I'm not sure."

And when the water did recede, what would be left behind? Sodden clothes, ruined furniture acquired a bit at a time on her meager salary. And the rocking chair, oh that precious wooden chair snatched up at a garage sale when she shouldn't have spent the money. How many hours had she spent in that chair after Gracie went to sleep, studying her nursing coursework, dreaming about the future she imagined she was providing for her daughter.

A lump formed in her throat.

"Where are we gonna sleep, Mommy?"

The question danced away, unanswered on the wind. They watched an inflatable Zodiac boat, guided by two firefighters, as it approached the bluff carrying an elderly couple swaddled in life jackets, their sparse white hair pasted in wet clumps to their foreheads. She searched the area for Dallas. What had happened to him?

Mia felt a hand on her shoulder.

She turned to find Dr. Elias wearing an orange vest over a long-sleeved denim shirt and jeans. Her mind was still dealing with the shock of seeing her whole life submerged and she wasn't sure what feeling floated to the top at the sight of her former employer.

"I'm sorry," he said, eyes somber. "The Army Corps of Engineers couldn't save the levee. They tried their best."

Mia nodded. "I'm sure they did."

"Hiya, Dr. Elias," Gracie said.

He smiled and knelt in front of her. "Well, hello there. I'm glad to see you."

"Our house is all watery now."

"Don't worry, honey. We'll find you a place to live."

Mia took Gracie's hand. "The doctor is here to help people who are hurt. Let him do his job now."

Dr. Elias straightened and put an arm around Mia's shoulders. "Really, I can help you find a place."

She didn't move, torn between shock and uncertainty. Was this the man whom she'd thought meant to harm her only days before? There was no longer a clear answer to any issue crowding her mind and heart.

Where would they go? She had maybe twenty dollars in her purse and a credit card on which she'd already charged a semester's tuition. "Why would you want to do that after you fired me?"

He sighed. "I told you I would help you, even if you couldn't work at the clinic. You lied to protect your child, not to hurt me. I'm sensitive about lying. A foible of mine."

How had the talk become about him?

He squeezed her shoulders. "I can fix you up in…"

A woman approached, dark hair cut into a stylish bob that remained neatly coiffed in spite of the elements. The fragrance of a floral perfume clung to her, odd and out of place at a disaster scene. Green eyes flashed under delicate brows. "Thomas, you're needed at the launch point. They're going out on a rescue for a possible heart attack in progress."

"Of course." He patted Gracie on the head and jogged toward the Zodiac that was being readied to embark on the rescue mission.

The woman gave Mia a tight smile. Her face was carefully made up to show her fortysomething years to full advantage, jewelry small and tasteful. "I'm Catherine Elias, the good doctor's wife."

The slight sarcasm left Mia off balance. "I'm Mia Verde and this is Gracie, my daughter. I work… I worked for your husband until just recently. We met at a party you were kind enough to host for the staff." Mia's eyes were drawn again toward the water. "That was my house down there."

Catherine's face softened, giving her a more youthful look. "I'm sorry. This must be hard for you. No job, no house and a daughter to care for." She seemed to consider for a moment. "I heard Thomas telling you he could help you find a place and I guess..." She shrugged. "Never mind. I'm tired, that's all. Our kids are almost finished with high school, but I remember how difficult it is when they're young. But sweet, too, those little ones." She looked wistfully at Gracie.

"Yes," Mia murmured, uncertain how to respond to the sudden change in mood.

"We have a small cabin up in the mountains here. It's remote, but you are welcome to stay there until you get another place."

"Thank you. That is incredibly kind of you, but we'll find something." Mia was amazed that her tone was calm and controlled. Inside, her gut churned like the gray water splashing against the bluff.

When? Where? And most of all how? She felt like dropping to her knees and praying, but she would not crumble. Not now. Not ever again. She would make a way, where there was none. "Where are the townspeople being evacuated to?"

Catherine pulled her gaze from Gracie. "The college gym just up the hill. It will work for a night or two anyway. You can walk up, or there's a van arriving in a minute to carry people."

"Great." Mia scooped Gracie up. "Mommy always

wanted you to go to college. You'll be the first four-year-old attendee ever. We'll just wait with the gang until the van arrives."

Feeling Catherine's eyes following them, she hastened toward the wet neighbors gathered in a forlorn group under a sodden canopy. She texted Tina, relieved when the girl answered back.

College classes canceled. Gone home to folks until flood's past. Kiss Gracie for me and try to stay dry.

"Hiya, Dallas," Gracie called over her shoulder.

Mia whirled, her spirit rising at the sight of Dallas loping toward her with Juno at his heels.

He gave Gracie a tight smile and she immediately crouched to administer an ear rub to Juno. Mud streaked his shirt, and Mia's eyes traveled downward, caught by the circle of bloody gauze tied around his forearm.

Her stomach clenched. "The man in the car."

"I'm okay, but he got away." Dallas seemed to weigh something in his mind before he leaned close and spoke in a low murmur. "He's keeping tabs on you for his boss."

She forced out the question. "Who is his boss? Never mind. It's Hector, isn't it?" Bitterness rose in her throat like a bubbling acid. "He's got people watching my every move. He'll never let us build a life without him."

"I don't think that's it."

Wind slapped her hair into her face. "Who then? Who would bother?"

"People who think Hector passed something on to you."

"Passed what?"

He didn't answer. Instead he showed her the picture on his cell phone. "Recognize him?"

Everything went fuzzy. She inhaled deeply, trying to stem the whirling in her head. "It's the man who broke into my house. I can't understand this. What is happening to my life?"

He embraced her then, and she let him. His arms pressed away the panic, the fear that grew with every passing day. The heat of his skin melted some of the numbing cold that gripped her.

"I'm checking into it. I'll have more answers soon."

"I've been in Spanish Canyon for months. Why would he come here now? What am I going to do?"

His embrace tightened. "Come back to the trailer. I'll keep watch. He won't get close."

Protection. Strength. Safety. And a delicious sliver of fascination. Dallas Black made all those things erupt in her belly. She turned so her lips touched the smooth skin of his jaw. His dark hair cocooned her face against the warm hollow of his neck. How her body craved the comfort of his touch, her soul cried out to have a partner to help her through the flood that she knew was far from over.

But she'd had that perfect union before. A God-blessed marriage, or so she'd thought, until she finally saw Hector for what he was. Now "until death do us part" sounded more like a sentence than a comfort. Never again. Never.

She stepped back, sucking in a breath. "I'm going to the college. They've got an evacuation shelter set up there."

He frowned. "You want to go sleep on the gym floor where anyone can get at you and Gracie?"

She took Gracie's hand. "We'll be safe there."

"Safe?" His face was incredulous. "This guy Archie was ready to kill me to get to you."

"There are lots of people going. We'll never be alone."

The muscles of his jaw jumped. "Absolutely not."

She stiffened. "We'll be in a group all the time. Never alone. Besides, you don't make decisions for me."

"Somebody should, because you're letting what happened to you with Hector color your judgment."

Cheeks burning, her stomach tightened into an angry ball. "I'm doing what's best for Gracie."

"Are you?" He fisted his hands on his hips, and she saw fresh blood welling through the white gauze when his muscles flexed.

Am I? Suddenly she wondered, but she couldn't reverse course now. Right or wrong she had to call the shots for Gracie. Just her and no one else. "I'll return your phone as soon as I can."

She pulled Gracie along to the van that had just wheezed up the slope, not allowing herself to look back. She knew what was behind her anyway. A disappointed German shepherd.

And one very angry Dallas Black.

EIGHT

"What?" Dallas barked into the phone.

Farley whistled. "Bite my head off, why don't you? Got a burr under your backpack?"

"Sorry. Bad day." Too bad to try to explain to Farley. He molded his tone into something that might pass for civil. "Do you have anything for me?"

"Seven P. Finnigans in the vicinity. Sending you those addresses."

"Thanks."

"And the car was rented to an Archie Gonzales, from Miami."

Miami. Not a surprise. "Okay."

"One more thing, man. Norm, over at the rental car place. I know him, and he's a crusty old codger. He's got trackers on the rentals."

Dallas's nerves quickened. "Illegal, of course,"

"Of course, but he's in favor of slapping a nice hefty fee on the cars if they're taken out of state. Anyway, it was easy to hack into his tracking system."

"Do I want to know how you did that?"

"Probably not."

"What did you find out?"

"Most of his routes were routine, except one I found interesting. Guess who he's been to see recently?"

"Not in the mood for guessing games."

"Dr. Elias."

"That's not news. I think he's been at the clinic shadowing Mia."

"Not the clinic. Archie's been to the doctor's house."

His house? Dallas struggled to put it together and almost missed the finish.

"At 3:13 a.m."

Not the usual time for social calls. "Thanks, Farley. I owe you lunch."

"Yeah, and a vacation in Maui."

"We'll start with lunch."

"All right, cheapskate."

Dallas disconnected. The next call would be to Reuben and Antonia. There was no more room to keep secrets. Mia needed to know everything. He swallowed, picturing her maddeningly stubborn brown eyes, the need for independence burning as bright as the hurt. When she knew, she would hate him.

But at least she'd still be alive.

Dallas's arm throbbed. He strolled as casually as he could through the collection of hastily parked cars on the grassy shoulder of the road, leaving Juno in the truck to catch a nap. He realized he was grinding his teeth when he passed Mia's battered car. If she'd listen to reason…if she'd consider the smart choice.

Like you did? His conscience flipped through the myriad prideful mistakes he'd made. Rival gang members he'd fought, threatened. Store owners he'd intimidated. Petty theft he'd committed to prove himself to his ersatz family. His damaged body would always be a reminder of that disastrous past.

Most of his shame came when he remembered the way he'd coveted the looks he'd gotten from people, the respect he'd imagined in their eyes. Turns out it was not respect, but fear. He'd been too blinded to turn from the smothering blanket of gang life.

In spite of his brother Trey's tough love born of experience.

With no regard for his mother's pleading requests and avalanche of prayers.

It had taken waking up in the hospital with part of his spleen missing and his knee on fire, shaking from alcohol withdrawal and his boyhood dream to become a Marine ruined, for him to fall on his face in front of the Lord. Maybe it was the humiliation of being handcuffed to the hospital bed, knowing he deserved to go to jail for many things, including possession of an illegal firearm and simple assault. Possibly it was the realization that he had shamed his mother, his brother and his father's memory. Undoubtedly, it was God shouting his name.

At rock bottom, there's no more room for pride. Only God.

Once he'd let go, God had shown him the goodness in people, the desperate love of his family, his own potential to be a man who lifted others, rather than striking them down. Somewhere along the way, he'd found there was goodness inside him, as well.

The fall had hurt, and he wished he could help Mia learn what he had without the dramatic descent. He sighed. *God's job, Dallas. Yours is to keep her safe.* It was a good reminder. No matter what the oddball storm of feelings brewing inside, Mia was his job, his mission. In spite of the pain from Archie's knife, and Mia's ridiculous desire to stay at the college shelter, he moved on through the sea of parked cars.

He saw no sign of Archie's rental, a small mark in their favor.

Sunset was not due for another hour, but the clouds succeeded in sealing the light away behind a wall of gray. Bad sign. The levees were similarly stressed all over Spanish Canyon and the rivers and catchments swollen to capacity. On an up note, the last weather report he'd heard called for only a mild rainfall in the next forty-eight hours. With that weather break, they might be able to stave off any more serious flooding and evacuations.

The flood lent strange odors to the air—the scent

of wet stone, sodden foliage and trees uprooted from centuries of packed earth. Mia's house was underwater to the eaves, and so was the picture that might shed some light on Cora's death. He guessed Archie had not been there in Mia's house looking for the photo, but searching for Garza's money. However the meeting between Elias and Archie still puzzled him.

He was about to return to his truck, parked well away from the others when a stealthy movement caught his attention. Trick of the cascading shadows? No, there was another pulse of motion near a well-appointed blue BMW.

He drew back, crouching behind Mia's car to watch as a slight figure stealthily opened the passenger door. Whoever it was wore a hat and a dark windbreaker. Pretty low for someone to take advantage of a disaster situation to rifle through someone's car. But it was true that disasters brought out both the best and worst in people. He was about to demand an explanation, when he realized this wasn't a stranger, not a total stranger anyway.

Easing closer, he could see Susan's profile well enough to be sure it was her, the red-haired woman who'd shown up at his trailer.

And snuck out with your knife, he reminded himself.

Still keeping low between vehicles, he crept nearer.

She sat in the passenger seat of the car, examining the pile of papers in her lap that she'd taken out of the glove box. So intent was she on her mission, she didn't look up until he wrenched open the door.

With a scream she bolted out, spilling the papers on the muddy ground. For a moment, she stood frozen, staring, chest heaving with panic.

"Breaking-and-entering a specialty of yours?"

She let out a gust of air. "The door was open. That's not breaking in."

"Whose car?"

Still no response. Keeping her in his peripheral vision he picked up one of the papers. Catherine Elias. "Why are you interested in Dr. Elias's wife?"

"She's a fake."

"A fake what?"

"She's living a lie, and I'm going to prove it."

"I thought you were interested in finding out who killed Cora."

She nodded, lips tight, eyes flat and hard as wet stones. "That's right."

"Do you think Catherine killed Cora?"

"Leave me alone, Dallas. This doesn't concern you right now."

He took a step toward her. "You're coming with me to the police. No more sneaking around breaking into cars. I'm out of patience with these guessing games."

She shook her head. "I'm not going with you anywhere."

He did not want to force a woman to do anything

against her wishes, but this particular woman was dangerous. He took her wrist, the tendons standing out against the skin, pulse slamming violently through her veins. "You need to come with me, Susan."

He'd prepared himself for her to pull away. Instead she surged close, her clawed fingers pinching his biceps, face so close her sour breath bathed his face. "Listen to me," she hissed. "There are dangerous people in this town, people who are not who they appear to be." Her mouth twitched at the corners, and he fought the urge to recoil.

"Like Mrs. Elias?"

She did not seem to hear him. "Dangerous people who will kill Mia Verde and her little girl, just like they killed Cora. If you try to go to the police, or anyone else, they'll just kill her quicker."

His stomach flipped. "Who? Tell me, and I'll help you."

She moved back slightly to search his eyes. "Ah, sweet boy. Are you going to protect me from a killer?"

"If I can."

"I'm not afraid to die," she said, releasing his shoulders. "It's the living part that's scary."

He felt as though he was stuck in a strange horror film. Was she crazy? Was he, for letting go of her wrist?

The sound of voices made them both turn. Susan

quickly returned the papers to the glove box and ducked down, yanking him to a crouch next to her. Through the window they saw Catherine Elias and an orange-vested volunteer consulting a clipboard as they walked toward the car. Catherine pointed to something on the first page and the two stopped to talk.

"Remember," Susan whispered, "if you tell anyone, Mia and Gracie will die. I'll contact you when I can." She sprinted off through the cars and ducked into a screen of trees. He scooted far enough away from Catherine's car that he would not be taken for a stalker, and then walked back to his truck where he sat on the front seat, brooding.

The obvious course of action was to go to the police, but they already suspected Mia of being involved in Cora's death. What would they make of his wild story about some mystery woman poking through Catherine's car?

Her words circled in his gut, cold and heavy. *"Dangerous people who will kill Mia Verde and her little girl, just like they killed Cora."*

Now his head pounded right along with the throbbing in his forearm. He should go home, back to the trailer to think it through, but he didn't want to be that far away from Mia and Gracie with Archie on the loose. If he checked himself in to the college evacuation center, Mia would be furious and possibly try to go find yet another unsuitable place to house herself and Gracie.

Juno poked his nose at Dallas, bringing him back. "What next?" his eyes inquired. The dog was eager to do just about anything Dallas requested except get his nails trimmed. That required several dozen treat bribes and some strong-arming from his owner. "Looks like we sleep in the truck again, boy, but I've got some kibble for you, don't worry."

He opened the door for the dog.

"Don't suppose you've got any notions on how to handle a stubborn woman, do you, Juno?"

Juno huffed out a breath and laid his head on his paws.

"Yeah, that's what I thought," Dallas said, giving his friend a pat.

Mia took the blankets offered to her and found her way to the side of the gym designated for women. She chose two cots together, but at a bit of a distance from the nearby family consisting of a wife and three teenage girls and a few older women who had already set up their makeshift beds. The two older women sat together, hands clasped, praying softly, one with wispy white hair. Perhaps they were sisters. Longing surged through her and she wished Antonia was there.

Gracie stared. "Is that Miss Cora? I want to go see her."

A pain stabbed deep inside. "No, honey. Just looks like her. The hair is the same color."

"Oh." Gracie said, looking up at the ceiling lights. "I don't like it here. Maybe we can go stay with Miss Cora. She prays nice, with songs and everything."

Tears collected in Mia's eyes, and she blinked hard. It hadn't dawned on her until just then that she had never prayed with Gracie, that she'd funneled her own anger into a deluge that kept her daughter far from the Lord, too. Her choice had bled down to Gracie, staining her with Mia's own sin.

"Gracie, I'm sorry. Do…do you want to pray with me?"

Gracie nodded, grabbing Mia's hands. "Okay. I'll say it. I know how." Gracie thanked God for Mia and Cora and the cheese sandwich and cookies she'd gotten from the volunteer who'd included an extra sweet for the little girl and the blue blanket and Auntie Nia and Uncle BooBen. "And thanks for Dallas 'cuz he says Daddy can be good again and thanks for Juno 'cuz he plays with me. Ayyyyyy men!" The last word came out in such an unexpected volume that the others shot amused glances their way.

Mia raised an eyebrow. "That was a big amen."

"Cora says you should always fill up the amen with joy," Gracie said. "So can we go see her?"

That innocent heart had never confronted death before. Certainly Mia would never have chosen to tell Gracie in the wake of losing every possession to the cruel water that engulfed their house. This time, she did send up a prayer of her own, a halting, awkward, stumbling effort.

Help me tell her.

Help her cope.

Mia forced out the words. "Honey, I have something sad to tell you."

Gracie regarded her soberly, bouncing a bit on the cot beside her.

"Miss Cora died. I'm so sorry. Her house caught on fire and the smoke got inside her lungs." Mia watched in fear as Gracie's brow puckered. "She's in Heaven now."

"Oh." Gracie considered the news as a full fifteen seconds ticked away. "Can we stay at her house until she comes back?"

It was as if her heart shrank smaller and smaller, concentrating the pain until it nearly choked her. "She's not coming back, baby," Mia whispered.

"Never?"

Mia took Gracie's small fingers in her own. "No, honey. Never."

"Mommy, I think that's not right. She's gonna come soon. Can I keep the blanket?" Gracie held up the blue blanket neatly folded at the foot of the cot.

"Yes," Mia said weakly. "The volunteers said you could if you want to."

Gracie wrapped herself up and laid down on the cot, singing softly to herself.

Mia watched her, filled with a river of tenderness that almost overwhelmed her. It would sink in, in time, that Cora was gone. Maybe that was a gift God gave his little children, a gradual realization that was kinder, somehow than the swift bolt of knowledge. Shadows crept along the edges of the gym, and quiet conversations gave way to silence. Mia found she could not sleep, though the cot was not at all uncomfortable.

She tossed and turned on the prickly choices she had made, ignoring Dallas's advice. His words floated back through her memory.

"Ever hear that verse from Proverbs? Starts with 'trust in the Lord' and ends with 'Seek His will in all you do, and He will show you which path to take.'"

She yanked the covers up around her chin. He could afford to believe such things; he had no one depending on him except for a dog. Dallas would not wake up tomorrow to a hungry child with not a single spare pair of socks, no place to live and nowhere to go. That was going to be Mia's scenario in the morning and she'd have to figure out how to deal with it.

A gleam of light crept across the gym floor. Someone entered carrying an enormous pile of towels, heading after a moment of hesitation, toward the locker room. She sighed. At least there was the possibility of a hot shower in the morning. Again she tried to force her body to relax on the cot. This time her wandering attention was caught by whispered conversation as two people talked by the light of a battery-powered lantern.

Giving up the attempt at sleep, she got up in search of a drink of water and caught a sentence of the conversation going on near the doors.

"She's practically a stranger," a familiar voice growled.

"No, she's not," Catherine Elias hissed. "That red-headed wacko is stalking me."

Dr. Elias reached for his wife's hand, but she jerked it away, nearly upsetting the lantern. "She lost her husband. I treated her some time later. She attached herself to me and Peter."

"Peter Finnigan? You never mentioned that."

Peter Finnigan? Mia's heart beat faster at the name from Cora's email. She wanted to ask, to step forward into the lamplight, but she decided to retreat from the private conversation instead. As she did so, she heard Dr. Elias continue.

"I didn't want to upset you, honey."

"What's her fixation with me?"

He sighed. "She wants to be with me, ever since I treated her all those years back. I've tried to keep her away because she's...unhinged."

Unhinged. Mia crept back toward her cot, but not until she heard Mrs. Elias's reply.

"She's dangerous."

Dangerous. They had to be talking about Susan,

the woman from the fire, who'd showed up at Dallas's trailer.

She was in such a state of confusion, at first she thought she'd gone to the wrong cot. "Gracie?" she called softy, turning in a quick circle.

Gracie's blanket lay on the floor, but the girl was nowhere to be found. She'd gone to the bathroom. That was it.

Mia made her way quickly to the ladies' room. Empty. Jogging now back out into the main gym, she raced through the rows of cots, peering intently to see if Gracie had mistakenly crawled into the wrong bed.

There she was—at the end of the row, curled into a ball under the blanket. Mia felt the weight of the world rise off her shoulders and she heaved out a gusty sigh.

"You scared me, Gracie," she whispered, laying a hand on the girl's shoulder. "You're in the wrong bed."

The child sat up, blinking dark eyes. The woman on the cot reached out a protective hand. "This is my daughter, Evelyn. Can I help you?"

Shock rippled through Mia. Gracie was gone.

NINE

Gracie's here somewhere. She's not gone. Mia began to run now, around the perimeter of the gym to the men's area, in case her daughter had gotten confused. She rechecked Gracie's cot, snatching up the blue blanket to prove to her hands what her eyes could not accept.

Gracie was not there.

"Gracie?" What started out as a whisper, grew in volume until people began to sit up on their cots.

Dr. Elias and his wife materialized, lantern in hand. "What's wrong?" the doctor asked.

"Gracie's gone."

Catherine scanned the room. "I'm sure she's here somewhere."

Fear clawed at Mia's insides, prickling her in cold waves of goose bumps. "What if she wandered outside?" Down the hill, to the edge of the bluff where there was six feet of floodwater to fall into?

"We'll look right now," Dr. Elias said, heading for

the door. "Catherine, keep searching inside." He put a hand on Mia's shoulder. "We'll find her."

At the moment, all her anger at the doctor dissipated in a cloud of hope.

We'll find her.

They ran outside, sprinting along the path to the edge of the bluff, looking down into the swirling, moonlit water. Mia's stomach was twisted into a knot. Would she see her little girl floating there, facedown in the merciless waves? Shaking all over she forced herself to look.

"No sign of her. I'll look downstream," Dr. Elias said, handing her a flashlight. "Would she have gone to the woods back up by the gym?"

"I don't know," Mia answered. "I'll check there." She turned toward the patch of trees, dark silhouettes against the sky. Why would she head out of the gym on her own? Gracie was not afraid of the dark, but she did sleepwalk sometimes. Mia looked for signs that Gracie had passed by, but the ground was littered with bushels of fallen leaves and downed branches. The darkness wasn't helping, either.

"Gracie?" Mia called, her voice tremulous.

She walked under the dripping canopy. Droplets landed on her face like tears. "Gracie?" she called again. There was no answer but the rustle of pine needles, the movement caught by her flashlight the result of debris blowing along the ground. Gracie wasn't here, Mia could feel it.

She had to be inside the gym, she'd fallen asleep somewhere or gone to look for a snack. Mia was beaming the flashlight ahead to find her way out, when a man grabbed her from behind. A hand, smelling of nicotine, covered her mouth, as a strong pair of arms held her in a tight clinch.

"Mrs. Sandoval, listen carefully because I'm not the patient type and I want to go back to Florida. We know Hector has sent you a stash of money and it belongs to my boss. He wants it back. I've already searched your home and followed you around like a tracking dog, and I'm sick of it so I decided we should have a little meeting. Now, I'm going to move my hand so you can tell me what I want to know. If you scream, I'll hurt you. Understand?"

Blood rushing in her ears, she managed a nod. He peeled away his fingers and she turned to face him. It was the same man who had tried to trap them in her garage. She didn't care. There was only one thing her mind screamed out to know.

"Did you take my daughter?"

Archie's expression was hard to read. "I asked you a question. Answer."

"I don't have any money from Hector, and I don't know where it is."

"Mr. Garza thinks otherwise."

Garza. Powerful. Ruthless. A man who ran the Miami drug trade. "I don't have it. If I did, would I be renting a house here? Driving a secondhand car?"

Archie shrugged. "Not my job to figure you out, just to return the money. Got a tip that you've hidden it somewhere."

"A tip from whom?"

He didn't answer.

"Please," she whispered. "Did you do something to Gracie?"

Flashlights played over the grass outside the gym. Archie stepped back into the shadows. "Think about what's important and what you will lose if you don't give me what I want."

He melted away into the wet trees.

She ran blindly, branches slapping at her face, back toward the gym.

Gracie, Gracie, her heart chanted as she sprinted straight into Dallas, rocking back off his hard chest.

"Gracie's gone. Archie got hold of me."

His fingers dug into her shoulders. "Did he hurt you?"

"No."

His eyes dropped to her hands. "Is it hers?"

"What?" She realized through her fog that she was still holding the blue blanket. "This? Yes, it's Gracie's."

He called Juno and held out the blanket to the dog. "Find."

Juno bounded over the grass, startling those doing the flashlight search.

"Can he smell her?" she whispered.

"He's air scenting, following her smell." They watched the dog jog up to the gym entrance, scratching to be let in.

Dallas eased the doors open and Juno disappeared inside. Mia and Dallas followed her in. The dog followed the scent to the girl's bathroom, but stopped before he made it to the threshold. Juno circled a few times and stood, nose twitching.

Mia pressed shaking fingers to her mouth. "He doesn't know where she is."

"Give him a minute. There are a lot of scents in here. He's an older dog, so he's better at thinking it out and taking his time."

"Are you sure?"

"Trust the dog."

Trust a dog? With her baby's life? She wanted to yell, to scream at the top of her lungs as she watched Juno make a slow perusal of the room. Most of the occupants were awake now, helping look under cots and in corners, while others stood on the sides of the gym, giving Mia looks of abject pity.

She felt Dallas's hand take her hand and he squeezed hard. She clung to that touch as if it were the only thing that could keep her alive. Maybe it was. If Juno didn't find Gracie… She could not breathe, her ears rang.

She felt the room spinning, and Dallas forced her into a chair. "Deep breaths."

Waves of nausea and panic alternated through her body as she struggled not to black out.

Juno scratched at a darkened door in the back of the gym that Mia had not noticed.

"Stay here," Dallas said. "I'll check it out."

No way. Mia struggled to her feet, shoving down the dizziness by sheer willpower and staggered after him.

The exit opened onto a chilly hallway with metal doors at even intervals. Juno charged into the inky darkness.

Dr. Elias trotted behind them. "All the doors along this corridor are locked except the far exit door, for safety's sake. I saw to it myself."

"And the exit door? Where does it open?"

"Onto the parking lot," Elias said.

Mia ran to the end, ignoring the men. She was about to plunge through.

"Wait," Dallas said. He nodded at Juno who was pacing the corridor in regular arcs, nose quivering.

"You stay with your dog. I'm going to find my kid," Mia snapped.

"We might be wasting time," Dallas said. "Let the dog work, just for a minute longer."

"I don't have a minute," she shrieked. "Gracie might be out there in the water."

"This is why we train rescue dogs, Mia," Dallas barked. "They save time and effort and find a victim faster than a person ever could. You've got to trust the dog. Trust me."

For a long moment she stared at him. Seconds passed into excruciating minutes. Trust. She could not give it to him, not now, not with Gracie's life at stake. She pressed on the panic bar, just as Juno scratched furiously at one of the doors. Dallas opened it.

"So much for locked. It's a door to the stairwell." He held it for Juno who raced away. In a matter of moments, the dog returned, sat rigidly at Dallas's feet and barked exactly two times.

"It leads to the roof, I think," Dr. Elias said, voice low and hushed. "How did she unlock the door? Could a little girl climb three stories all by herself in a darkened stairwell?"

Gracie could. Hope and fear clawed together in her throat and she pushed forward, but Dallas had already plunged through the door, long legs churning up the stairs leaving Mia racing to catch up.

Dallas reminded himself as he ran that Mia did not know Juno like he did. Trust a dog? With his life. If Juno alerted, he'd found Gracie all right. The question was, in what condition? He knew she hadn't unlocked the door that led to the stairwell by herself. Dallas did not allow himself to dwell further on the thought. Three flights at top speed, following the sound of Juno's nails clicking on the concrete until he got too far ahead for them to hear. When they reached the door to the roof, Juno was sitting, nose shoved to the gap under the threshold, tail wagging for all he was worth.

I know, buddy. You found her.

With adrenaline surging his gut, he threw open the door and half fell onto the rooftop, Mia and Elias right behind him.

"Gracie," Mia screamed. "Where are you?"

Juno had already disappeared around a utility enclosure. When they rounded the corner, he was licking the tears off Gracie's face. The girl was sitting in a little ball, sobbing and hiccupping all at the same time.

His own sigh of relief was drowned out by the wail that came from Mia as she threw herself on her daughter, adding her tears to the mix.

Dallas called Juno and gave him a thorough pet and scratch. "Good boy, Juno."

"That's an excellent dog," Dr. Elias said with a winded laugh.

"Yes, he's the best air scenter I've ever worked with."

"And to think he does it all for kibble." Dr. Elias stared at Gracie and Mia.

Dallas caught something in the doctor's tone. "He does it for the joy of the find."

"How do you know he'll come back to you?"

"He's trained that way."

Dr. Elias nodded thoughtfully. "Good investment. You make a nice wage for that kind of work?"

Dallas tried to keep the disgust out of his voice. "We're all volunteer."

He nodded as if he'd just figured out why Dallas wore beat-up jeans and drove a ten-year-old truck. "My son, Jake, always wanted a dog, but we never caved in to that desire. We bought him lacrosse gear instead. Now he's the best on his team."

Dallas figured a lacrosse stick was a pretty poor substitute for a dog, but he refrained from saying so. He waited for a few more moments while Mia held Gracie so tight the girl squirmed for breath.

"Why did you come up here?" Mia said, at last pulling Gracie to arm's length. "You could have fallen. Why did you do such a dangerous thing?"

"It was dark and I was going to find the bathroom. A man told me they were closed and I had to go up-stairs. He opened the door for me with a funny stick thing that he stuck in the lock."

"What man?" Dallas said.

Gracie shrugged. "I don't know. It was dark and he had a hat on."

Mia let out an exasperated sigh. "Why didn't you come back to ask me to go to the bathroom with you?"

"You weren't there."

Mia's face whirled through a storm of emotions before she settled on grabbing Gracie again and hugging her close. Over Gracie's shoulder she shot Dallas a look.

Dr. Elias reached for his phone. "I'm glad that's over."

"It's not over," Dallas snapped. "Someone sent Gracie up to the roof on purpose."

"For what purpose? To steal something while we were all busy searching? Mia and Gracie have nothing worth stealing." He looked thoughtfully at Mia. "Do you?"

Mia tightened her grip on Gracie. "No, we don't."

"I don't suppose it's…" He shot a look at Gracie and lowered his voice. "Someone who is reaching out from prison, for some reason?"

"Why would it be?" Dallas said.

The doctor shrugged. "True, I guess that's letting the past color the present. The door must not have been latched properly. Probably her imagination about the man." He chuckled. "My son was convinced for months that there was a bear living in our attic." He looked at Gracie, bending to look her in the eye. "I'm very happy that you are okay, Miss Gracie. I would be quite sad if anything happened to you." Dr. Elias dialed his cell phone to report that Gracie had been found. "I'll head downstairs and get everyone settled again."

He wiggled his fingers at Gracie and departed.

Dallas knelt next to the child, while Juno rolled over so Gracie could scratch the dog's belly. "Gracie, the man who told you to come up here. Do you think it could have been Dr. Elias?"

"No." She babbled to Juno. "You're a good doggie for finding me. I'm going to get you some Goldfish and we can share my blanket."

"How do you know?" Dallas continued. "How do you know it wasn't Dr. Elias?"

"'Cuz Dr. Elias smells nice."

"And the man who sent you up here didn't?"

"Nope," Gracie said. "He smelled like cigarettes."

Horror filtered past Mia's eyes as she squeezed her daughter closer. "Oh, Gracie."

"I told him cigarettes are bad." Gracie patted her mother's back. "He said to tell you something."

Mia tried to speak, but no sound emerged.

"What did he say?" Dallas used the calm tone he employed whenever Juno located a traumatized victim, the "everything is going to be absolutely fine now" tone.

"He said he was going to see us again real soon," she said.

TEN

Mia would not stay another second. Heedless of anything but the need to get Gracie out of that awful gym, she waved away the well-meaning urgings from Dr. Elias and Catherine to stay until morning.

"It's dark and the roads are treacherous," Dr. Elias said.

"Not as treacherous as staying here," she snapped.

"Someone phoned the police. They're sending someone, but it's not high on their list since Gracie's been located," Dallas said, grabbing the stuffed animal someone had given Gracie as Mia plopped her on the nearest empty cot to wrap her in a jacket.

"They can come find me if and when they send anyone." She pulled up the zipper. "We're not staying here."

Dallas did not ask where she was going. Honestly, she didn't have the foggiest notion, but Archie would not touch Gracie ever again and if he showed up, he'd wish he hadn't. Fury had replaced the fear. Anger was good, much better than helplessness.

Dr. Elias started to follow her as she led Gracie out the gym doors, but his wife stopped him with a whispered comment and a hand on his arm.

"Do you have my number at least?" the doctor said. "In case you decide you can't go it alone?"

Mia whirled to face him. "Thank you for everything, but that's exactly what I'm going to do."

Dallas followed her out. She hoisted Gracie on her hip and charged toward the makeshift parking lot, stopping short when she peered into the sodden interior of her damaged car. The rain had sheeted through the broken window and the seats were now sopping, bits of glass she had not seen before sparkling on the tattered vinyl.

One more thing. Another small obstacle, but it felt like the last tiny nudge toward complete desperation. She tried to keep her breathing steady as Gracie launched into a round of sleepy questions, rubbing her eyes with a fist. "Where will we sleep? I'm tired."

"Just a minute. Let mommy think." Could she get a ride? Borrow a car? Wait for the police and ask them to take her somewhere, anywhere?

An unusual detail caught her attention through the tension rippling her insides. Gracie's booster, still buckled in the backseat, had been covered up in a plastic garbage bag. She stared for a long moment before she turned around to face Dallas.

"Didn't want it to get wet," he said simply, hands

in his jeans pockets. "Would have sealed the window, too, but I only had one bag."

The man had thought about something as menial and foreign to his world as a child's booster seat. "Dallas," she said, but a thickening in her throat kept her mute. She reached out very slowly and pressed her palm to the side of his face. He gazed at her in silence. She searched for signs of pity or disgust in his expression. There was nothing there but compassion and worry. "I am pretty sure that was the nicest thing anybody has done for me in a very long time."

"You deserve nice things, and so does Gracie." He stroked the back of her hand, tentatively, as if it were a bird that might fly away at any moment.

She reached up to press a kiss to his cheek, but his greater height caused it to land just below his jawline. The stubble on his chin tickled her lips. The pulse that revved up in his throat seemed to pass into her body, until her heart matched pace with his. "Thank you," she whispered.

He cleared his throat as she stepped away. "I know you don't want to come back to the trailer. I'll help you find another place in the morning, but we can't right now. It's all there is. It's all I have to offer."

He left the question unspoken. *Will you come with me?*

"Why," she whispered, giving words to the question she hadn't known boiled and bubbled in her broken soul, "is it so hard to do it on my own?"

A beam of moonlight caught his face, highlighting the strong chin, wide cheekbones and a boy-like vulnerability under the tough guy mask. "Maybe because you weren't meant to. No one is."

Mia sagged under the weight of the words and her daughter's limp form. Dallas stepped forward, taking Gracie from her. She fetched the booster and they made a quiet procession back to Dallas's truck.

She squeezed the booster into the backseat of the double cab, and Dallas put her in and secured the buckle.

Juno hopped in next to Gracie whose eyes were at half-mast, licking her when he thought Dallas was not looking. After what Juno had done, Mia would never discourage him from being near Gracie again.

Dallas opened the passenger door for Mia, his body close to hers, and she pressed herself into his arms. "I don't want this," she said into his chest, dizzy with the nearness of him and the relief that Gracie was safe. "I don't want to…need someone."

"I know," he said as he bent his head and kissed her. Electric warmth circled through her and pushed back a tiny corner of fear as her lips touched his. Breathless, she pulled away. "I should have said it sooner, but thank you for finding my daughter."

Eyes wide, he offered a tentative smile. "Juno found her."

"I'll pay him in Goldfish," she said, her own voice

tremulous as she chided herself mentally. "But I don't know how to repay you."

"There's no debt."

The softness in his eyes brought her back to the heady emotion of that kiss. She almost lost herself in the feeling again before she snapped herself back to reality. His kiss was just a physical expression of what they'd just been through. *Don't feel for him. Don't love him.* Deep breaths helped her stop the wild firing of her nerves as he shut the door and went around to the driver's side.

The first ten miles passed in silence until Dallas told her about Susan.

Mia gaped. "Is she crazy? Making it all up?"

"I don't know."

"I heard Catherine say she was basically stalking him. She couldn't get over her husband's death and she became fixated on the doctor after he treated her. They mentioned Finnigan's name, too."

They mulled over the situation for the next half hour. Dallas edged the truck past a monster puddle that nearly swallowed the road. "I don't know who is telling the truth, but maybe this Finnigan is the place to start since his name has come up a few times now."

"Should we tell the police?"

"That's the million dollar question." He shot her a glance, dark eyes unreadable. "Your call." They made the final turn into the trailer park. "But you'd better decide now," he said as Detective Stiving emerged from the police car parked in front of Dallas's unit.

Dallas tried to hide his dismay that it was Stiving and not Chief Holder who greeted them. He lifted the sleeping Gracie from the back and handed her to Mia. Stiving let Mia get Gracie settled inside, Juno flopped down on the floor next to her. He stood on the front porch with Dallas until Mia joined them, a blanket wrapped around her shoulders.

"Folks told me you left the college gym. Said something unpleasant happened. How about filling me in?" Stiving took careful notes about Gracie's disappearance and the encounter with Archie in the woods. Dallas waited to see if she would reveal what Susan said, but she did not, nor did she mention Peter Finnigan's name.

Stiving arched an eyebrow. "So the Archie guy from Miami. He thinks you've got money from your husband squirreled away somewhere?"

Mia nodded wearily.

"Is he right?"

"No," Mia snapped, "as I explained to him. I'm a single mother with next to nothing in my wallet, no house, a ruined car and only the clothes on my back. I don't even have a change of clothes for Gracie. That's it. And even if I got Hector's money, I'd send it back express mail because I don't want anything to do with my ex-husband, thank you very much." The last few words came out a near shout.

Dallas could not have been more proud. After all she'd been through, she would not be steamrolled.

To Dallas's surprise, Stiving smiled. "Got it. Archie from Miami is a misguided individual. Targeting you for no reason."

Mia let out a squeak. "Does it matter the reason? He sent my child up onto the roof. He could have... hurt her."

"And no one else saw the guy?"

"I did, earlier," Dallas said.

"You don't count," Stiving said without looking at Dallas. "But adding a menacing stranger isn't going to throw me off the trail of who killed Cora."

"Incredible," Mia huffed. "What kind of woman would I be to use my daughter to deflect suspicion from myself?"

"The kind of woman that married a drug dealer and lived in the lap of luxury until hubby went to prison."

Mia's face blanched and she took a step back. "You don't know anything about me."

"I know more than you think. Fire Marshal says the house burned due to a candle fire, so that we have to rule as accidental, but the toxicology reports are what I'm eagerly awaiting. That's going to make for some interesting reading."

"I would never poison anyone, especially Cora," Mia said, arms folded tight across her chest.

"You stabbed a man before. Poison, knife." He shrugged. "Both can be lethal."

Dallas stiffened. "Knock it off. She doesn't deserve that."

Stiving looked close at Mia. "How do you know what she deserves?"

Mia sucked in a breath, then without another word she slammed back inside the trailer, leaving Dallas and Stiving alone on the porch.

"That was low. She's a good mother, the best," Dallas snarled.

"Really? You sound so protective. Good friend?" He quirked an eyebrow. "Or more?"

He burned inside. "None of your business."

"Let's lay it out here, Mr. Black. You and I don't get along."

"No kidding. Because I made you look bad by doing your job for you? Finding the kid when you didn't think it was worth your time?"

The smile vanished. "No, because you're a hotshot who makes trouble in my town. Whatever you think of me, I'm a good cop. Thorough."

"So do your job and investigate. You'll see she's telling the truth."

"Could be, but I think it's more likely that your friend Mia Sandoval murdered Cora and when the lab tests come back and prove that the pills were doctored with poison, I'm going to arrest her. As far as this Archie from Miami thing goes, if he really is threatening her, it's just deserts."

"Just?" Dallas spoke through gritted teeth.

"Sure. She's experiencing the fallout of being married to a mobster. She probably had full knowledge of Hector's activities the whole time."

"You're wrong."

"Maybe, but I'm right about the murder and you'd better believe I'm going to look real carefully at you, too, since you're so tight with Miss Sandoval and everything." He grinned. "Gang boy like you? Arrest record and the whole nine yards? Real stand-up guy."

Dallas bit back his response. It wouldn't help Mia to shoot off his mouth. It probably hadn't helped her that her supposed protector was an enemy of the town's police detective.

"I'll be seeing you around soon," Stiving said as he walked down the steps.

Dallas felt a desperate need to act, to take some small step that would help shed some light. He took a shot. "Do you know a Peter Finnigan?"

Stiving stopped. "Finnigan? Why?"

"Do you know him?"

Eyebrows drawn together, Stiving chewed his lip before answering. "Guy of that name lives about an hour from here in Mountain Grove. Used to live in California until he bought a real nice cabin here in Colorado."

"Know him personally?"

"Read about him." He shook his head. "Witness in a case a colleague of mine worked on in California decades ago. Surprised I remembered it."

"What kind of case?"

"Why do you want to know?"

"Why did it stick in your memory? A case that wasn't even in your state?"

His eyes narrowed to slits. "This colleague talked it over with me. He thought something smelled funny about the story. Just like something smells funny about this one. So you're not going to tell me why you're interested in Peter Finnigan?"

Dallas remained silent. He was not going to get anything more and he wondered if he'd blown it by bringing Peter's name into the mess. Besides, he needed to check on Mia. Now.

Stiving started up the engine, still smiling, and Dallas tapped on the trailer door before letting himself in. Mia sat at the little table, elbows propped on the surface. He tried to read her expression. Angry? Wounded?

"Sit down and quit staring at me," she said.

Angry. Good. "Stiving has no sense. Ignore him. He did give me a tip on Peter Finnigan in spite of himself. I've got a town name to research."

She drummed fingers on the table. "He truly believes I am a murderer."

"Cops are like that. Don't trust anyone. Don't take it to heart."

"Easy for you to say. He doesn't think you killed Cora." She shot a hasty look at Gracie who slept peacefully. She stared at the little girl, face softening until it was so tender he had to look away.

"Dallas, you...you don't think I would ever put Gracie in danger on purpose, do you?" She turned those luminous eyes on him, and suddenly breathing was difficult.

"No."

"But what if I do it unintentionally? Trying to make a life here has only gotten us in trouble."

"Not your fault."

"I'm not so sure. My number-one priority is to give her a good life, you know?"

He nodded.

"But I look back over my life, and I can't believe some of the things I've done." She looked at her hands. "I stabbed my husband. I actually did that."

"You thought he was going to kill you and take Gracie, didn't you?"

Her sigh was miserable. "But I never imagined I could do such a thing—that I was capable."

It cut at him to see the self-doubt. "You were protecting yourself and your daughter. Don't let guilt twist it around."

She beamed a smile at him that lit up even the farthest corners of the trailer. He could have been sitting in a glorious cathedral and there would be nothing to rival the beauty he experienced at that moment, sitting in a trailer parked on the edge of a flood-threatened town.

"I appreciate your friendship," she said, "I really do, even if I haven't shown it. It's been a long time since I could trust someone."

Trust. The word fell hard on his heart. *But I haven't told you the truth, Mia. Not all of it.* He opened his mouth to let it spill. Tomorrow, everything would change because of the phone call he'd made outside that rain-soaked gym. He remembered the cascade of emotions she'd triggered in him with their kiss that seemed to live inside him long after her mouth was no longer pressed tight to his. Would it all be gone in the morning? Perhaps it was for the best. She needed a friend, not anything more. He would be lucky if she still counted him in that circle after tomorrow.

"What is it?" Mia said, squeezing his fingers. She looked so tired, circles smudging her eyes. He could give her one night of rest, of peace, before her world turned upside down and his did, too.

"Nothing. Get some sleep. We'll talk later."

She laughed softly. "'Oh, I've got miles to go before I sleep.'"

He found himself smiling back. "Robert Frost. You listened in poetry class, too."

"Yes, I did." She pressed the laptop to life. "And

I'm going to dig up some dirt on a certain P. Finnigan before I turn in."

He understood. She needed to do something, to manage one small element in a life that was spiraling out of control. "How about if I help?"

She slid over on the bench seat, and he settled next to her, his big shoulder pressed against her soft one, admiring her slender wrists as her fingers danced across the keyboard.

It took them two hours of following cyber bunny trails before they had the pertinent details.

Mia gathered her long hair to the side, eyes darting in thought. "So this Peter Finnigan was a dishwasher at a greasy spoon in Southern California. He's out walking one day and sees a man boating. The boater falls overboard and is caught up by a rip current and shouts for help. Finnigan tries to get to him, but is unable and fearing for his own safety he leaves the water and calls the authorities. By the time they show up, the man is swept away, body never recovered."

Dallas consulted the screen. "The drowned man is Asa Norton, a thirty-year-old small-business owner. He's presumed dead after the appropriate length of time. Survived by his wife—" Dallas leaned closer "—Susan Norton. There's a picture."

Mia crowded close, her cheek nearly touching his. It took everything in his possession not to turn his head and find those lips again. *Knock it off, Black.*

"Does she look familiar?" Mia breathed quicker. "Could that possibly be the red-haired Susan we know?"

"Could be, but it's a bad picture." He leaned away a little, to quiet the pulse rushing in his veins. He read on. "Susan received the ten million dollar insurance settlement for her husband's death." He scrolled down. "Nothing further about it."

Mia chewed her lip. "Something Cora knew about Finnigan troubled her. It has to be a clue as to who killed her, doesn't it?"

Dallas saw the kindling of hope in her eyes as if a light had been turned on inside, somewhere down deep. *Help me keep that hope alive, Lord.* "We'll find out." But would there still be a *we* tomorrow?

They were silent for a moment. Pine needles scuttled quietly along the trailer roof.

"Do you think Peter Finnigan has answers?" she said finally.

"Possibly, but it could also be dangerous to go track him down."

"Dangerous, how?"

"Take your pick. Floodwaters, Archie on the loose and Cora's murderer."

"Could Archie have done it? Poisoned Cora's pills?"

Dallas thought it over. "I don't see why he'd go to trouble. Let's say he suspected you'd left this treasure from Hector with her. He might have searched her house, but he could have done that while she was out. No need to bring attention to himself or the property by causing her death. He's here on Garza's behalf to retrieve Hector's stash, that's his priority."

Mia's breath caught. "But what if he was there searching for all this money he believes I have, and she stumbled across him?"

He saw where she was going. "Cora did not die because of you. Period."

"I wish I could be sure."

"I'll be sure for both of us." He got up from the table, put a hand on her shoulder, trapping some of her silken hair under his palm. Without stopping to think it out, he pressed a kiss to her temple.

She curled a hand up around his neck and held him there. He was certain at the moment, as the nerves tingled through his body, how blessed he was to know Mia Verde Sandoval. But there was a secret between them, a secret that would hurt her. Though it took every bit of will power he possessed, he pulled away. "You've got to get some sleep. Tomorrow will be a bear." *And I want to leave now, while you're still looking at me with that half smile on your lips and eyes that make my heart pound.*

"Okay," she said, a puzzled smile on her face. "Tomorrow has to be better than today."

He wished with everything inside him that it could be, but his brain knew differently.

"Good night, Mia. Sleep well."

He said good-night to Juno, made sure Mia locked the trailer door and settled into the old chair in his own unit, positioned to keep watch, the feel of that kiss still dancing on his lips. It was the last time he'd share a kiss with Mia. He pushed away the sadness and rustled up some grit. *Do the job, Dallas.*

If Archie came, he'd know it.

Protection was all he could give Mia.

And he'd give it with his dying breath.

ELEVEN

Mia awoke to the sound of sneezing sometime after eight o'clock. It took her a few moments of blurry-eyed confusion to figure out it was Gracie who lay in a tight ball on the bed. Juno poked his nose at her, tail wagging.

Mia padded over on bare feet across the sunlit linoleum. "Hey, baby. The rain stopped."

Gracie sniffed. "I gotta sore throat."

Pulling the covers back, she found Gracie pink-cheeked and nose running. "Uh-oh."

"I got germans?"

Mia laughed. "Germs. Yes, I think you're coming down with something." Her forehead felt warm under Mia's palm. She fetched a glass of water and encouraged Gracie to drink it. Fishing through her bedraggled purse, she was thrilled to find the slightly sticky bottle of grape flavored medicine purchased after Gracie's last go around with the "germans." Cora had tended to her through that illness, offering homemade chicken soup and plenty of read-aloud stories. Mia's throat thickened at the thought. In spite of the groans, Mia managed to get Gracie to swallow a dose of the medicine.

"I want my turtle slippers. Can we get 'em?"

"I'm sorry, sweetie. Your slippers are all wet at the house. I'll get you some more soon." Anxiety cramped her stomach as the worries attacked in full force. And how exactly would she get slippers, or Gracie's pajamas, let alone a house? Especially while evading a murder rap and a mobster who'd threatened a return visit?

We'll find Peter Finnigan, and he will have some answers, she told herself firmly.

She grabbed a pair of neatly folded socks that Dallas had left, along with a clean T-shirt. The socks went nearly to Gracie's thighs and they both laughed as she rolled them onto the child's skinny legs. Mia let her mind stray back to the kiss. Why had she allowed herself to be kissed, let alone to respond? She had no clue, other than it was the most amazing kiss she'd experienced in her whole life.

Juno shot to his feet and ran to the door. Mia froze, heart hammering, until there was a quiet knock followed by a familiar voice.

"It's Dallas. I've got some things for you."

Mia found that her spirits ticked up a notch as she went to the door, pulling fingers through her messy hair and straightening the big sweatshirt he'd loaned her before letting him in.

His dark brows rose at the sight of her. "I didn't know that sweatshirt could look so nice."

She blushed.

He held up a brown bag. "Trailer park manager gave me some clothes for you and some that might work for Gracie left over from her granddaughter's last visit. And guess what—" He shook a pink pastry box. "Anybody want doughnuts for breakfast instead of Goldfish?"

Gracie coughed. "Can't. I'm sick."

Dallas shot her a panicked look. "Sick? How sick?"

"Terrible sick," Gracie piped up, adding a cough on the end for good measure.

"Should we take her to the doctor? I'll get my keys." He turned to leave, but Mia grabbed his arm.

"Not that sick. Kids come down with things all the time. It's okay. I gave her some medicine. She'll be okay. I promise." Mia hid a smile at the uncertain look on his face. "Really, it's fine. Kids are tough."

"They are?" His lips quirked. "They're just so… small."

She took the pink box from his hands. "Gracie won't eat them, but I wouldn't want these doughnuts to go to waste."

Soon he'd brewed a pot of coffee and she'd devoured two sugar-glazed doughnuts down to the last crumb. Dallas sipped out of his mug, a look of amusement on his face.

She wiped her sticky fingers. "Don't you eat doughnuts?"

"No sweet tooth."

"You're missing out," she said with a sigh. "Doughnuts are nature's second most perfect food next to mac and cheese. I think they're even on the food pyramid."

"It was worth it to watch you enjoy them." He added in a low voice. "To see you smile."

She returned the grin. "You know, for a tough guy who lives with a dog, you've got a sweet side."

"Don't let it get around."

"Why? Are you afraid you might have girls pounding at your door? Surely there must be some woman who wants a chance to get to know the softer side of Dallas Black."

He flicked a glance out the window before he answered. "I don't usually let them get close."

"Why not?" She shouldn't pry, but for some reason it felt so natural to talk to him and she wanted to understand what made him tick, and why she could not get him out of her mind.

"Don't want to disappoint them, I guess."

"When the mistakes of your past come out?"

He sighed. "Something like that."

"It's funny. You're trying hard to keep moving, and I'm going crazy trying to put down roots."

Yet here they were, sitting in the same banged-up trailer while a storm of trouble whirled around them. She watched the steam from the coffee drift past the waves in his hair. God had sent her a friend in Dallas Black, she realized. A friend when she most desperately needed one. But why did her feelings for him seem like something else?

He fidgeted with his coffee cup. "Mia, listen. I've got to tell you something and it won't wait anymore."

She felt a tremor inside. "Okay. I've had two doughnuts to shore up my spirit, and I don't see how things could get any worse than they were yesterday. Go for it."

Juno barked, and a second later they heard a car approach. Dallas peeked out the blinds.

Archie? The police? Her mind ran wild.

His expression was inexplicably sad as he went to open the door.

Mia blinked incredulously when her sister stepped inside.

"Antonia," she cried, wrapping her older sister in a massive hug. "Why are you here? How did you know where to find me?" She pulled her sister to arm's length. "Is everything okay? Is Reuben all right?"

Antonia chuckled. "I think I should be asking those kinds of questions." She looked over Mia's shoulder at Gracie. "Hey, Gracie girl. How's my niece?"

Gracie waggled her fingers and squealed. "Hiya, Auntie Nia. You're here. Where's Uncle BooBen?"

Gracie was perfectly capable of pronouncing Reuben's name, but her toddler nickname for him had stuck fast and it always made Reuben grin. Antonia kissed her. "I'll tell you in a minute. Let me talk to Mommy first, 'kay?"

"'Kay."

During the exchange, the flutter of unease in Mia's belly grew as she put some of the facts together. Dallas had not been at all surprised to see Antonia arrive. What's more, they seemed to be at ease with each other, as though they'd been in frequent contact.

The three moved away from Gracie. "What's going on?" Mia demanded.

Antonia squared her shoulders and kept her voice quiet. "First off, I'm here because Reuben and I love you and we're worried about you. We know Cora is dead and the police think it's foul play. We also know Archie is in town because Garza believes you've got Hector's jackpot somewhere. Reuben has gone to the prison to talk to Hector and tell him if there is such a prize, he has to fess up, because he's put you and Gracie in danger."

Mia held up a hand. "Antonia, how do you know all this?"

Antonia exchanged a worried look with Dallas. "Because Dallas has kept us informed. We hired him."

She could not believe she had heard correctly. "Hired?"

Dallas sighed. "They asked me to come to Spanish Canyon and keep an eye on you."

It took several tries before she managed a response. "What?"

"There were rumors that Garza's men were looking for something Hector had stashed," Antonia said. "Reuben and I feared they would come after you and Gracie."

The information landed like a bomb in her gut. "That's how you knew about Gracie climbing the tree. Your informant kept you apprised."

Dallas flushed.

"My fault," Antonia said. "I hounded him for details about Gracie. I shouldn't have, but I missed her so much."

Mia folded her arms, trying to steady her pounding pulse. There was more. She could see it in their faces. "What else?"

"Cora was an old friend of Reuben's mother," Antonia continued. "When we heard you were thinking of settling near here to go to school, we contacted her and she offered to help."

Help? Cora? The truth started to worm its way through Mia. "So Cora helped me get a job, find a house to rent. She made sure Dallas had work fixing her roof so he could spy on me. What an amazing network to put together a life for one helpless woman and her kid."

Antonia touched her arm, but she shook it off.

"Mia, we knew you wouldn't accept any help because you're stubborn and desperate to prove you don't need anybody. I'm sorry. I didn't want to tell you like this, but that's the truth."

"You knew I wouldn't accept it, but you arranged it all anyway, didn't you? Totally against my wishes." Anger hummed through her veins. "All this, everything I thought I accomplished here, was just charity, set up by people I thought were my friends."

"I'd like to think I am your friend," Dallas said quietly, "no matter how it came to be."

Mia turned her eyes on him. "You don't *hire* friends." Each word fell out of her mouth, cutting like glass. She saw him flinch and she was glad.

Antonia's chin went up, as it had for every head-butting argument they engaged in over the years, from which breakfast cereal to eat to the dire consequence of dating Hector Sandoval. "Listen, Mia. I know you're mad at me and that's okay. I knew that was a price for trying to protect you, but Dallas isn't doing this for pay. As a matter of fact, he refused any compensation at all. He cares about you, like we do."

Cares about you. And lied just like Hector and her sister. She found it hard to breathe. "So, why exactly are you here now, Antonia? Dallas hasn't been feeding you enough information? You had to check up on me personally?"

"Dallas called us after Garza's man showed up at

the college. I came to try and convince you to come back to Florida with me, until the thing with Archie is resolved."

"Didn't your informant tell you I'm shortly to be accused of murder? I don't think I'll be able to leave even if I wanted to."

"We'll get a lawyer if it comes to that. Let's try to get you out while we can. It's safest for Gracie."

Mia exploded. "Don't tell me how to be a mother to Gracie, Antonia," she snarled. "That little girl is the only thing I've done right in my whole life. Please don't imply I've messed that up, too. I can't take it." Dismayed to find tears on her face, she dashed them away.

"I never would," Antonia said, eyes anguished. "Honey, you're a wonderful mother. You just need help right now. That's all."

The emotion on her sister's face, the moisture that shone in her eyes, was too much for Mia. The fire ebbed out of her body, leaving only a dark despair in its place. She sank down on the bench seat. Antonia was right. She could not make a life for herself and Gracie. She did not even realize that her whole world in Spanish Canyon was a setup, neatly arranged for a woman who could not manage on her own.

But Dallas… She could not even look at him. Everything she imagined he'd done for her out of kindness, or, she hardly dared admit it, love? It was a job. She was a job to him.

"I guess I'd better do what you say. I can't trust myself."

Dallas sat across from her. "Mia, you're stronger than anyone I know. What we did… It was only because you have too many powerful people working against you."

"No," she said, her own voice sounding strange and dull in her ears. "You did it because you and Antonia and Reuben all believe I could not manage my life on my own."

"No…" he started, reaching for her hands.

She would not touch him, not look at him. "I said 'All right.'" She fought the thickness in her throat. "You're both right, and I'm not going to argue. When do we leave?"

"I'll get us a flight tonight," Antonia said.

"Tomorrow." Mia glanced toward the bed. "Gracie's sick, and there's something I need to do first."

Antonia quirked an eyebrow. "What? There's talk that the weather might turn bad again. I really think tonight is better."

Dallas stood, hands on his slim hips, eyebrows drawn together.

Mia stared at the pink doughnut box, incredulous that only moments before she'd wondered if her feelings for Dallas could be more than friendly. *They're right. You can't trust yourself.* Dr. Elias's words came back to her.

"…you're afraid that you can't trust yourself, your

choices, your judgments." Even her former employer had been able to see her deepest fear that had now been proven true. But she would not walk away, not from the murder of an old woman who had been trying to help her purely out of kindness. She was not a coward, not yet. "I'm going to find Peter Finnigan. He may be able to shed some light on Cora's death."

"No way..." Antonia said.

Mia whacked her hand on the table, startling Juno. "No matter how it came to be, Cora was my friend and Gracie and I loved her. I have to at least try to find out if Finnigan knows something. Please allow me to do that. Will you stay with Gracie?"

Antonia chewed her lip. "Of course, but I don't think..."

"I'll go with Mia," Dallas said.

"You don't need to do that," Mia told him. "Your spy identity has been compromised."

He flinched as her arrow hit the mark. "I'll go."

She didn't argue. If she said no he would follow her anyway. It was his job, after all, she thought bitterly, and he would do it until she and Gracie boarded that plane to Florida the following day.

She knelt next to Gracie and smoothed her hair. "I'll be back soon."

"Mommy, are you mad at Auntie Nia?"

"No, honey. We just had a disagreement. Auntie's going to stay with you while I run an errand. Is that okay?"

"Yes. Will Juno stay?"

Dallas nodded. "I think that's best."

"When you come back are we going to Florida?"

Mia exhaled. "I think so, baby."

"Is that gonna be our home?"

Mia thought there was never such a perfect little face as that of her sweet girl, staring at her expectantly, trusting that no matter what, her mother would provide a home. Was Florida going to be that home? Would any place ever be?

"I'm not sure if we'll stay in Florida."

She sneezed. "Will Juno and Dallas come, too?"

She could not answer above the sudden wave of sadness.

"Hey, Goldfish girl," Dallas said. "You just work on getting better. We'll talk about it later."

"'Kay."

Dallas offered a hand to help Mia get to her feet. She pretended she didn't see. *I'm a job to you, Dallas. Let's keep it that way*, she thought over the grief washing through her body.

Dallas tried to open the door of the truck for Mia but she scooted around and got in herself before he had the chance. What had he expected? She believed he'd betrayed her—and maybe to a woman who so desperately craved independence, he had. He'd crossed many people in his life, disappointed dozens, notably himself, but what he'd done to Mia hurt her worse than any other offense he'd dished out. It had been wrong to deceive her, even though the reasons were right.

I'm sorry, Mia.

The distance between them seemed like miles instead of inches. She stared out the window as his tension grew.

Should he try small talk? Apologize again? Mention the haze of clouds that had started to gather along the sunlit horizon?

Talk about the weather? Stupid, Dallas.

He settled on silence, trying to ignore the leaden feeling in his limbs. He'd hoped in that idiot macho way of his the truth might blow over as the miles went by and he could start again, trying to show her how much she meant to him. Judging from the hard line of her mouth, he'd thought wrong. If only women were as forgiving as dogs.

"Why did you do it?"

He jerked a look at her, startled, praying he would not make it any worse with more idiotic conversation. "To protect you. At least that's what I thought I was trying to do."

"No, I mean why did you do it for nothing? Agree to take the job without pay."

Because to me, it's not a job. "Antonia asked me. I respect her and Reuben."

"You didn't move to a strange town because you respect my sister and brother-in-law."

He shifted, setting the seat springs squeaking. "I never care much where I am. One town is as good as another. Spanish Canyon offered a decent place to teach Search and Rescue classes. Why not?"

She turned gleaming brown eyes on him, skewering him to the seat back. "That's not it. You moved to this town, spent hours working on an old roof and living in a trailer, for no pay, to protect a woman you barely knew. Why did you do that? I think I deserve to hear the truth."

She did, but he knew it meant sharing messy, unformed feelings, incoherent ramblings of his heart that he himself did not understand. He flipped through the memories that had swirled through his mind almost daily since he'd seen her in Florida following the hurricane. "At Antonia and Reuben's wedding. I saw you talking to Gracie before the ceremony."

She waited.

He sighed. "I dunno, something about what you said to her got inside me and stayed there."

"What did I say?"

He tried to repeat the words exactly. "Gracie was little then, just a toddler. Is that what you call that age?"

She nodded.

"Anyway, she asked you where her daddy was and you knelt down, right next to her and told her Daddy was in jail because he made mistakes."

He heard her sniff. "Yes. I remember now."

"And she started to cry so you said, 'We're going to be a family, you and me, and Mommy's going to make it all right.'"

Mia lowered her head. "I haven't made it anywhere near all right."

He went very still, the sound of the tires creating a soothing cadence. *Lord, help me to put words to the feelings, words she can understand.* "You were strong then, and gentle, too, just like you are now. I knew how hard it was going to be, with your past, and starting all over with a daughter and Hector's legacy. I understood because I have wreckage in my past, too." He reached out slowly, praying she would not jerk away from his touch, and covered her hand with his. "I wanted to help you and Gracie have a better shot at making a way for your family. That's why I told Antonia I'd do it."

She looked at their joined hands and one tear splashed onto their twined fingers.

"My whole life has been about where. Where will I go next. This time…" He struggled to find the words. "This time it was about the who, about you and Gracie. I wanted you to have a life." He swallowed hard. "And I guess maybe I wanted to be a part of that in some way."

It was too much. She pulled from him. "I didn't ask you. You invited yourself into our lives and you deceived me."

It cut at his heart. "I'm sorry."

She fished for a tissue in her pocket. "I understand your motives were sincere. Hector was sincere, too, but he did not trust me with the truth, either."

Her words stung like acid. He'd been put on the same shelf as Hector, a manipulator, a disappointment. Had he permanently severed that delicate strand between them? He could think of nothing to say to repair the break, not one word of comfort to bring the warmth back to her eyes.

The miles droned by in miserable silence until he turned on the weather station just to break the terrible quiet. It was not good news.

"More rain is on the way from an unexpected grouping of storms rolling in. A series of flash-flood warnings and advisories have been issued. Mudslides are already being reported near Mountain Grove and Coal Flats where rainfall on burn areas is causing ground failure. Residents are advised to be ready to evacuate."

Dallas took comfort in the fact that at least the trailer park was high enough to keep Antonia and Gracie safe. For a while.

"We should…"

She shook her head. "I'm going to see Finnigan. If you want to head back, just let me out."

Right. As if he would even consider leaving her on the side of a mountain road. Women. He wisely kept his thoughts to himself and pressed on at as quick a pace as he could manage. The steeper the grade, the more he began to worry about the possibility of mudslides. Slopes already sodden with moisture needed only a tiny push from nature and gravity to loosen tons of debris on the road below.

Finally, they turned off on an uneven path that took them through acreage so densely crowded with lodgepole pines that he thought Farley might have ferreted out the wrong address, until they came to the edge of a swollen river with a striking house set beside it. The dark wood tones and forest green roofing material made it appear as if the house was a part of the mountainside behind it.

They got out in time to receive the first drops of rainfall.

"Peter Finnigan has a nice little piece of real estate," Dallas said, perusing the boathouse that perched at the waterline and the modern shingled siding on the house above. "And he doesn't like being too close to the neighbors."

"He must have found something better paying than being a dishwasher." Mia started up the graveled path toward the house. As he followed, Dallas noted a green car parked behind the shrubbery, and the muscles in his stomach tightened. He put a hand on the hood. Still warm.

"Mia," he said.

There was the sudden sound of breaking glass followed by a shout.

Dallas took off for the house at a dead sprint.

TWELVE

Mia was gasping for breath by the time she made it to the house, pulling up next to Dallas who had just about reached the front door when it was flung open. A short, balding man stopped short, mouth wide. His arm was half raised, as if to shield himself from a blow.

"Peter Finnigan?" Dallas said.

The man glared, the fleshy pouches under his eyes bunching. "Who wants to know?"

"We heard a scream," Mia panted, by way of explanation. "Glass breaking."

"There's nothing wrong," he said. "Everything's fine. Go away."

"Not quite, Peter" came a singsong voice.

Mia gaped as Susan stepped up behind Peter. She wore clean clothes, her hair in a neat twist, a placid smile on her lips. Dallas seemed equally at a loss for words until he managed, "Are you hurt?"

Susan laughed. "Such a gentleman." She gave Mia a coy look. "You should keep him."

Mia's cheeks burned. "Susan, what's going on?"

She waved them in with an airy gesture. "Come in, why don't you? I just came to see Peter. We're acquainted. He's the man who tried to save my drowning husband, so he says."

Peter scanned the porch quickly, as if he was assessing the likelihood of an escape. Then he mumbled something, stepped aside and allowed them to enter.

"I'm glad you're here. She's some loony who busted in. When I wouldn't give her what she wanted, she started throwing things. I'm leaving just as soon as I can get her out."

Mia noticed a floral fragrance in the air and there was something familiar in the smell. Peter pulled keys and a wallet from a small bowl. While his back was turned, Mia spotted an old photo on the floor, partially hidden by shards of glass that littered the hardwood floor.

The snapshot was old and grainy, but it showed Peter with a taller man, heavily bearded, standing in a small boat. A third man was seated, holding a net. Peter stood to the left of them, dangling a fish for the camera, grinning.

She saw Susan looking at her. Quickly Mia tucked the picture into her pocket.

"What got smashed?" Mia asked.

Susan waved an impatient hand. "I startled Peter

and he dropped his drinking glass. I was asking him what he knew about my husband's death."

He flashed a sullen look. "I dunno what you're talking about. She's crazy, like I said."

Susan sighed. "All right, I'll get the ball rolling. Let's stroll down memory lane. Fifteen years ago, you saw my husband, Asa, drown, didn't you? What a story you told the police about how you tried in vain to save him, battling the waves at your own peril. Made yourself look like a real hero."

Peter folded his arms, then unfolded them and shoved his hands in the pockets of his faded jeans. "You already know what happened, Susan."

"So," Susan said, her tone cheerful as if she was reciting a bit of poetry. "You lied. You and Thomas." She looked at Mia and Dallas. "Dr. Elias, as you know him. To me he'll always be Thomas. Peter arranged with Thomas to make it look like an accidental death. Thomas was hoping to get his hands on the life insurance money. He pays you to keep quiet. That's how you afford this lovely home, isn't it?"

Peter grimaced. "You're nuts, and you're not telling the whole story."

"I probably am nuts. I've had a hard life after all. It took me a long time, years and years, to find Thomas and you. I tracked him down to Spanish Canyon. What a surprise to find out he'd started a whole new life here as a well-respected doctor. And you, too.

Cora overheard Thomas threaten me at the clinic after I confronted him. She wanted to go to the police, but I told her they were on his side. She promised to help me find proof to take to the authorities."

"Cora?" Mia gasped. "Susan, tell us what happened."

Peter cut Mia off. "This is nuts. I'm not talking to any of you anymore. Get out, all of you."

Susan's face whitened and filled with hatred. "Thomas killed Cora because he knew she was looking into his past, and the truth was coming out. Now Thomas's going to have to eliminate anyone who can incriminate him and that means you."

"Are you insane? I've never caused him any trouble. I've kept my mouth shut about everything for all these years. He trusts me."

"Not anymore," she said quietly. "Not after he's had to murder again. This time he's going to button up all the loose ends."

Including Susan. Mia shuddered.

"Crazy, but I'm not gonna take the time to sort it out," Peter snapped, turning away. The back of his neck was red.

Mia's mind was still spinning, trying to put it all together. When Peter whirled back around, he held a gun snatched from his pocket.

Dallas stepped in front of Mia. "You don't need

to do that, Peter. We're not here to cause trouble for you. We just wanted the truth."

"I'm getting out of this whole business. I was going to leave because of the flooding anyway, so I'll just make it permanent. If any of you tries to come at me, I'll kill you. I don't want to, but I will."

Susan chortled. "You can't get out. You'll never get out."

"Shut up," Peter barked. "Move away from the door."

Dallas and Mia edged aside. Mia took Susan's skinny wrist. "Let him go, Susan." Surprisingly, she did not resist.

"He won't get away," she said softly. "You'll never, ever get away."

Susan allowed Mia to guide her to the corner. When Peter fled out the door and down the path, Dallas ran to the window.

"He's got a boat ready." Dallas was dialing 911 as he watched. After a minute, he disconnected with an exasperated groan. "No signal."

Peter thundered down to the edge of the dock where a motorboat was moored. He cast off the lines and began to putter out into the swiftly moving water. A duffel bag in the back indicated his departure had been planned out.

Keeping low, Dallas sprinted toward the boat-house. He was going to see if there was another boat.

"Stay in the house," he yelled.

Mia watched as Peter piloted through the rough waters.

She and Susan edged out onto the porch. Mia could not stand it a moment longer.

"You have to tell us everything, Susan. We have to know who killed Cora."

Dallas vanished into the darkened interior of the boathouse, emerging a moment later with hands on hips. There was no other boat. Peter would get away and take his answers with him.

Dallas began to jog back to the dock. Mia started down the steps, leaving Susan behind. Thirty seconds passed. A flash of light and an earsplitting bang shook the boards under their feet. Mia's ears rang. Following Dallas's horrified gaze she realized the explosion had come from the boat.

Peter's duffel bag was burning, along with the interior of the vessel. Peter lay facedown in the water, his shirt on fire.

Susan stared, hands jammed into her pockets.

Dallas finished his sprint to the dock and jumped in the water, arms chopping through the waves. Bits of flaming debris sprinkled down around his head as he pressed on. It was a futile effort. By the time he'd cleaved through the swirling river to the spot where the boat had exploded, Peter's body had been sucked away by the current. The swollen river jerked and pulled at Peter, tumbling him along like a discarded doll. Dallas swam after Peter, and Mia found herself shouting, stomach twisted in fear.

"Dallas, come back. The water's too strong." *You'll drown,* her heart finished for her. She doubted he'd heard over the swirling cacophony, but he must have come to the same conclusion. She watched with her heart hammering at her ribs as he fought the water back toward the bank and Mia grasped his forearms to pull him from the river.

He stood, head bowed, water running from his hair and clothes. His broad shoulders drooped and quite suddenly, she wanted to comfort this man who had betrayed her. She raised her arms to embrace him. *Strength, not emotion, you ninny.*

Instead, she snatched up a towel that lay drying on the wooden rail and draped it around his shoulders. His eyes were shocked, horrified, drawn to the river where Peter Finnigan had just lost his life. In spite of herself, she pressed her hand to his biceps for a moment.

He imprisoned her palm there, his own fingers cold. "I couldn't get him."

She allowed the touch to linger before she pulled away. "No one could."

He heaved in a breath. "I'm guessing there was an explosive device in his duffel bag. It was motion triggered." He paused. "Or someone set it off by cell phone."

Mia glanced into the acres of dark trees and shivered. Were there eyes watching from the shadows? Eyes glowing with satisfaction at the death they had just witnessed? As they moved back toward the house, she realized Susan was still staring out at the burning boat, spinning in helpless circles as it moved downriver.

"I told you, Peter," she whispered.

Dallas left a trail of water along the floor as the three of them searched for a phone with a landline. Nothing. His own cell was now waterlogged thanks to his instinctive plunge into the river and there was no chance of getting a signal anyway. In the course of their hunting, thunderclouds began to roll in along the river canyon, obscuring the mountaintops under a blanket of grey.

"We need to get out of here," Dallas said. "We'll keep trying to call on your cell as we drive."

Mia patted the photo still tucked in her pocket. "Come on, Susan. You can fill us in on the way."

"My car is here," she said. "In the bushes."

"We'll bring you back for it later." Dallas was not about to let the woman slip out of their grasp again. Especially not after what had just happened to Finnigan. He still burned inside with the knowledge that he had not been strong enough or fast enough to pull the man from the monster river. An epic failure and a life lost. Trying to keep watch for any sign of movement from the tree line, they returned to the truck.

He fought the urge to bundle both women back into the house and barricade them safely inside, but with floodwater rising all around them, it was not an option. "Let's move a little faster," he said, putting an encouraging palm on Susan's bony shoulders.

Back in the truck with Susan in the backseat, Mia didn't waste a moment.

"How did you know about Peter?"

Susan sighed. "I'm very tired." She leaned her head back on the seat.

"I'm sorry, Susan," Mia snapped. "But we just saw a man murdered back there. You need to start talking."

Dallas felt the tingle in his stomach at the strength in her tone, the fire in her words.

Susan sighed and tears welled up in her eyes. "I killed him."

Mia gasped.

Dallas gripped the wheel as Mia blinked in shock. "Who?" she managed.

"My husband, because I got involved with Thomas. He was a medical student, deep in school loans and credit card debt, but charming, and he seduced me. Made friends with Asa, or pretended to. He knew how unhappy I was in my marriage, but I never dreamed… How could I know Thomas would murder Asa? Actually murder him? I blame myself for Asa's death. I always will for bringing Thomas into our lives."

"You had no idea what kind of man he was?"

"None," she sniffed. "Thomas knew Asa had planned a fishing trip. Asa had a high-stress job running his own business, so fishing was his escape. I think Thomas drugged his bottle of tea so he became unconscious. Peter was waiting nearby, and he made sure Asa tumbled out of his boat and drowned and then he told the story of trying to save Asa so the police wouldn't look into it too closely."

"Dr. Elias did it, why? Out of jealousy? So you two could have a life together?"

Her voice hardened. "Nothing so romantic. Thomas knew Asa had a life insurance policy, and he figured after he killed Asa I would give him the money because we were, um, in love. At least I thought we were. Completely stupid of me, of course. Maybe Thomas figured once I received the payment he could kill me then, too."

What was one more murder for the guy? Dallas thought.

"When the insurance company signed off, I collected the money and ran as far and as fast as I could, but I always knew I'd make Thomas pay." An edge crept into her voice. "Thomas wanted to make a fresh start with a new identity, the good doctor beloved by all, but I found him. And Peter, too."

Dallas hit the brakes as a small pile of rocks showered down onto the road. He guided the truck around it, trying to process Susan's revelation.

"I confronted him, and Cora overheard and started checking into things. She told me she found a photo that she could use against Thomas, but before she could show me, she died. Thomas killed her, I'm sure of it." Dallas saw tears slide down her face. "He got himself a new life. And a pretty new woman."

He remembered finding Susan breaking into the BMW outside the makeshift evacuation center. "It's Catherine Elias, you've been following, isn't it?"

Mia jerked. "The floral perfume fragrance. I thought it was familiar. It's Catherine's. You followed her to Peter's?"

"I've been watching her house. I was curious to see if she knew what kind of man she was married to." Susan laughed. "She's scared of me. Anyway, she brought him the photo of Peter and Thomas. Don't know how she got her hands on it unless she was in on Cora's murder the whole time."

Mia took the photo from her pocket. "Who is the seated man in the boat?"

"Asa." She chewed her lip. "You see? Shows the three were acquainted, though Peter claimed to be a random stranger who saw Asa drowning. The photo proves a connection between them, and the police would connect the dots, I have no doubt."

"And why would Catherine take the photo to Peter? Blackmail? To set him up to be murdered?" Mia wondered aloud.

"Or she's innocent," Dallas said. "Could be she

found the photo after Elias took it from Cora and she became suspicious, wanted to check up on her husband."

Mia slid the photo in the visor, staring at it as they drove.

Rain slammed into the windshield. Susan turned her face to the glass and watched the water sheeting along the window. Her eyes drooped. "I'm too tired to talk anymore."

He did not think Mia was even breathing until she heaved a long shaky breath. "It's true. Dr. Elias killed Cora."

"And Asa, and Peter," Dallas said.

"And he'll do the same to me, if he gets hold of me," Susan said.

"But now we have proof." Mia's voice held a tone of wonder. "We can go to the police and expose him. I can have my life back."

The hope shone on her face and his pulse trip hammered. Where would that life take her? Back to Florida? To some other faraway place? Didn't matter. Wherever it was, it wasn't going to include him. He cleared his throat. "Try the police again."

She did, with no better result.

They made it over the top of the mountain and began the descent. Half a mile later, he pulled the truck to a stop behind another truck and an SUV. A gnarled ponderosa pine had clawed free of the earth and fallen, blocking the road in both directions. The road was hemmed in by a steep drop on one side and the mountain on the other.

Dallas got out to talk to the bearded man from the truck just ahead of them. The guy was fetching a chain saw from the covered cab of his vehicle. He introduced himself as Mack.

"Gonna have to chop it up and haul it off as best we can," Mack shouted to Dallas over the roar of the chain saw. "Folks are gonna be packing this road to get out of here if the rain don't stop."

"How much time you figure before they order evacuations?" Dallas called.

"If the storm don't turn ASAP, they'll be evacuating before nightfall. Rivers are full."

Recalling Peter's body whirling away on the swollen river, Dallas fought a pang of horror. He started in, hauling away the branches as the bearded man cleaved them from the trunk. The two from the other stopped vehicle, a father and his strapping teen son, set to work helping also.

"Got some orange cones in my truck," Mack hollered. "Put 'em out on the road so we don't have a pileup."

Dallas nodded and retrieved the markers. He walked past Mia who was still trying to get a signal on her phone. Susan appeared to be sleeping, her forehead pressed against the glass. He had thought she was deranged and he still wondered about her sanity, but he could not deny what she said made sense. Dr. Elias was a killer. And he had to be stopped.

Splashing through puddles, he set the cones down a few yards from the back of his truck to signal on-coming drivers. One more set around the turn in the road would be sufficient, he thought, as he slogged onward. Just in time as a dump truck eased to a stop. He got a glimpse of the driver's face, older, scruff of a beard.

But it was the passenger that made his blood run cold.

Archie Gonzales gave him a startled look as he leapt from the cab.

Dallas was at the passenger door before Archie had shoved it fully open. There was no time for Archie to reach for a weapon. Dallas grabbed him by the collar and slammed him against the side of the truck.

"Funny how you always turn up," Dallas snarled.

The truck driver appeared around the front fender. "What's going on?"

"Private business," Dallas grunted. His tone must have convinced the driver.

"I'm going to help clear the road," he mumbled, ambling away over the muck.

Archie tried to move Dallas's hands away, but he did not loosen his grip. "Wasted effort, man. I'm leaving town. My piece of junk rental got stuck in the mud, and I hitched a ride. Going to the airport."

"Leaving? Why?" It occurred to Dallas that he might have been wrong about what had happened at the river. "Did you arrange to have Peter Finnigan killed?"

"Guy who bought it in the river? No. But I have to say, I didn't see that coming. Nice piece of work. Cell phone trigger?"

"Yeah, and I'm sure you've got a cell phone handy."

"Who doesn't? It wasn't me, though. As I said, I'm out of here."

"Explain," Dallas said, applying pressure to Archie's windpipe.

He squirmed. "I was following you and Mia, like I'm paid to do. Don't know who blew up this Peter guy, but I'm thinking it's probably the doctor. He's the one who looped me in. Or maybe his wife."

Mia ran up in time to overhear, cheeks pink, rain rolling down her long hair. "Dr. Elias contacted you in Miami?"

"He contacted Mr. Garza. Tipped him off that you were in Spanish Canyon, and that's why I got sent here." Archie shot her a look. "What did you do to cross that doctor? He's more ruthless than my boss."

"Oh, no," Mia said. "He knew Cora was going to tell me, warn me about what she'd learned. He must have been tracking her emails."

He shrugged. "Don't care. Not my business. I was sent to find the stash."

Mia let out a cry. "But I don't have any money. How many times can I say it? Hector didn't leave me a thing. How can I convince you?"

"Already done. Seems brother Reuben went to see Hector and explained that you and tiny tot were in trouble. Hector came clean. His stash was in Miami all along. Mr. Garza has his money, and my job here is done."

Mia shook her head and let out a sigh.

"Not done," Dallas growled. "You led Gracie up to the roof. She could have been hurt. You have to pay for that."

Archie managed a choked laugh. "Lying to a kid isn't against the law. People do it all the time."

"We'll see if the police agree. You broke into Mia's house, too. Better get a lawyer."

Archie struggled under Dallas's grip. "Don't have time for that. This whole county's gonna be underwater and I want to go home."

"Well," Dallas said, anger at the fear Archie had caused Mia still bubbling in his veins, "this just isn't your day."

Rain stung his face as he turned Archie around. "Mia, there's some rope in the back of the truck."

She dashed through the rain back up the road.

A trickle of mud ran down from the mountainside and past Dallas's feet.

"I hate Colorado," Archie spat.

"Should have stayed in Miami." Dallas could not

prevent a feeling of satisfaction from sweeping through him. Maybe the cops wouldn't charge Archie with anything, but upsetting his easy escape was a small triumph. At this point, he'd take what he could get. Archie first, Dr. Elias next.

Another wave of muck flowed under the truck and across the road. Dallas looked through the sheeting rain. The mountainside was black, denuded a few years back, he estimated, by a wildfire.

The ground trembled under his feet.

Archie's eyes rolled as he tried to process what was happening.

There wasn't time.

With a roar the mountainside fell away into a river of mud that swept toward the truck.

He thought he detected a scream, Mia's scream, but it was lost in the rumble of movement as the mud carried Archie, Dallas and the truck over the cliff.

THIRTEEN

The river of black engulfed Dallas and Archie, the cacophony swallowing up Mia's scream as she struggled to keep her footing on the trembling road. For a moment, she thought the entire stretch would be sucked up by the massive flow, like a monstrous inverse volcano. There was nowhere to run.

As the movement of the earth slowed, the mighty roar ebbed to a murmur. The flow softened into a trickle and then, eerie silence. Her heart cried out for Dallas. She half stumbled, half crawled, along the edge of the road, wiping the rain from her face. Down below was a sea of mud, coating the steep slope, blanketing the trees, blotting out everything it touched. The upended truck had caught on a trunk, wheels spinning lazily above the black ooze that imprisoned it.

"Dallas," she screamed.

The truck driver and the man with the chain saw raced up.

"Two men are down there," Mia screamed, trying to discern a path she could take to reach them.

"Make that one," the truck driver said, pointing.

A mud-caked figure detached itself from the mess, struggling upright.

The men tied a rope to a tree at the edge of the road and lowered it down. The man grabbed it and hoisted himself up, hand over hand.

Was it Dallas or Archie? Mia found she was holding her breath as the victim fought to pull himself up from the pit. When he was within a few feet of the top, the men reached over and grabbed his arms.

With one synchronized heave, he was pulled over the edge. On hands and knees, he crouched, sucking in a breath. Mia pressed close, unable to force out the question.

"Man," Archie said, wiping a layer of mud from his face. "I really hate this state."

Mia's breath choked off as she ran to the edge again. There was no movement from below, no sign of Dallas.

No, Lord. Please, no.

"I'll try the radio," the truck driver said gently. "We'll call for help."

The other man helped Archie to his feet and moved him away from the slide. Mia stared down into the muck. *Think, Mia.* She spotted the place where Archie had emerged, just behind a stand of three trees that had caught the truck. The thick trunks would have deflected some of the force of the earth flow. If Dallas was there…

"Hey, lady," she heard someone call, as she climbed over the roadbed, clinging to the rope as her feet sank in the mud.

What am I doing? What if I drown in this smothering blanket?

What if she did?

What would she have to show for her life? A perfect daughter, yes, and a heart choked with so much anger, hurt and distrust that it was nearly drowned already. *I've wasted time being afraid. I'm sorry. So sorry.* Her soul offered up the words and it was as if they rose up to the clean, storm-washed air above, even as her body sank into the filth below. A sense of calm ate away at the panic. Mud oozed and sloshed around her, her legs sinking in up to her thighs and then her waist until she was more swimming through it than climbing down. When she came level with the truck, she pulled up the rest of the rope and tied it around herself, transferring her grip from the rope to the sturdy truck fender.

"Dallas," she called. The rain drilled tiny craters into the mud surrounding her. Everything was so monochromatic, a sea of black. She would have to edge around the front of the truck to be able to see beyond. Fingers cold and caked with slippery mud, she groped her way along. A metal shard on the fender nicked her palm.

A few more feet to go, sodden soil sucking against her every inch of the journey, she made her way around the fender.

As she'd suspected, beyond the stand of tightly clustered trees was a space relatively unscathed by the flow. He was not there. Body tingling with despair she scanned frantically.

"Dallas," she yelled again.

A small movement caught her eye. She'd been mistaken. Among the roots of one of the massive trees, she saw him, lying on his side, covered with mud, as black as the shadows that cloaked him.

She scrambled along, fitting between the trees, and made it to his side.

Breathing, let him be breathing. With a shaking hand, she brushed some of the cloying mud from his face.

His eyes blinked open, and it seemed at that exact moment, something inside her opened up, too. She leaned her cheek on his forehead. "Oh, Dallas" was all she could manage.

His eyes widened, the whites brilliant against his mud-streaked face. The breath caught in her throat, and she realized she'd never seen such a truly spectacular sight as those black irises, regarding her soberly, flaming to life as his senses returned. She reached out and stroked his face, running her fingertips along his forehead, his cheeks, again and

again, until she began to believe he was really and
truly alive.

Was it relief she saw in his eyes? She might have
thought it joy, but why would it be so? Her brain reminded her what her heart did not want to acknowledge: she was a job, and she had every right to be
angry at this deceiver whose hand she now clung to,
their filthy fingers twined together. He had tricked
her and withheld the truth from her.

Yet it was definitely not anger she felt, nor anything close to it. And that scared her more than the
mudslide. She let go.

His lips moved, but she couldn't detect any sound
until she leaned close.

"That was a wild ride," he muttered.

She laughed. It was absurd. Nestled in the mud
up to her knees with a man who'd nearly been buried under tons of mountain, rain sheeting down on
them both, she could not hold in the relieved giggle
that bubbled from her mouth.

"I thought you were dead," she said, biting her lip
to steady her frayed nerves.

"So did I, for a while there," he said, struggling
to pull himself to a sitting position, letting loose a
shower of broken twigs and debris.

"Are you hurt?"

"Dunno yet." Clods of dirt fell away as he moved,
the rain washing some of the grime from his face.
He stared at her, his gaze so intense it made her look

away. "I'm just glad you didn't get sucked down here with me."

"No, I got here under my own steam."

Eyeing the slope he shook his head. "Incredible. Why didn't you wait for help?"

She gave him a casual shrug. The truth was, she did not fully understand why she had done something so rash, for him, when the hurt still echoed inside. "Seemed like the thing to do after only one of you made it out."

He stiffened, as if remembering. "Archie?"

"He climbed up, unharmed, of course."

"Of course." Dallas tried to get to his feet. "We've got to get back up there. Go to the police."

He stood too quickly, staggering backwards. She quickly shoved her shoulder under his. "Slow. I can't carry you out of here, so don't push too hard."

He considered the slope and groaned. "That's a long way back up."

She showed him the rope tied around her waist, ridiculously pleased at the respect on his face.

"Smart thinking to tie the rope."

"I'm not as good at rescue as Juno, but I do my best."

He laughed, winced, and put a hand to his ribs. "Broken?"

"Probably bruised, but I'll make it."

She unknotted the rope from her body so they could both grab hold. They began the arduous ascent, first climbing around the ruined truck and then struggling up the slope, stopping every few feet to rest, sinking sometimes to their knees, sometimes to their waists in the sticky mud. When he stumbled back, she would grab his arm, holding him steady until he regained his balance. When she slowed, mired down by the cloying mass, he pulled her through the worst of it. Though she did not want his help, she was grateful. Now that the adrenaline from the rescue was depleted, every muscle in her body seemed to resent the effort it took to climb back to the road.

Mack met them halfway down, lowered on another rope fed to him by the truck driver. Mia could have cried in relief when the big man grasped her around the waist and they were hauled to the top by the men, and, to Mia's surprise, Susan.

Susan helped her to sit on the fender of Dallas's truck while Mack went back down the slope to assist Dallas. From somewhere Susan produced a handkerchief and wiped the grit from Mia's face as best she could.

The rain continued to thunder all around them, and now she found herself pleased with the downpour that washed some of the clinging film of mud off her clothes. She felt light and lifted inside, as if she'd somehow left some of her anger at the bottom of the cliff. She was not ready to forgive, not yet, but it did not stop her from enjoying the relief that came from putting down some of her burden. Quietly, she thanked the Lord for blessing her and Dallas with another day of life. How odd to feel thankful. How very strange and foreign.

Dallas was helped over the top, and he walked gingerly over to join her. "Archie's gone," he said morosely. "He got away again."

Mia shook away her strange ponderings, and rubbed at a scrape on her arm. "Good riddance. I never want to see him again. I hope he's right that Mr. Garza is finally satisfied."

"He's got no reason to go after you anymore," Dallas said. "Hector gave him what he wanted."

"Only when he had to."

"Because he heard you were in danger."

She felt shamed. "Yes, I guess so. He loves us, in his own fashion."

"That's one thing he has right." He held her gaze and she found she could not look away. Had the rain become warmer as it fell? The wind melodious as it swept along the road? Had Dallas become even more attractive, filthiness aside? Could be it was all colored by relief, she concluded.

Mack called out from the spot where the tree had fallen.

"I'm going to help clear the road," Dallas said.

"I'll help, too," Mia insisted.

He started to protest and then sighed. "It won't do any good to tell you to wait in the truck, will it?"

"Not one bit," she replied, walking straight to

Mack and the truck driver. "Thank you for helping us out of that mess. We're ready to pitch in and
clear the road."

Mack chuckled. "And I had you pegged for a city
girl."

Mia shot him a sassy smile. "A city girl who's
ready to get home to her daughter. Are you going to
fire up that chain saw or am I?"

Mack and Dallas exchanged amused looks. In a
matter of thirty minutes, Mack sliced off enough of
the fallen tree to allow vehicles to squeeze by. Mia,
Dallas and the truck driver hauled the branches out
of the way while Susan continued to try to get a cell
phone signal.

After a shaking of hands all around, Mack and
the driver loaded up in his vehicle and the others in
Dallas's truck. Mia could not hold back a sigh as she
slid onto the passenger seat and Dallas got behind
the wheel. The old, cracked vinyl felt like a cloud of
comfort compared to the scraping she'd enduring tra-
versing down the cliffside and back up again. It was
sheer bliss to be out of the hammering rain. The mud
clinging to her skin coated her with an earthy funk.

What she wouldn't give for her favorite lavender
lemon bath scrub that Gracie said smelled like candy.
She sat up, a current of memory stinging everything
inside.

"What?" Dallas said. "Are you hurt?"

"I just thought of something." Mia turned to Susan

in the backseat. "You followed Catherine to Peter's house. How long was she there?"

Susan considered. "Only a few minutes. She pounded on the door, but he didn't answer at first. Finally he opened up, they exchanged a few words, and Peter grabbed the photo out of her hand and slammed the door closed. She went around the back and looked through the windows but he refused to let her in. After she left, he came outside and that's when I caught up with him."

"It occurred to me that if Catherine lingered awhile, she also could have put something in Peter's duffel bag while Susan and Peter were inside."

Dallas let out a low whistle. "Is Catherine in on the whole business?"

Mia gave voice to the question that was burning inside her. Peter's duffel bag was already in the boat when they arrived. "Did you see Catherine put anything in Peter's duffel bag?"

"I couldn't see down to the water from where I was in the house," Susan said.

Mia bit back a frustrated sigh.

Was Catherine Elias an unwitting cog in Elias's schemes? Or did she have her own part in Peter Finnigan's death?

Though Dallas had the wipers set at full speed, they hardly kept up with the water sheeting across the glass. His head was pounding a rhythm that matched the throbbing in his ribs. There was no option to drive fast, though he had to fight the urge to ram the gas pedal down. Dr. Elias was a murderer. And his wife, Catherine, might be his partner in crime. Most likely, Elias had taken care of Finnigan, who could prove his guilt. But Mia and Susan could still expose him, and there was the photo tucked under the visor in his truck. The miles passed excruciatingly slowly back to Spanish Canyon.

√They headed straight for the police station, against Susan's wishes.

"That detective, Stiving, he won't hear anything bad about the precious Dr. Elias. He's protecting him. Could be the doctor has him on the payroll, even. We can't go to the police here."

"There isn't much choice, Susan," Dallas said. "We'll talk to the chief."

"And you trust him?" she demanded.

"He's given me no reason not to." But Stiving had.

Mia straightened, clutching her phone. "Got a signal. There's a message from Antonia. She got word to evacuate a half hour ago. She packed up Gracie and Juno. They're heading for the airport. She said she'll wait in the parking terminal until we get there." She groaned. "I feel like I should go meet them right now."

"As soon as we report what you…" He broke off as they took the main road into town. The paved surface was covered by inches of water. Shop owners and police officers worked side by side in the rain, filling sandbags. They were fighting a losing battle, as the water was already lapping the sidewalks. Soon it would be spilling through doorways and flooding the businesses all along the block. The police station was obviously evacuating, officers and volunteers carrying boxes and equipment to a waiting van.

Dallas tried to park nearby, but he was waved at by a drenched police volunteer. "Can't stop here. Cantcha' see we're flooding?"

"It's an emergency."

He eyed Dallas and Mia skeptically. "Wet and dirty, but y'all look fine to me. Nobody's getting into the station right now."

Dallas kept his temper with serious effort. "We have to speak to the chief. It's urgent."

"Chief's already gone to our mobile station in Pine Grove. Stiving's out on a call, and every available officer is assisting the fire department. Sorry, can't help you unless you want to drive to Pine Grove and see if they have time for you."

Dallas was about to fire off an angry reply when Mia took his arm. "We'll go to Pine Grove. It's on the way to the airport, anyway."

A pang of grief stabbed at his insides. The airport would be their goodbye, the last time he would ever see her and Gracie. He rolled up the window and drove through the water. Pine Grove and the airport. End of the line. There was no way to stop it. He knew it was better, anyway. Mia and Gracie needed to be safely away from the floods and Dr. Elias. Once they were away, securely settled in Florida, Elias would pay for what he did to Cora, Susan and Finnigan.

Dallas would see to it.

They took the road to Pine Grove, which would provide a higher elevation for the police to regroup. The locals told of floods that had occurred some twenty years before, but nothing like this, and the town was simply not prepared for such a magnitude of disaster.

"Where will you go, Dallas?" Mia said, breaking into his thoughts. "Will you wait until the water recedes and live in the trailers still?"

Why would he? The only thing that meant something was his Search and Rescue classes and he was only filling in for a temporary vacancy. The job would be gone soon, too.

"Dunno. I'll have to ask Juno what he thinks."

Mia smiled and closed her eyes as they drove. She looked very young with her wet hair framing her face, smudged with both dirt and fatigue.

His thoughts wandered. If things had been different and they'd met under other circumstances. Would he have risked a relationship with her? Would she have allowed him past the protective wall she'd built? Might he have stuck around long enough to chip away at it?

Maybe he wouldn't have been brave enough to

attempt it. He would have packed up his unfinished puzzle and his uncomplaining dog and left town rather than face his own vulnerability. He would never know if he would have let the most amazing woman he'd ever known walk out of his life because now it was too late. She was flying away, and it felt like she was taking his heart with her. Despair felt as weighty as the oppressive storm.

He almost didn't have time to slam on the brakes. A car he didn't at first recognize, was stopped in the road, doors open, hazard lights on. Juno stood next to the car.

"It's Antonia," Mia cried, leaping from the truck. He was behind her in a flash. Juno raced up to him, electric with some kind of excitement.

Antonia stood in the rain, body shaking, mouth tight with terror. "Oh, Mia. She's gone. She's gone." Tears rolled down her cheeks as Mia gripped her forearms.

"What happened, Antonia?" Mia demanded, voice hard as glass. "Where's Gracie?"

Antonia tried to answer, but no sound came out. Mia's hands tightened, viselike, around her sister's wrists. "Where is my daughter?"

Sucking in a breath, she tried again. "He took her."

"Who?" Mia's words rang with anguish.

"There was a chair overturned in the road. I got out to remove it. When I turned back, a man was there at the passenger-side door. He…he took Gracie and ran up the road. I heard him get into a car and then he was gone." She heaved in a breath. "Juno barked, but I had him leashed in the back and he couldn't get out. I called the police. They're coming."

"No." Mia's hands flew to her mouth. "No, no. This can't be happening."

"He always wins," Susan said, her own eyes round.

"I'm sorry, I'm so sorry," Antonia kept repeating.

"Who?" Dallas said. "Who was the man? Did you recognize him?"

The look she gave him was pure agony. "I know his face because I looked him up online when you told me he fired Mia." She swallowed. "It was Dr. Elias."

FOURTEEN

Mia saw the ground rush up to meet her as her legs failed. Dallas caught her before she hit the asphalt and carried her back into the passenger seat of his truck. She did not feel him lift her, she could not feel anything except a cold river of terror that seemed out to numb her limbs, her mind, her soul. He had Gracie. Dr. Elias had taken her baby.

"Sit for a minute," Dallas's soothing voice urged.

She felt pressure and realized that Antonia was gripping her hand, squeezing hard enough that her sister's nails bit into the tender skin of her palm. She was speaking, and Mia tried to follow. Antonia told the story in halting bursts. "After I called the police, I checked back with the trailer park. They haven't been ordered to evacuate, yet. It was a hoax."

Dallas said. "He probably pretended to be with the fire department. He told you there was an evacuation order so he knew when you'd be passing by."

Antonia nodded, grief stricken. "He must have been watching, parked around the turn in the road, waiting for us. I should have known. I never should have left her in the car alone. Oh, Mia, what have I done?"

It was as if Mia was watching it all from a distance, like a dramatic play unfolding on the stage in front of her. She should comfort her sister. Decide on the next step. Find a current picture on her phone to give to the police. Isn't that what the parents of missing children were supposed to do? The faces on milk cartons materialized in her mind. She'd seen the pictures, the sweet little faces printed there, smiling in moments of innocence while the world fractured into a nightmare for the parents who searched desperately for them.

She should take action. Every moment idle meant Gracie was that much farther away.

But she could do nothing but shake, her body vibrating to the rhythm of the shock which her mind could not grasp. The hands in her lap, the hair hanging across her eyes, did not seem to belong to anyone real. Gracie, her heart, the most precious person on the planet, was in the hands of a murdering madman. And Mia was reduced to a mindless zombie.

How could it be real? She was dreaming, in the grip of a nightmare.

The phone in Mia's purse rang. "You should answer it," Dallas prodded gently.

She could not force her fingers into life, so he

removed the cell from the outside pocket of her purse and thumbed it awake.

"Hello?"

"I'm glad I thought to get the numbers off your cell phone when you left it in the office. This is Dallas's number, isn't it? The loser? Mia, your choice in men is terrible. Did we learn nothing from the last criminal you became involved with?"

Dallas stiffened. "Elias? Where's Gracie?"

Mia sucked in a breath and forced her teeth to stop chattering. Dallas put the call on speaker phone and the four of them bent their heads together to listen.

"Don't talk to the police," Elias said. "I don't want them involved."

Calm, collected, as if he was orchestrating every terrible moment. "What have you done with Gracie?" Mia tried to shout. Instead it came out as a pathetic whisper.

"She's with me, as you are aware, I'm sure."

"This isn't going to accomplish anything," Dallas snarled. "It's all over. We know the truth about Asa Norton."

He paused. "The truth is relative. I want the photo. I will contact you soon with the location."

"Please," Mia said, her voice breaking. "Don't hurt Gracie."

His tone was slightly offended. "I don't want to hurt her, Mia. I'm a doctor after all." Elias sounded almost as if he was talking to a patient, discussing treatment options or surgical procedures. "This is strictly a matter of self-preservation. Practical. Keep the police out of it, give me the photo, and there won't be any need for me to use violence. She will be returned, in perfect health. I'll call you back soon."

"No," Mia screamed, grabbing for the phone. "I want my daughter. Give me my daughter!"

There was no answer. Dr. Elias had disconnected.

Panic burgeoned through her senses. *Gracie, Gracie, Gracie.*

Dallas was talking, saying something as a police car pulled in behind them.

"Mia." He pressed his mouth to her ear. "Do you want to involve the police? I think we should, but I don't know if we can trust Stiving."

The words circled slowly in her mind. *Police. Stiving.*

The police car ground to a halt on the shoulder. Stiving got out and walked over to them. "What's this all about?"

Antonia looked at Mia. She gave a slow nod. What choice did she have, especially after Antonia already called them?

"It's Gracie. She's been abducted." Antonia shook her head. "Aren't you here about my call?"

His gaze narrowed. "No, I'm here for Mia. Who's been abducted?"

Antonia stared at Mia. She felt Dallas's weighty gaze on her, also. They were asking what she wanted to do. Should she trust that this officer could rescue Mia from Dr. Elias? What was the alternative? She didn't even know where to start looking for her daughter. Panic constricted her lungs until she feared she was going to pass out.

"I'm here to arrest you," Stiving finished.

The words sizzled through her addled senses. Arrest her?

"What?" Dallas barked.

"The tests came back like we thought. Cora's blood-pressure medicine capsules were emptied out and filled with cocaine. It caused her to fall into a coma and stopped her heart. Fire Captain says she wasn't alert enough to snuff out the candle on her bedside table which started the fire."

"I didn't do anything to her medicine," Mia heard herself say. "I just picked it up from the pharmacy. Dr. Elias tampered with it. He must have taken it out of my purse at work while I was in the file room."

Stiving raised his eyebrows. "Pretty crazy scenario. A respected doctor in this town murders an elderly volunteer. With a street drug."

"Cocaine is used in nasal surgery all the time. He had easy access," Susan chimed in.

Stiving shot her a look as if he had not noticed her there until that moment. "And why would he do that, exactly? To gain what?"

"Because he's not the man you think he is," Mia

said desperately. "He's a murderer, and Cora was onto him. She—"

Stiving held up a hand. "All right. One thing at a time. You'll have a chance to tell me everything when I get you to jail in Pine Grove."

Dallas slammed a hand on the truck. "Listen. She's telling you the truth. He's got her…"

"Enough," Stiving snapped. "There are only two sets of fingerprints on that poisoned medicine, Mia's and Cora's. If the doctor has access to cocaine at the clinic, then chances are Ms. Sandoval did, too, not to mention the fact that she inherited Cora's property. All of that put together gives me more than enough to arrest her. We're going to jail now and if any of you interferes, you can join Ms. Sandoval."

Stiving was an enemy, Mia knew it then. By the time she convinced him that Gracie had been taken, that Dr. Elias was not the man he seemed, Elias might have killed her. The doctor's words came back to her again.

"You're afraid that you can't trust yourself, your choices, your judgments."

He'd seen right down deep into the core of her, the real essence of her weakness. He was a master manipulator, and he was still in control, still pulling her strings as if she was a helpless marionette.

Mia could not trust herself, nor her ex-husband, or the police officer who stood there with the satisfied half smile on his face. She could not trust in the life she had built for her child, the possessions she'd accumulated, the schooling she was so determined to complete. It was not even a certainty that the town of Spanish Canyon would still be there tomorrow, threatened as it was by the menacing floodwaters set to swallow it whole. There was nothing on this earth that she could count on.

From somewhere deep down in her soul, came snippets that she had heard long ago when she was a child, maybe not any older than Gracie.

Trust in the Lord with all your heart...
Seek His will in all you do...
He will show you which path to take.

Trust God. Could she do something so simple and ultimately so very difficult?

Trust God.

Standing in front of her were two people who had done exactly that.

Dallas let the Lord rescue him from a minefield of sin and come out the other side a changed man. Antonia gave up years of anger and bitterness and the Lord transformed her life and filled it to the brim with love. It was time to trust Him to show Mia the way. There was a reason He had given her life and kept her living and right now, that reason she believed with every tiny atom inside her, was to save Gracie.

Armed with that desperate knowledge, and a faith wild and untamed and new, she closed her eyes and surrendered everything to which she had clung so tightly, pride, independence, fear, anger, hurt. *Lord, I trust You. Help me.*

When she opened her eyes she knew. God was there, right there with her as he had been since the beginning. Even when she'd ignored Him. Even when she'd railed at Him and yes, when she'd hated Him. He would be with her through whatever the next few hours brought.

In a flash, she saw the way. There was one person who knew where Dr. Elias had taken her daughter. Only one.

But Stiving would not let her go there, nor would he follow her leads. He would deliver her to jail before he conducted any search for Gracie. If Mia waited, if she let him take her, she would lose her daughter forever.

Please, Lord.

With cold fingers, she slipped the phone in her pocket and stepped out of the car. "All right, I'll go."

"Mia," Antonia cried out. "There has to be another way."

Mia grabbed her in a tight hug. She saw over Antonia's shoulder the naked anguish on Dallas's face. "It's all right," she whispered to her sister. "Tell Stiving everything. Convince him, if you can."

"What?" Antonia mumbled through her tears. "Where..."

"I'm sorry," Mia said to Antonia and Dallas. She locked onto his wondrous black eyes.

Something in her tone must have told him what she was going to do. He shook his head, hand raised to stop her. With all her strength, she shoved her sister backward, causing her to stumble into Stiving, who toppled against his car door and they both went down in the mud.

Mia ran as fast as she ever had in her life, heading for the rain-soaked forest, running toward the only way she could think of to save her child.

Dallas was thunderstruck. Juno barked and raced after Mia, thinking perhaps that it was some sort of game, until Dallas called him back. He stared as Mia raced over the uneven ground, making for the crowded wall of trees. She ran, fleet as a deer, disappearing between the branches.

Dallas helped Antonia and Stiving to their feet, shock and disbelief rocketed through him in waves. Had Mia really just run from the police? How could she think such a rash move would help find Gracie?

But would he not have done the same thing to find his brother?

Or Mia? He swallowed. Yes, he would.

Stiving barreled toward the trees, making it only a few yards, stumbling and slipping, before he must have come to the conclusion that he had no hope of catching up with her. He turned back to the car, rage suffusing his cheeks with red.

Antonia stood in shock, hands pressed to her mouth, staring in the direction her sister had just taken.

"Bad move." Stiving was on the radio now, calling for assistance in apprehending Mia Verde Sandoval.

The radio exchange seemed to snap Antonia from her inertia, and she started in on him before he could get back in the car. "Her daughter's been kidnapped by Dr. Elias. Whether you want to believe it or not, that's what happened. Dispatch will confirm it. I called it in moments before you arrived."

Stiving's lip curled. "I will confirm it, after I bring your sister in."

Dallas offered up everything he knew about Peter Finnigan's death. Susan reluctantly confirmed the facts until Stiving held up his hands. Was it Dallas's imagination, or did he see the slightest sign of belief on Stiving's face?

"All right. I've got enough to look into. I'll send anyone available to help search for the girl, but you have to know that Mia made an idiotic choice running from the police."

"She wouldn't have done it, except that Gracie's life is in danger," Antonia fired back.

"Seems to me she used that bit before, when she took the kid and went on the run after she served her jail time."

"She knows that was a mistake. She wanted to keep Mia away from her father," Dallas said through clenched teeth.

Stiving ignored him, took pictures of Antonia's car and checked it thoroughly before he ordered her to move it off the road. "They just radioed me that they're ordering evacuations of Spanish Canyon. This road will be jammed. I have to go back to town. You three should head to Pine Grove and wait for me there."

"My sister…" Antonia began.

"Your sister is now a fugitive, and she'll be treated as such." He climbed in the front seat. "If you help her in any way, you're aiding and abetting. Remember that." Tires squelched across the road as he did a sharp U-turn and headed back toward Spanish Canyon.

Dallas considered for a moment, trying to corral the thoughts stampeding through his brain. Mia would not hesitate to sacrifice her own life to save Gracie. Right or wrong, she felt she had no other choice than to run. He had to intercept her. Urgency burned like acid through his veins. "Take Susan and go to Pine Grove."

"What am I supposed to do there?" Antonia demanded. The angry quirk to her lips was so like her sister he almost smiled.

"Convince them to look for Gracie. Get to the

chief if you can." He shot Susan a look. "And don't let this lady out of your sight."

"Where do you think he took Gracie?" Susan asked.

"I'm not certain."

"Promise me you won't hand me over to Thomas, even if you do find him," she said, staring at Dallas with those oddly haunted eyes. "You are not that kind of man, I think."

"You're right, and I'm hoping you're not the kind of woman who would walk out on a mother and child. We'll need your testimony to bring Elias down once and for all."

She looked away. "I don't know what kind of woman I am anymore. Before I was just angry, but now..."

"It's time for you to decide." He faced her full-on. "You've been hurt and lost your husband. Now there's a little girl involved." He heard Antonia gulp back a sob. "She needs her mommy, and you can help put things right, but not if you run away. Do you understand?"

She cocked her head. "Yes, I do."

"Then stay with Antonia. When we find Mia, we'll need you to back up her story." He reached out and squeezed Susan's forearm. "This time, the doctor is going to pay for what he's done, I promise."

She nodded slowly.

He started for the truck.

"But where are you going?" Antonia cried. "How can you help Mia?"

"It's my job to protect her, remember?" He opened the truck door.

"You're not just doing a job," she said quietly. "It's something much more than that."

He allowed a moment to acknowledge that she was right. Mia was not a job, she never had been. Not to him. "Juno and I are going to find her."

A freshening wind pulled at Antonia's wet hair as the rain continued to fall. "Do you know where she's headed?"

"I have a pretty good idea."

She came close and gripped his hands. "You have to find her. And Gracie."

"I will," he said, a sense of resolve turning all his fears and uncertainties into hard steel in his gut.

I will.

FIFTEEN

Dallas pulled the truck off the road, crunching across the tall grass, making his own trail to a rocky outcropping behind which he parked. He picked up Mia's purse and offered a sniff to Juno. It was probably completely unnecessary. He had always thought that Juno understood much more than the average member of his species. Juno already knew that he was going to look for the small, determined woman who had crashed through the heavy carpet of grass. Perhaps he thought it was one of their many training exercises where he would be sent to discover a prearranged "victim."

"Find," he commanded anyway.

Dallas watched him run, graceful loping strides over the uneven ground, tail wagging with sheer joy at the prospect of engaging in a search. Mia was no doubt heading for Dr. Elias's house to talk to Catherine. It would be feasible to go there and wait for her to turn up, but he did not want to leave her plunging through a heavily wooded area, wanted by the police and not in her right mind with worry about Gracie. She could fall, break an ankle, sustain a concussion. He shut down the worrisome scenarios.

Juno returned after a short while, alerted with his ear piercing bark, and then disappeared again, scrambling up a twisting road which might have once been a logging trail. Dallas hiked onward, the muddy ground clinging to his boots, rain dripping from his hair. The trail crested the top of a wooded hill and drifted back down toward the highway.

Every now and again, Juno would return and bark, a sign that he had tracked Mia and perhaps even found her already and why didn't Dallas get a move on it and pick up the pace, already? Dallas smiled. They'd cross-trained together, Juno and his awkward human, and the dog was fully capable of both tracking and trailing, and air scenting, but Juno always seemed to relish the opportunity to be off leash and following his impeccable nose toward a rescue. Other dogs could do the tracking on leash.

It never ceased to amaze him. With his paltry sense of smell, he could detect nothing but the odor of rain-washed ground and pine. Juno was easily able to discern the scent left behind by the 40,000 skin cells dropped each minute by his human quarry. Not only that, he could pick that scent from a world awash in odors. Dallas had worked with or known canines that detected everything from cadavers, to explosives, to smuggled fruits and vegetables. And now, his chance to find one small amazing woman lost in a sea of giant trees, all depended on Juno's amazing nose.

Dallas kept himself in high gear. In spite of the aching in his ribs and the pounding rain, he increased his clip until he was at a near jog, avoiding patches of slippery pine needles and puddles as best as he was able. She could not be that far ahead, but her pace was impressive, considering she too had survived a mudslide not many hours before.

Time ticked away, sucking up the minutes until sundown. It was edging toward six o'clock. One more hour of daylight. Juno could track at night, they'd spent enough hours training at it, but Dallas was not as surefooted in the dark, and neither was Mia. She had to be cold and terrified. And what about Gracie? Was she frightened? Had he hurt her? Bound her? The thought haunted him.

The way ahead was overgrown, thick underfoot with soggy debris and crowded overhead by tree limbs, weeping icy droplets down on him. And then, without warning, the trail was gone. They found themselves in a forest that showed no signs that it had ever been penetrated by humans for any reason. He listened to the incessant dripping. Wind played with branches and loosed more water down upon them which Juno blasted away with a vigorous body shake.

Juno stopped and nosed around for Mia's scent.

With still victims on fair-weather days, the scent rose in a neat cone, emanating from the search target. Today the rain, shifting winds and highly active target, was making the search more difficult. It seemed likely that Mia would stop at some point, perhaps to try and use the GPS on her phone to locate Catherine's house, or simply to rest, to hide.

His heart was pounding and muscles fatigued after the brisk climb. Falling away to his left was a small hollow of firs, clustered close enough together to protect from the rain. She would head there, to regroup.

"Mia," he called. No answer but a quick darting movement from behind the trees. He charged toward it.

Juno stopped him with an impatient bark.

"She's down there," he said as much to himself as the dog, ignoring another louder bark from Juno.

He half ran now, wishing his stiff leg and ribs would work in harmony with the rest of his limbs. He'd spent years, his whole adult life, really, combing through wild corners of the world, quiet forests and ruined buildings, creek beds and mountaintops, searching, searching. Sometimes he and Juno had found the target and he'd celebrated. Sometimes they didn't get there in time and they grieved together. After every mission, the need to search always returned. There would be another someone to find, another search to be taken on, a restlessness that told him he had not yet discovered the person he was destined to find.

"Mia," he shouted again, earning another bark from Juno.

He plunged into the clearing, moving so fast he skidded a good couple of feet before he stopped his forward momentum. The Stellar's Jays in the shrubs shot out with a deafening screech, taking refuge in the branches and squawking their displeasure. The air was heavy with the scent of wet grass and decaying leaves.

He completed a rough circle of the hollow, sinking up to his ankle in water at one point. Mia wasn't there. Bending low, he peered under the taller bushes, searching out any hiding places.

No Mia, nor any sign she had ever been there. Juno stared at him. Recrimination. He'd broken his own rule. Trust the dog. Dallas hadn't.

Early on in his career in search and rescue, a mentor watched him disregard a seemingly impossible positive alert from his dog. That's when Dallas had learned the term "intelligent disobedience."

If you've got a smart dog and you have learned to trust each other, let the dog think for himself. Juno had, and Dallas had disregarded him.

He dropped to a knee in the soggy grass and gave Juno a scratch. "Sorry, boy. I messed up. You're in charge now."

Juno accepted the apology by licking a raindrop

off Dallas's chin, before he sprinted back in the other direction. Dallas tried to do the same, stumbling on the uneven earth and slapping aside branches as the slope became steep. He'd lost time with his dumb mistake. He prayed it wasn't too late. As the terrain grew more and more rugged, he had to resort to using his hands to hold on to tree trunks and exposed roots as he hauled himself upward, arriving at the top to find they'd looped back to the road.

Fifty yards ahead a yellow truck was stopped, the passenger door open.

And Mia was just stepping in.

"Mia," he shouted. Juno had almost reached her when she pulled the door closed and the truck rumbled away down the road, leaving Juno and Dallas alone on the rain-soaked highway.

Mia's heart plummeted as she eyed Dallas in the sideview mirror, Juno trotting back over to him as the truck pulled out. He'd come to find her, to help her out of the excruciating mess she'd fallen into. Maybe he'd intended to talk her into going back to the police. Knowing Dallas, he'd more likely determined to help her enact her own desperate plan to find her daughter.

But she could not let him throw his life away on a fugitive. And that's what she was, she reminded herself incredulously.

She realized the woman at the wheel was speaking to her. "Where'd you come from? Popping out of the woods like that, I thought you were Bigfoot, till I realized you're too small and not hairy enough." She laughed, setting her gray curls bouncing. "Name's Fiona. You?"

She smiled, imagining she must look like a deranged hitchhiker. "My name's Mia. I'm trying to get to the Spanish Villa Estates, on the edge of town. Do you know where that is?"

"'Course. Nice digs up there." She eyed Mia more closely, gaze flicking over her jeans and torn windbreaker. "That where you live?"

"No." Mia tried to stick to the truth as much as possible. "My house flooded. I know someone who lives in Spanish Villa. She said she'd help us find a place."

"Us?"

Mia swallowed hard. "My daughter, Gracie. She's four." She could not stop the tears then, hot and fast they rolled down her face. "I'm sorry. We've had a difficult time."

"It's okay, honey," the driver said, patting her hand and offering her a tissue box. "I got three girls myself. All grown now with kids of their own, but I remember how hard it was. Especially when my husband split town." She offered Mia a thermos. "Hot tea. You drink some now."

Mia protested.

"Your teeth are chattering. Drink the tea. I got plenty more."

Mia poured and sipped. The tea delivered warm comfort through her body and it had the added bonus of keeping her busy. Most of all she desperately did not want Fiona to ask her any more questions about Gracie. She could not trust her emotions.

Just get to Catherine and find out where her husband has taken my child.

Fiona kept up a constant commentary about the flooding and the small trucking company that she owned. Mia checked her phone constantly for any message from Dr. Elias. There wasn't any. He was probably enjoying the thought of the agony he'd created.

"Built it myself from the ground up," Fiona was saying. "Got twelve trucks now, out of Pine Grove. That's where I'm headed. Heard they've got the police moved up there during the flooding."

Mia sipped her tea and stared out the window. What else had Fiona heard?

Fiona sighed. "Awww, man. Looks like we got a roadblock."

Mia stared through the water-speckled windshield. Four cars ahead of them were stopped at a set of blockades straddling the road. A police officer, or perhaps a volunteer, swathed in a yellow slicker was making his way down the line, speaking with each of the drivers.

Her hands went icy around the cup. Were they looking for her? Nerves jumping, she darted a glance at the door handle. She could yank it open and jump down. Run away from the road. Right, and broadcast her presence like a signal flare.

The officer finished with the first two cars and made it to the third. It was almost sunset, and he held a flashlight. To search the vehicles for her? The fugitive wanted for murdering Cora Graham?

Fiona shot her a curious glance. "Drink more tea, honey, you're shaking like mad."

She watched the officer straighten and splash along the road, his boots dislodging sprays of water under the rubber soles. As subtly as she could, Mia reached for the door with one hand, fingers gripping the metal catch.

With the other, she kept the cup at her mouth, hoping to help conceal her face.

Her stomach was a lead weight as the cop waited for Fiona to roll down the window.

"Hello, ladies." He peered at Mia. "Where are you headed?"

Don't tell him about Spanish Villa, she begged silently.

"Pine Grove. Shop's up there."

He nodded. "Road's flooded ahead. Going to redirect you east about ten miles and then you can double back."

Fiona sighed. "I should have listened to the weather reports more closely."

"More rain coming. Just evacuating the lower elevations now, but might need to expand that." He looked closer at Mia. "You all right, miss?"

"Yes, I'm okay. I needed a ride, and Fiona was kind enough to stop for me."

"That right?" He took in the bedraggled hair, the scratches on her face from her plunge through the trees. Was there a dawning of recognition on his face? Would there be a request for an ID next? The roar of her own pulse deafened her.

A slow smile spread over his face. "Great to see people helping each other in times of emergency, isn't it?"

"Yes," she said, her sudden movement spilling some of the tea on her lap. She wiped at it with her sleeve.

"You headed to Pine Grove also?" The officer pinned her to the spot with his hard look. Her breath caught and she could not hide the shaking of her hands.

"I..." Mia started.

Fiona broke in. "I'm taking her to see a friend who's gonna help get her and her little daughter fixed up in a new place." Fiona looked at her watch. "When do you think you'll wave us through? I'd sure like to get this old truck in the barn before nightfall."

The officer gave Mia another long look before he

consulted his radio. "All clear," he said and began to wave the drivers on to the detour.

She hardly dared breathe. As they rolled by she kept her gaze fastened out the front window, feeling the officer's eyes on her. How could he not hear the slamming of her heart into her ribs? Guilt had to be written all over her face in vivid ink.

Fiona gave the cop a final wave as she eased the truck by. When they were on the road, a good half mile past the roadblock, Fiona sighed.

"You want to tell me about it?"

Mia started. "No, I just can't. I'm sorry."

"It's all right." Fiona sighed. "I knew whatever it was that happened back there, you were anxious to get away from that guy and his dog."

She'd seen Dallas and Juno. And completely misunderstood. "They weren't..."

Fiona held up a hand. "I don't need to hear about it. You're anxious to get to Spanish Villa and just as eager to avoid the police, but you seem like a nice kid and I've got a soft spot for moms and daughters. Here." Fiona removed a plastic-wrapped sandwich from a bag. "We'll split it."

Mia was going to decline but just then her stomach let out a hollow rumble. Humbly, she accepted the sandwich. "Thank you so much, Fiona. How can I ever repay you?"

"You can tell me I make the best ham-and-pickle sandwich you ever ate."

Mia managed a grin. "I think it might be the only ham-and-pickle sandwich I ever ate."

Fiona laughed. "Close enough. We'll be passing Spanish Villa in about a half hour. Sit back and enjoy these luxurious driving conditions."

And Mia did, eating every scrap of the sandwich and clinging to the knowledge that with every mile, she was that much closer to finding Gracie.

Dallas and Juno endured a miserable hike back to the truck. Dallas kicked himself mentally every rugged step along the way. He'd distrusted Juno and lost his chance to catch Mia. Now he was playing catch-up in a big way.

He called Mia's phone again. No surprise when she did not answer. She didn't want to involve him further. *Involved? Mia I'm more than involved now. I couldn't walk away if I wanted to.*

The thought surprised him. He knew she did not want him in her life, nor Gracie's. And he would never force himself into a situation where he wasn't wanted. All true. But also true was the fact that like it or not, he felt deep down in the place where only truth can survive that he was meant to save Mia Verde Sandoval.

He phoned Antonia. She answered before the first ring had died away.

"Dallas? Did you find out anything?"

The Verde women were strong, determined, practical. It would do no good to sugarcoat, nor would he disrespect her by doing so. In the words of his mother, "Every woman's got a spark, Dallas, and adversity turns it to fire." And oh, how he'd fanned his mother's spark into flame. He'd seen it blazing in her eyes when she'd stumbled upon the gun hidden under the seat of his car. He blinked the memory away.

"I didn't catch up to her." Juno gave him the look. Full confession. "Juno found her but I messed up."

Satisfied, Juno set about licking his paws clean.

"I know where she's going, I'll meet her there. I need Susan to tell me where Catherine lives."

There was muffled conversation as Antonia consulted Susan. "She says it's a street in Spanish Villa." Antonia told him the address.

He set the wipers in motion and started the truck. "Are you both all right?"

"We're at a Red Cross shelter in Pine Grove. The chief is supposedly on his way, says a volunteer." She paused. "I'm hearing radio reports about the flooding. It's really bad—road closures all over and a bridge, the Canyon Creek span, is all but underwater."

Dallas let her talk as he headed off. When she ran down, she said what she most needed to get off her chest.

"I feel helpless. I should be searching since I was the one…"

"Antonia, stop right there. We both know who is at fault here and he's going to pay for that."

She let out a soft breath. "What if you're too late, Dallas?"

"I won't be."

"I'll pray for you."

"That's the best thing I could ask for."

The only thing.

SIXTEEN

Fiona let Mia out on a patch of moonlit road at the entrance to the Spanish Villa housing complex. Mia gripped her hand in thanks. "You've done more for me tonight than you know."

Fiona squeezed back. "Take care of yourself, honey. You're strong. You'll make it through whatever it is that's got you in the crosshairs."

One final squeeze and Mia hopped down, avoiding the mud. The sky was leaden with clouds, but the rain had tapered off to a heavy mist. Though she still felt the grit trapped under her jeans and top, her clothes were more or less dry and her belly was not grumbling, thanks to Fiona's gracious gift of a ham-and-pickle sandwich. Had Dr. Elias given Gracie anything to eat? Fear engulfed her in such a tight clutch she had to stop and fight for breath, steadying her shaking legs by locking her knees. One more check of the phone. Still no message and her battery wouldn't last forever.

Go find out where he's got her, and get your daughter back. She set off.

Enormous houses with red tile roofs and white stucco exteriors perched on well-manicured lots. It was a point in her favor that the houses were spaced far apart and the weather kept residents inside, perhaps packing in case evacuations reached even this higher elevation. She had only been to the doctor's house once, for a clinic party which included all the employees.

Fleeting memories trickled across her recollection of the event. White napkins, delicate cheeses and imported olives, plush carpets and a swimming pool in which Gracie had paddled for hours until her button of a nose was sunburned in spite of the cream. Mia's throat ached with unshed tears until a crazy idea flickered into her consciousness. Was it possible he'd brought Gracie here? Catherine had been at Finnigan's for some reason. If she was just as guilty as her husband, this might be the place they were hiding her.

New resolve flooded her with energy. She practically sprinted to the top of the hill, to the last house at the end of a lonely cul-de-sac. Dr. Elias's house.

Knock on the door? It would give them a chance to lock Gracie away or call the police on her. Heart thundering, she moved closer, trying to piece together some sort of plan. A set of arched windows with fancy iron grillwork decorated the side of the house. Most were dark, but golden light glowed from the farthest one. She moved silently to the edge of the neat stepping-stone walk, keeping to the shadows. Did the doctor have a dog? She didn't think so. Too finicky, too controlling. He wasn't the dog-loving type.

You weren't either, until you met Juno.

And Dallas.

Mia realized that she had changed in a lot of ways since encountering Dallas. She had been too far away to see his face, as she got into the truck and left him on the side of the road, but she could imagine the anger and frustration. It stabbed at her. Why were her feelings a jumbled spaghetti mess whenever she thought of him?

Jaw clenched, she pushed the hair out of her face and shored up her strength. *He shouldn't have followed me. His job is done.* It was all on her now.

Her and God.

She drew level with the window now, fingers on the cold metal grillwork. A quick look. She readied herself to move when a hand went around her mouth, muffling whatever scream she might have managed.

She thrashed against the strong arms holding her, iron bands that kept her fastened against a rock-hard chest.

"Quiet" came the hissed whisper in her ear.

Dallas held her there for a moment, captive against him, and then slowly he turned her around, uncovered her mouth and pulled her into the shadows behind a potted shrub.

She couldn't decipher her own rattling emotions. He looked down at her, moisture beading on his tousled hair, a scratch running the length of his cheek, hands on hips, lips hard with anger. "Mia…" he began, then with a sudden rush he pulled her close and kissed her, palms cradling her head.

The warmth rushed through her in a delicious wave and she kissed him back, forgetting for a moment, everything but the elation that swept through her. A tide of warmth, safety and belonging thundered through her, beating back the desperate fear. When they both ran out of breath, he pulled away and put his forehead to hers.

"Sorry. Shouldn't have done that. You're a pain in the neck to keep track of."

She laughed, a quiet, wobbly chuckle that emerged over the sparks still showering through her. "Where's Juno?"

"He's in the truck because he's not good at quiet. And he's massively upset about it. What did you see inside?"

"I didn't get that far."

He started toward the window.

She grabbed his wrist. "Dallas, I've thrown everything away to find my daughter. You shouldn't. You have a future without us. I don't want you going to jail for me."

The moonlight flecked his eyes with an inner glow. "Noted." He continued to the window and looked inside.

"Didn't you hear me?"

"Yes," he said, still peering into the house. "I heard you, but I'm not obeying. There's a difference."

She huffed, uncertain whether to be angry or pleased.

He moved away from the window. "Catherine's in the back of the house. It looks like there's a living room that opens onto the patio. Let's see if we can get in that way."

"What if Dr. Elias is inside?"

"Unlikely. His car isn't in the garage."

Mia sagged. "I was hoping that he brought Gracie here."

"Don't think so, but we'll find out where. Let's go."

"Dallas," she tried again to stop him. This time she put her palms on his chest, feeling the strong beating of his heart. How could she tell him what it meant that he had come to find her? And that she could not allow him to stay? "This is wrong, breaking into someone's house. If you help me do this, there's no going back."

"No, Mia," he said slowly. "This is right, that I'm here with you now and we're going to get your daughter back."

"It's not worth it for you. I can't repay you in money, or…" She looked at the ground.

He tipped her chin up, his thumb gently tracing the curve of her lower lip. "I know you have a life to build somewhere else. I understand that. This isn't about payment. It's about what's right."

She closed her eyes tight. "Everything's mixed up, Dallas. How can you be sure what's right?"

He waited until she opened her eyes. "You pray and you take your best shot at it."

"I haven't had a good track record figuring out what's right, but…" She faltered. "I've asked His help this time."

Dallas smiled, moonlight illuminating the joy on his face. "Amen to that." He opened his mouth to continue, but instead he pulled her into the shadows. "Security vehicle," he breathed in her ear. "Stay still."

Easy for him to say, she thought, from the circle of his arms. Pressed against his ribs, her chin next to his, her heart was puttering like a motorboat. She was sure it might give out altogether as it ricocheted between comfort at being near him and utter terror about what could be happening to Gracie, to an odd peace that came when she'd given the situation over to God. A mixed up spaghetti jumble to be sure.

When the car passed, she disentangled herself from Dallas and got to her feet, breathing still hitched and unsteady.

"Ready?" he said, infuriatingly handsome in spite of his sodden condition.

"Are you really sure?"

"Mia," he said, cutting her off. "If you ask me that again, you're going to go wait in the car with Juno."

She was not completely sure if he was joking or not, as he headed off toward the patio.

You kissed her? Again? What part of the plan was that, you dope? The woman was running from the law and terrified for her daughter. He had no business kissing her. He willed his gut to stop quivering like jelly at the residual sensation of her lips pressed to his. He felt like Juno when they first worked together and the dog was more interested in rocketing off after enticing birds than engaging in a search and rescue. Impulse had overridden his good sense. Yet he could not deny the irrational happiness that sprang up in his soul that Mia had invited God in.

Still, had he really kissed her? He had. The electricity still tingled through him.

Focus already, would you?

He pulled his mind back to the present. As soon as Catherine caught sight of them, she would call the police or bolt. Since there was no way he wanted to hurt her, that gave them only a few minutes tops to see if they could convince her to rat out her husband or, if she was an accomplice, to bluff her into thinking she and the good doctor were caught.

Not much of a plan, but he couldn't think of anything better.

They reached the patio just as Catherine Elias stepped out. Dallas and Mia watched from behind a screen of bushes as she turned on the propane gas, and a fire pit sprang to life. She watched it burn in silence. The flames danced high in the darkness.

Mia burst out into the circle of light. "Where's my daughter?"

Catherine screamed, hands pressing a file folder to her chest. "What are you doing here?"

Dallas stepped forward so she could see him, too. "Your husband kidnapped Mia's daughter, Gracie. We're here to find out where he took her. Mia said you have a cabin in the mountains. We need to know where."

Catherine's mouth opened in an *O* of surprise. Or was it anger? He couldn't tell. She took a step toward the house, but one step only, eyes shifting in thought.

"Why would he take her?"

She knew something. Maybe everything. "He wants us to hand over the photo that you took to Peter Finnigan that can incriminate him in Asa Norton's murder."

"Asa Norton? The man who drowned all those years ago?" She cocked her head as if listening to the sound of far off music. "Susan's husband."

"Are you helping him?" Mia fired off.

"Helping? You think I helped my husband kill Asa?"

"No, but he also murdered Cora Graham and Peter Finnigan. You might have pitched in for those."

Catherine's mouth went slack. "This is insane. I'm not a murderer."

Dallas could not be sure it was disbelief or lying. Women confounded him. He had no chance of reading her right, but he pressed on anyway. "You went to see Peter Finnigan, just before he was blown up."

"Blown up? What are you talking about? He was perfectly fine when I left him." She sank down on the brick patio wall, heedless of the moisture. "This can't be true."

"It is true," Mia protested. "You know I'm not lying, don't you?"

She chewed on a thumbnail. "I suspected something was going on when that woman Susan showed up, stalking me. He said he'd treated her for a minor injury after her husband drowned and she became fixated with him."

"But you didn't believe him?" Mia pressed.

"Not really. There have been other women," she said wearily. "I suspected Susan was another one of Thomas's flings and he was trying to cover up. But then things started to happen. Cora died. This thug from Miami showed up. And I found Thomas shredding files. These files taken from the clinic."

She waved the folder at them. "There's nothing in them now. They're Cora's. Most were destroyed, but I saved one without him knowing. The photo was in it along with a newspaper clipping about Norton's death."

The pieces were beginning to fall into place, Dallas thought. "You recognized your husband in the picture."

"Yes, that's why I went to see Peter Finnigan. I read the paper's account of how Finnigan supposedly tried to save Susan's husband that day. I can't prove it, but I think Thomas was giving Finnigan money, paying him to stay quiet. I found an envelope of cash one time, addressed to P. Finnigan at his Mountain Grove address. Thomas explained it away, but I always wondered about it."

"Did Peter tell you anything?" Mia asked.

"Nothing. As a matter of fact, he snatched the photo and tossed me out, but I didn't do anything to harm him. And now you say he's dead? Are you sure?"

Dallas nodded. He would never lose the memory of how Finnigan lost his life.

"Why kill Peter?" Catherine mused.

"Both were involved in Asa's death," Dallas said. "Peter must have threatened to tell, so Elias killed him."

"After all these years? Why?"

Mia hugged herself. "Something went wrong."

"Susan's no innocent in all this, you realize," Catherine spat. "She kept quiet about Thomas's involvement all these years instead of going to the police, not to mention the fact that she got millions when Asa died."

"But she can bring Dr. Elias down now." Mia shivered. "So he'll need to kill her, too."

"I didn't want to see it." Catherine looked up at the cloud-washed sky. "I mean, I knew about the other women. I'm not so blind that I couldn't figure that out. I didn't want to believe there was anything else."

"Why didn't you go to the police?" Dallas said. "If you're an innocent in all this?"

She turned haggard eyes on him. "I'm leaving him as soon as I can get my things together. He's a manipulator and covering up whatever he did in the past, but the man is the father of my children. Whatever Thomas has done, they don't deserve to live with his sin. Can you understand that?"

Mia clutched Catherine's hands. "Yes, so you can understand why I need to find my daughter. Please, Catherine, you've got to tell me if you know where he might have gone."

"I don't," she said, detaching herself.

"Where's your cabin?" Dallas watched her mouth tighten.

"He wouldn't abduct a child. He's a lot of things, but he has his own children. He wouldn't hurt Gracie."

"But he did," Mia said. "Your husband called me

and told me he had my daughter. You have to face it, just like I had to face the truth about Gracie's father."

"This can't be possible. I would have known I was married to a murderer." Catherine looked away. "What kind of woman wouldn't know?"

"A woman like me," Mia said. "I misjudged my husband, too, Catherine. You feel stupid, vulnerable. And then—" she shot a look at Dallas "—you forgive yourself and you move on."

"I loved him." A tear rolled down Catherine's cheek. "I really did. Maybe I still do."

Mia knelt next to her and took her hand. "Believe me I understand, but your husband has killed and killed again, and now he has my baby." Her voice broke on the last word. Dallas put a hand on her shoulder, trying to squeeze some comfort into her.

"But Thomas is a father himself," Catherine said. "How could he?"

"I think you know deep down that we're right," Dallas said. "That's why you were getting ready to burn this file, isn't it?"

"All the others are shredded. This one only has the clipping left. I…I figured whatever he's been up to, the less evidence the better for my kids."

Mia did not release Catherine's hand. "Even if you can't accept it, would you throw away Gracie's life? A mother couldn't do that to another woman's child."

Her face crumpled. "I'm not a bad person. Really, I'm not."

Dallas sensed they were near to breaking through her defenses. "Then tell her."

Tears cascaded down Catherine's face. "The cabin's near the reservoir, on Sentinel Hill Road."

"Thank you." Mia clutched Catherine in a desperate hug.

"Here," Catherine said, shoving the file folder at Dallas. "Take it. Maybe it will help you prove he's guilty."

Betrayal shone like an exposed wound deep in her eyes.

"I'm sorry," he said.

She waved him away. "I won't be here when you come back. If what you say is true, I'll never come back."

Mia and Dallas left her staring at the fire pit.

SEVENTEEN

Mia was panting hard by the time they made it to Dallas's truck, having had to stop twice to avoid detection by the security people. She still had twigs tangled in her hair from their leafy hiding spots and a new catalogue of scratches. Once Juno was finally convinced to move to the backseat, he could not stop pressing his wet nose to her neck, snuffling her hair until she batted him away.

"Stop, Juno. That tickles."

He responded in doggie fashion by licking her along the hairline which made her laugh.

"I think you blew his mind showing up like this when he was all set to locate you out in the woods."

"Sorry," she said, giving Juno a rub under the chin. "You'll just have to find me some other time." When she'd gotten Juno down to an occasional slurp from the backseat, she called Antonia and put her on speaker phone.

Her big sister alternated between giving her a tongue lashing and expressing heartfelt relief that

Mia was now in the company of Dallas and Juno. "I'm still waiting for the chief. Susan's gone to see if she can find a room somewhere for us, but the town is full of evacuees." She huffed. "It's driving me crazy. Every minute I'm thinking about you and Gracie and I want to be doing something to help."

Mia heard her sister start to sniffle. "Don't cry, sis, or I'll start, too. We're going to get her, Antonia, we got some info from Catherine," she explained, giving her sister the location of the doctor's cabin. Saying it aloud spread an eagerness inside that she felt would burst out.

"You can't go. This is too dangerous," Antonia said.

"What choice is there? He's got Gracie, and I'm a fugitive."

"We have to tell the police where you're heading," Antonia insisted.

Mia's head spun. "No, I won't risk it. I can't."

She looked to Dallas.

"You know where we're going, Antonia." He checked the time on the truck's dashboard. "Give us a two-hour head start, then tell them everything."

If we're not back…if we're too late. Suddenly she could not get enough oxygen. There was no outcome possible except that they would find Gracie, unharmed and get her away from Elias. Forcing a breath in, she grated out the words. "Tell whoever will listen, but you and Susan need to stay there where it's safe." She paused.

"Okay," Antonia said.

"I don't know if Susan is trustworthy," Mia said quietly. "She's unstable, and she benefitted from her husband's death financially."

Antonia lowered her voice. "If she was involved in the murder, why would she come back and blame it on Elias?"

"It makes no sense to me, but I wanted to warn you. I can't stand anything happening to you." She scrubbed at a spot of grit on the knee of her jeans. "I wish I could do this by myself and not endanger any more people."

"You've got help now, Mia. You're not alone. Dallas is there, and Reuben's flying here as we speak. He's devastated about Cora and...and Gracie."

Deep breaths. "I'm going to get her back, Antonia." Mia clutched the phone. "I am going to get my daughter back."

"Be careful, sister."

"I'm used to dealing with criminals remember? I used to be married to one." The joke fell flat. She was about to hang up.

"And I wanted to say—" Antonia rushed on "—I'm sorry I didn't tell you about Dallas. Reuben and I..."

"Were trying to protect me." She sighed. "And so was Dallas. I understand." And she did. Though

Dallas did not look at her, she knew from his kiss, from his willingness to risk everything, that he was with her because he cared for her. With a stab of anguish, she also knew there could be no future for them. When she found Gracie, she would move back to Florida and be the best possible parent to her child. She would play it safe and humbly accept any help from her sister and brother-in-law. No more striking out on her own. No more independence at all costs.

And Dallas? He would continue to bounce around the country finding the missing, and living the kind of unfettered freedom that was exactly what Mia and Gracie did not need. He found lost souls and returned them home. She would always picture him that way, even when they had separated for the last time.

A branch snapped loose from the trees and cracked into the windshield, shocking her out of her reverie. Find Gracie. That was all that mattered.

"Be careful," Antonia said. "Please, Mia."

She said she would and disconnected.

Dallas kept the truck at a slow speed which maddened her, windshield wipers slapping out their own relaxed rhythm. "Can't we speed up a little?"

"Roads are dangerous right now, and we don't need any cops or security people taking notice of us."

She huffed. "Why do you have to be so…logical?"

He offered a smile which died quickly away.

"What's bothering you? Aside from the insanity which you've gotten yourself into?"

"Finnigan."

"What about him?"

"The way he died. We know Elias killed Asa Norton and Cora. He used drugs in both cases. Neat. No blood. Almost a peaceful way to die. But Finnigan…"

She saw the explosion in her mind's eye, the bright flower of flame that blew away Finnigan's life before the river took his body. "A bomb seems out of place for Dr. Elias?"

"Maybe I'm wrong."

"Could Catherine be lying about everything? Is it possible she killed Peter for some reason and she's trying to hide it by shifting blame to her husband?" The rest remained unspoken. *Could we be driving into a trap right now?*

"That's part of what's bothering me. I don't know if Catherine or Susan can be trusted."

"The only thing I can be certain of is Susan didn't take Gracie and neither did Catherine," Mia said firmly. "And that's all I care about right now, getting my daughter back."

They ran into two detours which cost them time. It was nearing ten o'clock when Dallas finally started the ascent up Sentinel Hill. Posted signs warned of flooded roads ahead.

The more Dallas slowed, the more frenzy whipped

inside Mia. At the top of a winding road, he pulled to the side. "Hang on. Gonna climb up those rocks and check things."

He got out, Juno following. Clouds rolled over the moon, leaving only unreliable patches of light that played across the pile of rocks, marbled with shadows and moisture. Juno sat at the bottom, eyes riveted on Dallas's progress as he climbed.

He'd just scrambled to the top when Mia's phone rang. Dr. Elias.

She scrambled to press the button. "Hello?"

"My apologies for making you wait so long, but we developed car trouble on the way."

She fought for calm. "Where?"

"We're at the cabin, top of Sentinel Hill. Roads are flooded so you'll have to be creative. Bring the photo. If you aren't here by midnight, there will be consequences."

Consequences. Mia's nerves turned to trails of ice. "I want to talk to my daughter right now."

There was a sound of movement.

"Mommy?"

"Gracie." Tears rained down Mia's face, her heart rose up and twined itself with those two precious syllables. "Are you okay? Did he hurt you? Mommy's coming."

Dallas climbed down and joined her. With icy fingers, she held the phone between them.

"We're going on a boat 'cuz…"

The phone was yanked away. "Gracie!" Mia screamed.

"Midnight." The phone clicked off. Mia stared. "She sounds okay, like he hasn't hurt her. Yet."

Dallas pressed her shoulders. "She's all right. Hang on to that. Gracie is all right."

Inside she repeated the mantra. Gracie was all right.

Until midnight.

Dallas wanted to reach through the phone line and pummel the man. Mia did not resist when he urged her back into the truck. She clutched the cell as if it was somehow still connecting her with Gracie.

"He's desperate for the photo. He won't do anything to her until we deliver it."

She nodded mechanically, like an automaton. He wondered if she would withstand his next bit of news.

"This area is bisected by a river that feeds into a lake. It's all flooded. There's no way I can drive any farther."

Some flicker of life in her eyes. "Where is the cabin?"

"On the other side of that ridge. The place is flooded, and he can't drive out, either. He's going to try to boat out of here. He's probably booked a flight and has his escape all lined up."

Her eyes were dull, breath coming in harsh gasps. "Mia, are you listening?" Was she going into shock? "We need to hike in and probably swim, there's no other option. Let me go ahead, with Juno. You don't have to…"

She fired back to life, fixing him with a look more ferocious than some of the gang members he'd tangled with. "I'm going." He was smart enough to know any arguing the point would get him nowhere but left behind. Juno had no complaints either, even though the sky was delivering more rain. The dog would prefer monsoons to the backseat of a truck any day of the week. He didn't want Juno in danger any more than he wanted Mia to be, but there was nothing to be done about that either. He threw up a prayer and let out a sigh. "Text Antonia. Tell her to fill the cops in on the doctor's call. Okay?"

Her fingers flew across the keys. "All right, let's go."

He removed a pack from under his seat and shouldered it, handing her a bottle of water. "Drink."

"I'm not thirsty."

"Humor me and drink anyway." He poured some into his cupped palm for Juno, who lapped it up, tail wagging and ready to begin the adventure, and drained a bottle himself. He wouldn't suggest they eat the snacks he'd stowed in the pack, though his stomach was empty. He had a feeling it was going to be all he could do to keep up with her. From a supply in his stash, he handed her a plastic bag for her phone and two more for the photo which she double-bagged and stowed in his pack.

Juno gave an excited whine.

"It's okay, buddy," Dallas said. "This time we already know where to find her."

The question was, how would they handle it when they did? There was no more time to think about it as they started across the sodden grass toward the top of Sentinel Hill.

The ground had been transformed to a marsh by the relentless rains. Mud sucked at their feet and shins and each step was a struggle, though Juno seemed to have no trouble with it. There was just enough moonlight peering between the clouds to sufficiently light their way. Some half an hour later they made it to the ridge, flopped down on their bellies and scoped out the cabin.

It was what surrounded the neat, wood-sided structure that concerned him most. The lake, which was normally a stone's throw from the cabin, was now engulfing it, clear up to the doorstep. A boat rolled on the rain-speckled surface, tied to the porch support.

Dallas whistled low. "This place will be under water in a matter of hours."

Worse yet, the cabin was on the far shore, a good quarter mile across the lake. He didn't hazard a guess about the depth. Didn't matter. They had no boat and no car. Swimming was the only option.

She read the question in his mind. "I'm a good swimmer."

"A Miami girl? I'd be surprised if you weren't." He emptied the remaining water bottles out of his pack, keeping only the first-aid kit and foil-wrapped food.

She offered the sliver of a smile. "You travel prepared."

"Sometimes it takes a few days to complete a rescue. Conditions are bad more often than not." He felt her watching. "What?"

"I was so mad about how you ended up in my life and just now, I was wondering if God put you here in spite of me, to rescue Gracie."

He reached out a finger and traced the perfect line of her cheek and chin. "Maybe He meant for us to rescue her together."

Moonlight captured the tears gathered in her eyes, jewels that she would not let fall. It made them more precious, somehow, the strength that kept them captive there. Mia was a woman of breathtaking courage, who could not see the best things about herself. If she could see what he saw, only for a moment, it would take her breath away.

"You are an amazing woman, Mia Verde."

She blinked, then blessed him with a smile that would live inside his heart with all the most precious memories he possessed. "Coming from you,

I take that as a fine compliment. Thank you, Mr. Dallas Black."

What he wouldn't give to kiss her right then, with the rain covering them in glistening droplets and the moon gilding her hair with a million sparkles. He swallowed hard. "When we get across, try for the east side of the cabin where there's only one window. Okay?"

She nodded, stripped off her jacket and without another word waded into the lake. Juno, who had been busy sniffing, gave him a comical double take.

"Yeah, I know it's a strange time for a swim, but you're up for it aren't you?"

Juno, every bit as silent as Mia, ambled right into the water after her.

EIGHTEEN

Cold. It shivered through her body as she swam into the dark water. Juno paddled ahead, turning once in a while to be sure she was still following along. Dallas kept level at her side. She suspected he could easily outpace her, but he, like Juno, was keeping tabs, ever her faithful guardian.

Her muscles fell into a desperate rhythm. Each stroke, every kick and breath brought her that much closer to Gracie. She would force herself to cross this endless watery barrier between herself and her daughter. Despite her effort, goose bumps prickled her skin. Clearing the water from her eyes, she realized she was still no more than halfway across the expanse. Arms tired, legs leaden and she stopped, treading water.

Dallas was next to her in an instant. "Need a rest?"

She was too winded to respond.

He offered his back. "Hold on. I'll tow you for a while."

Sucking in a breath she shook her head, not wanting to add weight to a man she had already burdened so heavily. "I'm okay." She plunged ahead. More minutes, inching along, the void fighting against her in a strange nocturnal race. There was just the frigid water and her weakened body, battling for each and every stroke. Her heart traveled on ahead, calling Gracie's name into the night.

She remembered Hector and Gracie splashing in the warm Miami waters.

"Blow bubbles, *bebé,* like a little fishy." He'd held Gracie against the foaming sea and laughed at the baby kicks and clumsy wiggles she'd tried. "She's going to be a great swimmer," Hector announced, his face shining with love.

Gracie's soft voice echoed through her memory. *My daddy's a bad man.*

Hector was a man who had done very bad things, but also a man who loved Gracie Louise quite possibly as much as she did. It was a fact she had forgotten, or perhaps, she had not wanted to accept. Maybe someday the Lord could make Hector's path straight, too.

And hers. If she could just get to Gracie. There were so many things she had to tell her, to love her through, comfort her against and lift her over. So many waves to be traversed. *Lord, help me, help me.*

Water broke over her face and she sucked in a mouthful. What if Dr. Elias had hurt her? Or worse? Fatigue and fear started to paralyze her limbs. Her teeth chattered. Wind-driven waves splashed again, sending her into a coughing fit.

His arms twined around her, lifting her head out of the water. "I'll hold you. Rest a minute."

She tried to protest.

"We're in this rescue together, remember?"

"Old habits…"

He kissed the tip of her nose and for a moment, she thought he might press his lips to hers. Expectation rippled through her body, but then he turned and she clung to his wide shoulders, feeling the muscles moving along his back. Cheek resting against him, she watched the moonlight catch on the surface dappled by the pattering rain. Almost there. What would they find? She pressed her face harder into his back, strong and soothing, a partner in the lowest moment of her life.

Oh Lord, I don't deserve this man who's risking everything to help me. I have been hard-hearted to him and to Hector. Hector was a criminal, yes, and maybe he always would be, but at that moment with the water lapping against them, she prayed he would be redeemed. He was a sinner who could be good with God's help. Just like a small woman in a very big lake whom she now understood was just as much in need of a savior.

"Almost there," Dallas murmured, calling Juno closer as they neared the other side.

"And Lord, thank you for Dallas," she whispered, completing the prayer and giving it to God.

The wall of the cabin facing them had no windows, except a small one cloaked by heavy curtains. They climbed up on what used to be a wraparound porch which was now covered by six inches of water. Juno levered himself out of the water next to them, immediately shaking his sodden coat with such violence both Dallas and Mia threw up their arms for cover.

Dallas peered around the corner, Mia crowding next to him to see.

A motorboat was tied to the porch rail, and a faint band of soft golden light shone from under the drapes in one of the front windows.

"There's a bag and supplies loaded into the boat," he whispered in her ear. "He's ready to get out of here."

The front door was thrown open. Instinctively, Dallas moved Mia behind him.

"Don't be shy," Dr. Elias called. "Come on in."

Mia pictured Gracie inside. What had the monster done to her? She pushed forward but Dallas stopped her.

"If we don't leave with Gracie in a matter of minutes, the police are coming in," Dallas shouted back. "It's all over for you."

"Nice bluff," Elias said. "But it's not going to fly. I've been tracking you with binoculars since you started your swim. Now get in here before I lose my patience."

Mia's heart sank. It was a trap, and there was no choice. What had they expected anyway? To surprise the doctor? Snatch Gracie from under his nose? They splashed along the porch until they reached the door.

Dr. Elias held a small lantern in one hand which added a pool of meager light. He wore jeans and a flannel shirt. His face was marred with stubble and darkened by shadows that added years. He looked nothing like the self-assured doctor, a man respected by the townspeople. He looked, in fact, like a man on the edge of desperation.

He pulled the gun from his pocket. "Inside. Now."

Mia went first, Dallas and Juno following.

It was a small cabin, three rooms, a ratty sofa and an old rocking chair, the only furniture. A fire in the small stone fireplace gave off sooty smoke that burned her throat. "Where's Gracie?" Mia demanded.

"In a minute." Dr. Elias gestured to Dallas. "Put down the pack."

Dallas did so.

"You'd better have the photo I requested."

Mia hurried over, wrenched open the pack and thrust the plastic bag containing the picture. "There. I brought what you asked for, now give me my daughter."

Elias took the bag, flicking a glance inside, while

keeping the gun leveled in their direction. "Ancient picture. Old lady was thorough. I wonder where in the world she unearthed it." He tossed it into the flames. "The trouble is, of course, other people could follow the same trail Cora did. Maybe you even made copies before you came."

"We didn't," Dallas said. He wondered if Catherine had, for an extra bit of insurance in case Elias resurfaced in her life someday.

Elias sighed. "In this age of technology, you can't really obliterate anything can you? It's best if I disappear." He shook his head. "Such a waste. I created a good life here, a thriving practice. Raised my kids in Spanish Canyon. I hate to leave it, and them."

"Don't you dare talk to me about your children, after what you did to my child. I want my daughter," Mia shouted. "Where is she?"

Elias laughed. "I have always admired your spunk, Mia Verde Sandoval."

Mia started at a run toward the closed bedroom door which opened abruptly.

"She's here with me," Susan said, stepping over the threshold, holding Gracie's hand.

Mia screamed and ran to Gracie, snatching her from Susan's grasp and sweeping her into a smothering embrace. "Oh, Gracie, my sweet Gracie." Mia cried so hard the tears spilled over onto Gracie's cheeks as Mia planted kiss after kiss on her baby's face.

Gracie looked bewildered, but not physically injured. She wrapped her small arms around her mother and smiled. Dallas's heart tore a bit to see that innocent smile.

"Mommy, you're squishing me," she said. Juno poked a friendly nose at Gracie's leg. "Hiya, Juno."

Mia looked her over. "Are you hurt? Did he hurt you in any way?"

She shook her head. "No, but I want to go home. I don't like it here."

Dallas heaved a sigh. Gracie was safe and his spirit spiraled at the joy of it, but he could not ignore the dread that rose in his stomach as the cost of his error came to light. Somewhere inside, Dallas had known the truth about Susan. Why had he not thought it out before? "You rendezvoused with the doctor when you gave Antonia the slip by pretending to look for a room, I take it."

She nodded. "Easy."

"And you and Dr. Elias killed your husband together, didn't you?"

"That's so heartwarming, like something you'd see on the big screen." Susan was smiling, watching Mia and Gracie as if she was an adoring aunt, not a murderer. "Yes, we plotted to kill Asa together and afterward, I made the biggest mistake of my life. I bolted."

"Leaving me holding the bag," Elias snapped.

"I was young, and I didn't know what I wanted. I

apologized for that, Thomas, over and over," Susan said. "I panicked. But I never stopped loving you, not for one moment in all those years."

So it was some twisted form of love that brought her back to Spanish Canyon. The loathing in the doctor's eyes revealed it was purely one-sided. Whatever fondness Dr. Elias had felt for Susan once upon a time, had evaporated when she collected the insurance money and ran.

Elias's nostrils flared. "You should have stopped loving me. You should have gone on and lived your own life and left me to mine. That's what I told you when you came back but you would not listen."

"I couldn't do that. Our love is too deep." A strange guttural noise came from her throat. "Only I came back to find you had married someone else." Her eyes went hard and flat.

"Catherine is a good woman."

"She's a snoop. If she hadn't taken the photo out of Cora's file, things would have been much simpler." Susan considered a moment. "Well, we're all entitled to a mistake now and then."

Elias groaned. "If you'd stayed away, everyone would be better off. You got Cora's suspicions up and filled her head with stories that police were corrupt until she decided to confide in these two."

"And Peter?" Dallas asked. He darted a glance around the dismal room, trying to figure out how to keep Gracie and Mia out of the line of fire. "Did he get scared and threaten to tell?"

"He wouldn't have," Elias said, white-knuckling the gun. "Peter would not have said anything no matter how much these two pried, but you arranged for him to die anyway, didn't you?"

Susan gave him a wide smile, sidling around and putting her hand on his cheek. He flinched away. "It was prudent. When Dallas and Mia are gone, we'll have a clean slate. Peter might have decided to spill the beans someday. That's why we arranged this little kidnapping, remember? To clean up the loose ends, as they say in the TV shows." She laughed.

Dallas bit back a groan. She was the one who had, no doubt, alerted Elias when they'd retrieved the picture from Finnigan's, and who'd called the trailer park to arrange the kidnapping. There had certainly been plenty of time for her to do so while Dallas and Mia dealt with the mudslide.

Water crested the threshold, sending the first gush over the floor. Dallas looked for something he could use as a weapon. He saw nothing within easy reach.

"Floodwater's rising," Elias said. The waves quenched the flames in the fireplace with an angry hiss. "Reservoir's full, and it's dumping into the lake."

Susan's eyes were dreamy, her face soft. "We can go anywhere in the world, Thomas. I've still got plenty of money and we can live the life we were meant to. Finally, after all these years. That's what you want, too, isn't it?"

"Too late to ask me what I want." Elias pointed to a narrow ladder in the corner. "Get up in the attic, Mia. Gracie and your hoodlum friend, too."

"You can't," Mia started.

"The guy with the gun makes the rules," Dr. Elias said, "so that means I can. You get up in that attic and take your chances with the floodwaters, or I can shoot you."

It would not be much of a chance, Dallas knew. Locked in the attic, they would drown. No question about it. Antonia would tell the police what she knew, but by then Elias would be gone. "You're a doctor," Dallas said, edging closer and stepping in front of Mia. "You took an oath to save lives. Didn't that mean anything to you?"

A flicker of emotion rippled across his face. "I was a good doctor. I helped a lot of people, and they loved me in this town. I just made a mistake a long time ago."

Susan stepped back, frowning. "Our love wasn't a mistake."

He ignored her. He gestured with the gun for Mia and Gracie to start up the ladder. The water was now at shin level and climbing fast. Mia took Gracie's hand, fear strong in her eyes as she helped her little girl. "It's okay, honey. I'm right behind you."

"I'm sorry, Mia," Dr. Elias said.

She turned. "But you're going to murder us anyway?" Mia's chin jutted, her voice low so Gracie would not hear.

"As I said, I'm sorry. I really mean that."

Mia gave the doctor her back and continued up to the attic. Dallas figured he had one chance to turn the tide in their favor, but he had to make sure Mia and Gracie were far enough away.

"Up, Juno," he commanded.

Juno scrambled up the ladder with the ease born of hours of training in every possible situation from planes to boats to escalators. The dog sensed no danger, only another adventure awaiting him.

He heard Gracie giggle from up in the attic. "Good job, Juno."

The tear in his heart widened. They could not die. He could not let them drown.

"Now you," Dr. Elias said, swiveling the gun not to Dallas, but to Susan.

Her mouth fell open. "What? What are you saying?"

"I'm saying," Elias said, fury kindling on his face, "that you ruined me, my career, my marriage, everything. Getting involved with you was the worst day in my life and having you show up in Spanish Canyon was the second. You're going to die along with them, Susan. You should have died a long time ago."

Horror dawned in her expression, creeping up to overtake the love that had been there a moment before. "How can you say this to me? You are the only man I've ever loved. I killed Peter Finnigan and got these people here so we could have a future."

"I never even told Peter you were in on Asa's murder. He didn't even know we hatched that little plot together. He did not have to die."

"Well, he's dead, and that can't be changed," she said. "We have to think about the future."

"We have no future. Can't you understand that?" he said, voice like the last peal of a funeral bell. "You will climb the ladder and die with the rest of them."

The color disappeared from her face. "But I love you. We have a whole life ahead of us."

"I had a future and I threw it away for money and because I thought I cared about you. After I killed your husband, you ran. And you know what? I deserved that because it showed me I never really loved you at all."

"That's not true," she protested. "You did. You did love me."

"You were a means to an end, Susan, a shortcut I never should have taken. That's all." The words dropped like bullets.

With a cry, Susan took out a knife, the one she had stolen from Dallas's kitchen, and sprang at Dr. Elias. He deflected her, dealing a blow to the side of her head that made her cry out and fall backward, grabbing the rocking chair for support.

Dallas used the moment of distraction to launch himself at Dr. Elias.

He threw a fist, aiming for the doctor's face, but an incoming gush of water knocked him off target. His punch connected with Elias's temple, but not hard enough to do the job. Elias fired. Dallas felt a sharp trail of fire shoot through his body as he splashed backward into the water.

NINETEEN

The shot exploded through the cabin, and Mia felt as if the bullet bisected her own body. Instinctively, she shoved Gracie farther into the attic, the floor of which had been covered with plywood to provide a surface for storage.

"Dallas," she screamed, grabbing at the barking Juno to prevent him from going back down the ladder. He whined and looked from her toward his fallen master. She strained to see into the dim space. Had Dallas gone under? Had the bullet passed by him?

"He's not dead," Susan snapped. "You shot him through the shoulder. Terrible aim."

Mia's breath squeezed out in panicked bursts. He was not dead. Dallas was still alive. Her thoughts focused on that one paramount fact.

"I'm a doctor, not a sniper. Help him up the ladder, Susan," Elias commanded.

"I won't."

Juno continued to bark.

"Shut that dog up," Elias shouted, "or I'll shoot him, too. I can't think with all that racket."

Mia stroked Juno's head. "It's okay, Juno," she whispered. "Quiet now."

"Don't cry, doggie," Gracie added, petting his trembling flanks with her tiny hands. The lamplight glinted off the gun as Dr. Elias pointed it at Susan.

"Yes, you will get him up that ladder, because if you don't, I will kill you down here, and I don't think you want to be shot, do you?"

She didn't answer.

"Do you?" he demanded, louder. "You've never liked discomfort, Susan. Always enjoyed the nice things, the easy answers. I don't think a bullet hole would suit you."

Susan splashed over to Dallas and took his arm. His groan of pain shot through Mia.

"Gently," she could not stop herself from saying.

"This is crazy," Elias said with a strangled cry. "The whole thing is insane. How did it come to this?"

"You can stop it," Mia called. "You are an excellent doctor and you've helped lots of people. Catherine said you are a good father, too."

"She said that?" His tone grew soft. "Then I didn't totally destroy everything."

Mia felt a spark of hope. "No, you haven't. You could let us go. Then you would be able to see your children, maybe. Still be a father to them."

He paused. "Thank you, Mia, for saying that, but

it will be better for them if I disappear. I'm not going to withstand jail. I don't have that kind of strength. I wish things could have been different. I sincerely do."

"But…" She realized he was no longer listening. He moved aside, water splashing nearly to his waist as Susan staggered with Dallas to the ladder and they crowded up together. Mia reached out and eased Dallas as best she could into the attic space where he knelt, one hand on the wood for support, the other clutching his shoulder. Juno licked Dallas and turned in happy circles.

Mia immediately ripped off the bottom hem of her T-shirt and wadded it up, pressing it to the profusely bleeding wound. "Dallas, I'm so sorry. I'm so, so sorry."

He looked up, gave her a tight, forced grin. "Not your fault. Is Gracie okay?"

"I'm okay," Gracie said. "Didja' get shot?" Her eyes were round as quarters in the darkening attic.

"Yeah. Forgot to duck," he said.

"Silly," she answered.

Susan stood at the attic access, staring down at Elias. "You won't get away from me," she hissed. "You will not go anywhere without me."

He laughed. "Watch me." Then he shut the trapdoor. The sound of scraping wood indicated he'd secured it from the outside.

Susan pounded on the hatch, screaming obscenities. "I knew you were a coward, Thomas. Deep down, I always knew it. That's why I went to Cora's house, to be sure you had the guts to follow through."

Mia drew Gracie away and left the woman to her rant. It was more important to figure out how they were going to escape. Dallas was considering the same thing, eyeing the nailed plywood floor.

He ran his hand over the seams. "Try to find a spot where the boards have warped or broken."

Though she didn't want to tear her attention away from Dallas, she did as he indicated.

Gracie crawled into the low spots near the walls.

Splinters drove into Mia's fingers, but she continued to search feverishly.

"I can hear the water," Gracie announced, her ear to a crack between two boards. Dallas and Mia hastened over. Gracie had found a place where one of the boards had splintered away, leaving an inch gap.

"Good work, Gracie." Dallas shoved his fingers into the gap and began pulling on the weakened board, the effort dappling his face with beads of sweat. When he'd lifted the board enough for her to get her hands in, Mia added her strength, yanking on the old wood until it gave way with a crack and a puff of dust.

"Okay," Dallas panted. "Now we can pull up the other boards."

Susan joined in and soon they had cleared enough boards away to create a small hole. Dallas lowered himself into the opening and kicked away the Sheetrock.

"There's the water," Gracie said. "I see it."

The level was only a few feet below the attic floor. Mia shuddered.

Dallas sat at the edge, feet dangling into the opening. "I'm going to swim through the house and make sure there's an exit."

"Dallas…" But he was already done, dropping down into the water after sucking in a deep breath. Juno dove in with him.

Gracie peered into the water. "When's he gonna come back, Mommy?"

Mia wrapped an arm around her girl's shoulders, holding here there to feel the reassuring rise and fall of her breathing. "Soon."

The seconds ticked into minutes.

"Do you think he drowned?" Susan said.

Mia turned on her. "Don't say that. He's doing his best to get us out of here in spite of all the damage you and Dr. Elias have done."

Susan broke into a smile. "You love him, don't you?"

Mia turned away from the crazy woman who had her own twisted version of love. Susan's infatuation had turned into an obsession, and Dr. Elias a possession that she had to acquire.

Love wasn't like that. It was an overwhelming desire to see the other person happy, healthy and thriving. She wanted that for Dallas with all the passion inside her. She wanted him to find a reason to put down roots and allow himself to have the family she knew he would treasure, with a woman who wasn't on the wrong side of the law, mother to a child of a drug lord. He deserved more than that.

Susan would never understand. Love wasn't holding on tightly. It was letting go, even when it hurt.

Dallas surfaced, sucking in a mighty breath of air. Juno popped up next to him.

"We have to get to the front door. I wedged it open. Can you do it?"

"Of course," she said, but his eyes were not on her. He was considering Gracie. He reached out a wet hand for hers, wincing only slightly, voice husky with pain.

"Hey, Goldfish girl."

Gracie giggled and took his hand. "You're wet."

"Yep. And it's time for you to get wet, too. I need you to take a big breath and hold it and we're gonna swim to the door down there. Okay?"

Gracie's mouth tightened. "I'm scared to do that."

"Juno will be there with you. You can hold on to his collar. How would that be?"

"Okay, I guess, but what if my breath won't hold in that long?"

Dallas riveted his eyes to hers. "God made you a strong lady, like your mama. You're gonna be okay and that's a promise. We'll get Goldfish after."

"The pizza-flavored kind?"

He laughed. "Any kind you want."

Gracie nodded. She sat on the edge of the plywood and stuck in her feet. "Cold, cold."

Juno paddled over and rested his paws on her lap, which set her to giggling. Dallas switched on a button that made a red light blink on Juno's collar. "Now you can see him. Ready?"

She nodded.

He turned to Mia and Susan. "Straight down and to the right. Give us a couple of minutes then follow."

He held up an open palm, and Mia grasped it, pulling strength and comfort from those long fingers. Then she helped Gracie over the edge, heart pulsing with fear as she watched the water close over her daughter's head.

I must be getting old. Dallas had been a tough guy, once. Recovered from stabbings, alcohol poisoning and even a snakebite, which had been worse than any of it, but now he felt weakened, the pain in his shoulder swelling with every arm stroke. Or maybe it was the added worry about escorting a tiny child through eight feet of water when her eyes were wide and terrified; panic beginning to set in on her face.

She clung to Juno's collar as he swam. They bobbed up, skimming the surface just under the ceiling. Gracie pressed her face so it was nearly touching the plaster, sucking in fearful breaths along with some water that set her to coughing. When they reached the far wall, he called over the surging water.

"We're going under now, Gracie. Only for a minute and then we'll be out the door.

"No, no," she said, choking on a mouthful of water. "I don't wanna."

Dallas was not confident that his calm reasoning skills were enough to counter Gracie's growing fears. What would Mia do? She hadn't yet caught up and there wasn't time. In a moment, the gap would be inundated and Gracie would be breathing in water instead of air. No time, Dallas. What are you going to do?

He flashed on how his mother had handled things when Dallas or his brother had come home bleeding or with some sort of contusion. Quick and efficient, before there was too much time for fear to bloom.

He took Gracie around the shoulders. "All right. Deep breath with me. Ready? Go!" Dallas heaved in a breath in exaggerated fashion and Gracie did the same. Then he pulled her underwater and dove for the door.

It was slow going with one good arm and Gracie wiggling in terror, pressing on his bullet wound. Juno managed the dive ahead of them, and Dallas followed in the dog's wake. He could make out nothing but the red blinking light on Juno's collar.

Gracie's movements became more frantic.

Don't breathe in, he wanted to say.

She grabbed at his neck, then started to push away.

Time was up. She would be sucking in water in a matter of seconds.

He tightened his hold on her and made for the door, kicking as hard as he dared.

They surged through and rocketed out the other side. He propelled them both to the surface and nearly brained himself on the roof gutter which was inches from the crown of his head. He grabbed the edge with one hand and held Gracie's head above water with the other.

For the longest moment of his life, she didn't make a sound.

Terror balled in his stomach and shot through his nerves. "Gracie," he shouted, giving her a shake.

Her head came up and she started coughing, vomiting up mouthfuls of water in between anguished cries. It was the sweetest sound he'd ever heard.

"Good girl, Gracie. You did great. The scary stuff is over now."

She cried and clung to his neck. "I don't wanna do that again."

He laughed. "Me, neither. I'm going to put you up on the roof now and go get your mama."

She shook her head. "No, I don't want to."

"I heard you could climb up a tree." He gave her a sideways look. "But maybe I remembered that wrong."

"I can climb a tree," she insisted, indignation stiffening her chin.

"Let's see then. Pretend I'm a tree. Climb up on my shoulders and onto the roof."

She did, setting darts of agony zipping through his wound. She got up on the roof and crouched into a little ball. "It's scary up here. I don't want to stay."

"It will just be for a minute, and then your mommy will come."

Dallas removed the blinking collar light and wrangled Juno out of the water and onto the roof. The dog immediately sat down next to Gracie and licked her all over.

"Be right back." He sank back down in the water, hanging the red light to a nail that stuck out of the doorframe. He felt, rather than saw, the two women kicking their way down. He grabbed an arm, Susan's or Mia's he was not sure and dragged that person toward the door before he did the same for the other, orienting himself using the red light. For the second time he emerged, physically spent, just under the eaves of the submerged cabin. It was all he could do to catch his breath.

"Gracie," Mia cried, scanning frantically, as she broke the surface.

He pointed upward, still gasping.

Craning her neck, she must have caught sight of her daughter. Tears began to stream down her face and she closed the distance between them, and kissed all the pain from his body.

* * *

Mia was not sure how they would escape from the rooftop, but she simply could not bring her mind to fret about it much. Gracie was there, safe and sound, her skinny knees tucked under her as she threw pine needles into the water below. Juno kept a watchful eye on her. Susan and Dallas scrambled to the peak of the roof.

"There he is," Susan said.

Mia blinked out of her euphoric trance. "Dr. Elias?"

"Out in the lake," Dallas grunted. "Must have had motor trouble because he's rowing."

"He never was much of a sailor," Susan said with disgust.

Dallas peered into the darkness. "After all this. Can't believe he got away."

Susan continued to watch Dr. Elias make his escape. "We could have been together forever."

Mia noted the revulsion that bubbled in Dallas's eyes. "The police will arrest him," he grumbled. "I'll get my phone."

Susan removed a plastic bag with a phone inside.

"No need," she said, voice soft, fingers pressing the buttons. "I knew he was angry with me so I planned ahead." She sighed. "Of course, I thought he would see reason. I thought I could convince him we were meant to be together."

Mia flashed back to Peter Finnigan. "What do you mean you planned ahead?"

Dallas must have come to the same conclusion because he and Mia both lunged for Susan at the same moment. Too late. With a moonlit smile on her dreamy face, she pressed the last button. There was a deafening blast from out on the lake, and Dr. Elias's boat exploded into a shower of golden sparks.

TWENTY

"What was that?" Gracie said, standing up so quickly she nearly toppled off the roof.

Mia closed her mouth, and Dallas was once again amazed at the strength of mothers to make every circumstance all right for their children. "It was a little explosion. It's not going to hurt us."

He could not comprehend Susan, the woman who had just blown up the man she purported to love, the man for whom she had committed multiple murders. Love and murder. How could they go together? There was not much time to mull it over as two Zodiac boats roared up to the flooded cabin.

Mia waved frantically, and he would have helped if his shoulder hadn't been useless. As it was, he struggled to keep upright against the dizziness.

In a moment, one boat had peeled off toward the burning wreckage. The other was captained by Detective Stiving, who grabbed Antonia's arm and forced her to sit.

"You're going to fall out," he snapped.

Antonia stood again anyway and screamed. "Mia, are you all right? Do you have Gracie?"

Mia was crying so hard she could not choke out a response.

"Yes," Dallas called down. "Mia and Gracie are fine. Susan is here, too. She just blew up Dr. Elias's boat."

Stiving held up a pair of handcuffs. "We're ready for her."

With an elaborate combination of coaxing and lifting, Gracie, Mia, Susan and Juno were loaded into the Zodiac. Stiving wasted no time cuffing Susan. Dallas contemplated his useless arm. "I'm gonna jump," he said. "Too hard to climb down."

Stiving shook his head. "You always were a nutcase."

With that endorsement ringing in his ears, Dallas plunged feet first into the frigid water. When he surfaced, Mia and Antonia dragged him into the boat where he collapsed.

Mia pulled a blanket around him.

He tried to protest. "You need it."

She ignored him and opened Stiving's first-aid kit. Antonia sat with Gracie held tight in her arms, crooning some soft endearments meant for the child's ears only.

Susan sat in silence, staring out toward the ruined boat.

Stiving flicked a glance at Dallas. "Took one in the shoulder, huh? Not so agile as you pretend to be."

"Apparently not." He bit back a groan as Mia pressed a cloth to his shoulder. "And you're not as thick-headed as you pretend to be, Stiving. Did Antonia finally convince you we were telling the truth?"

He grinned. "Nah. Actually I did some research, called some colleagues and interviewed Catherine Elias. I even discovered that Susan's poor, drowned husband was a demolitions expert and his wife worked for the company. Interesting, don't you think?"

"It explains her prowess in blowing people up."

"So you see, I really am a good cop after all."

"*Good* is a relative term."

Stiving laughed. "Just be quiet and we'll get you to a hospital, Black."

He did remain silent for a while, the pulsing of the engine shuddering through him. Mia adjusted the blanket, fiddled with the bandages, and mopped his face all the way back to the landing spot where Susan was transferred to Stiving's police car. Gracie, bundled to the ears, was loaded into another official vehicle driven by a volunteer who gave Juno a skeptical look.

"Do I have to take him, too? His paws are muddy."

Juno responded with a massive shake that sprayed the volunteer with water from head to boots.

Gracie laughed. "Come on, Juno. Get out of the cold, quick before you catch germans."

Juno leapt into the car and settled himself on the backseat as the dripping volunteer grumbled his way to the driver's door.

"There's a National Guard rescue crew coming, but they'll be another few minutes," Stiving said. "Most direct routes here are flooded." He raised an eyebrow. "You aren't going to bleed out or anything are you? That would create way too much paperwork for me."

"I'll try to spare you that."

Stiving nodded and went to speak to the captain of the other Zodiac, leaving Dallas propped on a plastic tarp, his back to a boulder, Mia kneeling next to him. She wasn't crying, but her brown eyes were bright, water droplets glittering in her curling strands of hair.

"I can't say the words," she said, taking his hands in hers. "How can I tell you how incredibly thankful I am?"

His heart lurched inside. She was so beautiful, bedraggled, exhausted, bruised and utterly, incomparably beautiful. "We did it together," he managed.

She shook her head. "I've been trying so hard to fashion some sort of life for myself and you know what? I figured out that I already have one."

He stroked the satin of her cheek.

He heard her choke back a sound, the sort of vulnerable tiny peep that a chick might make when confronted with the edge of the nest.

"My whole life," she continued, "is Gracie and…" She stopped, looked away.

Dallas, the man who had never been able to decipher the first thing about women, wondered. Could the tenderness he saw in her face match the love buried deep in his own heart that swelled and undulated like the flood? He took her hand and cleared his throat. Fish or cut bait. Take the chance, or let his heart fly away to Florida. "You and Gracie…" He sucked in a breath and started again. "I hoped that it might be you and Gracie and me."

She jerked, mouth open.

Had he blown it? Scared her right into flight? Misunderstood a woman as he had countless times before? *Do it. Say it,* something deep inside him urged. "Mia, I'm not traditional father material, and you are an amazing mother who doesn't need any help parenting, but all my life I've been waiting for a partner to put down roots with."

She blinked, staring at him.

"You want roots?"

He sighed. *If you're going to bury yourself, might as well go all the way.* "No. I want you. And Gracie. And the life I know we could have together."

Silence.

"I've done bad things, Mia, things I can't sponge away or keep hidden, not from you. You know the good and bad of me and if you feel at all like you could love me, I would like to build a life with you and Gracie." He said it louder than he'd meant to. "I love you."

She gripped his hands. "But I've been to jail."

"Me, too."

"My ex-husband was a drug dealer."

"I know."

"I have control issues and a stubborn daughter and I eat too many sweets and I have terrible hand-writing."

"I love you."

Her expression remained frozen somewhere between amusement and something unidentifiable. Fear? Love?

"Dallas, I'm not sure what to say."

"Say we can build a family together as slowly as you need it to happen. I'm not good at following rules, I don't know how to make mac and cheese and I spend most of my time with a dog. But I'm patient. I've got that going for me."

She smiled, lighting a fire in his belly. "Say you love me, too," he choked out.

She leaned closed and stopped, her mouth a tantalizing half inch from his. "I love you, too, Dallas."

Then there was warmth where he was cold, relief for his pain, and the sun triumphing over the flood-waters of his soul as he gathered her close.

Over the crush of joy, he became aware of a high-pitched noise, the squeals and laughter of Antonia and Gracie as they watched the proceedings from the car window. Juno added a robust bark.

He smiled and kissed her again.

Mia turned her face to the sun, relishing the warmth that drove away the last remnants of the storm some two weeks after Gracie's rescue. Spanish Canyon and the entire county was an official disaster area according to the federal government. Efforts were underway for a massive cleanup. Mia was ready to begin her own restoration project.

Dallas looped his good arm around her shoulders and planted a kiss on the top of her head as they stared at the burned wreckage of Cora's house. Gracie poked a stick into the various mudholes she was able to locate with Juno sniffing right along behind. "You sure you want to tackle this?" he said, gesturing to the ruined structure.

She snuggled into his side, careful not to put too much pressure on his shoulder. "I think Cora would have been pleased to see another house built here on the property she loved so much."

"And the matchmaker in her would have appreciated the fact that we're doing this together."

"For our future." Ours. The thought thrilled through her like the spring breeze. If all went well, the house would be built and the beautiful flower beds restored in time for their fall wedding. Closing her eyes, Mia could imagine the details. Gracie with her little basket of flowers, probably followed closely by a four-legged, hairy attendant. Antonia and Reuben would be there to add their heartfelt blessings along with Dallas's friends from the Search and Rescue school where he had signed on to work indefinitely.

"Still," Mia said, an ache in her throat. "I wish Cora was here to see it."

"She'll see it," Dallas said. "And she'll have the best view of all."

"Dallas," she said, turning to face him and marveling once again at the strength and gentleness she saw there. "This place was where I lost my dear friend. I thought I'd never come back."

"And?"

"And now it's the place where I am going to start my life over again. Pain and joy, all in one place."

"Blessings are like that, I think."

She kissed him, pressing him close, her future husband and irreplaceable blessing.

"Hiya," Gracie said, coming over with her muddy stick. "I'm hungry."

Mia laughed. "You're always hungry."

Dallas retrieved a package from the stash in his truck. He handed the pizza-flavored Goldfish crackers to Gracie. "Don't feed too many to Juno," he said, voice stern but eyes twinkling.

"Okay," Gracie agreed.

"And don't fill up before lunch," Dallas said, taking one more item from the truck. He shook the blue box. "We'll go back to the trailer you and your mom rented and I'm going to cook up some mac and cheese. This time, I'm following the directions."

"Hooray," Gracie squealed and Juno barked along with her. "But just in case, can Mommy help?"

Mia and Dallas laughed as Gracie raced off to chase a pair of butterflies.

"I dunno, Mr. Black," Mia teased. "Rebuilding a house is one thing, but tackling mac and cheese?"

"Don't worry," Dallas said, sliding his arms around her again. "Even an old dog can learn new tricks."

"That's what they say." She kissed him. "But I think I'll stick around to help."

His eyes reflected the light as the sun broke through the clouds. "I wouldn't have it any other way."

* * * * *

Dear Reader,

Floods, fires, famines, earthquakes! We live in a violent world prone to catastrophes. In this last book in the Stormswept series, Mia and Dallas must navigate floodwaters and the torrent of violence that follows in the wake of a decades-old crime. In real life, no matter what type of environment we live in, we're all prone to dangers both external and spiritual. The only life preserver we can hang on to is our loving God who is our safety in the storm and our guarantee of salvation.

Friends, I hope you are swept along in the story and, as always, I am blessed that you spent some of your precious time reading my book. Feel free to contact me via my website at www.danamentink.com if you'd like to chat. There is also a physical address there if you prefer to correspond by letter.

God bless,

Dana Mentink

Questions for Discussion

1. Mia and Dallas both struggle with their previous choices. Is it possible to escape a difficult past? What advice can you offer someone who is crippled by past situations?

2. Dallas and Juno have a unique bond that surpasses dog/owner. Have you experienced such a bond with an animal? Explain.

3. Dallas and Mia are both hampered by fear in different ways. How does it impact their life choices?

4. Dallas has disrespect for rules. Do you know anyone like that? Describe them.

5. What kind of mother is Mia Sandoval?

6. Do you think Hector Sandoval has really repented? How is it possible to tell if a person's repentance is sincere or a form of manipulation?

7. What was Dallas's motivation for getting into gang life? Why do you think he stayed in it, in spite of his brother's efforts to extricate him?

8. What is behind Dallas's "restless urge to move on"?

9. Why do we so desperately cling to our own plans, even when they appear to crumble around us? Is there a better way?

10. Do you think Antonia did the right thing by hiring Dallas to keep watch over Mia without her knowledge? Why or why not?

11. Gracie believes her daddy is a bad man. How would you describe Hector Sandoval's actions to his young daughter?

12. What spiritual battles do believers fight on a daily basis?

13. Why is it so hard to do things on our own? What does God have to say about this?

14. Mia is afraid to trust her choices and her judgments. Have you ever felt this way? What is the antidote for that fear?

15. What do you imagine the future holds for Mia, Dallas and Gracie?

LARGER-PRINT BOOKS!

GET 2 FREE
LARGER-PRINT NOVELS
PLUS 2 FREE
MYSTERY GIFTS

Love Inspired

Larger-print novels are now available...

LILPDIR13R

ReaderService.com

Manage your account online!

- Review your order history
- Manage your payments
- Update your address

*We've designed
the Harlequin® Reader Service
website just for you.*

Enjoy all the features!

- Reader excerpts from any series
- Respond to mailings and
  special monthly offers
- Discover new series available to you
- Browse the Bonus Bucks catalog
- Share your feedback

Visit us at:

ReaderService.com

RS13